Wrestling with Randi

Wrestling With Randi

A sheriff's daughter good girl meets a dirty-talking, alpha, pro wrestler bad boy, instalove, pro sports romance.

Heart's Destiny Book 2

Leah Mae Wright

Copyright

Contents

Dedication

To my Aunt Rhonda and Uncle Ben.
Thank you for being like a second set of parents to me.

Introduction

Randi Mae Lee felt like she was stuck in a rut and had no idea how to crawl her way out of it. She'd tried to portray herself as outgoing and confident all her life, but she felt awkward in the good girl role everyone expected her to play as the sheriff's daughter. After a traumatic lecture from her parents as a teenager, she mostly repressed her sexuality and any part of her personality that she thought might cause a repeat. She struggled with feelings of guilt anytime she acted on her baser instincts, never letting a boyfriend turn the relationship sexual until after at least a month of dating, and always breaking up with them within a few days of their first time together. Randi secretly longed to find a way to start standing up for herself and living life on her own terms. She wanted to find her dream job and break her bad relationship cycle, but fear kept holding her back.

James Hunter lived a pretty great life. After an idyllic childhood on the family homestead in the small town of Heart's Destiny, Texas, James had completed his college degree before going on to act as a bad boy of professional wrestling. He teamed with his brother as the Dangerous Twins, an outlaw biker tag team, for the Galactic Wrestling Association. He was living the dream, traveling the world while working at a job he loved. The only drawback was the feeling of jealousy he had at seeing the married wrestlers who traveled with their families. At twenty-five, he was starting to feel like it was time to cut back on the nights out at bars and start settling down to build a family. Random one-night stands weren't fulfilling anymore, but it was hard to find *The One* when he was traveling three-hundred-and-twenty days a year and not in one place long enough to really start a relationship.

When good girl meets bad boy, sparks fly. Fate seemed to be pushing him in the right direction the night James met Randi. It was instalove for the pro wrestler and the sheriff's daughter. They fell hard and fast for each other, but could they maintain their love when his travel schedule reduced them to a mostly texting romance? Or could they find a way to be together more than the nine days they got together for his Thanksgiving vacation and her sister's wedding to his other best friend?

He was the dirty-talking alpha man of her dreams, and she was the sexy, sweet woman of his. When a pregnancy mix-up pitted the lovebirds against her overprotective father, things looked bleak for their future together. Would James's love be enough to help Randi find and accept who she really was deep inside? Would he be able to pull back on his alpha tendency to take over her life and protect her from the world long enough for the wonderful woman inside her to shine when she's ready to show her true self to the world? When all is said and done, will James and Randi finally get their happily ever after?

DISCLAIMER: This sheriff's daughter, good girl meets a dirty-talking, alpha, pro wrestler bad boy, instalove, pro sports romance book contains profanity, graphic sex scenes, therapy to deal with childhood emotional trauma, and a surprise pregnancy for secondary characters that is temporarily believed to be the main characters' baby by several of their family members and the surrounding small town residents. It is intended for adult readers (18+) who are not easily offended.

Prologue

Saturday, September 29, 2018, almost midnight

James Hunter slammed the door of his hotel room and flopped down on the king-sized bed in frustration. He was a professional wrestler for the Galactic Wrestling Association, at the pinnacle of his career as one half of the world tag-team champions, the Dangerous Twins, with his twin brother, Dean. But instead of being as happy as he should be and staying out partying with his twin, he was brooding in his hotel room because he was sick of feeling alone even though he was surrounded by friends and fans constantly.

His brother didn't understand his feelings. Dean kept saying that James shouldn't feel lonely because they were two halves to a whole and were always together. James knew Dean meant well when he said that, but he still felt like there was something missing in his life. *Someone missing from my life*, he thought to himself.

Maybe it was because his mom had been dropping hints since their twenty-fifth birthday back in April that she was ready for her sons to settle down and give her grandbabies while she was still young enough to enjoy them. Or maybe it was that their best friend Anthony was talking about looking for his soulmate earlier that night in the locker room. James knew Anthony's sister, Becky, wasn't the someone he was missing, even though Anthony said she was interested in dating either he or his brother, Dean.

Damn, I hope Dean doesn't fuck up our friendship with Anthony by trying to date Becky!

After the show that night, Anthony had to go check in at the hotel, so he didn't go with Dean and James to hang out with the local wrestlers they worked with at the show. Normally, when they went out after a show, Anthony and James tended to fade into the background while Dean and the other guys tried to pick up a ring rat for the night. Not that James had never had a one-night stand on the road, but it was very few and far between because he wasn't as outgoing as his twin.

Their gimmick was that they were big, scary bikers with long hair, beards, and tattoos, who were willing to cheat to win. They played the role of the heels, the bad guys, if you will, in the scripted world of professional wrestling. It worked for him when he was working because he could be intimidating on television without having to say a word.

Unfortunately, his intimidating look often carried over to the real world. And most of the time, when he met a woman he was interested in, she looked at him with fear in her eyes instead of interest. He tried to smile and put them at ease, but it didn't always work. That was why he usually just faded into the background and let the women who weren't intimidated by his appearance come to him.

If only his brother and the rest of their coworkers were more like him and Anthony, maybe he wouldn't have felt so bad that night. He had to come to the hotel instead of going with them to a club after they embarrassed him for the second time that day in a restaurant. They flirted with every woman they met, whether she was interested or not, regardless of her age, marital status, or physical characteristics. It wasn't as big a deal when the woman flirted back or wasn't intimidated by them and cut their egos down to size. But when the woman got flustered or looked like she wanted to flee but felt trapped listening to them, James couldn't stand it.

Tonight wasn't as bad as earlier that afternoon because the waitress at the diner they went to after the show was much older than the waitress at the hotel restaurant that afternoon, but he still felt bad for her. Both servers tried to roast them instead of flirting back, but the one that night was more successful since she obviously had many more years of experience in dealing with assholes than the one that afternoon.

He really felt bad about the one that afternoon. Her name tag said Randi, but the guys kept calling her Blondie. The fact that the hotel looked like a castle and the restaurant had a medieval times theme, complete with suits of armor as decorations by the door, set them up for all kinds of lines about jousting for her hand and carrying her off to one of the castle towers. She got in a few good insults, but it was obvious she couldn't get away from their table fast enough, at least to James. For the first time in the almost two-and-a-half years he'd been traveling with the crew since starting with the GWA, he actually wanted to punch his brother and their friends to defend her honor.

He'd felt something the instant their eyes met when she walked toward their table. He adjusted his position, getting comfortable laying back on the pillows at the head of the bed as he went back to that first vision of her in his mind.

James looked up from the menu as their waitress approached the table. The way the overhead lighting hit the beautiful blonde made her look ethereal, like an angel walking toward him. He couldn't take his eyes off her. When their eyes locked, the jolt of arousal knocked the breath out of him.

She appeared to be experiencing the same feeling of connection, based on how she kept her focus on him, as she walked straight to his side without even acknowledging the other men at the table.

"Ah, our princess has arrived." With his first flirtation, Crockett brought both James and the waitress back to the moment when it had happened earlier in the day.

Not wanting to relive the uncomfortable conversation, James paused the fantasy in his head, backing up a few frames, as if he was watching a movie in his mind, and holding on the image of her standing by his side and looking down into his eyes.

His attraction to her was unlike anything he'd ever experienced before. It wasn't just that his dick instantly responded to her beauty, although she was gorgeous. James estimated Randi to be about five-foot-five, or maybe five-foot-six, so about average height for a woman but still petite enough to be intimidated by his six-foot-four, two-hundred-and-fifty-pound frame.

She had long blonde hair that she had up in a ponytail on the crown of her head, and it still fell down to between her shoulder blades. He wondered if it would feel as silky running through his fingers as it looked. Her long medieval style dress hid her curves a little too well, in his opinion, but he could tell she still had curves in all the right places.

Leah Mae Wright

Her most striking feature, though, had to be her emerald, green eyes. They were so vibrant and expressive that he couldn't look away from them even when she was focused on one of the other guys at the table with him. He was getting hard again, just lying there in bed thinking about her.

Just as he was about to undo his dress pants and jack off to a fantasy about the beautiful, blonde Randi, his phone buzzed in his pocket with a text notification. He pulled it out and looked at the display.

Anthony: Hey James, are you at the hotel?

James: Yeah. Why?

Anthony: Did you eat dinner at the hotel restaurant? Have a hot blonde waitress?

James: Yeah. How'd you find out? Which asshole told you about her?

Anthony: Nobody told me about her. I'm at the hotel bar & she's here.

Anthony: She's telling her sister about you.

James: No way. I didn't even really talk to her.

Anthony: That's why she was telling her sister about you.

Anthony: Wished you'd have come into the restaurant alone so she could have gotten to know you.

James: Seriously? She was too busy turning down Dean, Josh, Red, & Crockett to notice me.

Anthony: Dude, she's so into you that she just described you to me with so much detail she was trying to figure

**out your racial breakdown to get that golden-brown
skin.**

> **James: You sure she didn't mean Dean?**

Anthony: No, she said he was too flirty.

**Anthony: She likes the shy, quiet type apparently.
Probably because she wants to be the outgoing one in
a relationship.**

> **James: You think I have a chance with her?**

**Anthony: Yeah, definitely. If you get your ass down here
to the bar before she & her sister finish their drinks.**

> **James: On my way.**

Holy shit! James thought as he bolted up out of bed. He ran to the bathroom to quickly brush his hair and teeth and made sure his clothes didn't look wrinkled from lounging on the bed. He decided his tan button down and dark khakis still looked fine before going down to the hotel bar to see if it was really Randi that Anthony had met there.

Within ten minutes, he was making his way through the crowd of people at the bar to where he saw Anthony sitting with Randi and a woman James thought he recognized as the hostess from the hotel restaurant earlier.

"I love classic rock music and played bass in a rock band when I was in high school," Anthony told the other woman as James walked up behind the three of them at the bar.

"We rocked back then." James remembered back to when he was the drummer in their fledgling little band. Dean had played lead guitar and was the only one willing to sing when they had a rare gig.

"'Bout time you got here, James." Anthony and the little brunette next to him turned toward James. James was right in his recognition of her from the hotel restaurant that afternoon. "Since you didn't get a proper introduction earlier, this is Kay and her sister, Randi. Ladies, this is one of my best friends, James."

"Nice to meet you." Kay tentatively extended her hand. James could tell she was wary of him, so he gently shook her hand, but he quickly released it to turn to Randi.

"Hi." Randi raised her hand to wave at him.

Damn, she's adorable, he thought, liking how she looked in a t-shirt, jeans, and sneakers, and especially with her flaxen hair down, cascading low on her back.

"Hi," James returned the simple greeting as he smiled at her. James and Randi didn't break eye contact as Anthony told Kay that James and his twin Dean had been his neighbors since birth and his best friends since they were all toddlers.

"I hope your shift got better after my buddies left," James said to Randi as the two couples seemed to pair off to have separate conversations.

"Not really." Randi smiled coyly. "You left when they did, so my shift pretty much went downhill when I lost my chance to give you my number."

"Well, we can rectify that right now." James pulled his phone out of his pocket and opened his contact list before handing it to Randi. "You can give me your number now, so we don't miss that chance again."

She deftly entered her digits, then swiped to send herself a text from his phone before handing it back to him. "Now I have your number too, so I don't have to wait to hear from you again before I sext you."

Surely, I heard her wrong, James pondered. *She said text, not sext. Just because I'm thinking about sex with her doesn't mean she's thinking the same thing.*

"It's, um, kinda loud in here," James pointed out, smiling at Randi. "Wanna go somewhere quieter, so we can actually hear each other?"

"Sure!" Randi hopped down from the barstool. "What did you have in mind?"

"Anyplace you wanna go, Angel." James led her out of the bar. He probably shouldn't have started using the term of endearment so soon in their first real conversation, but with her halo of golden blonde hair and how innocent she looked in her pale pink t-shirt, she looked like an angel to James, even more than she had earlier at the restaurant.

"How long are you in town?" Randi asked as they made their way to the hotel lobby.

"Just overnight," James replied, dropping his hand from her low back once they were out of the crowd. "We fly out to California in the morning."

"Then why don't we drive around? And I'll show you some of my favorite places in Tulsa while we get to know each other." Randi smiled shyly.

James agreed, and they made their way out of the hotel to his rental car. He opened the passenger door for her, waiting to close it once she was in the vehicle before walking around to the driver's side to get in the car himself. He hoped Randi wasn't put off by what modern society seemed to consider an outdated custom, but he couldn't break himself of the gentlemanly behaviors his parents had instilled in him from a young age.

As she directed him where to go, they started asking each other about all their favorite things, finding they had a lot in common when it came to tastes in music, television, and movies. He was two days older than her, being born on April eleventh when she was born on April thirteenth. They thought it was interesting that James was the oldest sibling in his family, even though it was only by a few minutes, and Randi was the youngest sibling in hers, where Anthony and Kay were the exact opposite.

A few minutes into their drive, Randi changed their conversation to asking Would-You-Rather questions, telling him about the game her family played on long road trips.

"Would you rather read a book or watch the movie made about the book?" Randi inquired, after pointing out a historic building on their drive.

"That's a tough one." James tried to think back to when he'd last done either. "I'm gonna say read the book because I can do that on the plane while we're traveling between cities, and if I don't finish it, I can pick it back up the next day. It's hard to get to the movies with my schedule, unless there's a midnight showtime."

"How exactly does your schedule work?"

"We wake up every morning to go get on the plane to go to the next city." James hated that he was going to have to tell her he wouldn't be off the road to be able to see her again until Thanksgiving. "Once we land, we go to the new hotel to check in, have lunch, and hit the weight room. Then we report to the arena between four and five to get our assignments for the night. We spar for an hour or so, then rehearse for the show that night if we're performing. We usually only wrestle three or four nights a week, but we have to stay at the arena to do promos, or in case someone gets hurt and we have to make a last-minute change to the card. We have dinner in catering and watch the show on the monitors in the back when we're not in the ring ourselves. Then once the show is over for the night, we either go back to the hotel or go out to a club or whatever. Then try to get a few hours of sleep to do it all again the next day."

"So, you never have a day off?" Randi's jaw dropped as if she was in shock over his unusual schedule.

"Yeah, we get time off…" James trailed off pensively. "Like I said, we're only really working three or four days a week. We just have to be available in case we're needed more. Plus, Memorial Day, Fourth of July, Labor Day, Thanksgiving, and Christmas, we're off from the Saturday before to the Sunday after to actually spend time at home with our families."

"But even though you may not work the show tomorrow night, you have to be with the company at the arena and can't stay in Tulsa until the next time you're actually scheduled to wrestle." Randi shook her head like she couldn't believe his schedule.

"Yeah," James muttered, trying to figure out how to change the subject. He knew it was too soon to say if they had a chance at being more than a one-night stand. He just hoped the fact that they'd have to spend at least the next couple of months only communicating over the phone while he traveled for work wouldn't prevent her from being open to possibly being in a more serious relationship with him in the future. And he had no idea how to communicate that to her without sounding like an egotistical ass.

After a couple of minutes of silence, he finally asked her another question in their game. "If you were gonna perform in a talent show, would you rather act out a scene from a play or sing on stage?"

"Act, for sure," Randi giggled. "I can't carry a tune in a bucket, so I couldn't win if I tried singing for my talent."

"Really?" James looked at her with surprise. "I like listening to you talk, so I assumed I'd like listening to you sing, too."

"Yeah, I'm not going to subject your poor eardrums to my singing, so you'll just never know how wrong your assumption is." Randi grinned at him. "My turn and I'm bored with the normal version of Would You Rather, so we're switching to the naughty version."

"There's a naughty version?" James felt his dick rise, as if he was going to answer Randi's naughty questions.

"Oh, yeah, and it's a lot more fun." Randi turned in her seat, so she could watch him as she asked her next question. "Would you rather do it rough and rowdy or slow and sensual?"

Holy fuck, maybe she did say sext earlier. James shifted in his seat, needing to adjust his pants to make room for his growing erection, while he contemplated the question.

"That's a tough one," he finally supposed, trying to keep his focus on the road in front of them so he didn't wreck the car from trying to watch her reaction to his answer. "I wanna say both, because it depends on the specific situation and who I'm with at the time as to which I'd prefer. But I don't think I'm allowed to not pick one or the other in the game, am I?"

"Nope, you have to pick one or the other." Randi popped her P as the word "nope" passed her lips, mischief gleaming in her eyes, even on his brief glance in her direction.

"Then I'm gonna say slow and sensual," James replied. "At my size, I wouldn't wanna take a chance on hurting my partner if she couldn't handle rough and rowdy."

"Normally, I'd say that was a wrong answer, but since I like your reason why, I'll allow it," Randi grinned. "As long as you're willing to change that answer with a woman who wants rough and rowdy."

"Absolutely!" James smiled, just as Randi's phone rang.

"Ugh!" Randi groaned when she pulled it out of her pocket and saw who was calling. She swiped the screen to decline the call. "I've gotta get my dad to get this idiot to leave me alone."

"Someone harassing you?" James wished she would have answered the call and handed him the phone to deal with the asshole for her.

"Yeah," Randi huffed. "I broke up with him like a month and a half ago, but he was apparently too focused on the hunting expedition he was packing to go on and didn't hear me. He just got back into town earlier this week and has been blowing up my phone ever since, trying to say we're still dating. As if…"

She was cut off by her phone ringing in her hand again.

"Want me to answer it and get rid of him for you?" James extended his hand to her, so she could hand him the phone. When she placed it in his palm, he noticed the contact's name was "Ballless Billy" and had to stifle a chuckle before swiping to answer the call. He made sure it was on speaker, so they could both hear the whole conversation.

"What the fuck do you want, Ballless?" James used his deepest tone of voice as he spoke. The tone that he usually only used for cutting promos at work was his most intimidating way to engage the prick over the phone.

"Um, who's this? I-I'm trying to reach my girlfriend, Randi," Ballless Billy stuttered over the phone. "Who are you? And why are you answering her phone?"

"I'm James Dangerous and Randi isn't your girlfriend." James seamlessly went into character as his wrestling persona. "She's mine now. And if you call my girl again, I'll make sure that you won't be physically able to call anyone ever again."

"Um, uh, so, sorry," Ballless Billy stuttered out in response to James's threat.

James swiped the end call icon and handed Randi her phone. She burst out laughing as her fingers brushed his palm when she took the phone. He felt tingles in his hand where her fingertips barely touched him.

"Oh. My. Dog!" Randi exclaimed through her raucous laughter. "That was way better than having my dad threaten to arrest him!"

Oh my dog? Damn, she's cute, James mused, chuckling along with her. *Too innocent to curse, but hinting she wants rough and rowdy sex. Makes me wanna sneak her on the plane in the morning, so I can see just how dirty we can get together.*

James's inner monologue was interrupted by her phone ringing again in her hand. Randi didn't hesitate to answer the call.

"Hello," Randi giggled, angling the phone, so James could see her sister's name on the screen as she swiped the speaker icon.

"Hey, Sis," Kay greeted Randi through the phone. "I didn't see you leave, so I wanted to make sure you were actually safe at home before I leave the Camelot."

"You didn't see me leave?" Randi continued laughing. "I don't think you saw me at all once you locked eyes with Anthony." Randi took a couple of breaths, like she was trying to control her giggles. "Yeah, it was too loud to talk in there, so we left. We've just been driving around talking for the last half hour or so."

"So, you're not home yet? Do I need to wait here for him to bring you back? Or is he taking you home?"

"He's taking me home," Randi giggled into the phone. "Eventually!" More giggles. "Don't worry, I'll be home in time for church in the morning."

Her laughter was just getting more and more uncontrollable, so he wasn't sure her sister understood her "Bye, Sis," as she disconnected the call.

James was starting to understand what people meant when they said laughter was contagious. He was fighting to keep from laughing with her, but he had to so he could continue safely driving.

"Oh, oh!" Randi waved one hand in her face, still trying to stop laughing while pointing with the other. "Turn here to go into Chandler Park."

He followed her directions as her giggling subsided and they made their way through the park. They followed the paved drive around various playgrounds and sports fields until they came to an area that was more rustic with huge boulders that almost looked like they were placed there by an artist instead of being naturally occurring in the environment.

They parked and got out of the car to go exploring the trails through the boulders while Randi explained some of the history of the park.

"Back in the fifties, all this land was part of a rock quarry." Randi motioned to the area around them. "My grandpa worked there and when Mr. Chandler donated the land to the city, it was grandpa's job to move all these rocks from the area where they were putting in the playgrounds and picnic areas. It's my favorite part of the park because I'm still amazed that he was able to move such huge rocks."

James agreed that moving those huge boulders was an impressive feat. He thought about the rocky part of the family homestead that had once been a quarry for the stone used to build some of the first buildings in his small hometown, and wondered what could be done with the area to make it more of a park-like setting, similar to the park they were walking through. Maybe when he finally retired from wrestling, he could impress Randi by building her a park down in Heart's Destiny.

"It's your turn to ask me a Would-You-Rather question," Randi reminded him, bringing him back to the moment.

"Would you rather give or receive oral sex?" If she wanted to switch to the naughty version of the game, then James was more than willing to start asking her naughty questions.

"Receive," Randi replied rapidly. "Because I've never received it before, so I wanna know if it's really as good as I've heard."

"Seriously?" James stopped in his tracks to turn to look at Randi. "You've never…"

"Nope, never," Randi confided, cutting him off.

"You've been dating all the wrong men." James shook his head at the tragedy of her never having experienced one of his favorite sexual activities. He wanted to offer to drop to his knees right then and show her how good it would be, but he figured it was too soon in their potential relationship. The opportunity was lost when she asked her next question.

"Would you rather watch other people have sex or be watched while you're having sex?" Randi took his hand and pulled him farther along the trail between the boulders.

"You keep asking questions where I wanna answer both," he chuckled, reveling in the feel of her hand in his, as they walked down the rocky trail. "I guess I'll say watch, because A, I'm a guy, so of course I like to watch, and B, with my travel schedule, I'm more likely to watch porn than to actually have sex. But I will say that with the caveat that if I was with the right person and she wanted to be watched, I would be okay with being watched, too."

"Good answer." Randi smiled brightly. "I wouldn't ever wanna go be on stage at a sex club or whatever, but I like the idea of sex in public, where we're risking being seen but not likely to have an audience."

"You mean like in a deserted park in the middle of the night?" James's cock threatened to bust the seams of his slacks to fulfill the fantasy he was imagining with Randi right then.

"Exactly like that," Randi whispered, her voice sounding a little breathy.

They bantered back and forth for a few minutes with questions about various positions that they ultimately decided they couldn't answer under the rules of the game because they were both open to trying any and all new positions with the right partner.

Anthony had implied that Randi wanted to be the more outgoing person in a relationship, but James got the impression that she was actually uncomfortable taking a leadership role with a significant other. It was like she had to push outside her comfort zone to express her interest in the sexual acts their conversation had led to. Like she was adorably shy about her sexual desires, but she desperately wanted not to be. Like she almost needed permission to admit to what she wanted before she could enjoy it.

James had always held himself back, allowing whatever woman he was with to take the lead, not wanting to risk his inner caveman scaring or hurting anyone. As much as he tried to constantly control his primal urges, James wasn't sure he'd be able to keep those urges leashed with Randi. If she kept blushing so innocently with every sexual reference they made, he feared he'd release the beast and take charge of Randi and her sexual exploration. The shy, innocent side of her that he kept seeing glimpses of was calling out to his repressed dominant side in a way no other woman ever had. He longed to take control and lead her through all their wildest erotic fantasies.

"Okay, I'm gonna get us back on track with the game," Randi declared, as they climbed up on top of one of the boulders to sit and watch the stars while they talked. Once they were both reclining on the flat top of the rock, she asked, "Would you rather us stay platonic friends who talk via text once in a while, or bang like bunnies tonight and every chance we get when you can come back to town?"

James was glad he was mostly laying down when she finished her question. Had she asked that as he was still climbing up onto the boulder beside her, he would have surely fallen from the shock of her asking the question without blushing the way she had previously every time she mentioned anything sexual. It took him a moment of opening and closing his mouth like a fish out of water before he was able to verbalize a response.

"Fuck like bunnies," he finally blurted, turning to smile at her. "But not just tonight and when I can come back to Tulsa. Over Skype and anytime I can get you to come see me while I'm working, too."

"Perfect answer," she cooed, leaning into him, so their lips could meet for the first time.

James let her take the lead, enjoying the feel of her confidently kissing him. He loved the feel of her hands as they stroked over his pecs to his shoulders, eventually ending with her arms around his neck and her fingers weaving through his long hair.

As hard as he tried to keep his dominant side reined in and let her take the lead, there wasn't a force strong enough to stop him from wrapping her in his arms and pulling her on top of him. He laid all the way back, resting his head on the boulder beneath them, as he ran one hand through her silky soft hair and the other down her spine to cup her perfect ass. He probably squeezed her ass cheeks a little too hard, but he couldn't fight his need to press her pelvis into his own. He only hoped the feel of his hard cock pushing up against her pussy felt as good for her as it did for him, so it would be worth any accidental bruising he might have just caused.

Their tongues tangled, dueling for control of the kiss. She writhed on top of him, spreading her legs, so they rested on the rock on either side of his, as she rubbed her core over his rock-hard cock.

"Fuck, Angel," James growled as they pulled back from the kiss to take a breath. "Lose these jeans and sit on my face, so I can eat your pussy."

She quickly scrambled off of him to lose her shoes and jeans, taking her panties off with them, so he didn't even see what color they were before she was straddling his head. James was grateful for the bright light of the full moon, so he could see her pretty pink pussy and the little landing strip of blonde curls that he wouldn't mind finding mixed in with his beard the next time he looked in a mirror.

"Don't let me fall off this rock," Randi cautioned, looking down at him nervously.

"Never, Angel," James reassured her, gripping her hips to hold her in place.

He didn't waste time telling her how beautiful she was or how much he loved the musky scent of her arousal mixed with the lightly floral yet lightly fruity scent of her perfume. He dove in to devour the sweetest treat of his life. He licked from her slit to her clit. He sucked on her nubbin of nerves, teasing it lightly with his teeth, before fucking her with his tongue. He tightened the tip, swirling it around inside her, trying to get deep enough to stimulate her G-spot.

"Oh, my, dog!" Randi screamed, falling forward, and catching herself with her hands on his forehead. James tightened his grasp on her hips to make sure she wouldn't fall any further when she came. "Oh, yes, James, yes, right there."

He focused on her internal trigger with his tongue while he rubbed her clit with his thumb, wanting to make sure she was stimulated in all the right places to explode in his mouth. It didn't take long before she was chanting his name repeatedly while he swallowed down her sweet cream as her inner walls clamped down on his tongue.

As soon as the waves of her orgasm subsided, so he could actually pull his tongue out of her tight pussy, James picked her up and moved her down his body, so he could cradle her to him and keep her safe from falling while she recovered from her climax.

He was thinking about how to get his wallet out of his back pocket and his pants down enough that she could ride him without disturbing her as she recovered, when she lifted her head from his shoulder and changed his plan for how they'd have sex the first time.

"That was better than I ever imagined," Randi breathed out, smiling shyly. "Do you think we could maybe try to fulfill another of my fantasies?"

"Absolutely, Angel," James affirmed, brushing her stramineous strands of hair out of her face. "I'll fulfill any fantasy you want."

"I want you to chase me through the trails and take me up against one of these boulders like a wild animal when you catch me," she requested breathlessly, looking at him like she was nervous he would refuse.

As if he could ever refuse her anything. She may not know it yet, but he would prove to her eventually that he would do anything for her. She was it for him, the woman of his dreams, his future wife and mother of his children. He knew she would probably be freaked out if he told her that right then, so he put his plans for their future to the back of his mind and focused on fulfilling her fantasy instead.

"You want me to take you, even if you're fighting and telling me no?" James needed to be perfectly clear on what she wanted, so he could deliver exactly what she desired.

"I wouldn't actually say no." Randi bit her lower lip and her cheeks turned slightly pink. "I don't think, anyway. I mean, it's not really a rape fantasy, more of an I-want-to-tease-you-until-you-can't-take-it-anymore-and-have-to-have-me fantasy."

"Okay, Angel, how about we have a safe word, something you wouldn't normally say, so if you accidentally say no while you're getting into it, I won't stop when I shouldn't." James felt harder than he'd ever been in his life, extremely aroused by her dirty desires.

"Octothorpe," Randi stated, smiling as she started to sit up, so they could climb down from the top of the boulder.

"Octothorpe?" James chuckled at the strange word, wondering what it meant.

"It's the proper name for the hashtag symbol," Randi clarified, as if she read his mind.

"Alright, my brilliant Angel." James grinned at the gorgeous woman. "If I do anything that makes you uncomfortable or hurts in any way, you say octothorpe and I'll stop. Now put your shoes back on, so you don't hurt your feet running from me on the trails. I'll carry these with me, so we don't have to come back here for you to get dressed later."

James grabbed her jeans and rolled them up with the panties still in them. He tucked them under his arm like a football as he climbed down off the boulder.

As soon as Randi had her shoes back on, he reached up and helped her down, so she didn't accidentally scrape her exposed parts on the rock face to climb down. He loved the feel of her sliding down the front of his body as he lowered her to the ground.

Although, he did regret that she was still wearing her t-shirt and bra. He resolved to at least push them up and get his mouth on her mounds once he had her in his arms against a boulder.

He pulled his wallet out of his back pocket and removed one of the condoms he carried there.

"Why don't you start teasing me by putting this on me before you take off running?" James held the condom out to her with one hand while he put his wallet back in his pocket with the other.

Randi reached out and took the condom, then placed it between her teeth to hold it while she used both hands to unfasten his belt and dress pants. She pushed them and his boxer briefs down just enough for his cock to spring free. The eager appendage was hard as steel and aimed directly at her, already leaking precum from how aroused he was from what they'd already done.

She tucked his boxer briefs under his balls, then softly trailed her fingertips over them as she moved her hands. One hand moved to stroke his cock from root to tip in a firm grip. The other went to the condom package in her mouth, which she opened with her teeth, before that hand tucked the condom wrapper into his front pants pocket and joined the other on his dick.

"Fuck, that feels good, Angel," James groaned, loving the feel of her hands on him as she teased him before rolling the condom on.

Once the rubber was completely in place, she pulled his slacks back up and fastened the button at the waist, leaving his hard-on poking out through the zipper fly.

"Can't have you tripping and falling with your pants down around your ankles," Randi taunted, pushing up on her tiptoes to kiss him on the cheek before she took off running down the trail.

Like I can really run with my underwear tucked under my balls, James inwardly chuckled as he took off after her, making sure to keep her jeans tucked tightly under his arm. He wasn't sure if she was a really slow runner or if she was just going easy on him, since his loafers weren't exactly the right shoes to run the trails in, but he caught her easily only twenty or thirty yards down the trail.

He dropped her jeans as he scooped her up into his arms. She was so light it was easy for him to spin her around and bring her legs around his waist as he moved toward the wall of rock beside the trail. She wrapped her arms around his neck, allowing him to unfasten the button on his pants without risking dropping her.

His pants fell to his knees, effectively getting out of the way, so they wouldn't end up stained from her dripping wet pussy while they fucked. The tails of his shirt were already separated from covering her thighs, so there was nothing between his cock and the heaven between her legs other than the latex. He pushed her back against the rock wall and gripped the globes of her ass as he entered her for the first time.

"Fuck, you're so tight, Angel," James moaned as he tried to work his way inside her without hurting her. *Fuck, I should've spent more time getting her ready! One O from oral wasn't near enough to prepare her for taking all of me. Why would she talk about wanting it rough when she's clearly not ready for that?*

"No, you're just too big, Jimmy," Randi shuddered as she rocked her hips, trying to take more of him, like she was trying to rush to the finish line when he wanted to take his time and savor every moment.

No one else had ever called him by the nickname because he'd thought it sounded too juvenile, even as a child. He didn't think it sounded juvenile at all on Randi's lips as he slowly worked his way into her tight, wet sex, inch by agonizing inch.

He showed his appreciation for her giving him the nickname by bringing their lips together in a passionate kiss. She opened for him instantly, so he could explore the depths of her mouth with his tongue. She returned his ardent kiss, sucking his tongue briefly before tangling it with her own.

Wanting to get her more aroused, so he could get further inside her without hurting her, he adjusted his left hand to cradle her ass as he used his right hand to push her t-shirt up. He broke the kiss when her pink lace bra was exposed, so he could lick his way down her neck. He pulled his head back to go over the bump of her shirt at her collarbones, but returned to trailing his tongue on the soft skin of her cleavage. He pushed the cups of her bra down, exposing her perky pink nipples.

"Fuck, you're gorgeous, Angel," James crooned just before he latched on to her left breast. Her breasts weren't huge, but they weren't small either. Definitely more than a mouthful, which was just about perfect in James's opinion. He suckled and savored her left breast for a few minutes, noticing how much wetter she got as her pussy relaxed enough to finally let him all the way in, before giving equal treatment to her right breast.

Once he was balls-deep inside her, he held still for a moment to make sure she had ample time to adjust to accommodate him. He adjusted his hold, gripping both globes of her gorgeous ass, so he could have total control of how fast and hard he fucked her.

"Oh, dog, oh, James," Randi chanted when he started moving in and out of her tight little pussy. As he ramped up the intensity, she started digging her fingernails into his back through his shirt. "Yes, Jimmy, right, yes, there, yes!"

"You're mine, Angel," James shouted as he lifted his head from the perfect pillows on her chest. Their eyes locked, his gray to her green, their connection strengthening as he pounded into her against the granite wall of rock.

"Yes, James, yes," Randi panted as her inner walls tightened around his cock.

The way she clamped down on him like a vise as she came made it impossible for him to hold back his own release. They repeatedly shouted each other's names as they both went over the edge to ecstasy before sealing their union with another impassioned kiss.

They clung to each other for several long moments, catching their breath after their explosive orgasms. Once they recovered, James backed away from the wall of rock, so Randi could unlatch her feet where she had them hooked together over his ass and lower them to the ground.

Since they didn't have any way to clean up within the wooded area of the park, James carried Randi's pants and only pulled his up enough to be able to walk, as they made their way back to the SUV he'd rented when the GWA had landed in Tulsa that morning. He opened the passenger door and shielded her body between his and the vehicle while they wiped up with the napkins he found in the glovebox. He disposed of the condom in one of the napkins, walking the whole bundle they'd used to the nearest trashcan after they were both fully dressed again.

They climbed up on the boulder nearest the parking area to sit and talk until sunrise. They talked about anything and everything they could think of, continuing their naughty Would-You-Rather game some, comparing their favorite things some, about their childhoods, their college experiences, and their plans for the future. She explained her creative cursing, how she tried to always use substitute words, in case her parents or nieces might overhear her. He teased her about how he was going to work on getting her to talk dirty to him, until she finally conceded and whispered, "Fuck me, Jimmy," in his ear to instigate round two on top of the boulder.

Since they were so close to the parking area, they tried to stay as covered as possible. She only took one leg out of her jeans and panties, and he only pushed his pants and boxer briefs down to his mid-thighs. After he retrieved his second (and last) condom from his wallet, she straddled him where they were sitting, using his shirttails to cover where they were joined.

He couldn't really thrust from the seated position atop the boulder, but he loved being able to wrap his arms around her and kiss her as she ground down on him. Knowing that she was probably already going to be sore from how rough he'd gotten the first time, he tried to control his primal urge to shove his way into her. Just the thought of possibly hurting her silenced the demon inside him and allowed him to relinquish control to her for their second coupling.

Randi was excellent at taking the reins and riding him like one of the stallions in a rodeo. With her expert skill in the saddle, it didn't take long for them to both be flying over the edge together, moaning each other's names as they simultaneously climaxed.

Since they were out of napkins from the SUV, James tied off the condom to throw away as they walked back to the vehicle. He used his shirttail to wipe up between her luscious legs, and let his boxer briefs soak up anything left on him as they got dressed again.

Their conversation resumed as they sat there cuddling and enjoying the afterglow. They didn't label their relationship, but they agreed that they were open to seeing where they could go in the future together. He wanted to make plans for when he could see her again, but she wasn't ready to commit to flying out to wherever he was with work for the next few weeks or planning what they would do when he had time off for Thanksgiving. They planned to talk via text, phone calls, and Skype video calls, and would figure out when they could see each other in person again as they got to know each other better.

Once they watched the sunrise over the rolling hills around them, they left Chandler Park to go have breakfast at a local diner that Randi recommended. There was never a lull in their conversation as they ate or drove around West Tulsa.

He dropped her off at her house a little after eight that morning. He walked her to her door and left her with another passionate kiss. He hated having to leave, knowing he was going to miss her even though they would be in constant contact with their phones.

James knew that Randi Lee was his one true love. He just had to be patient as he convinced her that he was also hers.

Chapter One

Sunday, October 7, 2018

Randi Mae Lee reflected back on the interesting week she'd had since meeting James Hunter while she got ready to go meet her parents at church. Being raised as the baby of the family with two uber-religious parents, she knew better than to mention her new boyfriend, where either her mother or father could overhear her. They would definitely not approve of their youngest daughter, who they thought was still a virgin, dating the long-haired, tattooed, bad boy of professional wrestling. Even with those dates only being over the phone, since he left town within an hour of dropping her off the previous Sunday morning.

If her parents had even a whiff of what Randi and James had done in the eight hours they were together the previous weekend, they'd be mortified. They were adamant in wanting to raise their daughters to be *"good girls"* who didn't ever say a foul word or have sex outside of marriage, and only for procreation. When Randi's sister, Kay, had gotten pregnant at the end of her sophomore year of college, they were livid. Randi was only twelve years old at the time, but she remembered how they reprimanded Kay, even though she was nineteen and technically an adult. Randi honestly believed that Kay wouldn't have married her ex-husband if she hadn't been coerced by her parents.

That was why Randi kept as much of her dating life from her parents as possible. She still remembered the teenage dating lectures she'd endured and didn't want a repeat of them at twenty-five. To keep from being chastised for her casual relationships, she only informed her parents of the name of someone she dated if she absolutely had to, like when she needed her dad to get an ex to stop calling her after a break-up. Thankfully, that hadn't happened but a couple of times since she was a teenager. Randi was especially thankful that James had dealt with the latest ex-idiot, so she hadn't had to tell her father about him.

Thinking back to how James had answered her phone and dealt with Ballless Billy for her, led to her standing in her bathroom daydreaming about everything else they did that night. How they talked about anything and everything. How she felt butterflies in her stomach just looking at him. How connected she felt to him when they were intimate. It was the most intense feeling of bonding that she'd ever felt with anyone.

Their instant connection was so different from what she normally felt with men she'd dated in the past that she completely abandoned her normal timeline for meeting and getting to know someone before allowing the relationship to turn physical. *Were we even in a relationship the first time we had sex?* Randi wondered. If a relationship required being in the same location together the whole time, then what they had would probably be better classified as a one-night stand.

In fact, that's what Randi had thought it would be at the time and had been proud of herself for feeling confident enough to ask him to fulfill her fantasies, when she wasn't sure they would ever be more. It was the first time she'd been intimate with someone she'd just met. While she'd had some feelings of guilt at first, knowing that she would be considered a slut for not only having sex with James so soon, but also for how much she enjoyed it, his claiming her while they were joined and telling her that he wanted more between them in the future relieved a lot of those feelings of guilt.

Talking to her sister the next day had relieved a few more, especially when her sister confessed to having similar fantasies about Anthony, even though they didn't act on them that first night. She would probably still feel guilty if her parents ever found out, but she wasn't going to dwell on that possibility right then. She'd rather reminisce about her time with James and bask in the afterglow of reliving her dream come true night with him.

Feeling like I can really be myself with him is the most amazing part of our relationship. Randi remembered back to how she'd shared her dirtiest desires without feeling bad about herself for having those fantasies.

In the past, she'd let her boyfriends lead the way when their relationships had turned sexual, never sharing her own sexual desires with anyone in her past. She'd never initiated anything in her previous relationships. She'd never shown an interest in someone first, never leaned in to kiss a boy until he kissed her first. Even when she dated someone more than once, she held them off for at least six weeks before letting them do more than kiss her goodnight, and never let them do anything kinky once their clothes came off.

But with James, she felt like she could trust him with her innermost secrets from the moment they met. When they were together, she didn't feel guilty for her sexual desires for the first time ever in her life. With James, she actually felt free to explore her sexuality in a way she'd never imagined. Instead of making her feel dirty when she was brave enough to share her fantasies, James showed her that her sexual desires were nothing to be ashamed of, at least with him. He was not only aroused by all the same things she was, but he also wanted to explore every kinky thing they could think of together.

And boy, did we explore some kind of kinky stuff this last week! He even got me to say fuck and feel comfortable dirty texting, not to mention the mutual masturbation via Skype! But as wonderful as all that has been, nothing compares to how thoroughly he filled me when we fucked against the rocks in Chandler Park!

Randi fanned herself to try to cool down from the memory of their steamy, hot sexcapades in Chandler Park. Watching her cheeks flush in the mirror, she opted to add more concealer to her face, so that if she drifted off daydreaming about James while in church, like her sister, Kay, had about Anthony the previous week, her bright red blush wouldn't be apparent to everyone around her.

She thought back to their sizzling sexts, where they shared their dirtiest fantasies all week to make sure her makeup covered everywhere she flushed. When she thought she was good to go, she recalled their late-night Skype sex, where they watched each other masturbate over video chat. Only to realize that she needed to cover the flush that went down her neck and across her chest, too.

"I need a better-paying job if I'm gonna hafta use this much makeup every day to keep anyone from knowing how bad I'm blushing while thinking about James," Randi scoffed to her reflection as she applied the additional concealer and foundation to everywhere that wasn't covered by her dress.

"Or maybe you need a job where you can telecommute so you can travel with him," her housemate, Amy, suggested from the doorway of their shared bathroom.

Randi had been best friends with Amy Lawton since they were assigned as roommates in the dorms at OU for their freshman year. Randi had gone to college on a cheerleading scholarship and graduated with a bachelor's degree in multidisciplinary studies three years ago. While she loved cheerleading, she had no desire to become a cheerleading coach, and the pay for professional cheerleaders wasn't worth pursuing it as a career after college.

She struggled to pick a major because she honestly had no idea what she wanted to do for a living, even three years after graduating from college. After her time at OU, she came home to Tulsa and went to work full time at the restaurant in the Camelot Hotel, where she'd been working part time in the summers when she was home from college. It wasn't what she wanted to do long term, but she didn't have any other ideas for what she really wanted to do with her life, so it was good enough for now.

Amy, on the other hand, got her degree in chemical engineering and had a really great job at a company downtown. Randi knew Amy worked in a lab developing new chemical products, but Amy's actual job was way too technical for Randi to understand any of the specific processes she performed each day.

"Yeah, I don't have a clue what I'd be qualified for that would allow me the flexibility to travel the way he does," Randi replied to her friend while finishing putting on her makeup.

"Maybe you can be his personal assistant," Amy recommended with a shrug. "Or keep his social media updated?"

"I'm not gonna ask him for a job," Randi sighed. "I want him to be my boyfriend, not my boss. Besides, I'm not actually gonna change jobs until I figure out what I wanna do as a career. I have a long solid work history with the Camelot that'll look good to my future employer, and I wanna keep it that way, so I don't have any strikes against me when I finally decide what I wanna do for the rest of my life."

Once she was finally ready, she got in her ten-year-old Honda Accord and drove to the Baptist church she'd attended her entire life to meet her parents. As she drove, she thought about potential career options. She could probably get a job in the secretarial pool at any number of businesses in Tulsa, but she had no desire to work in an office every day. While waitressing was just as tedious as office work, at least it allowed her to meet new people every day while being active in her job, instead of sitting at a desk working with the same people day in and day out.

She wanted something where she could stay active. She hated sitting still for too long. She also wanted to do something creative and fun. She'd thought about being a writer at one point, but it required too much sitting still to write out the stories she came up with, so she ruled it out after only one semester of creative writing in college.

She'd also considered being an artist, thinking she could work on big canvases to make it more active, but her first art class had taught her that she wasn't talented enough to make a living painting as a profession. She'd even thought about acting, having loved the acting classes she'd taken in college. But there weren't many opportunities in Tulsa that actually paid well enough to make it a viable career.

That was the major problem she had with deciding what to do with the rest of her life. Everything that sounded enticing was completely impractical. If she tried to make a career of any of the things she enjoyed as hobbies, she wouldn't be able to pay even the bare minimum of bills and her parents would never quit treating her like a child. So, above all else, whatever career she chose for her future would have to be something practical that showed she had truly matured. If she found a really grown-up job, maybe her parents would start treating her more like the adult she was, instead of continuing to treat her like a teenager.

She shook off the wandering thoughts as she got out of her car and made her way into the chapel. She looked around for her parents, but they weren't where they normally all sat together. People were still milling about, though, so Randi just went to their normal pew to take her seat, expecting her parents to be there any minute. Or at least her dad, since her mom would be going up to play the organ for the musical portion of the service before joining them in the pew for the sermon.

Leah Mae Wright

As people started taking their seats, Randi saw her mother go up to play the organ. She looked around, but still didn't see her father anywhere. When he didn't show up at any point during the musical portion of the service, she started to get worried. She wanted to ask her mom where he was as soon as she took her seat for the sermon, but she didn't get a chance to, since the preacher started speaking immediately after Mary Lee and the members of the choir were seated with their families.

She shouldn't have wasted so much extra makeup since she wasn't in danger of blushing from daydreaming about James when she was so worried about her dad. She sat there with her knee nervously bouncing as she imagined all sorts of scary scenarios for why he wasn't at church. His job as the sheriff for Tulsa County usually wasn't dangerous. He was more of a team leader and not normally on the front lines in risky situations as crimes were occurring, but he might have had to go in on his day off if something really horrible happened. She hoped he was safely coordinating the actions of his deputies from a safe distance, and not actually close enough to a crime scene to be in the line of fire if there was an active shooter situation.

As soon as the pastor ended the service, Randi turned to her mother and demanded, "Where's Daddy?"

"He's at Kay's house," Mary Lee answered, gathering her Bible and purse before standing to leave.

"Why is he at Kay's house?" Randi grabbed her own belongings to follow her mother out of the pew toward the exit of the church. She hadn't been worried about her sister not being at church, since she knew it was Mark's weekend with the girls and that Kay would probably try to work an extra shift at work, if she wasn't otherwise occupied with Anthony coming back to Tulsa for the weekend. But hearing that her dad was at Kay's house made her wonder what was going on that kept her out of church that morning, too.

"Because he's supervising the forensics team before replacing her front door," Mary stated matter-of-factly, like it was a normal daily occurrence.

"Mom!" Randi shouted, grabbing her mother's elbow to stop her from walking away before explaining what exactly was going on. "Where are Kay and the girls? Why is Daddy having to have a forensics team at her house? Why does her front door need to be replaced?"

"Randi Mae Lee, lower your voice," Mary whisper-shouted, looking around at the crowd around them. "Follow me to the house and I'll tell you what I know, but I'm not going to share information about your father's investigation with all of West Tulsa."

"I don't want information about his investigation," Randi whisper-shouted back at her mother. "I'm worried about my daddy, sister, and nieces."

"They're fine," her mother replied, giving her a pointed look. "I'll explain everything when we get to the house."

"Okay," Randi relented, releasing a breath she hadn't realized she was holding. "Your house or Kay's house?"

"Ours," Mary snapped, pulling her daughter along behind her as they exited the chapel into the vestibule. "We can't go in Kay's until it's released."

Until it's released? Randi thought her mother's wording was peculiar at first, until realization dawned on her. *Until the crime scene is released! Sugar, my sister's house is a crime scene!*

She dutifully followed her mother home, feeling like her whole body was vibrating from her anxiety. She bolted out of the car almost before she had it in park and turned off because she was so worried about what exactly was going on. She beat her mother to the front door, even though she was parked behind her in the driveway.

As soon as Mary Lee unlocked her front door, Randi rushed in behind her and shut it, so they were alone and could finally talk. She wanted to scream when her mom didn't immediately start explaining what was going on, but she knew that wouldn't do any good to get the news faster. So, she waited, somewhat impatiently, while her mom put away her things before walking back into the formal living room to sit on the sofa before talking.

"Have you talked to your sister since Friday?" Mary inquired from her daughter as she took her seat on the other end of the couch.

"No," Randi admitted, nervously bouncing her right leg. "Last I saw her was when I was going in to work Friday just as she was leaving, and we haven't even texted since then."

"Well, unfortunately, Mark was drunk when he tried to pick up the girls Friday night," Mary stated. "Your dad had to go over there when

Leah Mae Wright

Tia called him to get Mark to leave in a cab. He impounded Mark's car, but he apparently got a ride from someone last night to break into the house. When we drove by this morning, it looked like he'd destroyed everything in the place. Not that I could see much, though, since your dad wouldn't let me do more than look in from the front porch before he was sending me on to church and calling his team."

"But you said Kay and the girls are fine." Randi felt faint with worry for her sister and nieces.

"Yes, they left town yesterday morning with that man, Anthony, she met last week." Mary reached over to put a hand on Randi's knee to stop the nervous bouncing. "I'm not sure if your dad has even notified her yet about the break-in, but they were already out of the state before it happened, so they are safe and sound, I'm sure."

"Should we call her to make sure?" Randi queried, wanting to do something to help her sister.

"As much as I want to hear all their voices to reassure myself that they're okay, I think we should wait until your dad says it's safe for us to contact them." Mary patted her daughter's knee. "He wouldn't even tell me where exactly they were going, just that Anthony was setting up some job interviews for Kay in Texas, so they could stay safe from whatever Mark tries next. But with what he was saying about Anthony's job, I'm not even sure they'll be staying in Texas more than a few days."

Randi remembered what James had told her about the schedule for anyone working with the Galactic Wrestling Association, and wondered what job her sister might be qualified to interview for with them to be able to travel all the time to stay ahead of Mark if he tried to follow them out of Tulsa. While she wished she could interview for the same position, so she could be with James all the time, she knew her sister needed the job more to be able to keep herself and her daughters safe from her obviously crazy ex-husband.

Kay had been worried about Mark escalating to more than just the verbal abuse she told Randi about the previous weekend. Hearing that he'd *destroyed everything* in Kay's home, Randi understood Kay's fear. *Yep, he's definitely escalating. Thank goodness, they're safely out of his reach, so he can't physically hurt them, too.*

She talked with her mother for a few more minutes before hugging her and heading home for lunch. As she pulled out of her parents' driveway, she turned the opposite direction from the way she came in from church, so she could drive by her sister's house to see what her father would allow her to see of the damages.

He was standing on the front porch as she parked on the street. She couldn't pull into the driveway because of all the law enforcement vehicles already occupying the space. She barely got her car door open before her father was marching toward her, his long strides making quick work of crossing the lawn.

"Don't even get out of that car, young lady," Charles Lee bellowed in his most commanding sheriff's voice.

"I just wanted to see what I can do to help," Randi asserted as he approached her car.

"You can go home," he retorted as he put one big hand on the top of her car and the other on the top of the driver's door, effectively blocking her from exiting the vehicle. "And stay as far away from anyone in the Fox family as possible."

"Do I need to be worried that Mark or his brothers will break into my house, too?" Randi looked up to her father and tried not to look as scared as she felt.

"I don't think so," her dad replied, shaking his head. "They might come by to see if Kay or the girls are at your house, but I don't think they have any reason to break in. If any of them do show up at your place, don't answer the door and call me immediately."

"Okay, Daddy." Randi stood up so she could hug her father. He returned her hug, cracking her back in the process, before releasing her to leave. "Let me know when it's safe to call Kay," she beseeched, as she got back in her car and buckled up to drive home.

"Will do, baby girl," he agreed as he shut her car door. "Love you."

"Love you, too, Daddy," Randi returned the affection through her open window as she started her car to pull away.

She went straight home and as soon as she got in the front door, she texted James to call her as soon as he had a free moment to talk. Even if he couldn't really do anything to protect her from Albuquerque, New Mexico, where he was wrestling that night, just hearing his voice for a few minutes would make her feel safer, so she could quit shaking in fear, jumping at every unexpected noise, and looking over her shoulder like she expected Mark or one of his brothers to jump out at her from anyplace they could have hidden between Kay's house and her own.

<center>~~~</center>

Tuesday, October 9, 2018

As soon as James got back to the locker room after the afternoon sparring and rehearsal session in the ring, he had to pull his phone out of his locker and text Randi. He hoped it was at least late enough that she would be off work and able to reply. But with what she'd said the night before about the mess she was dealing with at work since her sister left town with Anthony, he wouldn't be surprised if in addition to making her cover her sister's shift as hostess, her boss also made her stay and work her own shift as a waitress again.

> **James: Hey, Angel. Today any better at work? It was for me since I met your nieces. Text me as soon as you're free to chat.**

James laid his phone down on the bench beside him while he changed into his wrestling tights, boots, and a Dangerous Twins t-shirt. The GWA's television show, ***Tuesday Night Takedown***, was airing live that night, so he had to go ahead and dress for the gimmick to do promos early before wrestling in the main event. It was going to be a busy evening, and he hated that he could only text Randi in between his work duties, instead of getting to head to the hotel early to call or Skype with her.

Just as he was starting to lace up his wrestling boots, his phone buzzed beside him on the bench. He looked down to see Randi's name on the display and smiled before picking it up to see her message.

> **Randi: Work was Work. {Face with Rolling Eyes Emoji}**

> **Randi: Tia & Maria are at your show tonight?**

30

James: Yeah, & Kay got a job with the GWA today.

Randi: Thank Dog! With what her ex pulled this
weekend, she needs a job far from Tulsa. What's she
doing?

James: I'm not sure. Something with the flight crew so
she can be on the same schedule as Anthony. I thought
both flight crews were full, though, so I don't have a
clue what the job actually is.

Randi: You think it's a real job?

James: Yeah, why wouldn't it be?

Randi: Just the way my parents were talking about Friday
night.

James: I thought you said they all agreed that it was best
for them to leave town with Anthony, especially after
her ex trashed her house.

Randi: Yeah, but the way Dad talked made it sound like
Anthony made up the job possibilities to get Kay to
agree to go with him.

James: Maybe if it were a job at Burleson, Inc., but I don't
think Rick would go along with it if Anthony had made
up a job with GWA.

Randi: What's Burleson, Inc.?

James: Anthony's family's business. If he asked them to
make up a job for Kay, I'm sure they would with no
questions asked. But I don't think my boss would

actually hire her for a job if it wasn't a real job he
needed to fill.

Randi: If you say so, but I can't think of a single thing Kay
would be qualified to do on a flight crew, so I'm still
reserving judgement.

James: I'll ask about it some more, so I can set your mind
at ease. Who knows, maybe it's something you can do
on the other flight crew, so you can come travel with
us, too. ;)

Randi: Yeah, I know I'm not qualified to do anything on a
flight crew. {Woozy Face Emoji}

James: You get air sick?

Randi: No, but I'm the reason they pass out little bottles
of booze. Too nervous a flyer to be able to do a job in
the air.

James: Nothing to be nervous about, Angel. If you ever
agree to fly off with me, I'll hold your hand the whole
time. Or convert our pods for privacy and join the
mile-high club with you as a distraction from your
nerves.

Randi: Just how private are those pods? Soundproof?
{Ear Emoji} {Kiss Emoji} {Eggplant Emoji}

James: LOL Maybe not soundproof, but we can sit in the
back as far away from everyone else as possible & try
to be quiet. {Devil Emoji}

Randi: That might be fun on a plane with a bunch of strangers, but I don't think I could do it on the same plane as my sister and nieces. {Flushed Face Emoji}

James: Then I guess I'll have to look into chartering us a private jet sometime so we can join the mile-high club together. ;)

Randi: Maybe one of these days. So, what's your schedule tonight? Any chance we can call or Skype?

James: Dinner in catering, cutting promos, & wrestling the main event tonight. Show is airing live tonight, so the closest we can get is you watching while I work.

Randi: It's not as good as naked Skyping, but I'll settle for seeing you in tights on TV. {Star Struck Emoji} {Face Blowing a Kiss Emoji}

James: What's your schedule for tomorrow? Maybe we can Skype then?

Randi: 7a.m. to 3p.m. as hostess and 3p.m. to 10p.m. as waitress. What about Thursday? Only 7a.m. to 3p.m. work then for me.

James: We'll definitely find the time to Skype Thursday. :D Going to eat now but keeping my phone with me until my match later. Text me your thoughts on my promos.

Randi: Break a leg! {Leg Emoji} {Smiling Face with Heart Eyes Emoji} {Face Blowing a Kiss Emoji}

James wished his wrestling tights had a pocket, so he could carry his phone more discreetly as he made his way to catering. Now he understood why so many old-school wrestlers wore fanny packs. He thought about tucking his phone in his waistband where he could cover it with his t-shirt, but knew that if he did, he would either get an inappropriate erection when it buzzed from Randi texting, or break it when one of the guys started roughhousing and didn't know it was there. So, he just carried it in his hand, resting his plate on it while filling it at the buffet table, and then put it on the table beside his plate while he ate.

He knew from the week and a half he'd been texting Randi that she wouldn't text him anything while he was working that shouldn't be seen by his coworkers. While he didn't delete any of their texts, so technically one of his friends, or more likely his brother, could scroll back through their never-ending conversation to read their fantasies, they already had a system for sending sexy selfies through a more private app. And they only used it when they were alone in their individual bedrooms for the night, so there was no chance that anyone else would see his naughty naked nymph.

So far, he thought they were progressing nicely in their relationship. They were texting daily, carrying on a constant conversation where neither of them actually said *"goodbye,"* opting to do like they had earlier with explaining what was going on as to why they couldn't respond immediately, and picking up the conversation again as soon as they were free to text again.

Her schedule had been a little worse this week, with having to cover her sister's former shifts at the restaurant in addition to her own, so they were having a harder time actually calling or Skyping than they had the first week. But they were still going to be able to schedule two or three days when they could have the privacy for more intimate conversations and sexy Skype sessions. *Fuck, I love Skype sex with Randi!* He had to quit thinking about that, or he would have a wardrobe malfunction at the dinner table that was quickly filling up with his coworkers and their families.

The only issue he had with their relationship was that she still wouldn't agree to take some vacation time to come meet him at a show. Even though he'd told her about the pay-per-view weekend that was happening at the end of the month, when he would be in the same city from Friday afternoon until Monday morning, so they could spend several days together, she still refused to come to him. He didn't know how to convince her to either.

"Yo, Bro." Dean sat down beside James. "You're more quiet than normal tonight. Everything okay?"

"Everything's fine. Just trying to get in the right headspace for the show tonight," James lied. It wasn't that he was embarrassed to be caught thinking about Randi, instead of mentally preparing for the performance that night. He just wanted to keep her all to himself as much as possible, and that meant not sharing anything about her, their relationship, their private conversations, or his feelings about her with his brother and coworkers.

"Whatever, man," Dean grumbled, shaking his head at James before digging into his plate. "You're worse tonight than you and Anthony combined last week. Maybe now that Kay is traveling with him, at least he'll join back into normal conversations with the rest of us."

"Dude, when did I not join in on normal conversations?" Anthony sat down across the table from James, with Kay and her daughters beside him.

"Last week," Dean accused between bites of food. "There were even a couple of nights when you didn't even come to the arena, or you cut out as soon as possible. And neither one of you," he pointed back and forth between James and Anthony with his fork, "have gone out with the rest of us after a show since Tulsa."

"Sorry, Bro," James apologized, feeling slightly guilty for neglecting his brother since meeting Randi.

"Yeah, I'm not apologizing for having better priorities than going out partying with you after a show." Anthony shrugged his shoulders. "But I am sorry if you felt ignored when I was here, but focused on texting Kay instead of whatever conversation you wanted to have with me."

"I suppose you do have better priorities now," Dean acknowledged, smiling at Kay's daughters. "So, how have ya'll liked your first day with our crazy crew?"

"It's been, um, interesting," Kay responded with a shy smile. "And maybe a bit overwhelming."

"We're not all as bad as my brother," James quipped, knowing Dean wouldn't be satisfied that James was engaging in conversation unless he was giving him shit. They both knew they were intimidating and often threw each other under the bus to put others at ease. While Kay wasn't acting as timid as she had the weekend they first met, she was still acting a little uncomfortable around all the guys. James hoped she would relax some around them as she got to know them all. "In fact, most of us are just big teddy bears, who only pretend to be big, scary bad guys on TV."

Tia and Maria giggled as Dean glared at James.

"Did he just insinuate that I'm not one of the big teddy bears who only pretends to be a bad guy?" Dean rolled his eyes as if he was one of the girls.

"Yes, I think so," Tia giggled, bobbing her head. "But I think he's just trying to help you sell your character, so you don't show your teddy bear side on TV tonight."

"Exactly," James laughed, leaning across the table to give Tia a fist bump. "You're learning the wrestling world so fast that I bet you'll be booking the shows for us before you're old enough to actually wrestle on them yourself."

"How old do you have to be to wrestle?" Tia inquired, looking at James like she was thinking about a possible future career.

"Eighteen," James guessed as Rick Robertson, the owner of the GWA, walked by their table. "Right, Boss?"

Rick turned to look down at the table as a whole before asking, "Right about what?"

"I can't wrestle on your shows until I'm eighteen years old?" Tia arched an eyebrow, looking up at Rick curiously.

"Yes, that's correct," Rick smiled at the little girl. "But once you turn eighteen, you'll have to go through training before you can even get a tryout."

"But federal labor laws say that I can get a job at sixteen," Tia stated matter-of-factly, looking up at Rick with an expression that could only be read as determination. "If I train with Anthony, Dean, and James for the next three years and eighty-three days for my physical education credit for school, I should be ready for a tryout on my sixteenth birthday."

The entire room went silent, focusing on watching the boss to see how he countered Tia's logical argument. Rick looked like he was about to speak, opening his mouth as if to answer her, but he just closed it again, as if he had no idea how to respond. After he floundered a couple more times, a few people started to giggle, starting with Kay, and spreading to several of the people at the table.

"Don't fight it, Boss," Anthony chortled. "Tia's gonna be an attorney when she grows up, so I'd schedule her tryout for her sixteenth birthday if I were you. Otherwise, she might sue you for age discrimination."

Rick finally broke and laughed with the rest of them then. "Fine, but if you make the roster, you have to wear a lucha mask, so nobody can tell how old you are, and protest our shows."

"Awesome!" Tia shouted, a huge smile spreading across her face. "Wrestling will be a fun first job. And it should pay well enough to cover the costs of law school."

James picked up his phone, needing to share this conversation with Randi. He knew she'd get a kick out of hearing her niece's future plans.

> **James: Bet you can't guess what your niece just told us that she's going to do for her first job to pay her way through law school.**

> **Randi: Tia?**

> **James: Yes, Tia.**

> **Randi: No telling with that girl. Probably whatever Kay is doing with the GWA now.**

> **James: Nope, guess again.**

At least he didn't think Kay was signing on as a wrestler for the company. Just to be sure, he asked Kay, "So, Kay, tell us about your new job with the GWA?"

"Oh, um," Kay sputtered, looking first at Rick's retreating back, before turning to look nervously at Anthony. "I'm going to be a flight attendant, but I don't know what all it actually entails yet. I'll be learning on the job starting tomorrow."

Leah Mae Wright

"Is Janice leaving the crew?" Dean looked back and forth between Kay and Anthony.

"No," Anthony answered, which appeared to relieve Kay, probably because she hadn't met the other flight attendant on the crew yet. "Rick is adding a second flight attendant to the crews."

"He said my job will be more of a mother's helper position." Kay half-shrugged one shoulder. "Like I said, I'm not sure what all that means yet, but I think it means I'll be focusing on helping take care of the kids while we're on the plane more than a traditional flight attendant role."

"Cool," James nodded, wondering if that meant there was another opening on the other flight crew that he could possibly convince Randi to apply for in the future, if he could help her get over her anxiety about flying.

His phone buzzed in his hand, so he went back to his text conversation with Randi as the rest of the people at the table carried on the majority of the conversation around him.

> **Randi: Getting her pilot's license at the same time she gets her driver's license so she can be the co-pilot on the plane?**

> **James: No, but it wouldn't surprise me if she eventually changes her mind to do that instead of what she said tonight.**

> **Randi: Okay, I give up. What did my brilliant niece say she's going to do for her first job?**

> **James: She convinced my boss to give her a tryout on her sixteenth birthday so she can be a professional wrestler.**

> **Randi: Seriously?**

> **James: Yep, already has it planned for Anthony, Dean, & I to train her as her P.E. credit for school for the next 3**

years & 83 days, so she'll be ready for her tryout on her
16th birthday.

Randi: Only my brainiac niece could figure out exactly
how many days she has to train. {Rolling on the Floor
Laughing Emoji} {Brain Emoji} {People Wrestling
Emoji}

James: And only you would find a wrestling emoji. Now I
have to look those up.

Randi: You're welcome for the emoji addiction. {Smiling
Face with Halo Emoji}

James: You should use that one as your signature, Angel.

Randi: Only with you. Nobody else thinks I'm an angel.

Randi: Did you find out what Kay's new job is?

James: Yeah, she's going to be a flight attendant, but
focused on helping the parents with kids that travel
with us while we're in the air instead of the normal
flight attendant stuff.

Randi: Oh, she'll be good at that!

James: Still think you couldn't do the same job?

Randi: Definitely not. I can't calm down crying kids when
I want to cry right along with them.

James didn't know how to reply to Randi. He wanted to know what
her issue with flying was, so he could comfort her and help her get
past it to eventually be able to travel with him, but didn't know how to

ask her about it tactfully, so that he didn't trigger her into putting up walls between them and pulling away from him.

He looked up and noticed that Kay was watching him where he was texting Randi. *I wonder if she knows her sister's issue with flying and would be willing to share it with me?*

"Kay," James choked out her name. He took a drink of his bottled water to allow him time to formulate his words. "Do you know why Randi doesn't like to fly?"

"No, why?" Kay tilted her head at him inquisitively.

"We were talking about flying some and she said she's a nervous flyer."

"Oh, I thought you were setting me up for a joke," Kay snickered, shaking her head. "Like you were going to say that her arms got tired too soon to get very far or something."

"No." James chuckled at the joke Kay was expecting. "She didn't tell me why she doesn't like to fly. I thought you might know if she had a bad experience flying in the past, so I wouldn't risk upsetting her by asking about it and bringing up bad memories for her."

"Not that I know of." Kay bobbed her head from side to side, looking thoughtfully at James. "But we haven't been on a flight together in the past fifteen years. She could've had a bad experience while she was in college. I know she flew to cheerleading competitions and a couple of bowl games then."

"Okay, well, then I guess I'll back off on the subject for a little bit, until she's more comfortable telling me more." James hoped his smile would reassure Kay that her sister was safe with him.

The conversation continued with more small talk as they finished dinner. James and Dean went together to the makeshift interview area backstage to record their promos. James sat his phone on a side table out of the camera's view. They got into position for the backstage reporter, who happened to be one of the wrestler's wives, to interview them.

"Dean, James," Tiffany greeted them just after the light came on the camera, showing they were live on air. "What do you think of Red and Dark Chocolate teaming up to try and take your titles tonight?"

"What do I think?" Dean shouted into the microphone. "I think Red used to be a good wrestler, but him turning his back on the Dangerous Twins to team up with Dark Chocolate shows that he's not as ring savvy as he thinks he is. Red being on the opposite side of the ring from us tonight is making me see red. As in the red cloud of anger that focuses me on destroying my opponents. Tonight, that red cloud of anger will be focused on Red, the washed-up wrestler!"

Tiffany turned the microphone toward James for him to cut his part of the promo. James looked directly into the camera and smirked before speaking.

"While my brother is focusing his anger tonight, I'm gonna indulge my sweet tooth," James growled into the microphone. "Dark Chocolate Dion Davis, tonight I'm gonna turn you into a chocolate cream pie."

The Dangerous Twins walked away, stopping just outside of camera range to turn and watch Tiffany flounder with a moment of speechlessness before sending the show back to the ringside announcers. As soon as the light on the camera went dark, the area around them erupted in laughter.

"Chocolate cream pie?" Dean choked out through his laughter. "Bro, you made it sound like you're gonna eat him after our match."

"No, I'm gonna flatten him like a pie crust and then whip him into pudding," James proclaimed, chuckling with his brother and the camera crew.

"You really should've elaborated more there," Tiffany giggled. "My first thought was that you were gonna give him a sex change center ring and I wanted to make sure you weren't wrestling my husband anytime soon."

"This is why I keep telling you that we need to script our promos," James pointed out to his brother. "You took the easy one with seeing red. All I can come up with for Dion's gimmick are food references. Chocolate pie, chocolate cake, chocolate donuts, chocolate eclairs, chocolate syrup, chocolate ice cream, and I haven't even cycled through all the chocolate candy bars. But if we keep this feud up for very long, I'll probably refer to all of them because I don't have any serious sounding ideas for promos against Dark Chocolate."

"Fine, let's go see if we can get one of the writers to help us out before we cut the promo to end the show tonight," Dean acquiesced, leading the way back to the office area.

Leah Mae Wright

James picked up his phone on the way out of the interview area and noticed a message from Randi. He swiped the screen to open the text thread.

Randi: That was hilarious! Next time, tell him you're going to whip him into chocolate frosting for your girlfriend's birthday cake. {Birthday Cake Emoji}

James: That would imply that I'd be feeding him to you, which I would never do. {Angry Face Emoji}

Randi: Better than sounding like you'd be eating him for dessert after the show. {Men Wrestling Emoji} {Fork and Knife Emoji} {Pie Emoji} {Face Savoring Food Emoji}

James: Maybe you need to come on the road & write my promos for me.

Randi didn't reply before he got to the area where the writers were congregated, so he dimmed his screen to talk to them about how to cut the final promo of the night to end the show after they won their match. He started to get a little worried that he might have overstepped by suggesting she travel with him, when she didn't reply before he had to put his phone in his locker to go wrestle in the main event.

They had a good match, wrestling against two of their favorite people to work with in the ring and coming out on top to retain their titles at the end of the night. James ended the show by telling the crowd, "While I did whip him into pudding, Dark Chocolate is way too bitter for anyone to ever wanna eat that pie, so we had to toss him out with the rest of the garbage."

Once they made their way back to the dressing room, Dion and Liam joined his brother, Dean, in ragging him for the ridiculous pie promo.

"Dude, seriously, next time say I look like I'm going soft from eating too many chocolate treats," Dion chortled, shaking his head as his laughter died down. "You can tweak the wording and replace the pie with donuts or ice cream or whatever and cut the same promo a dozen different ways. We can keep people laughing for months with this feud."

"You'll have to sit in on the meeting I have tomorrow with the writers to help me come up with better promos," James implored Dion, slapping his friend on the back before heading to the shower.

At least he had a viable plan for future promos, since Randi had changed the subject without commenting on his idea for her to write them for him, when he checked his phone after getting dressed to go to the hotel.

Randi: Are you wrestling against the same guys you ate with at the Camelot 10 days ago? How am I supposed to believe you really want to beat each other up when I keep remembering the way ya'll were laughing and joking around as friends? {Confused Face Emoji}

James: Alas, Kayfabe is dead. {Disappointed Face Emoji}

Chapter Two

Randi woke up really irritated with her boss and had no idea what to do about it. The week before, he about worked her to death by having her cover Kay's hostess shifts and her own waitressing shifts, even if that meant she worked doubles several days. This week, he'd just scheduled her to cover Kay's hostess shifts, but then hired a new hostess that she spent Tuesday training and told her she wasn't needed for those shifts the rest of the week. Which meant that she wasn't scheduled to work again until he added her back to the schedule for the week beginning on Monday the twenty-second. If he added her back to the schedule at all.

She decided to start searching for job ideas and carried her laptop to the dining table to search while she ate breakfast. If Mr. Brooks was going to punish her for Kay having to leave town without notice, then she needed to come up with some ideas for ways to make up her lost income on these weeks when her hours were cut short. *A lot of good my seven years of job history does for me if I can't make ends meet on reduced work hours,* she thought, just as Amy walked into the kitchen.

"What are you doing still home?" Amy poured herself a travel cup of coffee. "I thought you were scheduled to work mornings all week."

"Yeah, I was," Randi huffed. "Until I trained Kay's replacement yesterday, and now, they don't need me anymore this week."

"Seriously?" Amy's jaw dropped in astonishment.

"Yep," Randi sighed. "That's why I'm searching for something else online now. I mean, I can see both sides of the situation with Kay leaving. It sucks for her that she had to leave, and it sucks for the restaurant to not have her there, but I didn't have anything to do with it, so I don't know why my boss is punishing me for something I had no control over."

"Yeah, that's just petty." Amy started gathering her things to go to work. "If the lack of hours puts you short and you need me to cover a little more of the bills this month, just let me know."

"Hopefully, it won't come to that," Randi lamented, going back to her online job search as Amy walked toward the door.

"Well, just know that it's an option if needed," Amy reassured, just before stepping out of the kitchen. "Good luck with your search today. See you later."

"Thanks," Randi replied as she waved her friend goodbye for the day.

Nothing she was finding online seemed appealing. The only things she found that she was even qualified for were other waitressing gigs or secretarial work. She was really sick of waiting tables, and had no desire to sit at a desk all day, so she didn't bother to apply for any of the jobs she saw online.

Just as she was switching her browser over to check her social media accounts for the day, her phone dinged with a text notification. She knew it wasn't from James because of the time of day. He was either on his way to the airport or on the plane going to the next city. But thinking of him did make her wonder how serious he was about the possibility of there being a job available for her to write promos for the GWA.

I know I can't do that flight attendant thing like Kay, but if they need writers, maybe I can get over my anxiety on planes and train with Tia to eventually perform on the shows. I mean, wrestling is just athletic acting. It checks both of my most important boxes for the perfect career—active and creative—so, maybe I should consider it as a potential career, even if it's not really a practical grown-up type of job like Mom and Dad want me to find.

Her phone dinged again, bringing her out of her possible career thoughts. She picked it up and saw it was her sister texting. Kay certainly seemed more chatty via text since she got her new phone the day before.

Kay: Hey, Sis, how do you feel about being a bridesmaid in my wedding next month?

Kay: Consider this your save the date notification to come to Texas the weekend after Thanksgiving. Barring any complications with court, we're planning to get married here on Sat., 11/24.

Randi: Wow! Prince Anthony really swept you off your feet fast! :) {Person in Tuxedo Emoji} {Person in Veil Emoji} {Family: Man, Woman, Girl, Girl Emoji} {Bouquet Emoji} {Wedding Emoji}

Kay: Okay to give your number to my future MIL for dress measurements/options?

Randi: I'd be honored to be in your wedding. {Beaming Face with Smiling Eyes Emoji} Yes, give her my number.

Kay: You don't think it's too fast? I know you thought I was being swept away by my fairy-tale dreams when we first met.

Randi: Yeah, but that was before you filled me in on everything that's happened since you left Tulsa. Now I'm starting to believe in your fairy tale being real. {Princess Emoji} {Prince Emoji}

Kay: How much do you believe in your own real fairy tale?

Randi wasn't sure how to respond to her sister. Could James be her fairy-tale prince? Maybe? He certainly swept her off her feet the night they met. If every day with him could be like that magical night, Randi would have easily agreed that she was living a real-life fairy tale, too, much like her sister.

But if they only got to see each other in person the forty-five days a year when he wasn't traveling with the GWA, she didn't think it would be possible for them to really make a go of a relationship. Even with all their electronic communication over the last eighteen days that they'd known each other, Randi didn't feel half the connection to him that she felt the night they met, when he felt like the missing half of her heart.

Even with him adamantly claiming that he wasn't interested in even talking to other women, she couldn't imagine he would really be faithful to her, when he was probably being hit on by beautiful women in every city he went to in the three-hundred-and-twenty days a year he was working. If the local guys she'd dated couldn't remain faithful when they saw each other daily, she wasn't sure she could ever believe a long-distance boyfriend would be able to keep it in his pants.

Regardless, though, she had to reply to her sister, so she estimated the odds as if she weren't able to get over her issues to be able to travel with him eventually.

> **Randi: I'm about 90% on yours & only about 40% on mine. {Kissing Face Emoji} {Frog Emoji} My frog can't exactly turn into a Prince when we won't actually be in the same city until your wedding. :(And then he'll be gone again 2 days later.**

> **Kay: But you think James could be your Prince if ya'll could just spend more time together?**

> **Randi: Maybe? I really like him. I mean I LIKE, LIKE him. But I don't know if I can really fall in love over texts, phone calls, and Skype sessions, ya know. {Confused Face Emoji}**

> **Kay: Yeah, I understand that. I was unsure about Anthony the first week when that's all we had. And even the second week when I felt like we were in the Friend Zone. Not that the only reason I think I've fallen in love with him is because of sleeping with him every**

night, but it's hard to really feel the connection with a
soulmate when the physical intimacy is missing.
{Hugging Face Emoji}

Randi: Exactly! {You Get Me GIF}

Kay: You just need to figure out a way to see each other
more. Want me to talk to my boss about job
opportunities for you?

Randi: No. James already mentioned that they haven't
hired anyone for your job on the other flight crew, but I
don't think I can do that. Not sure I could handle flying
that much.

Kay: Why don't you like flying? Have you had a really bad
experience on a plane? Or just general anxiety in a
plane?

Randi: No real bad experiences. I just feel sick the whole
time. I think it has to do with seeing the planes on 9-11
when I was too young to comprehend it. Intellectually,
I know that most planes don't crash, but when I get on
a plane, I can't stop worrying about being on one of the
few that do.

Randi: That's why I haven't taken James up on his offer to
fly me out to meet him, even though I have a few days
off when I could.

Kay: Gotcha. Wish there was something I could do to
help you with that. Are you going to be able to fly
down for my wedding? Daddy said he's making the
arrangements, so you might want to let him know if he
needs to schedule driving time for you.

Sugar! I didn't think about having to fly to her wedding! Randi felt nauseous just at the thought of having to fly to and from Texas less than a week apart. *Maybe I should see a therapist to deal with my anxiety? Or maybe a shrink to get on anxiety meds? I need to go get my next birth control shot next week, so maybe Dr. McShane can refer me to someone then.*

> **Randi: Yeah, surely, I can get into the doctor for anti-anxiety meds in the next 5 weeks so I can fly w/o {Woozy Face Emoji} {Nauseated Face Emoji} {Face Vomiting Emoji}.**

Kay: Well, then we'll see how well they work when you come down for the wedding & if they're a possible solution, so you can fly away with your Prince to your happily ever after, too.

> **Randi: I'll call her and make the appointment now. ;) {Crossed Fingers Emoji}**

Kay: {Crossed Fingers Emoji} Okay, going to see what I can do to prep our new home for painting now. Love you, Sis!

> **Randi: Have fun! Love you, too!**

Randi pulled up her contact list and called her doctor's office to schedule an appointment. She wondered if her primary care physician could prescribe something for her anxiety when she got her shot, so she could make sure whatever was prescribed for her anxiety wouldn't impact her birth control's efficacy. She had to make sure she could handle flying before she thought anymore about possible career options with the GWA, so she could be with James and work in a career she truly loved.

She surfed the net, perusing social media for a while, specifically looking at pictures of James that were added to his "James Dangerous" profiles, since the company put up mostly pictures of him wrestling in those tight spandex pants and without a shirt. She loved looking at his body. He was big all over, but not fat in any way. The tattoos running down his arms disguised how veiny they were from being so muscular, but even with tattoos covering them, his broad shoulders still looked like boulders.

One of the first pictures was from behind as he stood on the ring apron waiting to tag into the match. Randi loved looking at the intricate artwork on his wide expanse of back muscles, but especially liked how the spandex pants he wrestled in showed off his fine derriere. She really wished she would've had the chance to get her hands on his butt when they were together back in September.

Her favorite, though, was the one from his after-match interview where his chest hair was soaked in sweat. It was matted down over his perfect pecs and led down to a happy trail in the middle of his chiseled abs that were at least two or three ridges past a six-pack. Even though he was thicker through the middle than every other man she'd ever dated, he still had that sexy V-taper of cut muscles that aimed her eyes directly toward his wonder down under that she still couldn't believe actually fit inside her without hurting. She knew he wasn't aroused in the online photo, but he still filled out his wrestling tights more than most of his fellow wrestlers.

Randi wasn't a prude, no matter how her parents tried to raise her to be, so she had seen her fair share of penises. She hadn't had sex with all of the dozen guys she'd dated since high school, but the few who lasted longer than six weeks of dating to get into her pants were nowhere near as anatomically impressive as James.

She'd thought she'd gotten over the shame of having her parents burn her dirty poetry when she was in high school to eventually lose her virginity and explore her sexuality while in college. She thought her prior experiences had taught her that size didn't matter as much as how a man used his pleasure wand. She'd even enjoyed sex with boyfriends who were below average in size when they knew how to wiggle their worm.

Her one night with James was making her rethink her previous belief that size didn't matter, though. He was long and thick and hit spots inside her that nobody had found before. Even though she'd told him she wanted it rough and rowdy, she was glad he took his time at first to stretch her opening enough to accommodate his triple extra-large erection.

I wonder if that's why porn is rated XXX? Randi grinned and giggled at the thought. *Because the guys have to have XXX-large boners.*

After spending a couple of hours drooling over James online while fantasizing about all the ways she wanted them to be together, she closed her computer to go clean her house. It wasn't super dirty, since she and Amy were both good about keeping things picked up. But since she had a free afternoon, she figured she could use it to do the deep cleaning tasks that normally got skipped, like actually mopping the kitchen floor instead of just hitting it with a wet Swiffer.

That was the only chore she got done on her afternoon off, though. Because James texted her just after she finished mopping to see if she was free for a midday Skype sex session. *Yes, please! That's definitely a better way to spend the afternoon than cleaning the house!*

Randi: Give me 15 minutes to get my computer set up in my bedroom. {Smiling Face with Hearts Emoji}

It didn't really take her that long to get her computer set up, as that was simply a matter of moving it to the bed and turning it back on. She really needed the time to check her hair and makeup in the bathroom mirror, and change into a set of sheer black bra and panties to entice him over their video connection.

Once she felt like she was as dolled up as possible, she propped up on the pillows on her bed and opened her laptop to log-in to Skype for their video chat. She positioned the computer between her feet, so James could see everything from her bent legs up to her face. It didn't take long for James to show up on her screen in a very similar position to the way she was lying on her bed.

He was already naked and stroking his erection in his large hand, which caused Randi to flood her sheer black panties. Her nipples felt like they were hard enough to cut through the matching bra.

"Fuck, Angel," James groaned, stopping his strokes to squeeze his dick. "You're so hot in that sexy lingerie that I almost don't want you to remove it."

"Oh, I'm not planning on removing it, Jimmy," Randi teased, her voice sounding breathy to her own ears. She ran her hands over her thighs, then up to her flat abdomen, trying to torment him by not actually touching herself in the intimate areas he wanted to see her fondling.

"Such a naughty girl," James growled in a deep, almost rough voice that made Randi's skin tingle as if he was the one touching her. "You really shouldn't hide those tantalizing titties and pretty pink pussy from me. Fuck, I can already see how wet you are for me. Your panties are soaked, Angel."

As much as Randi loved hearing him talk dirty, she struggled with her own ability to reciprocate the dirty talk. It was really hard to overcome years of programming by her prudish parents that, *"good girls don't use those words,"* to be able to say the words she usually kept buried deep in her head, where nobody knew she even thought them to chastise her for being bad.

The one time before meeting James that she'd tried to let out her inner dirty thoughts and use the raunchy words, she wrote them out in erotic poetry when she was fifteen and still a virgin. Her mother found her hidden poetry notebook and lectured her for over an hour before her father got home. Once he got home, he continued the lecture and then burned her spiral notebook in the fireplace while slut shaming her, as if she'd done all the things that she wrote about, instead of just writing them out. She was grounded for a month with no phone, no internet, and no extra-curricular activities other than the cheer practice and games that were mandatory for her to stay on the squad. It was the worst month of her life.

In one of their earliest conversations, James had asked her about why she used substitute words instead of the usual curse words. She tried to explain to him about how her parents expected her to behave, even telling him about her teenage writing, and the consequences of her parents seeing her dirty thoughts. She explained that even the milder words like *"pissed"* and *"sucks"* that she would use around her sister and friends were banned when her parents were present. It was like her parents thought she was still fifteen instead of twenty-five.

James had appeared angry on her behalf, but he didn't say a negative word about her parents, like some of her ex-boyfriends had in the past. Instead, he just said he would talk dirty enough for both of them, until she finally felt comfortable enough with him to say the raunchy words back in their intimate moments.

Randi had even surprised herself when she'd been able to whisper the word "fuck" to James that first night. She'd been able to text him using variations on that word along with the other curse words she'd struggled to think to herself previously, but she still struggled to say them loud enough for him to hear them over Skype. He seemed to enjoy teasing her until he coaxed her into saying them louder for him, though, so she knew he would eventually get her to feel comfortable saying them louder without prompting.

Hopefully, I won't ever get so comfortable saying them that I accidentally say them in front of Mom or Dad, though.

"Randi, look at me," James ordered in that deep, commanding tone that brought Randi back out of her head. "Quit thinking so hard, Angel. Look at me while you touch yourself. Imagine it's my hands on your body. Do what you want me to do the next time we're together."

"Sorry, James," Randi apologized, starting to move her hands again on her body, where she'd stopped while getting lost in her head.

"Nothing to apologize for, Angel." James's lips turned up slightly in what she classified as his sexy smile. "We'll get them completely out of your head, eventually. It'll just take time and lots of practice at focusing solely on each other. Now lose the lingerie so I can see my naughty nymph."

Randi returned his sexy smile as she reached up to remove her bra as he instructed. She lifted her legs straight up in the air so she could shimmy out of her panties without having to move the computer from its position on the bed. Once she was completely bared for him, she repositioned herself so he could see everywhere she was touching herself for him.

He continued his dirty talk, giving her instructions for using a firmer hand when she was only teasing him with a light stroke of a single finger over her breasts and outer folds. She loved having him tell her what to do, like she wasn't doing anything *"wrong"* or *"shameful"* because it was what he wanted his *"Angel"* to do.

Angels are the ultimate good girls, after all, so I can't be bad when I'm being his Angel.

It didn't take long for his dominant demands to bring her to the brink. Her first orgasm ripped through her so suddenly that Randi didn't believe it had anything to do with how or where she was touching herself. It was almost certainly, one-hundred percent, from his deep, dark, dirty words and commanding tone of voice.

"Fuck, Angel, you're so fucking sexy when you come," James moaned as Randi was coming down from the heights of bliss.

"You didn't come with me," Randi whined, noticing that he was still slowly stroking his XXXL erection.

"No, Angel, I wanna watch you come a few more times before I let go," James proclaimed with a sexy smile. "So, don't stop, keep finger-fucking your tight little cunt."

Randi did as she was told as James continued to growl out his dirty thoughts, saying "I can't wait to feel your perfect pussy squeezing my cock again," and "I wish I was there sucking on your pretty pink nipples," among many other things that made Randi feel like the sexy siren he described.

She came two more times before he finally let go. She was barely able to keep her eyes open as she floated in a cloud of ecstasy to watch him release rope after rope of thick, white cum on the rippled muscles of his abdomen. After they both caught their breath, Randi threw on a robe, so she could go to the bathroom and clean up while James stepped away from his computer to do the same.

When they got back to their computers, James playfully pouted about her wearing her pink fluffy robe, instead of letting him see her beautiful body the whole time they were talking. Randi knew she was blushing from head to toe, and just couldn't undress again to let him see everything when they weren't going for another round of Skype sex.

They mostly talked about the mundane things that happened in their daily lives, only coming close to a second round of sexy time when he suggested they should get some toys for their mutual pleasure over Skype.

"I can't go buy sex toys," Randi objected, picturing the mortification she would suffer when her parents found out about them. "West Tulsa is like the gossipiest small town you can imagine. It's bad enough that I have to go across the river to buy underwear, so I'm not embarrassed going through the line at Walmart and having people

I've known my whole life see that I prefer colored lace instead of plain white cotton. If I go within a hundred yards of an adult store, everyone will know it."

"Then maybe I should order something for you, and have it shipped in a plain, unmarked box, so nobody can guess what it is," James suggested. "I'd love to watch you ride a dildo that looks like my cock when we Skype. Or use a little vibrator that fits on your thumb to stimulate your clit while you have your fingers buried in your pussy."

Yep, it's official. I'm a brighter shade of pink than my robe. Hopefully, he can't see it through my makeup.

"Yeah, and just as soon as you do that," Randi argued, shaking her head. "My Mom will show up to check on me and carry in my mail for the day. I wouldn't put it past her to open it before I got the chance to hide the box."

James opened his mouth as if he was going to say something, but then just closed it again. Randi knew he was fighting with himself not to say something derogatory about her overprotective parents, and her inability to be an adult and stand up to them. That was yet another thing about her that she felt she would have to overcome before she could ever really be in a relationship with him. Not that she wanted to curse when they were around, but that she wanted to be able to tell them about dating James, without being afraid of being lectured about it, or made to feel guilty for being in a sexual relationship.

Instead of letting him flounder for a few minutes and eventually figure out how to word his unkind thoughts about her family dynamics, she changed the subject. "Since I'm not working at the Camelot again until next week, I started looking at jobs online this morning. I don't really wanna wait tables anymore, so it looks like I might be stuck in an office job for a while, until I find something more active and fun like I really want."

"Yeah?" James raised an eyebrow and made the word sound as if it was a question.

"Yeah," Randi replied with a shrug of her shoulders. "There were a half dozen receptionist jobs I found this morning, so I'll probably spend some time this week while I'm off revamping my résumé to be able to apply for them. At least a receptionist has the chance to meet people outside the company that walk in to do business and isn't just stuck in an office, only interacting with one or two other people in the company all day like an admin would."

"Have you thought about being a personal assistant instead?" James sat up on his bed and moved his computer, so she could see his face up close.

The view made his eyes appear more gray-blue than the brown they'd looked the night they met. She made a mental note to ask him if he wore colored contacts for work and missed what he was saying. She shook herself out of her mental musings and asked him to repeat himself.

"I said that a personal assistant does more errands for their employer than office work, so it might be more what you're looking for to stay active and not be bored at a desk all day." James gave her an encouraging smile.

She loved his smile, even though it was hard to see sometimes when he didn't trim his beard but once a week. That was one of the reasons she normally didn't go for guys with facial hair. The others being that she didn't want to get hair in her mouth from kissing and she thought it would be scratchy against her skin if he kissed her anywhere else. James had proven her last objection to facial hair incorrect the night they met because he kept his beard just long enough to be soft and not stubbly, so it was more of a soft caress against her skin when he kissed her intimately. She had to shake herself out of her jaunt down memory lane to reply to his suggestion for her future employment.

"Yeah, that would be great if I could find a job as a PA, but there weren't any available on the job boards I was looking at this morning." Randi hoped he couldn't read her mind to realize she was thinking about how his beard almost tickled her inner thighs on the night they met.

She felt her nipples pucker and her sex start to weep from the memory of her first and only oral O. She almost suggested a second round of sexy time, but just couldn't make herself say the words. "I'll be checking the web daily, though, and will definitely apply for any PA jobs I see."

He started asking her about her other interests, trying to find a way to incorporate them into her search for the perfect career, and the mood passed to more of a friendship vibe between them, instead of the strong sexual connection from the beginning of their Skype session.

Randi wasn't sure how she felt about the way the conversation turned. On the one hand, it was nice to be able to be friends with a romantic partner because long-term couples needed that when they got old, and their parts stopped working as well. But on the other hand, she felt like they were disconnecting from one another, when he was helping her find a job in Tulsa, where he couldn't be with her most of the time because of his travel schedule for work.

She finally just resigned herself to enjoy her time with him while it lasted, knowing that it would be best to focus on being friends with him, so they wouldn't be awkward around each other after their romance ended. Knowing that she would have to be around him for a long time into the future with her sister marrying his best friend, Randi decided it was safer for her heart to consider him a friend with benefits, and to try to stay friends after the benefits ended.

James had skipped his normal midday weight training session with his brother and fellow wrestlers, so he could Skype with Randi. He knew they would probably give him hell when he got to the arena to run through their choreography for the show that night, but he didn't care. The two hours he got to spend seeing his sexy Randi was worth it, even though she covered her scrumptious body immediately after their mutual masturbation session.

They didn't just have a strong sexual connection, though that was stronger than he'd ever felt with anyone in the past. They were also aligned in their priorities. They both wanted to have strong, loving relationships with their families, which included not only with the family members they already had, but also their future spouses and children. They both wanted at least two children, but not for at least another five years. Even though he couldn't stand how her parents still treated her like a teenager, he still respected her desire to be close to them. So, as much as he wanted her to defy them and explore her dirty desires more with him, he wouldn't push her to do more than she was comfortable doing.

Maintaining strong, loving family relationships wasn't the only priority they shared. They both had a strong work ethic, wanting to find meaning in their careers. Although she hadn't figured out exactly what that was for her, he found it in knowing that he helped millions of people around the world escape from reality for a few hours a week when they watched him wrestle, either on television or at a live show. While they were both intelligent and capable of any kind of work, they both preferred more activity than a typical office job for their careers.

After hearing how she was searching for another job due to the way her current employer had cut her hours that week, James really wished he could convince her to look into options with the GWA. But he understood how her anxiety around flying would prevent her from considering any at the moment. He was glad when she confided in him during their earlier Skype session that she was looking into options for controlling her flying phobia. If she found an option that worked for her when she had to fly down to San Antonio for Kay and Anthony's wedding in a month, she said she would be open to options for visiting him at work in the future.

While he really wanted to have her travel with him all the time, he could be patient and wait for her to be ready to do more than just the occasional trip to see each other. Just thinking about the possibilities for the future put a smile on his face as he finished changing into his workout clothes to go to the ring to rehearse for the evening show.

The Dangerous Twins match was being taped for the weekend television show, but it would only make it to production if the local wrestlers they were working with were as good as Rick expected them to be from watching their promo tapes. James loved wrestling against local independent talent to give them a shot at making the GWA roster. It was how he and his brother had interviewed for their jobs almost three years back. They were offered jobs that first night, but had to wait a few months to finish their final semester of college before they could actually accept them. It was an honor to have worked their way up the ladder in the company in only two short years for Rick to trust them to evaluate the potential new talent trying to join the company.

"Uh-oh, he's got that goofy grin on his face again," Dion mimicked a lovesick expression, as James joined the guys at ringside. "Maybe we should change the lineup tonight, so the new guys don't get hurt while James is daydreaming about his woman, instead of focusing on the match? I swear that's why he screwed up that promo last week. He was thinking about her cream pie instead of what he was saying about me."

James glared at his friend. He was never going to live down the chocolate cream pie promo. He honestly didn't mind his buddies joking around with him about it, knowing they all delighted in picking on one another because they were such good friends. He just didn't like them bringing Randi into their jabs at him.

"Naw," Dean disagreed, slapping both James and Dion on the back. "I'm sure he got plenty of pie via Skype this afternoon, so he can focus on wrestling for the rest of the night."

"That's why you didn't show in the weight room earlier?" Josh Parker, the wrestler with a surfer gimmick, jumped down from the ring.

"Would you have been in the weight room if you could've been in your hotel room having Skype sex with a hottie?" Brent Crockett, the wrestler with a lumberjack gimmick, gave Josh a dumbfounded look from inside the ring.

"No," a chorus of the guys cried out in unison.

Soon, he was being inundated with questions about his relationship with Randi from all the guys. The single guys who remembered her from their late lunch in Tulsa were asking if she would be joining them on tour anytime soon, and if she could bring a friend or two when she did. The married wrestlers were asking James if he would be joining their ranks in the near future. When they found out that the woman he was sort of seeing was Kay's sister, they asked if he and Anthony were considering talking them into a double wedding.

James just shook his head at the antics of his fellow wrestlers. He was really glad when the local talent arrived, so they could all focus on their rehearsal for that night's show. Rick actually walked down to the ring to introduce the potential new additions to the roster to the GWA wrestlers they would be working with that night.

James and Dean were paired up with Mason Scott and Noah Adams for their match that night. Mason and Noah were both local to the Birmingham, Alabama area and had been wrestling part time for about five years with a gimmick name of the Bama Boys, after training for two years prior to that. All four of the guys were about the same age, but the Dangerous Twins were a little bigger than the Bama Boys. Like maybe two or three inches taller and twenty pounds heavier.

The four of them sat at ringside for a long while and talked about each of their individual styles in the ring and favorite maneuvers. That allowed them to plan out their match choreography to highlight the strengths of the guys trying to get a job with the GWA, even though they would lose to the GWA tag-team champions.

Once they had a general idea of how the match would go, they all got in the ring to do a run through, so they would all be comfortable with any tricky spots they planned, with ideas for how they could change anything that didn't go as planned in the actual match, if needed. They worked on their timing and making the moves look seamless for about half an hour before vacating the ring, so some of the other wrestlers could have their turn to choreograph their matches for the night.

It wasn't long after they got out of the ring and continued their discussion at ringside that it was time to head backstage for dinner before the show started. Mason and Noah both joined the Hunters in catering, so they could all keep talking about their match and the potential futures for all their careers. James really hoped that Rick would hire the two new guys after the show that night. They seemed like really good guys who loved the business and would be good additions to the roster.

When he changed into his wrestling gear for the night, he checked his phone, eager to tell Randi about his late afternoon and early evening. She hadn't texted since their Skype session earlier, but he wasn't expecting her to, since she knew he would be busy with rehearsals and wouldn't be able to text until he was watching the rest of the show on the backstage monitors while waiting for his turn in the ring.

James: Good evening, Angel. Have a good nap this afternoon?

Randi: Yes, 3 O's for lunch was exhausting. {Grinning Face with Big Eyes Emoji} {Yawning Face Emoji} {Sleeping Face Emoji} Did you get in trouble for missing weight training?

James: No, it's not mandatory. Besides, I hate trying to
wrestle on days I'm sore from weight training.

Randi: So, we can have a nooner every day you wrestle if
I don't have to work then? {Crossed Fingers Emoji}
{Smiling Face with Hearts Emoji}

James: Absolutely, Angel! {Grinning Face with Smiling
Eyes Emoji}

Randi: Tonight's not a TV night, is it?

James: Not live but being taped for the weekend show.
Only Tuesdays and PPVs air live.

Randi: But you didn't actually wrestle last night. :(I only
got to see you in biker gear to do that run-in to
interfere in the other guys' match, not in your
wrestling tights and shirtless.

James: You saw all of me this afternoon to make up for it.
;)

Randi: Yeah, I did! {Beaming Face with Smiling Eyes
Emoji} Who are you wrestling tonight?

James: Some new talent from here in Birmingham. It's
their tryout to see if they can join the GWA roster.
That's why I didn't text earlier. I've been working with
them all evening to plan our match.

Randi: Think they'll be good enough to make TV this
weekend?

James: Yeah, I do. It wouldn't surprise me if they were on the plane with us out of Birmingham in the morning.

Randi: Really? They could be hired that fast? I thought you said you had to wait 6 months after your tryout match to work with the GWA.

James: Yeah, but that's because we were committed to finishing college before we accepted the jobs. Unless they have other commitments that delay their start date, Rick usually brings people into the company immediately after their interview/tryout.

Randi: So, Kay starting work the day after her interview wasn't as unusual as my Dad thinks?

James: Nope, perfectly normal for the GWA.

Randi: Cool. I feel better about her getting the job now, but that may have more to do with her telling me to save the date for her wedding next month than you reassuring me that it's a legit job.

James: They set a date for the wedding? I know Anthony was talking to Rick about options last week, but with them being off this week, I didn't know they'd officially set a date.

Randi: Yep, Sat. Nov. 24th right after Thanksgiving. {Turkey Emoji} {Wedding Emoji}

James: I guess that means instead of planning to come to Tulsa for my Thanksgiving break, we'll have to meet up wherever they're getting married. Did she say where?

Randi: Texas, I'm guessing your hometown, unless
     something happens in court before then to change the
     plans.

          James: Then I'll look forward to showing you around
          Heart's Destiny like you showed me around Tulsa while
                         we're both there. ;)

Randi: Ya'll have a park like Chandler? {Face Blowing a
     Kiss Emoji}

          James: Not unless you count the picnic area by the
          church, but I have a 10000-acre family homestead that
          has a secluded, rocky area you might like. {Winking
                         Face with Tongue Emoji}

Randi: Where you can do that thing with your tongue
     again? {Mouth Emoji} {Tongue Emoji} {Kiss Mark
     Emoji}

          James: Where I will definitely do that thing with my
                         tongue again!

"You're up," the production assistant barked as he walked by where
James was sitting with his brother and the new guys and pretending to
watch the monitors of the rest of the show.

          James: Time to go wrestle. BRB!

Randi: Break a leg. {Leg Emoji} {Men Wrestling Emoji}

James had to chuckle at her use of the old acting superstition as he
put his phone in his locker before heading out to the ring. *She's so
adorable,* he thought before schooling his expression to get into
character for the show.

They all played their parts perfectly and put on the match of the
night. That wasn't just James's opinion or his brother's ego talking,

either. Rick gave them all a standing ovation as they walked back through the curtain to the backstage area and asked the new guys to find him after they showered and changed to negotiate their contracts. James welcomed Mason and Noah to the GWA before heading off to get his own shower and text his girl.

Chapter Three

James followed his brother Dean into the locker room to change into their workout clothes, so they could go to the ring to spar. And, possibly, rehearse, if they were needed for a match that night. As they walked in, they found their friend Anthony already there. He was in the men's locker room changing out of his workout clothes and back into his dark gray suit, since he was skipping their sparring session to go help his future stepdaughters with their schoolwork for the afternoon.

"While I've got you both here," Anthony got their attention as he sat on a bench and slipped on his loafers. "The wedding is gonna be Saturday, November twenty-fourth. So, if you wanna be my groomsmen, I need you to get with my mom to give her whatever measurements she needs to order your tuxes."

"Congrats, man," James and Dean offered in unison as they each slapped a big hand on Anthony's shoulders.

"It's gonna be in Heart's Destiny?" James wanted to verify what Randi had assumed when she'd told him about the wedding date earlier in the week.

"Yeah, hopefully…" Anthony trailed off, looking a little unsure of his answer. "Barring any craziness in court before then."

"Randi was telling me a little about the shit with Kay's ex," James admitted, hoping his friend would understand that he was offering his support in dealing with the issue and not trying to pry into his fiancée's personal business. "Made me wish we could all go to court with you to kick his ass."

"Yeah, I don't think that would help the situation," Anthony chuckled. "It's gonna take every ounce of self-control I have to control my temper when we're there, but I know that's the only way Kay can win in court. And she has to win this, so I can eventually adopt the girls, so I'm determined to be on my best behavior in court."

"Who all's gonna be in the wedding?" Dean inquired as he removed his jacket and hung it in a locker. He effectively changed the subject before James could ask Anthony more about the possible adoption, or how the wedding location might change based on the court ruling.

"I'm not completely sure," Anthony shrugged. "Kay mentioned two bridesmaids, her sister Randi, and her best friend Deanna. But we haven't talked about anyone else yet. I'm sure we'll wanna have the girls participate too, but I'm not sure how yet. I figure we'll go over all that next week when we're home planning everything else with Mom."

"Since James will probably be escorting Randi, I'm guessing I'll be escorting Deanna." Dean continued to change into sweats and a t-shirt from his business casual traveling attire.

"Yeah, probably," Anthony affirmed as he finished tying his tie and putting on his suit coat. "I don't know much about her, other than she's been Kay's best friend since sixth grade. And apparently, my cousin JJ knows her because she works with an oil company in Tulsa that he's had dealings with for Burleson Oil."

"I guess that old song is right," James mused aloud as he plopped down on the bench to put on his tennis shoes. "It really is a small world, after all."

"Something like that," Anthony laughed with his friends before excusing himself to go meet the girls in the classroom.

James and Dean stored their gear in their lockers before heading down to the ring. It was crazy how much stuff they had to carry to the arena. Even though they left their larger suitcases at the hotel, they still had to bring two bags each, a duffle and a garment bag, to the arena for all the different outfits they had to change into during the time they were there.

It was company policy that they had to dress professionally for traveling because Rick wanted to bring the business aspect of their company to the forefront, instead of appearing to still be stuck in the carnival sideshow days of professional wrestling. That meant at least business casual clothes when they were on the plane, in the airport, at the hotel, or traveling to and from the arena or any of those places. While James thought Rick preferred to have them in a suit most of the time, he only wore the jacket in the winter when they were in a city that got cold enough to need it.

In addition to their business casual clothing, though, they also had to bring workout clothes and sneakers for sparring and rehearsals, wrestling tights, boots, and any gimmick t-shirts or jackets they wore to the ring to perform, and an outfit to match their gimmick persona, which meant jeans, t-shirts, leather jackets, and biker boots for James and his brother's bad ass biker gimmick, in case they needed to record an interview or interfere in a match when they weren't actually wrestling.

While they could technically wear their gimmick attire when out in public, like at lunch in the hotel or when they went out after a show, James tended to stick with the business casual clothing, so he didn't have to wear the heavy leather jacket when it would be too hot. He only wore the leather jacket for the few minutes he needed to for the show, or if he went out when it was below freezing outside, but he still had to have it hanging in his garment bag at every show.

James checked his phone for messages from Randi before stuffing it in the side pocket of his duffle and locking it up while he was in the ring.

"I seriously think you're addicted to texting your girl," Dean mocked, shaking his head as they walked out of the locker room together.

"Well, there are worse things to be addicted to, so I'm okay if she's my only vice," James confided, smiling at the thought of all the ways he could be addicted to Randi.

Addicted to texting her, to talking to her, to Skyping with her, to kissing her, to touching her, to licking her sweet pussy, to fucking her, to watching her come multiple times a day. Yep, I'm definitely okay with being addicted to her in every way possible.

The guys continued ribbing him for his goofy grin when they got to the ring, but James still couldn't stop smiling while thinking about Randi. Instead of getting upset with his buddies for picking on him, he almost felt sorry for them, knowing they were just giving him shit because they were jealous of what he had with Randi, and they were still missing in their lives. He let them have their fun for a few minutes before redirecting the conversation. "So, what do you think we should plan for Anthony's bachelor party?"

"Not sure," Dean mumbled, scratching his head as they sat at ringside, watching the group that was already in the ring and waiting for their turn. "It's gonna depend on what all they have going on the week before."

"Yeah, I was thinking that with the wedding being on Saturday, they'd for sure have the rehearsal and dinner the night before," James speculated, picturing a calendar of events in his head. "I wouldn't wanna do it the night before the wedding anyway, since I wouldn't want him to get married while hungover."

"And the day before that is Thanksgiving," Dean pointed out. "So, even if the bar is open, we'll all be too stuffed from eating all day to wanna go out then."

"Any idea what the hours are at Tully's earlier in the week?"

"No, but I'm sure they aren't open as late as they are on Friday and Saturday nights." Dean shook his head.

"We'll be home the Friday before." James wondered if the weekend before the wedding might be best for the bachelor party. "But with everyone having to drive to Heart's Destiny from the airport in San Antonio before even checking in at the B and B, I doubt any of these guys will wanna go out that night. Maybe Saturday the seventeenth?"

"Yeah, that sounds good," Dean agreed before whistling to get the attention of all the wrestlers in the vicinity of the ring. "Hey, guys, we're trying to plan Anthony's bachelor party for Saturday, November seventeenth. Are any of you planning to spend your whole Thanksgiving break in the area for the wedding to be able to attend then? Or are you going home for Thanksgiving and just coming to town the actual weekend of the wedding?"

There were mumblings amongst the group with a lot of "haven't really thought about it" and "staying wherever we land on the sixteenth" and only a few references to "going home for the holiday and not attending the wedding," making it seem like a lot of the guys would be available and attend the bachelor party on the seventeenth.

"So, the seventeenth is good for the bachelor party for most of you?" Dean questioned the group as a whole.

He was answered with a resounding "yeah" from the majority of the guys, so at least they had that part figured out. James wasn't sure what else he would need to do as far as planning for the party, but he decided to wait until closer to the event to worry about it.

He took his turn sparring, but since he wasn't wrestling that night, James opted to run the stairs in the arena for an extra cardio workout, instead of sitting ringside to watch the other guys rehearse for the show that night. Since his legs were already going to be sore from his earlier weight workout in the hotel gym, he figured it wouldn't take long to completely wear them out, so he was only suffering from leg soreness once that week, instead of splitting the workouts up and being sore in different ways twice that week.

Once he felt like he was ready to collapse into a sweaty lump at the bottom of the stairs, he hit the shower and put on his gimmick wear, minus the hot leather jacket, in case he was needed for a run-in later in the night. He grabbed his phone from his locker to text Randi while eating dinner and watching the show on the backstage monitors.

James: Good evening, Angel. How was your day?

Randi: Boring. {Expressionless Face Emoji} Cleaned the house & sent out résumés all morning. Then spent the afternoon meeting all of Kay's future in-laws in a group chat where we've been sharing pictures of dresses & ideas for the wedding. Now I'm flopped on the couch to watch you wrestle, even though I already know you're going to win the match. Maybe you shouldn't give me spoilers for these taped shows, so I can enjoy them more. {Zipper Mouth Face Emoji}

James: So, I shouldn't tell you that we aren't scheduled to lose a match until 12/16 at the PPV in Providence, RI?

;)

Randi: {GIF of the words *Spoiler Alert* flashing in red, white, and blue alternating with the lights on a police car} You are so bad!

> **James: Does that mean you won't come see me that weekend to help me get over the loss of our titles?**

> **Randi: Only if I can jump in the ring & be the reason you lose the titles. {Rolling on the Floor Laughing Emoji}**

If I thought she was serious about actually coming to the pay-per-view, I'd ask Rick if we could make that happen, James thought as he started to type his reply.

> **James: We could book it that way if you want. Like my girlfriend is worried about me getting my ass kicked & jumps into the ring from the audience to hit my opponent over the head with her purse & gets us disqualified. We'd have to make it a special stipulation to lose the titles on the DQ, but that's definitely doable.**

> **Randi: {Face with Rolling Eyes Emoji}**

> **James: But you'll have to be prepared to start acting as our manager afterward. We can do a bunch of vignettes where Dean & I teach you how to be sneakier when cheating for us, so we don't keep getting DQ-ed.**

> **Randi: Don't be ridiculous. I'm not even sure I'll ever be able to get on a plane to go to one of your shows, & I definitely don't have the training to get in the ring.**

James wanted to tell her that her college acting classes were all the training she would need to act as their manager, and he could teach her anything she needed to know to safely take a bump or pretend to knock out one of the guys. But he knew she wouldn't even consider that possibility until she conquered her fear of flying. If only he could convince her to try to fly out to see him before the wedding to get her started on overcoming that anxiety.

James: When is your doctor's appointment to learn your
options for your airplane anxiety?

Randi: Tuesday afternoon. Is it bad that I scheduled it for
then so I could tell my boss not to schedule me for the
evening shift that day so I can be home to watch you
wrestle on TV? {Smiling Face with Horns Emoji}

James: Nope, that's not bad at all. You're still my Angel.
{Smiling Face with Halo Emoji}

James: Any chance they'll give you some good options to
try that will require you trying to fly before the
wedding?

Randi: IDK but probably not. If she recommends therapy,
I'm sure it will take at least a month before I'll have
had enough therapy to be willing to fly to the wedding.
And if she prescribes meds, I don't want anything so
strong that it will impair me from driving or whatever,
so it will probably need to have time to build up in my
system to keep me from having a panic attack on the
plane. I don't think there's anything that will work
immediately & not leave me too loopy to walk onto the
plane. {Woozy Face Emoji}

With his hopes of seeing Randi before the wedding dashed, James
changed the subject, asking her what she thought of the bridesmaid
dresses that were in the group chat and about the jobs she'd applied for
earlier that day. They texted about mostly irrelevant things. like her
opinion on the pre-taped match she was watching on the GWA's
Saturday television show, and what color she and her roommate were
going to paint their toenails that night.

Regardless that it was all lighthearted discussion, James enjoyed
every minute of the evening spent interacting with Randi. He didn't
even care that his brother and a few of the other guys were making

Leah Mae Wright

jokes about him being a lovesick puppy. *I may be a lovesick puppy,
but at least I'm happy.*

~~~

James was glad he had another night off from wrestling, since he was
so sore from his double leg workout the day before. He took a quick
shower after the afternoon sparring session, so he wasn't a sweaty
mess to put his black slacks and button-down shirt on to go hang out
with his friends in catering. Rick had seen how stiff he was in the ring
earlier and told him not to worry about wearing his gimmick attire,
since he was in no shape to even do a run-in if needed that night.

"I think they should wear white to match your Navy dress
uniform," Kay said as James walked up to the table where she was
sitting with Anthony and a couple of women who were wives of some
of the other wrestlers. He noticed their kids were all seated at the next
table over, leaving room for James and his brother and a few other
wrestlers to sit with the adults talking about their upcoming wedding.
He took the seat on the opposite side of Kay from Anthony, so he
could get in on the discussion about the wedding attire, since he would
have to wear whatever they picked. "And they should have royal blue
bow ties to match the bridesmaids' dresses, but I don't know if we
should go with a cummerbund, or a vest, or neither because they won't
match your uniform."

"You know I can't wear a tie with my dress whites," Anthony
pointed out after flipping through the bridal catalog in front of him.
"If you want them to wear a royal blue tie, maybe we should pick one
of these more traditional tuxes, instead of trying to find one with a
mandarin collar like my uniform."

"Or maybe you could put them in blue tuxes," one of the women
suggested as she scrolled through her phone. James thought she was
married to Jeff, but he couldn't remember her name. "If you're both
going to be in white and the bridesmaids are going to be in blue,
maybe the groomsmen should match the bridesmaids and leave the
~~~

white just for the two of you. If you put the groomsmen in white tuxes, it could look like you have three grooms."

"Oh, I hadn't thought about that," Kay admitted, just as her phone buzzed with a new message. When Kay opened it on her phone, James could see from his seat beside her that someone had sent her a picture of a royal blue with black trim, mandarin collar, four button, men's tuxedo.

"Send me that picture." Anthony pointed at Kay's phone. "That way I can show the guys without seeing any of the wedding dresses in your phone."

"Is that tux blue?" James pointed at the picture that Kay was sending to Anthony.

"Yeah, and currently, it's the front-runner for your tuxes for the wedding," Anthony acknowledged as he pulled the photo up on his phone and handed it to James behind Kay's back, since he was sitting on her other side.

"I thought you said we would be in white tuxes?" James passed Anthony's phone to his brother Dean, who just sat down on his other side and hadn't heard the reasoning for why the tux color might change.

"That's what we were thinking at first," Anthony explained in response to Dean's question. "But while looking at the different options for tuxes, these have a similar style to my dress whites but match the bridesmaids' royal blue dresses."

"So, we get to dress like Smurfs for your wedding?" Dean smirked.

"Can I see the tux?" Tia turned in her chair to tap Anthony on the shoulder. Dean passed Anthony's phone back down the table and Anthony passed it to Tia. "That's not a Smurf tux. Smurfs actually wear white clothing, and their skin is a lighter blue than that tux."

Tia handed the phone back to Anthony before turning back to her dinner. James couldn't contain his grin at the precocious child.

"I guess that means we'll be the only ones dressing like Smurfs for the wedding," Kay giggled, pointing at herself and Anthony. She leaned into his side and whispered, probably thinking only Anthony could hear her, but James understood every word, "But any blue body paint will have to wait until the honeymoon."

"I think I'm too hairy for body paint," Anthony whispered back to her and they both chuckled. "And I'm not too fond of blue body parts."

"Oh, yeah, we definitely don't want that," Kay replied as a sharp laugh burst from her.

"Alright, now, share with the rest of the class," Dean admonished, waving his fork in Anthony and Kay's direction. "What's so funny?"

"Nothing," Kay chirped, still struggling not to laugh.

"Did you get with Ma about what measurements she needs from you?" Anthony effectively redirected the conversation away from his and Kay's discussion of body paint.

James didn't say a word about his sudden change of subject. He understood that his friend wouldn't want to talk about blue body parts loud enough that the kids could hear. And he had absolutely no desire to embarrass Kay by letting her know that he'd heard their entire conversation.

"Yeah, she said we need to go to any men's formalwear store we can find and have the professionals measure us and send the measurements to Benny's," James informed Anthony between bites of food.

"That's the same thing she told Randi and Deanna in our group chat," Kay affirmed. "The girls and I will get our measurements done on Friday, when we go to Destiny Dresses to look at samples of the dresses I've liked best in our group chat."

"What about your Dad?" James asked Kay. "Is the sheriff gonna be okay with wearing a blue tux to walk you down the aisle?"

"Oh, Dad's not walking me down the aisle," Kay replied before taking her next bite.

"Why not?" Anthony questioned, looking a little nervous.

"Because I want the girls to walk me down the aisle," Kay proclaimed with a smile. "I had originally thought we'd have Maria act as the flower girl and Tia as my maid of honor, but then we'd have to find a ring bearer and another groomsman. I didn't know who to ask that would be age appropriate, since neither of us have little boys in our extended family." Kay paused to take a drink before continuing. "Now that we're putting the guys in blue tuxes to match the bridesmaids' dresses, I think it will look best if the girls stand on either side of us for the vows and family unity candle, and they can walk back up the aisle together at the end of the ceremony."

"Yeah, I suppose it would be lopsided to have them both lined up with the bridesmaids," Anthony agreed.

"Besides, I didn't like the flower petal options Hazel sent me," Kay divulged, her nose wrinkling up in aversion. "In order to be royal blue, they had to be fake or painted. Flowers that are naturally that shade of blue, like bachelor's buttons, have long thin petals, not the wide petals like roses that are normally used for tossing by flower girls."

"You've been able to find the right shade of blue flowers for the bouquets, though, right?" the other woman at the table queried. James thought she was married to Matt. He really needed to start learning some of his coworkers' wives' names, especially if he wanted to be able to introduce them to Randi, if and when she finally agreed to come see him at a show.

"I think so," Kay affirmed. "They look like the right shade in the pictures Hazel has sent me, but I still have to stop at the florist on Friday to verify which ones I like best, so they can order everything they'll need for the bouquets and the arrangements for the church."

"Where are you doing the reception?" Dean inquired.

"Hazel said we could do it in the fellowship hall at the church," Kay shrugged. Her expression made James think it wasn't the option she really wanted for their wedding reception.

"Have they redecorated the church recently?" James shook his head as the question passed his lips, not thinking the fellowship hall would project the elegance they'd want for a wedding reception. "From what I remember of the fellowship hall, it's really just a big extension off the kitchen, and not nearly fancy enough for a wedding reception."

"Nope," Anthony answered. "But it's not like we have a ballroom in Heart's Destiny to have it in. The only other options are the high school gymnasium or the rodeo arena."

"Actually, there is a ballroom in Heart's Destiny," James grinned. He turned to his brother before continuing. "You think Mom and Dad have enough time to get the brush cleared out and the old plantation house cleaned up before the wedding?"

"Oh, man, I forgot about that place," Anthony interjected, looking at James skeptically.

James thought back to when they were kids and were convinced it was a haunted house. The last time Anthony had seen it was when they were fifteen and the Hunters dared him to spend Halloween night in the spooky old mansion, so James understood his skepticism. What Anthony didn't know, though, was that James's parents had been slowly refurbishing the plantation house to add on to the bed and breakfast for the last decade. Eventually, his mom wanted to open it up as a wedding and event venue.

"That place was falling apart ten years ago. Do you think it's structurally sound enough to have the reception there?" Anthony still looked like he wasn't sure it was a viable option.

"Oh, yeah," James beamed, smiling at his memories of their teen years. "After our Halloween Spooktacular ended up with all of us needing tetanus shots, Dad hired Walker Construction to refurbish the place. The first year they just got it to where it was structurally sound, which is why we didn't go back the next Halloween. It took them three more years to get all the electrical and plumbing redone and up to code. Mom took over then and started redecorating it with plans to rent it out for weddings and maybe even moving the B and B to it, instead of our great-grandparents' place where she's been, or maybe expanding to use both."

"I wonder why Hazel didn't mention that option?" Kay questioned. "She's mentioned your mom and even said something about the B and B being the only hotel in town, if we have more out-of-town visitors than will fit in the extra rooms on the ranch."

"Knowing Mom, she probably didn't mention it to anyone," James confessed. "The plantation house is over a hundred-thousand square feet, and she's only done a little at a time while mostly focusing on the bed and breakfast. The last I heard, she only had the first floor redecorated. And I don't think she'd mention it to anyone until at least the second-floor bedrooms were done and she had someone redo the landscape around it."

"So, it's not really usable space, yet," Kay faltered, her shoulders slumping as if her hopes were dashed.

"Maybe not all the extra bedrooms, but the first floor where the ballroom and kitchen are should be usable," Dean chimed in, pulling out his phone. "But let's call her and see if it's close enough that we can make it work."

He put his phone on speaker and sat it on the table as it started to ring. "Hello," their mother, Mandi Hunter, said through the phone.

"Hey, Ma," Dean hollered, leaning over toward his phone, so she could hear him over the sounds of the other GWA staff and families talking and eating. "James and I are sitting here with Anthony and his fiancée, Kay, talking about their upcoming wedding."

"Oh, well, hello everyone," Mandi chirped. James could hear the happiness in her voice, even through the phone.

"They're having a problem finding a place big enough to have the reception," James blurted, hoping to keep the conversation on track, so his mother didn't sidetrack them with all the other questions about the upcoming wedding that she would no doubt have.

"I'm not surprised," Mandi chuckled. "Hazel has pretty much invited the whole town. She's so excited about her baby boy getting married. She's been bragging about her new daughter and granddaughters all over town."

"Yeah, that's why I called you," Dean confessed, scratching his head. "We thought the ballroom in the plantation house might be big enough to hold the whole town for the reception."

"Oh, um, maybe," Mandi sputtered, sounding a bit unsure. "I did finish the first floor, but we haven't needed the extra rooms for the bed and breakfast, so I quit working on the second floor a couple years back, thinking I wouldn't ever have enough business to expand because of the cost of retrofitting an elevator to make it ADA compliant."

"Any chance you could get some help to make it usable before Thanksgiving?" James entreated his mother. "Rick's planning on bringing the whole company to Heart's Destiny for our Thanksgiving break so we can all attend the wedding. And I'm pretty sure the bill for all those rooms will be enough to cover the elevator cost."

"Oh, my, how many rooms do I need to have ready?" Mandi's voice quavered, sounding a little overwhelmed.

Anthony waved Rick over to their table and asked him how many rooms the company usually booked for everyone on the payroll and their families.

"We normally reserve a block of fifty rooms plus fifteen two-bedroom family suites," Rick replied.

"We don't have family suites," Mandi divulged. "And we only have thirty rooms in the B and B. I did have them configure the top two floors of the plantation house to make fifty bedrooms over there, but I've only got the first ten of them furnished."

"Is this the B and B in Heart's Destiny you were telling me about for the wedding?" Rick looked at Anthony.

"Yes," Anthony answered at the same time Dean spoke up saying, "Yeah."

Anthony pointed to Dean, gesturing for him to introduce their boss to his mother.

"Mom, that's our boss, Rick. Rick, our mom, Mandi Hunter, runs the B and B, which is the only hotel in Heart's Destiny." Dean handled the introductions, pointing at the phone on the table as if Rick didn't realize that he was being introduced to the woman on the other end of the line.

After they both exchanged pleasantries about how nice it was to meet each other, Rick whistled to get everyone's attention in the backstage area.

"Show of hands, who all is planning to spend their Thanksgiving vacation in Heart's Destiny for Anthony and Kay's wedding?" Rick inquired and started counting families.

James looked around and noticed it was only about half of the people who worked with the GWA who raised their hands. Mostly the parents and children that Kay and the girls had interacted with in their short time with the company, a few single wrestlers that Anthony had become friends with through hanging out with the Hunters, a couple of the tutors, and the rest of the flight crew.

"You don't have to count Dean and I for rooms," James pointed out to his boss as he was counting the hands raised for people coming to the wedding. "We each have a cabin on the family homestead."

"Mandi, do any of the rooms in the B and B connect to each other for families to not have to cram into a single bedroom?" Rick asked as soon as he finished counting.

"Yes, they pretty much all have Jack and Jill bathrooms, so we can put families in connecting rooms," Mandi replied.

"Then I'd like to book all forty rooms you have available from the evening of November sixteenth to the morning of November twenty-sixth," Rick stated. "That should be plenty for the people we have staying in town. Anyone who isn't going to the wedding can stay at our normal hotel in San Antonio, on the nights they have to be there before their flights home and after they come back to meet us to fly out. Would you like my credit card information over the phone now? Or would you prefer a wire transfer to book the rooms?"

"Oh, we don't need to do all that," Mandi announced. "My boys have told me what an upstanding man you are, so I trust you to pay the bill when you check out on the twenty-sixth."

"Baby, what's wrong?" Anthony prodded Kay. James looked back and forth between them and noticed that they both looked worried about something

"How many spare bedrooms are there on the ranch?" Kay looked especially stressed.

Oh, shit, she's worried there's not enough room for her family to have a place to stay, James supposed, not sure what could be done if there weren't enough rooms on the ranch to accommodate her family.

"There's at least a dozen empty bedrooms between my folks and Uncle Jon and Aunt Susan's houses, plus at least one extra bedroom at each of my siblings' and cousins' places. And if that's not enough for everyone, then we have a second bunkhouse that hasn't been used since we quit breeding rodeo bulls."

"That should work for everyone I've invited," Kay assumed, still nibbling her bottom lip like she wasn't one-hundred percent sure it would be enough rooms. "I just have to make sure my parents know they can't invite half of West Tulsa, like I'm afraid they're planning to do."

"Why don't we give them a call when we get back to the hotel to confirm the guest list?" Anthony appealed to Kay.

"Yes, and maybe conference in your mom, so she has a heads up about needing to have rooms ready for more than just my parents, sister, and Deanna," Kay confirmed as they stood and started to clean up from dinner.

Should I tell her that Randi can stay with me? James wondered. *And can I get there with enough time before she arrives to clean and air out my cabin that's been closed up since Labor Day?*

Leah Mae Wright

James pulled out his phone and texted Randi, deciding that it was better to make the offer directly instead of going through her family.

James: Have you scheduled your trip to Heart's Destiny for the wedding yet?

Randi: No, my Dad's doing that for us.

James: My boss just booked the whole B&B, so I wanted to make sure you knew you're welcome to stay with me.

Randi: My Dad's not going to be able to get us rooms? {Worried Face Emoji}

James: Not at the B&B. Anthony & Kay are setting it up for your folks & any other family traveling down for the wedding to stay on the Burleson Ranch. But if you don't want to stay with Anthony's family, you can stay with me. I'll get there the 16th and won't leave town until the 26th.

Randi: Yeah, I don't think I'll be able to get away with not staying where my parents do. And I'm not even sure what day we're going to get there yet. I think maybe the 21st through the 25th? But I'm not 100% on those dates. I need to find out for sure so I can schedule the time off from work. {Pensive Face Emoji}

Fuck! James cursed in his head. *She's not even gonna be there the whole time I actually have time off. And her parents are probably gonna chaperone any possible time we can spend together in those five short days we're both there.*

James: When are you doing the bachelorette party? We're planning the bachelor party for the 17th and

thought it might have to be a combined event since there's only one bar in town.

Randi: Fudge! {Angry Face Emoji} I hadn't thought about that. We can't do it the 22nd because Thanksgiving or the 23rd because Black Friday. I guess the 21st?

James: I'll call Tully's to find out their hours that Wednesday.

Randi: And I'll try to talk my Dad into going down there the 17th, just in case. {Crossed Fingers Emoji} {Folded Hands Emoji}

James: Any chance we'll be able to find some alone time, or will your folks be constantly watching us?

Randi: {Eyes Emoji} But I don't think they'll come to the bachelor/bachelorette party. How secluded is your place? Maybe if I sneak over there after the party, they won't find us until we come out of hiding for the next wedding event? {Partying Face Emoji} ;)

James: It's not in the main cluster of buildings that make up the B&B and older family homes, but it's not exactly hidden either. They might not know you're there if you ride with me and don't park a strange vehicle there, but they might come knocking if they see my truck there.

Randi: UGH! I love my sister, but I hate that her wedding is interfering with our only time to be able to see each other. If it was anyone else getting married, I'd suggest we skip town together instead, but I can't miss my sister's wedding. {Shushing Face Emoji}

James: Maybe we can go away together for Christmas?

Randi: You capable of breaking me out of my parent's vacation cabin without getting caught? I'm already sentenced to be there Dec. 22nd-26th, with no possibility of parole. {GIF of a Cat Sneaking through a Baby Gate with a caption of *Jail Break*}

James had to laugh at her goofy GIFs, even if he didn't understand why she couldn't defy her parents when they treated her like she was still a teenager.

"What's so funny?" Kay inquired, bringing him back into the conversation going on around the table.

"Your sister is sending me jail break GIFs, suggesting that's what it'll take for us to be able to spend any time together during our holiday break," James admitted with a smile. No point in burdening Kay with his frustration over not getting to spend any time with Randi, so he tried to make his expression appear like they were joking around instead.

"Sorry, I didn't think when we were planning things," Kay giggled slightly. "I should've realized that Randi would get stuck with my parents dictating her time, like they do when we go to their cabin for holidays. I'm so used to her being so much more outspoken at work, since that's where I usually see her most of the time, that her not arguing with them about whatever they plan for us at Thanksgiving and Christmas even surprises me for the first few days we're all together."

"So, I should be prepared to meet a different version of Randi when your parents are around than the outgoing, free spirited, wonderful woman I met in September and have been texting and talking to for the last three weeks?" James arched an eyebrow at Kay.

"I wouldn't say different, exactly," Kay stammered, looking pensive. "Just quieter and a little more going with the flow, instead of doing her own thing. You have to understand that our parents are both really great people, but they have a lot of old-fashioned beliefs that they expect us to live by, even as adults. We've both learned over the years that it's best if we behave accordingly whenever they might be around. To be honest, I'm a little concerned about them coming to town before the wedding and realizing that Anthony and I are already pretty much living together."

"Yeah, her Dad still thinks I'm sleeping on the couch or in a separate hotel room while we're traveling," Anthony confessed with a smirk. "I figured we'd have to put an extra pillow and blanket on the couch in the music room to keep them in the dark the week before the wedding."

Fuck! James exclaimed in his head. *Thanksgiving week together is gonna be tougher than even the time we've spent in separate cities. We won't even be able to Skype if her parents are in the room next door to hers.*

Chapter Four

Monday, October 22, 2018

Randi hated working Monday evenings in the Camelot Hotel restaurant. They were usually the most dead shift all week. Any guests who had stayed over the weekend had already checked out to go home. Plus, anyone coming to stay there while in town for work would schedule their business dinners closer to the downtown corporations where they were working, not at the castle themed hotel restaurant over by the Arkansas River.

If she had to work a night shift, she preferred the weekend shifts, when the restaurant was busier. But even on the weekends, she preferred the day shifts, when they hosted princess parties for little girls who wanted a themed birthday celebration at the castle hotel.

Since her boss was still taking out his irritation at her sister on Randi, though, she was stuck with only three days that she was scheduled to work that week. Monday, Wednesday, and Thursday, all in the evening, and all during the week when the restaurant was mostly empty. So, she had little hope of making enough in tips to be worth her time.

Maybe it's a good thing I applied to some of those boring desk jobs this weekend?

Randi stood at the hostess stand, killing time by rolling silverware. Since there were so few customers at the restaurant, Mr. Brooks had sent the hostess home for the night. Her boss expected Randi to cover for the hostess, while also waiting on the one table of customers in her section, should anyone else come in to eat that night.

Randi basically had to stay at the hostess stand to watch for anyone coming in the door, while watching the window to the kitchen to know when the food was ready to go to the table, and also keep an eye on the table to know when they needed drink refills. How she was supposed to watch three places at once, she didn't know, but she thought she was doing a pretty good job of it. At least, until a group of guys walked in that prevented her from keeping her eyes on either the kitchen window or her table of customers.

Mitch Fox, the brother of her sister Kay's ex-husband, stomped up to the hostess stand. He was flanked by two other guys that Randi didn't know. The two strangers were a little more intimidating than Mitch, since they were at least each over six feet tall, even though they were all super skinny.

"Randi Lee," Mitch bellowed with a scowl. "Not exactly the woman I hoped to see here, but you'll do for now. Where's your bitch sister and her brats?"

"Welcome to Camelot," Randi chirped with a fake smile, trying to stick to the script for being the restaurant hostess and not respond to Mitch's hate speech. "How many in your party?"

She quickly finished rolling the silverware in her hand and reached toward the menus, so she could grab as many as she needed to escort them to a table on the opposite side of the restaurant from where she was working.

"We're not here to eat, skank!" Mitch spat at her as he stepped around the hostess stand toward her. "We're here to find Kay, so tell us where she is, and nobody has to get hurt!"

Randi backed away from him as fast as she could, wishing she'd held onto that bundle of silverware, so she could use it to defend herself if needed. But he was still easily able to grab her by the upper arms, his bony fingers digging into her biceps enough to leave several finger-shaped bruises.

"I don't know where she is," Randi croaked as she tried to wrench herself away from his painful grasp. "But she's not here, so if you aren't here to eat, then you need to leave."

"I'm not going anywhere until you tell me where the bitch is!" Mitch shouted, shoving Randi back into the table closest to the front of the restaurant. Her low back slammed into the edge of the table, causing an immediate stabbing pain, and probably more bruising. "I need to find her, so she can drop the bullshit charges she filed against Mark, and he can come back home. So quit being a bitch and tell me where the fuck she is!"

Randi was glad there weren't any customers at the table in danger of getting hurt in the scuffle, but she hoped that at least one of the patrons seated farther into the restaurant, or one of her coworkers, would notice what was happening and, at least, call nine-one-one for her.

"No, Mitch," Randi yelled back at him as she struggled to escape his hold. "I already told you that I don't know where she is. Now let me go and leave before I have to call my Dad to press charges against you for assault."

"What's going on here?" Mr. Brooks finally spoke up from somewhere behind Randi. She had no idea how much of the confrontation he had seen, but Randi knew from how far away his voice sounded that he probably hadn't heard most of it.

"Tell your bitch sister to drop the charges against Mark before anyone else has to get hurt," Mitch growled in a low tone right in Randi's face before shoving her to the ground and storming out of the restaurant. His two friends followed close behind him, without having said a word the whole time.

"Ms. Lee," Mr. Brooks screeched as he finally arrived at Randi's side, where she was still sitting on the floor from Mitch shoving her down. "Fighting with our customers is unacceptable."

"Whoa!" Randi shouted, jumping up from her position on the ground to be able to stand eye to eye with her boss. She pointed her finger toward the door as she continued speaking. "I wasn't fighting with a customer. I was just assaulted by a lunatic, who flat out said they weren't here to eat. He was here looking for someone else and attacked me when I couldn't tell him where she is. I didn't fight with him. I didn't hit him. I didn't lay a finger on him. He grabbed me. He shoved me to the floor. So, instead of getting mad at me for fighting with a customer, get mad at the criminal who just assaulted one of your employees, and be grateful that I was the one he attacked instead of you."

Mr. Brooks stood there, red faced, and floundering, as if he had no idea how to respond to Randi or what to do about the situation. "Buh-but you called him by name," her boss finally stuttered out. "So, he was obviously here to see you. Therefore, you're responsible for the actions of your guests on the premises."

"Just because I know his name, doesn't mean he was here to see me," Randi tried to explain to her boss. "I know your name too, Paul, but you aren't here to see me."

Randi turned to look around the restaurant to see if anyone else had seen what Mitch had done to back her up, since her boss was obviously too much of an idiot to comprehend the situation. "Did anyone call nine-one-one?" she inquired of the room as a whole, hoping someone would have her back. "Or do I need to do that myself, too?"

"I called nine-one-one," one of the older women seated across the restaurant hollered back. "The dispatcher said the police are on their way."

"Thank you," Randi beamed, smiling at the sweet little old lady.

"We couldn't hear everything he said, but it was obvious that he was the aggressor," one of the other women at the same table added. "We all saw everything and will be glad to stay and tell the police officers what happened."

"Thank you," Randi smiled again, relieved to know that, at least, she had witnesses to back her up.

Before anyone else could say another word, two Tulsa Police Department officers walked into the restaurant.

"We had a report of an altercation here this evening," the first officer reported.

Randi looked at the name tag on his uniform, so she could address him by name. "Yes, Officer Butler," she acknowledged the officer just as Mr. Brooks tried waving them away by saying, "No, it was just a misunderstanding."

"You hush," a chorus of older women reprimanded as they walked up to the area where Randi was standing with her boss and the police officers. One of them actually slapped Paul Brooks on the arm as she reached the group, making Randi need to stifle a giggle at the older woman scolding him like a child.

"I'm Betty Clark," the woman who had called the authorities introduced herself. "I'm the one who called you when I saw this young lady being attacked. I knew we wouldn't be much help in fighting all three of them off of her, but we could at least call the police to help her, since none of the men in this place were brave enough to come to her rescue."

Leah Mae Wright

"What exactly did you see, ma'am?" The second officer addressed Betty, pulling out a notebook so she could take notes of everyone's statements.

"We had just finished placing our order when three guys walked in," Betty stated, pointing out where they had been. Randi noticed the phone still in her hand as she continued to use her hands while she talked to point out where each thing happened as she described it. "This young lady was standing at the hostess stand. I couldn't hear what was said until the short one grabbed her by the arms and started yelling. He shouted, 'we're not here to eat,' and called her a bad word I won't repeat. Then he said, 'we're here to find Kay, so tell us where she is, and nobody has to get hurt here,' and started shoving her back into that table."

"Could you hear what she said back to him?" Officer Dennis inquired of Betty while making notes in her notebook.

"No, she wasn't yelling, so I couldn't hear her," Betty replied, shaking her head. "But she was shaking her head like she was telling him 'no,' so I assume she was telling him that she didn't know where Kay was, whoever Kay is."

"Kay is a former employee," Mr. Brooks grumbled, looking down his nose at Randi. "So, this whole scene was just because she wouldn't tell him where her sister is, but since he and his friends left without anyone getting hurt, I don't think we need anything further from you, officers."

"I already told you to hush once," the older woman who had slapped Paul's arm earlier admonished him once again. "And you don't know that nobody was hurt, since we had to have our waitress go get you from back in the kitchen and you didn't see what was happening. She could have a broken tailbone from the way he shoved her into the table and then to the ground, or at the very least bruises on her arms. Even scrawny little twerps can have a strong enough grip to cause bruising."

"Alright, let's all calm down," Officer Butler instructed, stepping between Mr. Brooks and the little old lady, who was swatting at him and telling him off. "Let's let Ms. Clark finish giving her statement and then we'll take turns getting everyone else's statements, one at a time."

"Thank you, Officer," Betty nodded at Officer Butler, smiling at the male officer before turning back to the female officer to finish her statement. "Next he shouted 'I'm not going anywhere until you tell me where the bleep is,' only, he didn't say bleep. He said the B word that rhymes with witch."

Betty shook her head as she continued. "He kept shouting when he said, 'I need to find her, so she can drop the bull bleep charges she filed against Mark, and he can come back home. So quit being a bleep and tell me where the bleep she is.' The first bleep was the S word, the second bleep was the B word again, and the third bleep was the F word."

Betty reached over and took Randi's hand before continuing. "That's when this sweet girl finally yelled back at him. She said, 'no, Mitch, I already told you that I don't know where she is. Now let me go and leave before I have to call my Dad to press charges against you for assault,' while struggling to get him to let go of her arms. I couldn't hear what else he said before he shoved her down and took off. That was when this one," Betty pointed at Mr. Brooks, "came out of the kitchen asking what was going on and started accusing this sweetheart of fighting with customers."

"At what point did you call nine-one-one?" Officer Dennis queried Betty, pointing at the phone still in the older woman's hand.

"As soon as the one she called Mitch grabbed her," Betty replied, handing the officer her cell phone. "You can ask the dispatcher; I was telling her word for word what he was saying the whole time I was on the phone with her."

Officer Dennis looked at the phone before putting it up to her ear and speaking. "Are you still on the line? Yes. Yes, send it to Officer Dennis at the twenty-third precinct. Thank you." She disconnected the call before handing Betty back her phone. "Thank you, Ms. Clark."

"I'm assuming the rest of you will have the same story as Ms. Clark?" Officer Butler looked around at the group of older women around them. When they all nodded in agreement, he continued. "Then I'll just take down each of your names and phone numbers in case we need to call you in to testify or identify the culprit in a line-up."

Leah Mae Wright

As each of the older ladies gave Officer Butler their information, Officer Dennis motioned for Randi to step away from everyone else to speak to her.

"Since you mentioned calling your dad to press charges against your assailant tonight, I'm assuming you're related to a member of law enforcement." Officer Dennis arched an eyebrow inquisitively at Randi.

"Yes, ma'am," Randi crooned, smiling at the officer. "I'm Randi Lee. My father is Sheriff Charles Lee."

"And who was the man who attacked you tonight?" Officer Dennis looked down at her notepad, taking more notes.

"Mitch Fox, my sister's former brother-in-law," Randi informed the officer. She briefly explained the issues Kay was having with her ex-husband. How Mark had turned abusive and vandalized her home, as well as how the sheriff's department was trying to locate him to arrest him for multiple warrants and charges. She told the officer that Kay had taken a much better paying job with the GWA that allowed her daughters to travel with her and provided private tutors for their education, so they could all stay safely away from her abusive ex-husband.

"Apparently, his family is upset that he's probably gonna be doing some prison time once he's arrested, and his brother thought he could intimidate me into convincing my sister into dropping the charges," Randi explained to the officer. "What Mitch was too dumb to realize is that it wasn't actually Kay that pressed the charges against Mark. It was my dad, the legal owner of the house he vandalized. And there's no way on earth that Daddy will ever drop those charges. The only thing getting Kay to come back to town would do is increase the charges against him to add the assault on her from right before she got her new job."

"As the injured party tonight, do you wish to press charges against Mitch Fox?"

"Can I?" Randi looked hopefully at the officer. "I mean, I might have some bruising, but I don't have any broken bones or anything that I need to go to the doctor for as injuries. I wanna make sure he doesn't try anything like this again, but I don't know if a few bruises are enough evidence to warrant a charge big enough to earn him a sentence that would actually be an effective deterrent to doing it again."

"Oh, yes," Officer Dennis assured her with a smile. "We can definitely charge him with felony assault and battery with pictures of bruises as evidence. Do you have a locker room or restroom here, where we can go take the pictures now?"

"Yes," Randi nodded, motioning toward the back of the restaurant, where the employee break room and restrooms were located.

"I'll document your injuries tonight and then we can get together again in a day or two when the bruising looks the worst to take additional pictures," Officer Dennis clarified as the two of them walked back toward the employee restroom.

Randi noticed as they walked by that the other waitress had already taken the food to the one group of men that had been sitting in Randi's section of the restaurant that night. She met her gaze from across the room and mouthed "thank you" to the other woman. She would have to come up with some way of showing her gratitude after she was finished with the officer.

I'll pick her up a gift card to her favorite coffee shop tomorrow, Randi decided while the officer was taking pictures of her arms, lower back, and buttocks. Thinking about how to show her fellow server her appreciation for covering her table was a good way to distract herself while standing in her underwear in the employee restroom at work and being photographed. Randi wasn't nearly as self-conscious with the female TPD officer as she would have been had it been her father or one of the sheriff's deputies who worked for him taking the pictures of her bruises, but it still wasn't completely comfortable for her to be so exposed while on the job.

As soon as they were done taking the pictures, she put her uniform dress back on, so they could go back out to the front of the restaurant and finish up with any other questions the officers had for her. Thankfully, they only had a couple, just wanting to know what she'd said to Mitch and his friends that Betty and her brood hadn't overheard.

"I greeted them the same way we greet all our customers," Randi explained. "Welcome to Camelot. How many in your party? That sort of thing, not acknowledging Mitch's question about Kay or the other bile he was spewing. When he grabbed me, I told him I don't know where Kay is, which I don't. Like I told you earlier, Kay is traveling all over the country with her new job. She's in a different city every day, and I don't have her schedule to know where she is, where she's been, or where she's going. Then, after he said they weren't here to eat, I told him that if they weren't here to eat, then they needed to leave. And Betty already told you what I said when he shoved me into the table, and I finally got mad enough to yell back at him."

"Why didn't you fight back?" Officer Butler looked at her with pity in his expression. "The witnesses all said you tried to pull out of his grasp, but you didn't kick him when you had a clear open shot."

"Because he didn't hit me or kick me first," Randi shrugged, not wanting to admit to her momentary fantasy of stabbing him with a fork. "He grabbed me. And while it was painful, he didn't try to knock me out, or drag me out of the restaurant, or rip my clothes off so he could rape me. If I'd have kicked him in the balls just because I had a clear shot at them, I would've been the one escalating the aggression, and my dad taught me to only use as much force as necessary to get out of the situation without escalating it. If I'd have escalated it by kicking him, then his two friends probably would've come after me next. And who's to say what they'd have done, or what weapons they might have pulled, that could've put everyone else in the restaurant in danger, too. So, I did what Daddy taught me. I stayed as calm as possible and tried to get them to leave without making things worse."

"Do you know the names of the other two men?" Officer Butler snapped off his quick question without acknowledging that Randi had handled the situation correctly.

"No, I've never seen them before," Randi reported before describing them both for the officers. Not that it really mattered, since they hadn't said a word or done anything that would be grounds for charging them with anything, but Randi hoped that having descriptions of all three of them would make it easier for the officers to find Mitch, so they could at least arrest him.

Once the officers were satisfied that they had everything they needed, Randi started back up toward the hostess stand to continue working. Mr. Brooks, however, told her that he'd already clocked her out for the night and that she should just go on home, since she hadn't worked for the last hour anyway.

As irritating as it was to Randi to not get paid for most of the night, she knew she had to call her father and tell him about the events of the evening anyway. So, she didn't mind all that much that she was sent home early.

As soon as her phone connected to the Bluetooth in her car stereo, she called her dad, relaying the events of the night as she drove home. To say he was livid would be an understatement, but Randi wouldn't say the words that would really describe how he reacted to Mitch attacking her. At least, not where he could hear her.

"I'll have my guys run extra patrols by your house," her father, Charles Lee, barked, his deep voice rumbling through her speakers. "And what were the names of the officers? I'll get with them tomorrow to make sure they're pushing for an order of protection for you, too."

"Dennis and Butler," Randi replied, knowing it would be useless to tell him not to bother the officers, who had been so kind in helping her at the restaurant. "I think Officer Dennis said she works in the twenty-third precinct."

"They sent a female officer out to an assault call?" Charles sounded worried on behalf of the officer.

"Yes, Daddy," Randi cajoled, hating how sexist his last question sounded. "And I'm glad they did, since she had to take pictures of me in my underwear to document the bruises on my arms, low back, and bottom. I would've never been able to let one of the male officers do that to be able to press charges."

"Oh, um, yeah," Charles stuttered out. "I guess that makes sense then. I just hate the thought of any woman, even a well-trained policewoman, trying to take on an aggressive perp."

"I know, Daddy," Randi sighed, not wanting to rock the boat any by telling him how outdated she felt his beliefs were. "I'm gonna let you go, since I just pulled into the driveway and my phone will disconnect as soon as I turn off the car. Love you."

"Love you, too, baby girl," Charles repeated just before they disconnected.

As soon as Randi got inside her house, she sent James a text, not even caring that she was texting while walking down the hall to her bedroom.

Randi: Home from work early. Any chance you can actually talk instead of texting me back? I need to hear your voice.

She'd barely dropped her purse on her dresser when her phone rang in her hand. Seeing James's name on her screen brought tears to her eyes, knowing that he was calling her even if he wasn't completely alone for the night yet, just because she wanted to hear his voice. She blinked them back as she swiped the screen to answer his call.

"What's wrong, Angel?" James prodded before she could even say "hello" to him.

"I've just had a really bad night," Randi confessed as she flopped onto her bed, not even bothering to change out of her uniform to get comfortable for the call. "Kay's ex-brother-in-law showed up at work tonight, trying to get me to tell him where she is. He caused a scene. My boss got mad at me over it and sent me home early. Thankfully, it was the Tulsa PD that showed up and not my dad or one of his deputies, so I at least had a female officer to take the pictures of my bruises."

"He hurt you?" James roared through the phone. "What's his name? I may not be able to get there until tomorrow, but I'll book the next flight to Tulsa and kill the son of a bitch for touching you."

"No, James," Randi shouted. "You can't come to Tulsa tomorrow, and even if you could come here, it would only make things worse, not fix it."

"But he hurt you," James groaned. "I'm sure Rick will be glad to give me a few days off to kick his ass."

"And then you'll be sharing a jail cell with him when you're both brought up on charges of assault," Randi pointed out with a sigh. "The TPD will be arresting him, as soon as they can find him, because I specifically said I wanna press charges. And I'm not really hurt, just some bruises from where he grabbed my arms and pushed me into a table and then down to the floor. Nothing's broken. I don't have any open wounds, or even any bruises where anyone will see them. So, stop overreacting and tell me about your day, so I can forget mine."

James didn't reply immediately, but Randi could hear his heavy breathing through the phone and knew that he was probably pacing around wherever he was, trying to calm down before saying anything more that might upset her. That was one of the main things she liked about James, how he was always thoughtful in how he spoke to her. He thought through what he was going to say most of the time, instead of just blurting out whatever was on his mind, making sure to put her at ease when she needed it most. He was a calming presence in her life that she hadn't realized she needed until she met him.

Even though her attack earlier in the evening was obviously upsetting to him, and he'd initially had a bad reaction, he was still trying to be her calm in the storm to help her get through the unpleasantness of the evening. It only took him a couple of minutes before he was back to breathing normally, and calmly telling her about the show that night, where he did a run-in to interfere with Dion and Jeff while they were wrestling a singles match.

Apparently, Jeff was married to one of Kay's new friends, and when James interfered in the match, it helped him turn heel when they double-teamed Dion. While all that was going on in the ring, Dean attacked Red backstage, so he couldn't come rescue his tag-team partner.

Randi was fascinated with the storylines they had going on, especially how they were planning things out months in advance. The more he talked about the creative aspects of his job, the more interested she became in pursuing a similar career. Not that she would tell him that, yet, though.

She had to get through her doctor's appointment the next day and, hopefully, find a way to conquer her fear of flying first. Once she conquered that fear, then she could tell him that she was interested in becoming a wrestler, so she could spend more time with him while working in a job she thought she would love. *But maybe I should look into the local wrestling company and see if they offer training to potential wrestlers?* It wouldn't hurt to start training before she was ready to fly, so she'd be more likely to get a tryout with the GWA as soon as she could get on a plane regularly without having a panic attack.

Leah Mae Wright

<center>~~~</center>

Randi was a nervous wreck as she sat in the waiting room at Dr. McShane's office. She thought it was ridiculous that she was so anxious about what was a mostly normal quarterly appointment to get her birth control shot. It wasn't like she hadn't been getting them every January, April, July, and October for the last several years. Just the thought of talking to her doctor about trying to find a way to overcome her anxiety while flying shouldn't be so nerve-racking.

Her right knee was bouncing, just as it always did when she was worried about something, and Randi had no idea what to do to stop the physical manifestation of her anxiety. She knew her blood pressure was probably going to be elevated, and would almost certainly alarm the nurse and doctor, if she didn't find a way to calm down before being called to the back. She pulled out her phone and opened a meditation app to try a two-minute breathing exercise to see if it would help her chill a little before going back. But she didn't even get to start it before they were calling her name.

She jumped up out of the chair and dutifully followed the nurse down the hall to the exam room. As soon as Randi was seated in the little room, the nurse reached for the electronic contraption that would read her blood pressure, pulse rate, and temperature.

"My blood pressure is probably through the roof right now," Randi told the nurse as she was wrapping the cuff around her upper arm.

"If it's too high, we'll let you relax for a few minutes and check it again," Jessie, the nurse, replied as she put the thermometer under Randi's tongue. Jessie put the pulse oximeter on Randi's finger on the hand opposite the blood pressure cuff, pushed a button on the machine to inflate the cuff, and started recording all the data.

Once Randi's vitals were recorded, Jessie removed all the probes and asked Randi all the usual questions about why she was there, her previous medical history, and current medications. Randi answered every other question before going back to the reason she was there.

"It's time for my quarterly birth control shot." Randi took a deep breath, feeling her nerves amp back up as she added, "and I wanna ask Dr. McShane about anxiety meds, or maybe a referral to someone who can help me with my anxiety, if that's not something she normally handles."

"Is that why your blood pressure is elevated today?" Jessie finished typing notes into Randi's chart on the computer.

"Yes," Randi admitted, fidgeting with her hands while trying to hold her knee still. "Normally it's just when I have to fly, or when I'm really worried about something. Like right now, it's hitting me because I'm worried about talking to the doctor about it, and possibly not being able to get it under control."

"I understand," Jessie comforted Randi by patting her hand and smiling as she stood to leave the room. "Try to relax while you're waiting for Dr. McShane. I'm sure she'll be able to help you find the best option for dealing with it."

As soon as Jessie left the room, Randi pulled out her phone again and started the two-minute breathing exercise on her meditation app. The doctor walked into the room as she was finishing the last deep inhale and exhale sequence, so Randi quickly shut the app and put her phone back in her purse.

"I love those apps," Dr. McShane confided as she sat down on the rolling stool in front of the computer. "Some days, I have to take a breather several times between patients, and they really do help."

"Yeah, I found that one when I was doing some online research about how to handle my anxiety," Randi confessed, still a little fidgety. "While it's enough to bring my blood pressure back down to normal on days like today, I don't think it's enough to help me get over my fear of flying, like I really need to do now."

"So, your anxiety is mostly centered around when you actually have to fly?" Dr. McShane made notes on the computer as they talked.

"Yes, but I also get nervous when I think about people I love flying, or if I worry about my dad working a crime scene," Randi replied, her nerves making her blurt out all her worst anxiety issues. "And my sister just started a job where she's flying seven days out of ten, and my nieces are traveling with her and her fiancé, so I worry about all of them constantly now. And I've sort of started seeing a guy who flies daily, and he wants me to come work with him, which would mean me having to fly daily, too. There's no way I can do that until I find a way to keep from freaking out at just the thought of getting on a plane."

"I thought maybe therapy would help, but I don't know if that would work fast enough," Randi continued, unable to control the bouncing of her leg, or the excessive word vomit spewing from her mouth. "I have to fly to my sister's wedding in less than a month. And I have a feeling that while we're all down there in Texas for a week, they're gonna introduce me to their boss and try to get me a job flying all over the world with them. I don't wanna hafta turn down what could be a dream job because I'm too much of a chicken to get on the company's plane, ya know."

"Okay," Dr. McShane interjected as Randi paused to take a breath. "It sounds like you've always had an issue with flying, but it's only gotten bad recently because of so many people you care about being on the same company plane."

"Yes," Randi adamantly agreed, nodding her head.

"If it was just an issue with you needing something to deal with a panic attack on an occasional flight, this would be an easy fix," Dr. McShane informed Randi as she typed on the computer. "We could prescribe something for you to take an hour before you had to get on a plane, but since you're having issues worrying about others, and are considering a job where you'd be flying daily, I don't think that's our best option."

"I don't wanna take anything that will have a lot of side effects or make me loopy either," Randi confided, wringing her hands in her lap. "Or anything addictive. That's why I was thinking about trying therapy, but I just don't know how effective that would be. Or how I could continue it if I got a job with the GWA."

"The GWA?" Dr. McShane sounded intrigued, while still looking at the computer screen like she was looking for something.

"Yeah, the Galactic Wrestling Association," Randi clarified. "My sister just started working for them a couple of weeks ago. She's a flight attendant, which is just crazy to me, but she seems to love it."

"And your new boyfriend works for them, too?" Dr. McShane pried, still scrolling on the computer.

"Yeah, James is a professional wrestler," Randi replied, smiling at the thought of James in his spandex wrestling tights. Just thinking about him was calming Randi down, but she didn't notice that her knee was no longer bouncing, and her hands had gone still in her lap, or even that Dr. McShane's eyes had widened at the mention of the GWA and James in particular.

"What's his wrestling name?" Dr. McShane turned from the computer to look directly at Randi, but didn't give her a chance to answer before continuing. "I went with my husband to the GWA show here in town last month. I wonder if he wrestled that night."

"James Dangerous," Randi finally answered when the doctor quit talking for a second. "He and his brother, Dean, are the tag-team champions."

Randi noticed the doctor's reaction that time, seeing the wide eyes and dropped jaw for a brief second before the doctor squealed in delight.

"Mike, my husband, is going to flip when I tell him I know James Dangerous's girlfriend!" Dr. McShane cheered with a giggle. "Especially when I won't tell him anything else about you because of HIPAA."

"Um, okay," Randi drawled, not sure how to respond to her doctor's unusual reaction to learning who she was sort of dating.

"And what will you be doing with the GWA when we get your anxiety issues under control?" Dr. McShane turned back to the computer and clicked the mouse.

"James has suggested that I could write his promos or be his manager, but I'm not sure I'm qualified to do anything with them," Randi shrugged. "But if you can help me get over my airplane anxiety, I'm thinking about looking into training to be a wrestler eventually."

"The thought of performing in the ring doesn't cause you any anxiety?" Dr. McShane inquired, again not giving Randi time to reply before continuing. "Because that would be what I would need anxiolytics for."

"No, it's just athletic acting, and I loved my acting classes and performing in plays in school," Randi responded, as the doctor finished what she was doing on the computer and stood to get a specimen cup from the cabinet.

"Well, then I'll look forward to watching you on television soon," Dr. McShane confessed, smiling at Randi as she handed her the specimen cup. "You know the drill. We have to have a urine sample to verify you aren't pregnant before we give you your shot. I'm going to print off your prescription and referral. Then I'll be back in to administer your injection and explain the medication we're going to try first."

They walked out of the exam room together. Dr. McShane pointed out the restroom to Randi as she walked by it on the way to her office. Randi went in the restroom and followed the standard procedures for giving a urine sample, making sure to wash her hands a second time after putting the specimen cup in the collection box in the wall. She barely made it back into the exam room before Dr. McShane walked back in with a stack of papers.

"First, this is a referral to a therapist that I think you'll like," the doctor explained as she handed Randi the first paper. "She does telehealth appointments for people who can't come into her office, so if you do get a job traveling with the GWA, then you'll still be able to meet with her from wherever you are in the world."

"Thank you." Randi took the first paper.

"Second, this is a prescription for a very mild anxiolytic. It doesn't have the side effects or dependency issues of benzodiazepines or antidepressants. I've started you on the lowest dose. I want you to take it every morning for the next two weeks and then message me on your online chart to let me know how it's working. If you're still having anxiety while thinking about your boyfriend or sister flying, then we can take it up to twice a day. When exactly do you have to fly to your sister's wedding?"

"I'm not sure of the exact date, but somewhere between the seventeenth and the twenty-first," Randi replied, taking the prescription and the packet of paperwork explaining all about the new medication, not remembering how her mother had said they would be flying the seventeenth in one of their recent group chats.

"Okay, we'll see how you're feeling on it in two weeks. And if we need to increase it then, we'll check again a week later, so we have time to make another adjustment before your flight," Dr. McShane decided. "So, I expect messages from you on November sixth and thirteenth, so we can discuss any changes before you fly out on the seventeenth. If you end up not flying out until the twenty-first, we can make another adjustment on the twentieth as well."

Before Randi could reply to thank her doctor, there was a knock on the exam room door and Jessie was walking into the room carrying the birth control shot that was Randi's original reason for setting the appointment. "You're good to go," Jessie confirmed as she handed the syringe to the doctor.

Randi removed her light jacket and pushed up her shirt sleeve, so the doctor could give her the injection. Randi had to explain the bruising on her arm from the night before in order for Dr. McShane to actually give her the shot. While she was slightly embarrassed to tell her doctor about her sister's ex-brother-in-law attacking her, it was way less mortifying than the doctor's original assumption that James had caused the bruising.

No, the light little love marks he left the night we met faded after only a couple of days, Randi mused, fondly remembering the faintest of hickeys on her breasts that had faded by the Tuesday following her night with James.

It only took a few more minutes for the doctor to verify that Randi had no further questions before the ladies were all exiting the exam room to go on with their daily routines. Randi made sure to schedule her next appointment for January as she was checking out at the front desk.

As soon as she got to her car, she pulled her phone out of her purse and called to schedule her first appointment with the therapist that Dr. McShane had referred her to, happy that there was an opening late Friday afternoon.

Surely, I'll be done Skyping with Kay at Mom's by then, Randi hoped. *I don't wanna hafta explain to them why I have to leave by four to go meet my therapist.*

She wasn't really embarrassed by seeing a therapist, but she didn't want to mention it around her mother. Kay had seen a therapist after her divorce and said it really helped her, so Randi knew her sister would be supportive of her taking steps to improve her mental wellbeing. But if Mary Lee heard Randi mention it, she would start asking all kinds of questions about why Randi needed therapy. Before she started her car to leave the doctor's office, she sent her sister a quick text.

> **Randi: Hey, Sis, just making sure we'll be done by 4 on Friday.**

Kay: Should be, why?

> **Randi: I have an appointment with a therapist at 4:30 Friday & don't want to tell Mom about it.**

Kay: Okay, I'll make sure we're done with plenty of time to spare. Is this what Dr. McShane recommended for your anxiety about flying?

> **Randi: Yeah, that and the prescription I'm picking up on my way home.**

Kay: You don't want Mom to know about it either? You know she'll support you in doing what you need to be able to fly down for the wedding, right?

> **Randi: Yeah, but not without a lot of questions & a lecture & I'm just not ready for all that.**

Kay: Okay, my lips are zipped. {Zipper-Mouth Face Emoji} But keep me posted on how it's all working.

> **Randi: Will do. {Crossed Fingers Emoji}**

Randi knew she could tell her mother that her therapy and medication was for her anxiety about flying, so she would be more comfortable flying down to Kay's wedding. But Randi knew her mother wouldn't believe that she'd go to such lengths for only a couple of flights. She'd push until Randi finally broke down and told her about James, and how she wanted to be able to go see him while he was working, and eventually be able to travel with him all the time.

As much as her parents were on her case about needing to find a better job, specifically saying she needed to find a worthwhile career, she knew they wouldn't support her in working in the wrestling industry. They'd wanted her to work at the church for a while, trying to convince her that it would be fulfilling to *"assist in spreading the word of God to others"* by being a church secretary or Sunday school teacher.

When she didn't volunteer for that on her summers home from college, they started pushing her to study nursing, thinking she would be fulfilled by helping others while working in a hospital. She had to remind them of how she passed out at the sight of blood to convince them that a medical career wasn't for her.

When she took a few business administration classes to finish out her final semester of college, they started pushing her to work in a corporate job. When Randi tried to explain how boring she thought a corporate job would be, her mother had switched tactics. Mary tried to convince Randi to just find an office job temporarily because it would be a good way to meet her future husband. Mary went as far as to say that once Randi was married, she could quit working and be a stay-at-home mom.

As if Randi wanted to sit around being lazy all day while letting some man support her. Not that stay-at-home moms were lazy. Randi knew they worked their butts off to take care of their families. But since she wasn't planning on having kids until she was at least thirty, she'd feel pretty lazy staying at home without kids for the next five years. And she wouldn't be attracted to any man who wanted her to stay home being a kept woman while he supported her.

That was another thing she liked about James. She knew he had a multi-million-dollar contract with the GWA, but he didn't act like a stereotypical stuck up rich guy. He didn't patronize her by suggesting she shouldn't work, and he respected her enough to treat her as if her lowly waitressing job was just as impressive as his high paying wrestling job. He treated her as if they were equals, even though he probably spent more on his wardrobe than she spent on her clothes, rent, and car combined.

She thought about the other things she liked about him as she stopped at the pharmacy to pick up her new prescription. He was wrestling on the live television show that night that was being aired from Columbus, Ohio. She might get a text or two from him after he was done with his rehearsals, while he was eating dinner or waiting backstage for his time to perform. But Randi figured he wouldn't reply yet if she texted him right then, since he was probably in the ring. She decided to wait a little while, maybe until he let her know he was available to talk, before she texted him, even though she was dying to message him to tell him about her doctor's appointment.

While she loved their sexy time Skype sessions, and drooled over his hot bod while watching him wrestle on television, she liked their normal daily conversations the most. They could literally talk about anything, from the mundane meaningless memes they found funny that day to all their hopes, dreams, and deepest darkest secrets.

Anytime even the slightest little thing happened in her day, she felt the need to tell James about it as soon as possible. Judging from the amount of texts he sent her about every little thing that happened where he was each day, Randi believed that James was just as desperate to tell her everything as she was him. While she was waiting for the pharmacist to fill her prescription, she pulled her phone back out of her purse and sent him an update to her day, unable to hold back a moment longer.

> **Randi: Done at the doctor. Waiting at the pharmacy now for new medicine that will hopefully be working well enough by next month that I won't panic while flying. And I have an appointment for therapy on Friday to tackle my anxiety that way too. {Crossed-Fingers Emoji}**

Randi thought about also telling him about getting her birth control shot, but she wasn't sure she was ready to tell him that she trusted him enough to ditch the condoms yet, and she was afraid that would be implied by the admission. She hadn't ever trusted a guy that far before, but she also didn't usually have sex with a guy the first night they met either. James had pushed her outside her normal comfort zone without even really trying.

He probably doesn't even know how unusual that night was for me. But if I'd have stuck to my norm and insisted on at least a dozen dates before doing more than chaste kisses, we probably wouldn't have talked nearly as much as we have the past few weeks. He would've just flown out to the next town to find the next girl who was willing to have a one-night stand, and I wouldn't have ever known that I was missing out on the best sex of my life.

But there was just something about him that night that I've never felt before. Something that connected us in a way I didn't even know was possible. Just looking at him was like looking at the other half of myself that I didn't even know I was missing before. And when we made love, that connection was even stronger. It's the only time in my life that I've ever felt like I was exactly where I was supposed to be—in his arms.

I hate not feeling that connection as strongly over the distance between us, even with all our electronic communication. I have to find a way to be with him more, because I need that bonded feeling with him again.

Dear Lord, please let this medication and therapy work, so I can fly without fear. Let me figure out how to get the training I need to be able to pursue a career in wrestling like James. Give me the courage I somehow found the night I met him to be brave enough to go after what I want in life. Amen.

Chapter Five

Wednesday, October 24, 2018

James and his brother, Dean, skipped their weight training session to follow Anthony, Kay, Tia, and Maria from the hotel after lunch to go find a men's formalwear store in Indianapolis, Indiana, so they could be measured for the tuxedos that Anthony would be ordering for them to wear in the wedding exactly a month away. They'd have done it sooner, but neither of them had a clue what measurements would be needed, so they preferred spending the afternoon hanging out with their friend and his future family to make sure they had the exact right measurements, since it was already so close to the date of the wedding.

Normally, James would have stuck to his normal routine of going to the hotel right after they arrived in whatever city they were in to get checked in, hit the weight room, and then have a late lunch before going to the arena. But he had to follow Anthony's new routine, so he could follow him to the formalwear store.

Anthony had switched up his routine since Kay and the girls were traveling with him. Instead of going to the weight room with the guys, they would check in and have lunch at the hotel, then get some sightseeing in before going to the arena, so Anthony could teach them self-defense in the ring before the wrestlers started to arrive for sparring and show rehearsals.

Since he'd eaten with his friend and they were doing these tuxedo measurements when they would normally go sightseeing, James hoped to get to help with the girls' self-defense training that afternoon, too. If Tia really wanted to learn to wrestle, then he wanted to work some time into his schedule to teach her the tricks of the trade, in addition to the self-defense she was already learning with Anthony.

That wasn't just because she was going to be his best friend's stepdaughter. Or even that she was Randi's niece and kind of looked like her aunt more than her mom. He genuinely liked the kids, both Tia and Maria, as well as their mother. But, since it would be a while before any kids he had would get to be their ages, he hoped that he could learn from his friend's family what to expect when he eventually had kids of his own.

I hope my kids are just like Tia and Maria in about fifteen years or so.

James parked beside his friend when they arrived at the store. Dean assisted Anthony in opening the car doors for Kay, Tia, and Maria, since he was on the passenger side and closest to their vehicle. So, James walked ahead to the door of the store to open it for everyone to enter.

"You guys do realize we're capable of opening doors, right?" Tia rolled her eyes at him as she walked through the door to the store.

"Tia," Kay admonished, sounding exasperated.

"Yeah, Squirt, I know you're capable." James hoped he was speaking fast enough that Kay wouldn't feel the need to reprimand the girl while he was explaining it to her. "We don't open doors or pull-out chairs because ladies can't do it for themselves. We do it because our parents and grandparents raised us to take care of the people we care about."

"Don't lie, Bro," Dean mocked as he brought up the rear of the line of people entering the store. "We do it because if we didn't when Ma or Meemaw were around, they'd whip us with a switch."

"Well, yeah, that, too," James admitted as they walked up to the counter at the front of the store. "But that's not the reason we were taught to behave like gentlemen. It's meant to show our respect and affection. That's why I held the door for you and Anthony, too, not just the girls."

"So, you won't get mad if I open a door or pull out a chair for you?" Tia gave James a skeptical look.

"Of course not," James replied with a smile at the precocious child, ruffling her hair. "Especially if you pull out a chair for me when I have my hands full in catering, so I can sit down without spilling my plate."

"Deal," Tia grinned. "I'll even save you a seat in catering tonight, so you can sit next to me at dinner, even if you're late getting there."

"How may I help you?" A gentleman in a three-piece suit, who looked to be about forty, walked up to the counter where they were all standing.

"I'm Anthony, I called about an hour ago." Anthony extended his hand to the salesman. "About getting my groomsmen measured by a professional, so we can order the correct size tuxedos."

"Ah, yes, I'm Jeffery," the salesman introduced himself as they shook hands. "Do you already have tuxedos picked out? I know you're just in town for the day and will be taking their measurements to your local shop to place the order for your wedding. But if I have the style you've picked in stock, it might be beneficial to see the gentlemen in them, so we can note the correct sizes in addition to their measurements."

"We're thinking of something like this." Kay showed the salesman a photo on her phone. "We want the groomsmen in royal blue to match the bridesmaids, but in a style similar to Anthony's dress white uniform."

"I have something similar in black." Jeffery nodded as he handed Kay's phone back to her. "It won't give you an exact match to the royal blue that you've already chosen, but I believe it's the same designer, so the sizes should be correct. If you'll just follow me, we'll get all the measurements done and have them try on what I have to make sure they fit properly."

Jeffery turned and walked back through the store, leading their group past racks of suits and tuxedos to an open area with mirrors all around in front of a row of changing rooms. Once there, he pulled a tape measure from his coat pocket and directed James and Dean where to stand, so he could do their measurements. When Jeffery walked over to a table off to one side and picked up a clipboard, Anthony told him that he would just log their measurements in his phone, so he could just call them out as he measured them and didn't have to write them down.

After only a few minutes of slightly uncomfortable touching by the older gentleman, James and Dean had both been measured. Although James silently agreed with the observations of the girls that they really only needed to measure one of them since their measurements were identical, he didn't say anything since it wasn't too invasive to be measured.

I'm still gonna ask Anthony to send me my measurements, though, so I won't have to do that again if Randi wants me in a tux for our wedding, James reasoned, not even realizing that he'd just imagined marrying Randi before saying, "Hey, send those to me in a text, will ya?"

"Sure," Anthony replied, arching an eyebrow at James. "You planning to buy a tux for something else?"

Holy shit! James freaked out in his head. *I wanna marry Randi and have daughters who look just like her! Fuck, we'd better have a couple of sons who look like me first to help me keep the boys away from our daughters when they're all teenagers.*

"Um, no," James lied to Anthony, hoping his friend couldn't read his mind. "Just thought it might come in handy to have my measurements to order some new suits, since we'll be spending the first couple of weeks of December in the northeast where I'll need something warmer than my summer travel clothes."

"Hey, that's not a bad idea," Dean blurted, unwittingly backing up James's lie. "Jeffery, can you ship some suits to us? We won't need them immediately, but it would be nice to pick them up when we're home for Thanksgiving break before the tour heads north again."

"Yes, sir, I can ship anything you pick out today," Jeffery confirmed as he handed them each a tuxedo to try on. "Do you have any preferences for cut or color? I can pull some options for you while you're trying on the tuxedos."

"Nothing as fancy as what you're wearing." Dean waved his arm up and down at Jeffery, who was in a charcoal gray three-piece suit that looked fancy enough to be only one step down from a tux. "We just have to look like we're going to work in an office for the company dress code, but maybe some thicker material than the lightweight stuff we're wearing now."

"What color are your eyes?" Maria tugged on James's sleeve to get his attention. "We can help him pick out clothes that will bring them out on camera."

James squatted down to look as close to eye to eye with her as possible. "They change color depending on what I'm wearing or what color they reflect back from my surroundings," James explained, staring directly into her aqua blue eyes. "But they're listed as gray on my driver's license."

"I've read about gray eyes," Tia professed, trying to get in on the eye contact with her sister. "I originally thought only hazel eyes changed color like that. I always thought mine were hazel because they change from blue to green depending on what's around me. But from what I read, hazel eyes usually only look light brown, gold, or green. Gray eyes can look blue, gray, brown, or green, so I think mine might actually be gray too. What do you think?"

James looked into Tia's eyes and compared them to her sister's. "Yeah, Tia, I think you're right. Your eyes look more gray blue with flecks of light brown and Maria's look more blue-green."

"No fair, I want gray eyes, too," Maria pouted with a cute little frown.

"Your eyes are probably classified as gray too," Tia reassured her little sister. "That's why they can change from blue to green."

"Cool, then let's go pick out shirts for James and Dean, so their eyes will look more blue-green, too." Maria grabbed her sister's hand to follow Jeffery through the store.

When he stood back up and started to go into the dressing room to change, James noticed Anthony shaking his head at him. "Guess you don't really need those measurements now, since you're ordering suits from here?"

James just shrugged as he went into the dressing room. *If Anthony doesn't send them, I'll just get them from Jeffery, since he'll probably have to write them down now to keep on file for any possible issues we might have with the suits we're buying today.* James changed out of his tan slacks and light blue button down and into the black tuxedo and silk shirt.

He really liked the look of the tux, so he snapped a couple of selfies in the dressing room and sent them to Randi before going back out to let Anthony and Kay see how it looked, even though it wasn't the right color for their wedding.

Once they'd approved the cut of the tux and took down the size for the blue one they would order for their wedding, Jeffery handed him the first suit that he and the girls had selected for him to try on. His phone buzzed as he was changing out of the tux, making him stop what he was doing to read Randi's reply to his selfies.

Randi: {Drooling Face Emoji} {Flushed Face Emoji} But I
thought Kay said she wanted you in a white or blue
tux?

James: Yeah, but this shop didn't have this style tux in
anything but black, so that's what we're trying on to
give them an idea of what size to order in blue.

Randi: I think I like the black better, personally.
{Shushing Face Emoji} Hate that I won't get to see you
in that one except in these pics.

James: Well, I haven't bought a Halloween costume yet
for the party next week. Maybe I should get this one
and say I'm James Bond for Halloween?

Randi: Maybe, depends on how many Bond girls will be at
the party. Where will you be on Halloween?

James: No Bond girls, unless you're coming to see me in
Billings, MT for Halloween.

Randi: Then yeah, that's a good costume, but no, I'm not
ready to fly yet. Only took my new med 1x so far & still
feel anxious just thinking about flying. {Nauseated
Face Emoji}

James: Med's not making you sick, I hope?

Randi: No, just thinking about flying. I haven't noticed
anything from the medicine, good or bad. But I've only
taken 1 pill and it's the lowest dose. Dr. McShane said
to let her know how I feel after 2 weeks on it, so I don't
expect to see much of a change until it's built up in my
system for at least that long.

> **James: Good, I'm glad you're not having bad side effects.
> And I think I'll go ahead and get the tux along with a
> couple of suits today, so I have a few things you might
> want to see me in next month.**

James finished changing into the first suit, a dark gray pinstriped suit with a royal blue shirt and sent Randi another selfie before going to show the girls. He enjoyed spending the next hour letting the girls pick out clothes for him to try on and getting Randi's opinion via text as to which outfits he should buy. He ended up with five new suits and shirts that he was having Jeffery ship to Heart's Destiny. And he carried the black tux and silk shirt with him.

"That's not really the right cut for a James Bond costume," Anthony asserted as James was paying for his purchases. "He normally goes for more traditional with a bow tie, doesn't he?"

James just smiled and shrugged. He didn't care if it wasn't the right style for a Bond costume. *Randi liked it, so even if I only wear it for a little role play with her, it was money well spent. But maybe I'll be able to convince her to let me wear it again for our wedding.*

He pulled his phone out of his pocket to check his messages while he waited for Dean to pay for the suits he'd also purchased.

> **Randi: Sorry, I have to cut the fashion show short, but it's
> time for me to leave for work. Have a great evening.
> I'll call you as soon as I get home tonight. <3**

> **James: No problem, Angel. I was done trying on clothes
> anyway. Stay safe at work. I can't wait to hear your
> voice tonight. <3**

As he pocketed his phone, he noticed that Kay was watching him intently. She'd been mostly quiet when they first arrived, but she'd really opened up and held her own in the banter as the guys were all trying on new suits. She'd even insisted on Anthony buying a couple of new suits for himself, teasing him about needing to replace the navy suit he wore on her birthday, after she ruined the pants by trying to get the stains out in the washer instead of taking them to the dry cleaners.

James wasn't sure they'd been completely honest when they said he'd spilled chili on them, because chili stains on his pants wouldn't have caused the blush on Kay's cheeks that appeared when the girls asked why she'd tried to wash them. James wasn't going to ask what had really stained Anthony's pants, though. He figured it was something that happened in their bedroom after the birthday party was over, and he didn't need to know. He did smile at Kay, though, when she continued to stare at him like she was trying to work up the nerve to ask him something.

"What?" James finally questioned her when everyone else started walking toward the door and she just stayed there examining him. He looked down at the front of his shirt to confirm he hadn't spilled any of his lunch without noticing. "Did I miss a button or something?"

"No, nothing like that," Kay denied, smiling up at him. "Just making sure the right emotions were crossing your face while you were thinking about my sister. And once I saw them, I was trying to picture the two of you together. I only saw you side by side for a few minutes almost a month ago. But the more I'm around you, the more I can really see you being good for her. I hope she's as good for you, too."

She turned and followed the rest of the group out of the store and got in the SUV that Anthony was holding the door open on for her before James could respond. *Yeah, I think we're perfect for each other, not just good.* James made his way out to his own rental vehicle and put his new tuxedo in the back seat before getting behind the wheel to drive with his brother to the arena for the show that night.

<center>~~~</center>

Friday, October 26, 2018

After spending the previous two nights working until almost midnight and then talking on the phone with James until two or three in the morning, Randi slept in Friday morning. She'd barely gotten up to take her medication and get a quick shower before Kay texted to tell her that she was on her way to the dress shop and would be Skyping her in about fifteen minutes.

113

"Sugar," Randi muttered as she brushed out her wet hair. She didn't take the time to dry it or put on any makeup before running back to her room to throw on some clothes, so she could rush over to her parents' house. Thankfully, they were only a couple of miles away, so it didn't take her that long to get there.

She'd just walked in the front door when her phone buzzed in her hand with the notification that Kay was calling on Skype.

"Hey!" Randi squealed as her sister appeared on her phone screen.

"Um, hang on a second, Randi." Kay turned to look at Anthony beside her, instead of the phone she was talking to Randi on. "I need to text pictures to Dee on this phone while we're Skyping with Mom and Randi on my new one. Can you, um, maybe do that for me?"

"Sure, Baby, no problem." Anthony took what Randi assumed was Kay's old phone and kissed the top of her head.

"Let me see them," Mary Lee demanded as she squeezed in close to Randi on the sofa, where she'd sat down.

"Hello," Kay finally greeted them when she turned back to them on her phone. "First, let me introduce you to my future mother-in-law, Hazel."

Kay turned her phone, so the woman that Randi assumed was Anthony's mother was on the screen as she made the introductions. "Hazel, this is my mother, Mary, and my sister, Randi."

They all said, "hi," "hello," and "nice to meet you" before Kay continued moving her phone to repeat the introduction process with Benny and Louella, the husband and wife who ran the dress shop and men's formalwear store in the small town of Heart's Destiny, Texas.

Then Kay focused the phone on the dresses Louella was showing her from the rack, only turning the phone back so that Randi could see her again to discuss each option. It wasn't too uncomfortable to snuggle into her mother like she had when she was a little kid, so they could both see everything on the screen and give their opinions. In fact, Randi almost missed snuggling on the couch to watch TV with her parents like she had when she was a child.

As they discussed their thoughts on each dress, Anthony read the text reply from Kay's best friend, Deanna Wolfe, where he was apparently taking pictures with Kay's old phone and texting them to Deanna. They all seemed to agree with Kay's pick for her favorite, but understood her reluctance to pick it because of not seeing a similar dress in the children's sizes her daughters would need.

"That's because that particular line doesn't publish a catalog for their flower girl dresses," Louella told them. "But we can get that exact same dress in children's sizes."

"Aren't the lace sections a little too revealing for children's dresses?" Hazel wrinkled her nose. Randi was glad her sister was turning the phone, so she could see who was talking when they spoke because the distant voices while looking at Kay or a dress were confusing as to who was speaking, since she didn't know the other two women well enough to recognize their voices.

"Oh, no, the lace sections in the skirt don't go above the knee on most people." Louella pulled out the adult version of the dress again. "The only reason you're thinking this is even slightly risqué is because this dress is meant for a woman at least five-foot-seven, so the lace inserts seem to go higher in the skirt to hit at knee level on a taller woman. With you and Kay both being petite, you have to imagine losing the bottom six or eight inches of this skirt to convert it to fit a petite person."

Louella held the dress up to Hazel and folded one of the lace panels up about six inches from the bottom and it did indeed look like the lace panel would still hit about knee-high on Hazel with the bottom of the shortest section of the asymmetrical hem still being about mid-calf. Unaltered the longest part of the dress would drag the ground on someone as short as Hazel.

"Well, I'm five-foot-six, so we'll still need to hem that one for me," Randi pointed out, thinking that she wouldn't really mind if the lace panels went a little above her knees.

"We'll actually order them specifically for your measurements," Louella replied to Randi.

"That's why I had you and Dee go get measured at the bridal boutique this week," Kay told her sister.

"Yeah, I did that on my day off Tuesday," Randi confirmed before rattling off her measurements from the note card that the local bridal shop had given her. Louella repeated the measurements back to Randi to double-check that they were correct.

Leah Mae Wright

"Here are the measurements from the other bridesmaid," Anthony said, and Kay focused her phone on him, so Randi and Mary could see him hand Louella a phone.

"I also have the Hunters' measurements for their tuxes." Anthony swapped phones with Louella, so she could get the guys' measurements from his phone.

"And I have sample tuxedos for you to look at," called out a male voice that Randi thought must be Benny. Kay panned over to him as he carried over three different blue tuxedos. "I figured you'd probably want to compare them to the dress you picked to find the closest color match."

"Oh my goodness!" Randi's mother, Mary exclaimed when she saw the blue tuxes. "I'm not sure your father will want to look like a blueberry walking you down the aisle."

Randi burst out laughing at her mother's imagery. Apparently, Kay did as well, because she was laughing just as hard as Randi when she turned the phone back to her face, so they could see her. When she got her giggles under control and caught her breath, Kay finally explained to their mom, "Dad tried to give me away the first time and I came back like a bad penny. This time I'm having the girls walk me down the aisle, only instead of them giving me away, we're going to claim Anthony as ours."

"I'm happy to be claimed," Anthony chuckled as he kissed the top of Kay's head. "And the groomsmen are fine with looking like blueberries as long as they don't turn into blueberries like that kid in the candy factory movie."

"Her name was Violet and she turned violet, not royal blue," Tia stated matter-of-factly. Kay turned her phone, so Randi and Mary could see Tia pointing at the blue tuxedos. "So, I think they'll be safe in royal blue suits."

"So, those tuxes are only for the groomsmen?" Mary arched an eyebrow inquisitively.

"Yes," Anthony and Kay answered in unison.

"Do you have anything picked out for the parents?" Louella inquired. "We have a nice selection of mother's dresses."

"I don't have any preference for what our parents wear." Kay turned to look at Anthony beside her, apparently wanting his opinion on the matter.

He shook his head. "Me either."

"Well, since the two of you will be in white and the rest of the wedding party will be in royal blue, maybe we should wear navy blue?" Hazel took Kay's phone from her, so she could talk directly to Mary. "I'm sure your husband is much like mine and has a classic navy-blue suit in the closet. And you and I can have fun shopping for new navy-blue dresses to match our spouses without being too matchy-matchy with the royal blue and white wedding."

"Excellent idea, Hazel," Mary replied, taking Randi's phone from her hand.

As they discussed the groomsmen's tuxedos, Randi pulled back away from her mom. She was still sitting beside her on the sofa, close enough to see what was on the phone screen to offer her opinions, but not so close that she would be seen on Kay's phone. Randi didn't want to appear too interested in the story Kay, Tia, Maria, and Anthony were telling them about going with James and Dean to get measured for their tuxes. She already knew most of what happened from texting with James while he was there and had the photos on her phone of how hot he looked in the black version of the tuxedos they were now looking at in blue.

While she hoped to one day see him in the sexy ensemble, so they could role play some sensual spy fantasies in the flesh, she had to stop herself from thinking about him, or what all they'd discussed doing while he was wearing the tux in their late-night phone calls the last two nights. If she didn't, her mother would wonder why she was blushing at the discussion of the groomsmen, and she might have to admit to meeting James and staying in touch with him while he was traveling.

Randi knew her mother would insist on seeing a picture of him, if she thought Randi was even slightly interested in him. She also knew her mother would object to his long hair and beard, even if she saw him in the tuxedo picture and couldn't see his tattoos. It wasn't that her parents would discriminate based on him having a darker complexion than them. They didn't care what race or color a person was who dated one of their children, only that they were good to the child they were dating. But with her father working in law enforcement for so long, they tended to try to steer their daughters into dating clean-cut men, who didn't look like they might have a criminal record.

Randi didn't think they would ever be okay with her dating James, even after they met him and his parents at Kay's wedding. She knew that they would learn about his prestigious family legacy, his business degree from college, and even that he earned most of his money from investing in a variety of businesses, both on and off the New York Stock Exchange, when they were all in Texas for a week before the wedding. But even with seeing him go to church with his parents and grandparents while they were all in town, her parents would still worry that his long hair, beard, and tattoos projected the wrong image to the world, and wouldn't be good enough for him to date their daughter.

Randi was brought out of her negative musings when Kay announced her choice of tuxedos for the groomsmen. After looking at them side by side with the other options and seeing that the three tuxedos that were all listed as being royal blue varied dramatically based on the material they were made out of and how much the material shimmered, she picked the one that best matched the bridesmaids' dresses. They were a linen blend that didn't sparkle, since it was closest to the chiffon of the women's attire. Randi agreed with her choice and couldn't wait to see James in the blue version of the same tuxedo he'd bought a couple of days before.

There was more shuffling of phones as Anthony was instructed to leave, so Kay could try on bridal gowns. Randi pushed in a little closer to her mother, so Kay could see her facial expression when she offered her opinions on the dresses. Kay tried on at least a dozen dresses in the next hour. While they were all beautiful, Randi didn't think any of them seemed exactly right for her sister. At least, not until she tried on the one that Randi had initially sent her in the group chat.

Randi recognized it as soon as Kay made her way out of the dressing room and back out to the stage that was set up with mirrors all around, so they could all see the dress from every angle. It was a trumpet style dress with an iridescent lace overlay. The white satin that provided the base for the majority of the dress stopped at the bottom of the sweetheart neckline, with only the lace coming up over the shoulders and down the arms as full sleeves.

"Oh, Kay," her mother, Mary, exclaimed, clutching her chest with the hand not holding Randi's phone. "That's definitely my favorite."

"It's exquisite," Hazel agreed.

"I think this is the one," Kay decided, beaming at them on the screen of the phone. "And with these shoes, I don't think it will even need to be hemmed."

"Let me see," Randi insisted, pushing in closer to her mother to get a better look at the dress and shoes. "Oh, Sis, it's perfect! Lift it up and let me see the shoes."

Kay lifted the front of the dress and poked out a foot to show off the satin covered stilettos.

"They'd be sexier if they weren't bridal white," Randi quipped when she saw the shoe.

Mary swatted Randi away from the phone. "Don't embarrass your sister or I with comments about sex and shoes," Mary hissed under her breath, like she didn't want anyone but Randi to hear her.

Randi cringed at her mother's admonition, not sure what had possessed her to be able to say the word "sexy" in her mother's presence.

"You look like a fairy princess, Mommy," Maria declared, while Randi bit her tongue to not respond to her mother.

"It's beautiful, Mom," Tia confirmed, a note of awe in her voice.

After they all agreed that it was definitely the wedding dress she should wear, Louella helped Kay try on the matching veil for more pictures before she went back to the dressing room to change. Once Kay had stepped away, Hazel turned the phone to face her, so she could talk with Mary. Randi leaned back on the couch, not wanting to get in the middle of the discussion about payment for everything related to the wedding.

Mary was trying to get Louella to take her credit card information over the phone because she thought it was her place as Kay's mother to pay for the wedding. Louella was explaining to the two mothers that Anthony had already left his card information to pay for everything, along with instructions not to let Kay switch it to her card, unless it was her card on his accounts. Hazel was trying to mediate, but she wasn't having much luck.

Randi tried to tune out the discussion, thinking that her mother wouldn't be trying to push so hard to pay for a wedding for Randi with

James as the groom. Even though Anthony and James grew up together and were both just as good natured as they could be, Anthony's hair barely reached his collar, he maintained a clean-shaven face, and he didn't have any visible tattoos to give the impression that he was in a biker gang.

Randi didn't think even knowing that James had only grown out his hair and beard and gotten his tattoos to play a role on television would dissuade her parents from having a negative impression of him when they saw him for the first time. And once they learned that his character often cheated to win, they would probably feel vindicated in their incorrect judgement of him as a person, even though the GWA storylines were all scripted.

Randi was brought back from her thoughts by Kay shouting "Mom," as she took her phone back from Hazel and appeared on the screen.

"Thank you for wanting to pay for my wedding," Kay remarked, as Randi leaned in a little closer to be able to hear her sister. "I love you and appreciate how you've always taken care of me. But I've learned in the last few weeks that I'm not nearly hardheaded enough to win an argument with Anthony, when he insists on paying for something that I think is my responsibility. So, I'm going to let him have his way anywhere he's already set up payment for wedding stuff, and let Daddy argue with him when ya'll come down for the wedding, if there's something you really want to pay for the wedding. They are much more evenly matched in the stubbornness department, so maybe Daddy can convince him to let ya'll reimburse him for some of this stuff."

"Don't hold your breath on that one," Hazel chortled with a smile as she looked over Kay's shoulder on the phone screen. "Burleson men are known to be very determined when it comes to providing for their families. Bob wouldn't even let my parents continue paying for my college classes once we started dating. The only reason my mother was able to buy my wedding dress is because we went shopping in Austin when Bob didn't know."

"Gracious, they sound a lot like my Charles," Mary grinned. "Alright, I guess I can't fuss over a good man wanting to take care of my baby girl."

Maybe I can get Kay to tell Mom and Dad about James? Randi thought as they wrapped up their Skype call with Kay. *Maybe she can start telling them all about Anthony's best friend that she wants to introduce me to while we're at the wedding, and they'll be so sold on her hyping him up that they won't be as quick to judge him based on how he looks.*

She didn't have the chance to message her sister about that possibility, though, because Kay was going to the florist, and Randi had to run home and do something with her hair and makeup before going to her first therapy appointment.

~~~

James waited impatiently in his hotel room for Randi to get finished with her first therapy appointment and call to tell him how it went. It was a pay-per-view weekend, so when they arrived in Minneapolis that morning, he went ahead and checked into the hotel, got in a weight workout, and ate a late lunch like normal, but he didn't have to go to the arena since there wasn't a show that night, so he was pacing around his room.

The ground crew was setting up the ring as usual, but they were configuring the floor space around it for the fan expo on Saturday instead of the normal ringside seating. They'd have to go break down the expo exhibits and set up the ringside seating Sunday morning before the actual pay-per-view show Sunday night.

James loved the pay-per-views that the GWA did every six or eight weeks. In addition to staying in one city from Friday to Monday, so he didn't have to get up early to fly for a couple of days, he loved meeting fans at the daytime expo on those Saturdays before the big shows on Sundays. And having two nights off in a row when he was free to have sexy Skype sessions with Randi was icing on the cake.

While there weren't as many people who lined up for his autograph at the expo, since he wrestled heel, as there were for the babyfaces, he still loved meeting each and every one of them. Most of the fans were smart these days, and they knew that the shows were scripted, so they knew they didn't have anything to fear with asking him or his fellow *bad guys* for an autograph. James appreciated meeting them and
~~~

hearing how they liked a specific maneuver or had dreams of becoming a wrestler. He tried to be as encouraging to the fans as possible.

Every once in a while, there would be an old school fan who would heckle the heels. James wasn't ever sure if they really still believed professional wrestling was real, or if they just wanted to be a part of the show so bad that they pretended it was, so they could mouth off to the wrestlers, like they wanted to do with a bad boss or irritating acquaintance and couldn't in real life. Either way, James loved being able to get into character to interact with them and enhance their experience as fans of the pseudo sport.

His absolute favorite fans, though, were the little kids who weren't quite sure they could believe their parents when they were telling them that James and his brother only played bad guys on TV, but they were really nice in person. Seeing them overcome their trepidation to say "hello" or ask for an autograph, reminded him of when he was a kid and nervous to meet his favorite wrestlers, when he went to a show with his grandfather, who he still called PopPop.

Back then, the wrestling industry was different than it is now. The wrestlers and promoters tried to make everyone believe it was a real sport back in the day. So, when James, Dean, and PopPop asked the biggest bad guy on the show for an autograph, he stayed in his heel character and refused, stomping away from where they were standing outside the arena trying to meet the wrestlers before the show.

James was glad that the industry had changed in the last twenty years because he didn't have it in him to be mean to a five-year-old, like the old school wrestlers had devastated him when they refused to sign his wrestling magazine. Instead, he tried to smile and wink and let them beat him at arm wrestling to give them a good experience at meeting the stars of their favorite *sport,* even though he knew they would boo him when he was in the ring. He even made a big deal about that with the little kids, telling them that they needed to really boo loudly, so he would know he was doing a good job of pretending to be mean in the ring.

James was pulled out of his internal musings by his phone ringing. He swiped to answer as soon as he saw Randi's name on the screen.

"Hello, Angel," he greeted her as soon as he got the phone to his ear.

"Hi, Jimmy," Randi practically purred in that sexy voice he loved hearing every day.

"How was your day?" James got settled on the bed, laying back to relax while they talked.

"Good," Randi replied. "I slept in and barely made it to Mom's before Kay Skyped me to show us the wedding dresses she was trying on. She also made the final decision on the bridesmaids' dresses and groomsmen's tuxedos."

"Yeah, how'd they look in blue?" James hoped she liked the selections.

"I think it's the exact same tux as the one you got on Wednesday, just royal blue," Randi replied. "It was the closest match to the dresses with the uneven hem that we all liked for the bridesmaids."

"Cool, did you get any pictures you can send me, so I can imagine you in the dress?" James was already trying to picture Randi in a royal blue dress in his head.

"Yeah, I can send you a picture," Randi cooed. "But I know you're probably only going to imagine it in a puddle on your bedroom floor."

"Naw, I'm gonna enjoy seeing you in it first, Angel." James's voice deepened with desire as he envisioned dancing with Randi at the wedding before taking her back to his cabin and stripping the dress from her delectable body. "I hope you'll be in comfortable shoes for dancing at the wedding, too."

"Sexy shoes, maybe, but I'm not so sure they'll be comfortable for dancing," Randi quipped with a little laugh.

"Maybe I should ask one of the women wrestlers where they get the ballet slippers they wear backstage, so I can bring you a pair to wear to save your feet at the wedding, like they do for the shows?" James mused aloud.

"No, you don't have to do that," Randi admonished, sounding a little irritated. "I still have to check with Kay to see what shoes I'm even supposed to get, so I match the other bridesmaid. Maybe since we're both so much taller than her, she'll want us in something with a lower heal like those ballet slippers for the whole day."

"Well, let me know if she decides on something uncomfortable, and I'll ask about the ballet slippers for you. I wanna make sure you're as comfortable as possible."

"That's sweet, but not necessary." Randi still sounded a little off to James.

He hoped it wasn't something he said that had her upset, but he didn't want to keep making it worse if it was, so he changed the subject.

"How'd it go with meeting the therapist?" James prayed she wasn't in a bad mood because of therapy not going as well as she'd hoped.

"Actually, really good," Randi admitted, her voice already sounding a little lighter. "She gave me some suggestions about things to do to stop a panic attack, if I have one when I go to get on the plane next month. Since I haven't really had a traumatic experience on a plane, that was really all she could do for me to help with the airplane anxiety. But we spent the rest of the hour talking about other stuff that I think she'll really be able to help me with. I really liked her and I'm looking forward to our next session."

"That's awesome, Angel." James was glad to hear her back to her normal chipper tone of voice. He wanted to ask what other things they discussed, but he knew that if she wasn't ready to tell him about them, asking about it could cause her to pull back from him. Since he didn't want to risk that, he simply said, "I'm proud of you for being brave enough to talk to her and work through whatever you feel is holding you back from being your best self. I mean, I already think you're pretty awesome already, but I can't wait to see you soar once you've overcome your anxiety."

"Thank you." Randi sounded even happier. "Me, too. I was talking to her today about not feeling like I have any idea what my ultimate goals in life should be, about not having a clue what I should do for a career. We figured out that some of that is because I have anxiety about disappointing my family, if they don't approve of what I wanna do with my life. I told her about how my parents were so strict when I was a teenager and how they still treat me like I'm fifteen instead of twenty-five. She's gonna help me come up with some strategies for how to figure out what I really want, as opposed to what I think I want just to defy my parents, and how to be more myself, even if my parents don't agree with my plans or behavior."

"That's great, Angel," James praised, wanting to be as supportive as possible. "Let me know if there's anything I can do to help you with that."

"I appreciate that, James," Randi sighed. "But you can't fight my battles for me. I have to be able to tell them who I am and what I want with my life. I have to be strong enough to set boundaries with everyone, you included, not just my parents."

"Absolutely, Angel," James agreed, hating that she thought he was trying to take over her life like her parents had. "I have no plans to fight your battles for you. I just wanna be there to support you, like your cheerleader on the sidelines, or your sounding board when you need to practice what you wanna say to them."

"You just wanna hear me say bad words," Randi teased with a giggle. "But even though I'm getting more comfortable saying them in my head or with you, I'll probably never cuss in front of my parents."

"Angel, I don't cuss in front of my parents either," James chuckled. He thought it was cute that she could text the word "fuck" or "fucking" when they were talking about their fantasies and had even whispered it in his ear that first night, but still used words like "sugar" or "hello" in place of curse words, even in texts when she wasn't specifically having a sexual conversation with him. "And I think it's cute how you use substitute words most of the time. I just want us to be more real when we're talking dirty, not so clinical. Ya know?"

"Yes, I know," Randi affirmed with yet another sigh. "And I'm working on it. I've actually started thinking of your penis as your wonder down under in my head."

"My wonder down under?" James chuckled. "You know I'm not Australian."

"No," Randi giggled. "I mean he's wonderful and down under your pants."

"Yeah, he's only down because he can't get under your pants until next month," James taunted as he laughed with Randi.

"Speaking of next month, have you figured out how we're gonna get you in my pants while we're there?"

"Other than the first night after the bachelor and bachelorette party, no," James replied. "I mean, it'll be easy for us to leave that together and go to my cabin, but with you not actually staying with me all week, it'll be more difficult to sneak away from the other activities."

"Well, maybe my therapist can help me figure out how to tell my parents about you during one of the three sessions I have scheduled before we leave, so staying with you can become a possibility."

James wanted to be upset that they'd been in a relationship for almost a month, and she hadn't said anything to her parents about even meeting him. But he hadn't said anything to his parents about her either, so he couldn't really be upset at her for doing the same thing he'd done himself. Although, he'd only spoken to his mom on the phone a couple of times in the last month, both of which were when Dean had called her and put her on speaker, so they could both talk to her. And the only time he'd talked to his dad in the last month was actually a business call about his stock portfolio.

When he thought back, the last time he'd spoken to his Meemaw and PopPop was when he was home for the Labor Day break. James resolved to get better about checking in with his parents and grandparents while he was traveling for work. But even if he called them all during his downtime in the next couple of days, he wasn't sure he should mention Randi to them. He hadn't ever really talked about anyone he'd dated with his family. Even Dean only knew about the girl he dated in college because of seeing them together.

James wondered if mentioning that he was seeing Randi to his family would imply that he was more serious than she was ready for to his parents. He didn't want his mother to do like Anthony's mother had and start pushing to plan their wedding the first time she met Randi. That would go over like a fart in church, if she said something about them in front of Randi's parents when they didn't even know who he was, much less that he was seeing their daughter.

James decided he would have to think more about all that later, he needed to focus on talking to Randi right then while he had her on the phone. To keep from worrying her about his thoughts, he changed the subject yet again.

"So, what are you planning to get them for a wedding gift?"

"No clue." Randi rolled with the subject change like she didn't even notice it. "Kay hasn't registered for gifts anywhere, yet. I'll remind her to do that the next time we're all on the wedding planning group chat and let you know when she does it, so you can get some ideas, too."

"Thanks, Angel." James loved how she was able to do little things like that to take care of him, and her sister, and probably half of the people in his hometown, who would all need to know what to get them for the wedding.

"I'm thinking I'll order her a gift card for an online lingerie shop to give her at the bachelorette party. If she doesn't register somewhere soon, I may do that for the wedding present, too. Gift cards are much easier to take on the plane than the actual presents, too, so maybe I'll do that regardless of if she puts up a bridal registry somewhere."

"We're supposed to do presents for the bachelor party too?" James tried to come up with some ideas of his own for that one.

"I have no idea what the etiquette is for bachelor parties, but I've always seen the bachelorette party as the right time to give the more risqué gifts like lingerie and sex toys, when the parents aren't around to see them open them. Then the gifts at the bridal shower and wedding are more household goods. At least, that's always been what has happened when my other friends have gotten married."

"Yeah, well, Anthony is the first of my friends to get married, so I have no clue what I'm expected to do for any of it. I was hoping you'd clue me in, and I could pass the info along to Dean and the other wrestlers that are coming to the wedding."

"Seriously, you've never been to a wedding before?" Randi sounded surprised.

"Maybe when I was a kid and too young to remember it, but as an adult, no," James replied, running a hand through his hair, like that would help him remember a distant relative's wedding. "I mean I've seen them in movies enough to have a general idea of what I'm supposed to do, but I don't think Anthony wants a wild bachelor party like in the movies."

"Definitely not," Randi snorted with laughter. "Bachelor parties in movies are always a disaster! And with it being co-ed, I can guarantee my sister won't want any strippers there."

"That's good, since I wouldn't have a clue where to find strippers to hire for the night," James smiled. "I was thinking low key, like just sitting at the bar having a few rounds of drinks, maybe a toast or two, but mostly just hanging out like we used to do after work."

"Yeah, that's pretty much what I planned to do, but with party favors like a sash that says 'bride-to-be', or tiaras for all the bridal party," Randi agreed. "I thought about the penis straws and raunchy games my friend Autumn had at her bachelorette party, but since it's co-ed, I didn't figure Kay would be okay with that in front of all the guys from Anthony's family and work."

"Yeah, probably not," James chuckled, remembering how Kay blushed every time Anthony whispered something to her when there were other people around, who she probably didn't want to overhear their sexy talk.

"Normally, it's just the women that have to buy gifts for the bridal shower, but it's also normally like six months in advance of the wedding," Randi told him. "But since they're doing a co-ed wedding shower the Sunday before the wedding, I'm guessing you guys will have to bring gifts to that, too."

"Yeah, nobody's told me about that yet." James wasn't sure what a wedding shower entailed. "Maybe it's not really co-ed since the groomsmen haven't been invited to it?"

"No, it's definitely co-ed and both my parents will be there," Randi huffed. "Apparently it's gonna take the place of the normal potluck dinner after church in the fellowship hall, so anyone who goes to church that Sunday will be invited to the wedding shower."

"Well, they can't expect gifts at a wedding shower if they don't invite anyone until the day of and only minutes before it starts." James wondered if he should ask Anthony about all of these things.

"I think Hazel said something about announcing it in the church bulletin when it changes next week and the women in the group chat are responsible for informing anyone who won't see it in advance," Randi replied. "I think my Mom is doing the same thing with the church bulletin in Tulsa in case anyone from our church wants to attend the wedding or send a gift."

"You think there will be a lot of people who wanna come down for the wedding?" James really felt guilty for having the whole bed and breakfast booked by the GWA and not leaving any open rooms for Kay's out-of-town guests.

"I have no idea. Maybe a few of my parents' closest friends, but they might not wanna come down when they have to get a hotel in San Antonio."

"Yeah, I'll call my Mom later and see about getting a crew from Walker Construction out to help her finish a few more rooms in the plantation house. And I'll give Brent Deere a call to see how many bedroom suites he has available that I can order for her to fill them with, so there will be more availability at the B and B. Since I can't be there to help her get it all done in person, the least I can do is pay for the things she needs to be ready for being overrun by the GWA."

"How many more rooms do you think she'll be able to get ready? I mean, it seems like an awful lot of work for her in the next three weeks for rooms that probably won't be needed again anytime soon."

"Currently, she has thirty rooms in the original building and ten more in the plantation house." James realized that if they finished out the rest of the rooms in the plantation house, they would more than double the number of rooms she usually had available, since she didn't normally rent out the ten in the plantation house. "And there are about forty more in the plantation house that just need to be painted and decorated."

"You really think they can paint and furnish forty rooms in three weeks?" Randi sounded incredulous at the amount of work that would need to be done in such a short amount of time. "That's gonna cost a fortune, if it's even possible. And way too much work for your mom to maintain on her own if she ever rents them all out at once."

"Yeah, it would be, but Ma doesn't do all the work herself on the thirty rooms she's been renting out. She runs the place, but she has staff to do the cooking, cleaning, and stable work. She's wanted to expand for years and turn the plantation house into a wedding and event venue. She's talked about conventions and business retreats and how many rooms she wished she had ready on rodeo weekends for years, but I think the wedding coming up so fast is gonna finally push her into doing the expansion, since she hasn't been able to push herself to really do it before."

"You're all about pushing people to do things out of their comfort zones today, aren't you?" Randi's voice sounded slightly higher than normal. "Your mom to rapidly expand the B and B and me to get over my anxiety. What are you doing to push yourself out of your comfort zone?"

"I'm not trying to push anyone out of their comfort zone," James objected. "I just want the people I care about to have everything they've ever dreamed of. I'm sorry if you think I'm pushing you, I don't mean to. I just wanna help you, Angel. But while I can easily pay for the crew and furniture to help Ma with her expansion dreams, I doubt you'll let me pay for whatever you need to achieve your goals and dreams. That's why I offered to be your sounding board instead, because that's the only way I know to help you that you might not reject."

"I don't mean to make you feel like I'm rejecting you," Randi groaned. "Gaw, why do I feel like we're fighting over something that I was actually trying to thank you for helping me with?"

"Probably because it's hard to really communicate over the phone," James replied, shrugging even though he knew she couldn't see him. "It's hard to tell what you're really feeling by the tone of your voice when I can't also see your facial expressions."

"I'm sure that's part of it," Randi sighed. "We could switch to a video call and then you can see for yourself how much I want you to help me get over my anxiety about saying those dirty words you like so much."

"That's an excellent idea, Angel." James sat up and started to strip off his clothes. "Are you already home, so we can do that now?"

"Oh, yeah, I didn't call you until after I got home," Randi admitted, her voice sounding more like the seductive purr he loved the most. "In fact, I've been soaking in a nice, hot, bubble bath the whole time we've been talking."

"Fuck, Angel," James growled as the last of his clothing hit the floor and he flopped back down on the bed. His free hand was already around his cock at the thought of Randi covered in nothing but bubbles. "Switch us to video, please. I need to see you in the bathtub."

"Move your phone, Jimmy," Randi giggled. "I wanna see more than just your ear when I click this button."

James laughed as he pulled his phone down to hold it where he could click over to video with Randi. When her image appeared on his screen, it looked like she had her phone propped up on a table or counter to look down at her in the bathtub. He could only see her face for all the bubbles, but it was still one of the sexiest scenes he could imagine. Since he didn't have a way to prop up his phone to give her a view of all of him, he opted to aim the phone at his face at first and would show her anything else she wanted to see when she asked to see it.

"I think I like this better when we Skype on our computers." Randi smiled up at him from the tub. "I can't see as much of you on the phone."

"No, but I can always aim my phone at whatever part of me you wanna see." James smiled back at his water nymph. "But only if you use the right words to ask to see more than my face."

"Oh, so I have to use their proper names, like pectorals and abdominals instead of saying I wanna see your chest and abs?" Randi batted her eyelashes like she was trying to playfully overdo the flirting.

"I'll accept any of those if you just wanna see my chest and abs." James panned down with the camera on his phone and flexed his pecs and abs to give Randi a show. "But I won't accept clinical names for my cock."

"Can I see your wonder down under?" Randi blushed slightly.

"Nope, that's not the right word either," James chuckled as he aimed his phone back at his face.

"Your disco stick?" Randi grinned mischievously.

"I don't own a disco stick," James replied, deadpan.

"Oh, I know, I need to use the words they use in romance novels." Randi sat up straighter, so her shoulders appeared above the bubbles. "Can I see the throbbing, purple, mushroom shaped head of your manhood?"

James almost dropped his phone as he burst out laughing. "Do books really describe it like that?"

He couldn't remember ever feeling like laughing while being naked with anyone but Randi. It was one of the many things he loved about her. They could be serious and intense one second and laughing with each other the next.

"Some of them do," Randi confirmed through her own giggles. "At least, the older books in the library do. The more contemporary authors just use the slang words and don't try to be so descriptive about color and shape."

James looked down at his cock in his hand and realized that the description was at least pretty accurate, even if it did sound silly when Randi said it out loud. "Yeah, well, as accurate as that description is, that's not what you need to ask to see."

"Fine." Randi exhaled with a playful huff that blew some of the bubbles away from her face. "I wanna watch you stroke your cock, Jimmy."

She may have said the word "cock" a little quieter than the rest of her sentence, but James didn't care. He gladly panned the phone down to show her as he stroked his cock from tip to base and back again. He stroked himself a few times for her visual enjoyment before giving her some direction for what he wanted her to do. "Sit up a little more, Angel, so I can see your titties and imagine covering them with my cum."

His thoughts were derailed as soon as Randi lifted her arms out from under the bubbles to rest them on the sides of her bathtub to push herself up above the bubbles. She had prominent bruises on both upper arms from where she'd been assaulted on Monday night. He hadn't had a chance to see them since that first night because of their conflicting work schedules keeping them only communicating via text and phone calls. Now that he could see the black and blue marks on her porcelain skin, he was furious all over again, and he couldn't continue the sexual conversation because he needed to make sure she was safe from another potential attack.

"Angel, have you met with the police again to find out if that guy has been arrested?" James released his grip on his dick to sit up and grab his pants to put back on.

"Yeah, I met with officer Dennis this afternoon, so she could get pictures of the bruises at their worst," Randi replied, pulling her arms back into the tub and sinking down below the bubbles again, like she was ashamed to have James see the bruises.

"And have they arrested him yet?" James prayed they had, so he wouldn't have to keep worrying about the guy going after her again.

"No, they haven't found Mitch or his buddies yet," Randi admitted, biting her lip like she was afraid.

"Did they say if they have any leads on where he could be? Have you talked to your Dad about it? Is he looking for him too? Does he have a protective detail set up for you?" James decided he'd contract with a security company to have someone watch over her if he needed to, so she'd be safe when he couldn't be by her side to protect her.

"No, they aren't gonna tell me anything about what they're doing," Randi glowered, looking pissed, and James hoped she wasn't pissed at him for bringing it up. "The police are doing all they can, and I don't wanna talk about it anymore."

"I'm not trying to upset you, Angel," James consoled in what he hoped was a soothing tone of voice. "I just wanna make sure you're safe. I wish I could be there to protect you, but since I can't, maybe I could hire a bodyguard for you, so they can't get to you again."

"No, James," Randi seethed, sitting up, so he could finally see her tantalizing tits over the bubbles. "I'm perfectly safe. I don't need you to protect me. I don't need a bodyguard. And if you don't drop this, I'm gonna hang up, so you don't get to even see me touch myself tonight."

"Fine, consider the subject dropped." James held up his free hand to show his surrender, exasperated. "But you have to stay above the bubbles, so I can see you play with your tits."

"Oh, I have better plans than just what you can currently see," Randi teased as she stood up in the tub. She bent over and pulled the plug to drain the water. "I have my phone in a waterproof case on the counter, so you can see me rinse the bubbles off and it won't matter if I don't keep all the water in the tub."

Fuck yes! James shoved his pants back off while watching Randi turn on the shower. She reached up and pulled down the sprayer for the shower massager and gave him a show.

"Fuck, Angel, you're so fucking hot," James moaned as he palmed his cock while watching her rinse off. Soon he was giving her directions for where to aim the spray of the water and how to touch herself with her free hand at the same time.

She didn't ask to see his dick again, but he still showed it to her as he instructed her to use the power pulse massage setting on her clit. He held his phone, so he could still see her on the screen while she watched him jack off. It didn't take but a moment with that pulsing jet setting to send her over the edge. Watching her come took him over the edge with her. It took a little longer for them to each come back to earth after their mutual orgasms.

"It's too bad you're not here with me so I could rinse off your stomach," Randi giggled, aiming the massage sprayer that was now on a more gentle rain shower setting at her own flat stomach.

"If I were there with you, my stomach wouldn't be what needs rinsing off." James aimed the phone back at his face, so she could see his wicked grin.

"Oh?" Randi was acting more innocent than James knew she was. "And what exactly would need to be rinsed off instead?"

"Your perfect tits, Angel," James decreed, his voice gravelly from arousal. "Or maybe your sexy as sin ass."

"I'll look forward to you rinsing me off in your shower next month then," Randi smiled. "Do you have a shower massager in your cabin?"

"No, but I can order one to be waiting on us when we get there," James replied. "Anything else you want me to have on hand to fulfill your fantasies with, Angel?"

"Not that I can think of at the moment." Randi turned off the water in her shower and started to dry off with a towel. "But I'll let you know if I get any ideas before then."

They signed off for the moment, so James could go get a quick shower to clean up from their mutual release. He smiled through the fastest shower he'd ever taken and rushed to get some sweats on, so he could call Randi back.

They talked late into the night about the new show she was binge watching online, about actual paper books versus an e-reader, and about the training strategies he used to stay in ring shape. James loved that they could talk about anything, and especially, the way she seemed as interested in the topics he introduced as he was interested in what she had to say.

He felt closer to Randi than he'd ever felt with another person, even his twin, and it wasn't just sexual chemistry. Even when they talked about things that had nothing to do with sex or them being together as a couple, he was fascinated by everything she said. He just wished they could find a way to spend more time together in person instead of only via electronic communication.

Chapter Six

Randi was sitting at her dining room table looking up job opportunities online when she got an unexpected Skype request from James. Because it was a pay-per-view weekend, she knew he wouldn't be on a plane midmorning like his normal schedule, but she wasn't sure what his day looked like to know if it was safe to accept the Skype call while in a common area of her home, where her roommate could walk into the room at any minute. She decided that she could easily pick up her computer and run to her bedroom if he was naked when she connected the call, so she didn't hesitate too long before clicking the icon to accept his video chat.

She was surprised when the image appeared on her screen, and it wasn't his face or naked body that she saw. Instead, he had his phone aimed at the arena floor, where there was a wrestling ring set up in the middle of several booths of tables and various things that almost looked like mini stages, or possibly a video game convention with televisions and gaming chairs. It seemed like he was at the very top of the cheap seats in the bleachers, or maybe even up on the lighting scaffolding, to get high enough to show her the whole arena from above.

"Um, James, what's going on? Where are you?" Randi felt slightly nauseous about the potential precariousness of his current position.

When he turned his phone around, so she could see his face, she realized that he was indeed sitting in one of the cheap seats at the top of the bleachers in the arena. Her nausea dissipated when she realized that he would just have to walk down a whole lot of stairs to get back to the arena floor and not have to risk anything by climbing off the lighting scaffolding.

Leah Mae Wright

"Morning, Angel," James greeted her once they were looking into each other's eyes. He'd informed her that his eyes were gray when she asked why they looked brown sometimes and blue others on one of their previous Skype sessions and that gray clearly showed in his eyes through her up close look on her screen. "I just wanted to show you around the fan expo before the fans arrive."

"What's the fan expo?" Randi was intrigued by this event she didn't know anything about before.

"It's basically a meet and greet for the fans," James explained as he stood and started walking down that long set of steps to the floor of the arena. "We're all here to rotate out between booths, where we sign autographs, play video games, and work with the fans, so they can cut their own promos or tape their own ring entrance."

"So, you're gonna be hanging out with your fans for the day?" Randi both liked and disliked the idea. She loved the thought of little kids getting to hang out with their favorite wrestling heroes for the day, but she wasn't so sure about James hanging out with a bunch of gorgeous wrestling groupies, who would probably be flirting with him when she wasn't there.

"Angel, what's that scowl for?" James deflected instead of answering her question. "I thought this would be something you'd like seeing. I thought you might be able to help me convince some of the skeptical kids that I'm really a nice guy when I'm not having to be James Dangerous, bad guy biker, on the show."

"Is it really gonna be kids there?" Randi hated the green-eyed monster of jealousy that she probably resembled to James at the moment, and not just because her eyes were actually green. "Not a bunch of grown women groupies?"

"Uh, um," James stuttered. "I mean there might be a few ring rats who show up today, but the majority of fans that come to the expo are families, and the majority of single adults who come are guys, who wanna know how to get into the industry."

Randi wasn't sure she believed his estimates of who the majority of the fans would be that attended the expo, but she didn't want to argue with James. Or let him know just how threatened she felt by the women he referred to as *"ring rats."*

He would either be the faithful boyfriend he claimed to be, or they would eventually go their separate ways and it wouldn't be an issue for her in the future. So, she dropped the subject, opting to ask him to show her around the various booths and tell her what he would be doing when he went to each one.

He showed her one that was set up like their backstage interview area, where fans could cut promos like the wrestlers did between matches on the weekly television shows. He introduced her to the camera operator who was setting up to be able to videotape the fans, who wanted to imitate their favorite wrestler's ring entrance. He showed her a couple of booths, where they had televisions set up with video game systems, so the fans could challenge the wrestlers in virtual matches on the GWA video game.

After about twenty minutes of walking around and introducing her to various crew members, including a few other wrestlers and a couple of their wives, one of which was the backstage interviewer that she recognized from watching the weekly shows, James finally took a seat at a table to sign autographs. His brother said "hi" from over his shoulder as he joined James in the booth, and Randi almost didn't recognize him as the over-the-top boisterous guy he'd been the day they ate at the Camelot Hotel restaurant. Dean was acting more reserved than James as they sat there waiting for the fans to make their way through the other booths to line up for their autographs.

"Is Dean okay? He's being awfully quiet over there."

"Yeah, he's fine." James slugged his brother in the arm. "Just pouting because he doesn't have a hot girlfriend to introduce to the fans."

"And no chance of finding one for the night unless the name of our hotel has been leaked to the ring rats on social media," Dean grumbled as he slugged James back. "And since Rick has banned us from leaking the name of our hotel, there's very little chance of that tonight either."

"Seriously?" *I guess he's not as interested in the new woman on the roster as James claimed the other day. Either that, or he's trying to keep anyone from realizing he's caught up on her, so he can maintain a little of his bad boy image for their wrestling characters.*

Randi giggled at their goofball antics as they scuffled in their seats. Apparently, James had propped his phone up on the stack of photos he would soon be signing, so he had both hands free to fight with his brother. "Why would he tell you not to leak the name of your hotel? I would think he'd like to have extra fan interaction to increase ticket sales."

"Because so many of the guys travel with their families and he doesn't want any of the kids to be at risk of a bad interaction with a crazy fan," James explained, straightening in his seat like the playful scuffle with his brother was over.

"And the ring rats won't buy tickets to the shows if they know where to find us afterward," Dean clarified, leaning into the camera view, so Randi could see him as he spoke. "They'd just hang out at the hotel all evening, trying to convince a hotel employee to let them into one of our rooms, or harassing whoever went back to the hotel early, which would more likely be one of the married guys and his family."

"Wow, I hadn't thought about any of that." Randi wondered if her impression of wrestlers having their choice of women in every city was wrong. "So, how do you normally meet women while you're on tour?"

"I don't," James claimed as Dean spoke over him saying, "They follow us from the arena to wherever we go to eat after a show, or to whatever club we go hang out in, and eventually back to the hotel after all the good boys like James are already safe in their rooms, where the ring rats can't bother them."

Randi couldn't contain her bark of laughter at the expressions on James and Dean's faces. Especially when they changed so rapidly into broad smiles to mask their conversation from the fans they were greeting.

James turned his phone around, so Randi could see the line forming to get his autograph. Then he introduced her as his girlfriend to the family of four that was first in line. It was surreal meeting his fans, especially when the little girl asked her why she wasn't there to wrestle, too. She fumbled through an explanation of having to be in Tulsa for work.

The more she interacted with the kids asking her about James, the more she wished she could be there with him in person. When his hour signing autographs was up, they disconnected, so he could focus on his next task at the expo—losing to fans while playing the GWA video game.

James probably didn't realize just how much his morning video call had affected her and her career aspirations. Anytime she spoke with James, he brought out her passionate side and not just sexually. Anytime he talked about his job, his exuberance for the field spoke to her, reminding her of how passionate she'd been about performing in her teens and early twenties. Him introducing her to his fans and making her feel like a part of the show already, struck a chord deep inside her, strengthening her desire to throw practicality out the window and plan for a future career in the squared circle.

Randi stood and stretched for a few minutes before sitting back down at her computer on her dining room table to look into the local professional wrestling organization. She hadn't even been on her new medication for a week yet, but since she was already feeling less anxious about her loved ones flying every day, she wanted to see if she could start some kind of training locally to be a little more prepared to possibly get a job with James in a month or two.

Mid-American Wrestling didn't have anything on their website about training, but they did have an email address listed with their contact information. Randi clicked on it and sent them an inquiry about options for training to become a professional wrestler. Even if they didn't train new talent, maybe they could point her in the right direction for where their talent had trained locally.

~~~

Monday, October 29, 2018

The Galactic Wrestling Association was back to their normal schedule after the **Halloween Horror** pay-per-view show on Sunday in Minneapolis. They flew out to Fargo, North Dakota on Monday morning, and James went back to his normal routine of going to the hotel to check in, getting a weight workout in the hotel gym, and having a late lunch before going to the arena for sparring, rehearsals, and the evening show.

Since he had the night off from wrestling after he and Dean had successfully defended their tag-team titles on the pay-per-view the night before, James changed into his gimmick clothes after sparring.
~~~

He went to catering early while the guys who were actually wrestling that night stayed in the ring to rehearse for the show. While he was there, Anthony, Kay, and the girls arrived to check in with Rick before taking over as the flight crew the next day.

As soon as they'd checked in with Rick, James asked Anthony if they could talk for a few minutes while Kay took the girls to the classroom area to check in with the tutors.

"What's up?" Anthony didn't waste time with small talk, wanting to know what James needed to talk to him about just as soon as they were alone in the area where James had been sitting.

"Just wondering if you've heard anything from Sheriff Lee about the asshole who attacked Randi last week," James prodded as Anthony sat down.

"No, but let's call him right quick and see what the status is." Anthony pulled out his phone and swiped across the screen to place the call. He put it on speaker and sat it on the table just as it started ringing.

"Anthony, perfect timing, I was just about to call you," Sheriff Lee greeted from the phone on the table.

"Oh, good news I hope." Anthony smiled at the phone where his future father-in-law was speaking.

"Yes, we have Mark in custody," Sheriff Lee announced, his voice sounding happy to James. "He'll probably get out on bail later this week, but it will still look bad for him in court next week with charges pending against him."

"That is good news," Anthony exclaimed with a smile.

"What about Mitch?" James couldn't stop himself from asking. "Were you able to arrest him at the same time?"

"Um, Anthony, did your voice change? Or is there someone else there with you?" Sheriff Lee chuckled.

"Sorry, Charles, I should've mentioned sooner that I have you on speaker," Anthony apologized for the confusion. "My best friend James is sitting here with me. He met Randi the same night I met Kay."

"I see," Charles drawled, his voice deepening, like he was concerned about discussing things with James able to hear the conversation. "And what exactly are your intentions with my youngest daughter, James?"

"Um, uh," James stammered, feeling suddenly put on the hot seat with Randi's father. "Doing everything I can to make sure Randi is happy and safe, sir."

"Happy and safe, huh?" Charles chuckled again. "So, you're not going to give me any lines about love at first sight like Anthony did about Kay?"

"I hadn't planned on mentioning anything like that with you, sir," James admitted, running a hand through his hair, like that would calm his nerves at talking to Randi's father for the first time. "But I wouldn't disagree with the sentiment either."

"Anthony, does James look as nervous as he sounds?" Charles's laughter was apparent in his tone of voice.

"It's kinda hard to tell if he's turning green, or just going really pale under his beard. But yeah, I'd say he does look a little nervous to be talking to you." Anthony confirmed with a broad smile.

"Beard, huh? You are gonna make him shave that before he stands up for you at the wedding, right?" Charles sounded more serious than James hoped he was at the moment.

"It will be neatly trimmed for the wedding," James interjected before Anthony could reply. "But I can't shave or cut my hair because I have to maintain my biker gimmick for work."

"What exactly do you do for work, James?" Charles's tone continued to sound way too critical to James.

"I'm a professional wrestler," James answered, knowing that Randi's straight-laced father probably wouldn't approve of the character he portrayed in the ring, but hoping he could redeem himself with his college degree and stable business investment strategy. "My brother and I are the GWA tag-team champions. Our characters are bad guy bikers, hence the reason for the long hair, beard, and tattoos. But my degree is in finance, and I've actually more than tripled my income with my investment portfolio."

"Are you trying to tell me that you aren't just a dumb punk, who spends his nights losing brain cells in pointless fights?" Charles hypothesized in a gruff tone of voice.

James looked at Anthony, trying to figure out how to reply to Randi's father. But Anthony wasn't any help, since all he was doing was trying to hide his laughter behind his hand.

"I'm not a boxer, sir," James quipped. "So, I'm not getting punch drunk and losing brain cells. Professional wrestling is choreographed and staged like any other television show, not like the actual sport of amateur wrestling like in high school, college, or the Olympics. We pull our punches, so we don't risk concussions or more serious traumatic brain injuries. As for who I am as a person, I'd say I'm an intelligent twenty-five-year-old, who saw the opportunity to transition from my amateur wrestling days in high school and college into the athletic acting of the professional stage, where I could use my size, appearance, and skill to earn a seven-figure annual salary while having fun with my brother and friends. I've invested that salary wisely, so it's now an eight-figure yearly income that keeps growing and should be in the ten-figure range by the time I'm too old to wrestle anymore."

"Impressive," Charles acknowledged, his voice a little lighter than before.

"But I didn't ask Anthony to call you to discuss my character, my career, or how soon I'll be a billionaire," James retorted, ready to be done defending himself and make sure Randi was safe. "I'm concerned for Randi's safety. It's been a week since she was attacked and she's still telling me the same thing she told me the night of the assault about what's being done about it—that the police are handling it. She won't let me hire a bodyguard for her and she doesn't answer when I ask if you've been doing anything to protect her. And she has no idea how close anyone is to arresting Mitch. I can't stand the thought of her still being at risk while going about her normal day, so I need you to tell me what's being done to keep her safe and get that jackass off the streets before I completely lose my shit and quit my job to go camp out in her driveway to protect her myself."

"Whoa, dude!" Anthony held up his hands to James like he was trying to calm him down. James wasn't sure why, since he didn't think he'd even really raised his voice and didn't feel like he was acting out of control in any way.

"Let me put your mind at ease then, James," Charles bellowed through the phone, still laying on the table between James and Anthony. "Since the responding officers were from the Tulsa PD, I have no information on the status of their case. And they won't share it with me as a professional courtesy, even though I'm the sheriff, because they don't want me to act like the angry dad I am and jeopardize their ability to prosecute him. That being said, I've had my deputies making extra patrols through our neighborhoods to ensure the safety of my daughter, my wife, and any of their friends, who might also be targeted by the Fox brothers or their buddies. My department is on the lookout for Mitch and will turn him over to the TPD, if we're able to arrest him before they do. When we arrested Mark today, I put his other brother, Matt on notice that they all need to stay away from my family. I also told him that it would be in Mitch's best interest to turn himself in to the Tulsa PD before I find him. So, hopefully, it won't be long before he does just that."

James let out a breath he hadn't realized he'd been holding as Charles explained what he and his department were doing to keep Randi and everyone else in their family safe. "Thank you, sir," he said sincerely, feeling a little less concerned since Sheriff Lee was doing all he could legally do to keep Randi safe.

"No need to thank me for doing my job and taking care of my family," Charles insisted. "So, have you been back to Tulsa since you met my daughter back in September?"

"No, sir," James answered honestly. "I don't have any time off until Thanksgiving to be able to see Randi in person again."

"But you've been talking to her regularly since then?" Charles sounded skeptical.

"Yes, sir," James replied, trying to decide just how much he wanted to tell Randi's father about his relationship with her. "We talk and text pretty much every day."

"Alright, well, you sound like a decent enough guy to be allowed to continue talking and texting with my daughter, but you might want to rethink that wrestling job if you want to actually date her," Charles cautioned just before an alarm blared from his end of the phone conversation. "Duty calls, ya'll stay safe and I'll see you next week, Anthony."

"Bye, see you next week," Anthony replied as they disconnected the call without giving James a chance to say goodbye or ask what Charles meant by saying James needed to *"rethink that wrestling job if you want to actually date her."*

"What do you think he meant about needing to rethink my job if I wanna date Randi?" James questioned Anthony instead, since he couldn't ask Charles Lee.

Leah Mae Wright

"No idea," Anthony shrugged. "I mean you pretty much shut down any argument he could have about it not being good enough of a job for Randi when you informed him of your salary, but he could still be looking down on it based on your gimmick and that you wrestle heel. Or he could just be commenting on the fact that your schedule keeps you from actually being able to go on a date with her."

"Well, hopefully, it's the latter, and he won't try to keep me from taking her on a few dates while we're all in Heart's Destiny the week of the wedding," James wished aloud, trying to think of some date ideas for Monday, Tuesday, and Wednesday of Thanksgiving week.

He already knew he would see her at the bachelor and bachelorette party on the Saturday before the nuptials, and at church and the wedding shower the Sunday before the ceremony. He figured that they would get everyone together for Thanksgiving and then the rehearsal and rehearsal dinner the day after Thanksgiving, and of course, the wedding on the following Saturday. So, he wanted a plan for the three days that week when they weren't already scheduled to be together.

Before he could ask Anthony's opinion on the ideas in his head, the catering area started filling up with all the families meeting up for dinner between tutoring sessions, rehearsals, and the actual show that night. Instead of talking to Anthony about his possible plans with Randi, James joined in on the conversations around him. He listened to what his friend and his new family had done on their time off, appreciating their reports about how the crew he'd hired to help his mother was doing at getting the plantation house set up for the wedding and the expansion of the bed and breakfast.

He wanted to text Randi, missing being able to talk to her while she was at work. She was working an eleven a.m. to seven p.m. shift, so it wouldn't be much longer before she got home from work and would text him, but that didn't stop him missing her while she was unavailable.

It's not too desperate to text her and tell her I'm missing her, is it? James wondered as he pulled out his phone to send her a text message.

James: Hey Angel, missing you and couldn't wait another minute to text you. Hope you had a good day. {Face Blowing A Kiss Emoji}

~~~

Randi was dragging when she left work at seven o'clock. Not because it had been a day of hard labor, but because the shift was so slow that it seemed to drag on without enough to do to keep her mind occupied. So, other than the noon rush when she served plenty of lunch customers, she spent most of the shift watching the door to the restaurant, worried that Mitch or one of his brothers or buddies would show up again. That meant her adrenaline was elevated and her head was on a swivel to watch out for anyone out of place the whole way home.

Already being on high alert, she was exceptionally concerned when she pulled into her driveway and saw her father parked behind Amy's car in his sheriff's cruiser. She passed his car to pull into her own parking spot under the carport, but barely got her car shifted into park and turned off before she was jumping out to go see why he was there.

"What happened? Is everyone okay?" Randi demanded as soon as her father opened his car door to exit his vehicle.

"Everyone's fine." Charles Lee stood to his full six-foot-two height, looking down at her with a curious expression as soon as he closed the cruiser's door.

"Then why are you here?" Randi didn't quite believe him. "You normally call before you come over, so you know I'm home first. Coming over without calling first means something's wrong."

"Nothing's wrong, baby girl," Charles denied, pulling his daughter into a much-needed hug, trying to calm her down. "I was just driving by on my way home and when I didn't see your car, I pulled in to send you a text to find out when you'd be home tonight. Just as I went to pull my phone out of my pocket, I saw you pulling in, so I didn't bother to go ahead and type it out."

"Oh, okay." Randi relaxed into her father's embrace, even as she squeezed him back. "I started some chili in the crock pot this morning before I went to work, if you wanna come in and sneak a bowl, without the beans Mom insists on putting in hers, before going home."

"You know me so well," Charles chuckled, clicking the lock button on his key fob before following Randi into her house. "I know she's
~~~

just trying to get more fiber in my diet by adding the beans, but I don't think she realizes just how much we dislike them."

Randi didn't bother to try to dissuade her father from thinking her mother didn't know they hated beans. She'd been complaining about how gross beans were since she was old enough to remember eating chili the first time. If her mother hadn't gotten the hint in the last twenty-plus years, she never would.

As a child, she couldn't argue with her mother about not caring how good they were for her or make her understand that she didn't want to eat them because she didn't like the taste. But as an adult, she'd found a chili recipe she liked that didn't include beans and would sneak bowls to her fellow bean-hating family members whenever she got the chance to. She didn't feel like she was really being rebellious to her parents in doing so, since she mostly snuck the bean-free bowls to her dad.

Once they were settled at the table with their chili, cheese, Fritos, and tall glasses of sweet tea, her father finally explained why he'd stopped by to see her.

"I wanted to let you know that we arrested Mark today," Charles reported between bites. "He was with his brother Matt, so I told Matt to make sure Mitch knows it's in his best interest to turn himself into the TPD before one of my deputies finds him."

"Oh, well…" Randi let her words trail off, gathering her thoughts and feeling a little relieved that at least one of the Fox brothers was behind bars for the night. "That's good news. Have you gotten any updates from the TPD on how close they are to arresting him?"

"No." Charles shook his head in frustration. "The chief actually told me that he didn't want me to go after Mitch in *angry dad mode* and jeopardize his case, so he's not sharing any information with me. It's like he thinks I'm planning on doing something other than having my deputies detain him until the TPD can pick him up from us if we find him first."

"Sorry, Daddy," Randi tried to console her father, understanding his frustration, and hoping to diffuse the moment with humor. "Next time someone tries to attack me, I'll make sure they do it outside the official city limits, so it's in your jurisdiction. I might have to beat them up and stuff them in my trunk to drive them out into the county, but I'll make sure I only talk to you or one of your deputies when I give my statement from now on."

"I'd rather you just not get attacked again," Charles chuckled at his daughter's attempt at humor. "And after the phone call I got today, I'm thinking I'm not the only person who wants to make sure nobody gets a chance to hurt you again."

"Oh, what did Mom tell you to make you think that?" Randi grinned at her father, thinking it had to be her mother that he'd spoken to on the phone about her situation.

"It wasn't your mother who called me." His expression turned serious and worried Randi. "Anthony called me, so James could ask about what's being done to keep you safe."

Sugar! Fudge! Donuts! Randi thought her creative alternative words for cussing in her head, freezing in place with her spoon halfway up to her gaping open mouth. *What the Hello was he thinking? James knows I haven't told my parents about him, so why on earth would he wanna call and talk to my Dad?*

"Are you going to take that bite, baby girl?" Charles pointed at her spoonful of chili. "Or would you rather tell me about your new boyfriend?"

"He's not my boyfriend," Randi choked out as she put her spoon back in her bowl. *We haven't labeled what we are to each other, so I'm not really lying to my Daddy,* she justified herself in her head, even knowing that she thought of him as her boyfriend. "We met the same day Kay met Anthony and exchanged phone numbers, so we've been talking and texting, but we're not dating. He's just a friend."

"That's not the impression he gave me over the phone." Charles went back to eating his chili. When Randi didn't say anything because she had no idea what to say to her father about James, Charles swallowed his bite of chili and continued speaking. "He sounded like he wants to be more than a friend to you."

Randi opened her mouth to respond, but she couldn't figure out what to say, so she just repeated opening and closing her mouth like a fish out of water for a moment before giving up and taking a bite to have an excuse not to speak. She wasn't sure exactly what her dad thought about James from their conversation, but she knew his opinion would be negative as soon as he saw James, either in person or in a picture. *Daddy doesn't like long hair on men, or beards, or tattoos, so I know he'll hate James on first sight.*

"Do I need to call him back and make it clear that you just want to be friends, so things aren't awkward at the wedding?" Charles inquired as Randi kept filling her mouth, so she couldn't speak. "Or do you think you can make that clear to him yourself?"

Sugar! I shouldn't have taken such a big bite, Randi realized as she shook her head at her father. *I can't let Daddy call James and tell him I don't want to be anything but friends. I know that's all Daddy wants between us, but it's not what I want. And until I can convince Daddy that James isn't a low life like he'll think based on appearance, I'll just have to keep hiding my real feelings about him.*

She chewed and swallowed as quickly as possible, so she could say, "No, Daddy, don't call James. I'll talk to him myself, just as soon as we're through eating, and I get the kitchen cleaned up, and can go to my room to call him in private."

"Alright, sweetheart," Charles sighed, after finishing his last bite of chili. "Let me know if I need to step in and get him to accept no as an answer like I had to do with that boy a couple of years ago."

He stood and carried his dishes to the sink, rinsing them off before kissing the top of Randi's head, telling her "goodnight, sweetheart," and leaving her sitting at her kitchen table feeling overwhelmed.

She sat there stewing for a few minutes as she finished her dinner. Amy walked into the kitchen from the hallway that led back to their bedrooms, carrying her empty dinner dishes.

"Why'd you eat in your room?" Randi looked at her roommate in confusion when Amy put the dishes in the sink and started rinsing them.

"I was getting a bowl of chili when I heard you pull in the driveway," Amy shrugged as she opened the dishwasher and started loading it with the dishes in the sink. "When I realized your dad was here too, I figured you'd want some privacy to talk to him about the assault case, so I decided to eat in my bedroom to give it to you."

"Yeah, well, next time, don't," Randi blurted as she got up to rinse her own dishes, help load the dishwasher, and put away the leftovers. "He blindsided me by telling me he talked to James today, and I could've used the backup to know what to say in response."

"Shit, girl, seriously?" Amy held a bowl in midair over the dishwasher like she forgot she was putting it in there. "Who told him about James?"

"James," Randi barked, throwing up her hands in frustration. "He had Anthony call Daddy to find out what's being done to keep me safe. And apparently, they had a nice long conversation, where James made it clear to Daddy that we're more than friends. I'm so mad at him right now, I could spit nails."

"Why are you mad that he wanted to know you're safe?" Amy finally started moving to continue loading the dishwasher.

"I'm not mad that he wants to know I'm safe," Randi clarified as she poured the leftover chili from the crock pot into a plastic bowl that she could put a lid on and store in the refrigerator. "I'm mad because he knows I don't tell my parents about anyone I date, unless I have to have Daddy get rid of someone when it's over, and he went behind my back to tell Daddy that we're dating, when he knew I didn't want Daddy to know anything was going on between us."

"Okay, I can see your point," Amy conceded, looking thoughtfully at Randi. "But maybe you should ask him why he did it before you decide whether to be mad or not."

"You really think there's a reason he could give me that would be valid enough that I shouldn't be mad at him for outing us to Daddy, when he knows I don't want either of my parents to know who I date?" Randi finished up cleaning the kitchen by wiping down the counters.

"Yeah," Amy replied as she closed and started the dishwasher. "I mean you can't really get mad at the guy for caring so much about you that he didn't think before he acted to make sure you're safe. That's just a typical boneheaded guy thing to do, but it's not malicious. Now if he outed you to your dad because he wants to end things with you and doesn't have the balls to do it himself, then you have every right to be pissed at him and give him hell for it."

Randi wasn't sure she agreed with Amy's assessment that she couldn't get mad at him for being a *typical boneheaded guy,* but she would rather fight it out with James than her roommate. So, she excused herself to go to her room to hash things out with James in private.

Leah Mae Wright

As soon as she was behind her closed door, she pulled her phone out of her purse and saw his text message and quickly typed out a reply.

James: Hey Angel, missing you and couldn't wait another minute to text you. Hope you had a good day. {Face Blowing A Kiss Emoji}

Randi: Yeah? Is that why you called my Dad today? Thanks a lot for that! I appreciate so much how you respect me & don't do anything to cause me to have to sit through a lecture like I'm still a kid. Or NOT!

James: Shit, Angel, I'm sorry.

James: I just wanted to make sure you were safe. I didn't think he'd lecture you about having a friend who was worried about you.

Randi: Yeah, well, according to him, you made it very clear that we're more than friends! I'm under strict orders to make sure you know that's all we'll ever be & to let him know if you don't believe that from me so he can convince you himself to stay away from me as anything more. What the Hello did you say to him to make him hate you without even meeting you?

James: Fuck, Angel, I don't know. I didn't get the feeling that he hated me when we talked. In fact, right before he hung up, he told me that I was a decent enough guy to be able to keep talking & texting with you, but that I should rethink my job as a wrestler if I want to actually date you. Anthony thought that meant he liked me but my traveling all the time would keep us apart.

Randi: He didn't say any of that to me tonight. He was telling me about arresting Mark & trying to get his other brother Matt to tell Mitch to turn himself in & when he was talking about the lack of communication from the TPD, he said something about knowing he wasn't the only person who wanted to protect me based on the phone call he got today.

Randi: That's when he asked me about you. I told him that we just met the same day that Kay met Anthony & had exchanged phone numbers to talk & text while you're traveling for work.

James: Yeah, that sounds like word for word what we said today too.

Randi: Well, when I said we're just friends, he said that you made it clear that you want to be more than friends with me. I didn't know what to say to that & when I didn't say anything he asked if he needed to call & tell you that we're only ever going to be friends so things aren't awkward at the wedding or if I could tell you myself. So, you had to have said something else to make him think you're pressuring me into more.

James: Right after Anthony said we met the same night he met Kay, he asked me my intentions with you. I told him that I want to do everything I can to make you happy & safe. Then he asked if I was planning to tell him a line like Anthony did the first time he talked to your dad about falling in love at first sight. I told him that I wasn't planning on saying anything like that to him, but I couldn't completely disagree with the sentiment.

Randi: You should have left off the end of that
statement.

James: Then he asked Anthony if I looked as nervous as I
sounded, & Anthony said he couldn't tell if I was
turning green or going pale under my beard. Then he
said something about me needing to shave before
standing up for Anthony in the wedding. When I
explained that it would be neatly trimmed for the
wedding, but I couldn't shave it off because of my job,
he asked what I do for work.

Randi: Oh DOG, no wonder he doesn't like you. I thought
I could maybe talk you up to him in the next couple of
weeks so that he wouldn't hate you when he saw you.
But Daddy thinks Anthony's hair is a bit too long, so if
you told him about needing the long hair, beard, &
tattoos for work, he's going to think you're a low life
criminal based simply on your wrestling gimmick & will
never accept us dating.

James: Yeah, well, I did tell him all that, but I also told
him that I'm not a "dumb punk losing brain cells in
senseless fights" like he said he thought of professional
wrestlers. I told him about my degree in finance &
how I've already invested my 7-figure salary from my
athletic acting job & turned it into an 8-figure income,
& that I'll be reaching billionaire status from my
investments by the time I'm ready to retire from
wrestling. He even said that was "impressive."

Randi: My Dad said that was impressive? That doesn't
sound like him. And it's certainly not what he was
saying to me tonight about you.

James: Yeah, well, that's what he said. But then I was losing it because it's been a week since you were attacked, & you couldn't tell me anything more was being done to keep you safe than you'd said the first night. I may have said a couple of bad words about Mitch & wanting to come kick his ass myself to protect you before your dad told me about the extra patrols of your neighborhood & how he threatened his brother to get him to turn himself in.

Randi: He threatened Matt? Daddy said he told Matt it would be in Mitch's best interest to turn himself in, but he didn't say anything about threatening him.

James: I don't know exactly what he said to the guy, but when he told Anthony and I, it sounded like he threatened Mitch with bodily harm if he or his deputies arrested him before the TPD could.

Randi: No way! That's not Daddy's style. You must have misunderstood him. Honestly, none of the things you've said he said when you talked to him sound like him at all. And they definitely don't match up with what he was telling me tonight.

James: I don't know what could have changed in the 3 hours between when I talked to him & when you talked to him. What do I need to do to fix it so we can be together without him giving you any more lectures? Do I need to call him again so he can get to know me?

Randi: NO! Do not call my Daddy! Do not call my Mom either! The only people you're allowed to talk to in my family are my sister and nieces & that's only because you work with the same company. Everyone else is off limits for you to talk to!

James: That's gonna be kinda hard when we're all at the wedding. And won't do anything to let them get to know me so they can see how good we are together as more than friends.

Randi: Yeah, well, tough. You ignored my boundaries, so now we can't be more than friends.

James: Angel, please tell me you don't really mean that. We are a hell of a lot more than friends!

Randi: No, we're not. I'm not sure I can even be friends with someone who cares so little about my feelings that he stomps over my boundaries without regard to the consequences I'll have to face for his actions.

James: Angel, please. I said I'm sorry. I had no idea that asking about what's being done to keep you safe would cause you to have to be lectured tonight. If I had known that was a possibility, I wouldn't have said a word while Anthony was talking to your dad.

James: Please tell me how to fix this.

Randi didn't know how to reply to James. She had no idea how to fix anything in her life. Not her relationship with him, not her relationship with her parents.

Hello, I can't even find a new job, so I can keep from draining my savings to pay my rent. Maybe I should just quit James cold turkey, so I can focus on job hunting instead of getting sidetracked by talking to him, or thinking about him, or stalking his social media, instead of going through every job posting online and sending out more résumés.

Her phone buzzed with another new text.

James: You mean the world to me, Angel. I can't lose you. Please tell me what you need me to do to make this right between us.

"There's nothing you can do," Randi cried into her pillow, not able to stop the tears that started flowing down her face.

She wasn't entirely sure of all the reasons she was crying. She knew part of it was because she felt like James had disregarded how his actions would impact her like she'd told him in their text conversation. She wasn't sure she wanted to be in a relationship with someone who didn't respect her boundaries or who acted without thinking about her at all beforehand.

She also thought that part of it was because of her screwed-up relationship with her parents. She cried because she didn't think she was strong enough to tell them what she wanted in life, or who she wanted to be with, regardless of their opinions. She wanted to be a strong independent woman, and hated the part of herself that still needed their approval more than she was willing to stand up for herself against them and their opposing beliefs of what she should be doing or who she should be with.

But the biggest reason that Randi thought she was lying in her bed crying her eyes out was that she thought she'd just broken her own heart by pulling away from James. She realized as she was lashing out at him that although she was telling him that she didn't think they could even be friends anymore, it wasn't what she truly felt for him.

Somehow, in the month they'd known each other, she'd fallen completely, head over heels, in love with him. But loving him wasn't enough to get over all the obstacles in their way of being together. Love didn't help her get over her airplane anxiety. Love didn't help her find the strength to tell her parents that she wanted to be with him or that she wanted to pursue a career in professional wrestling. Love didn't make her brave enough to do everything that she would have to do in order to actually live the dream of working with the GWA and traveling the world by his side.

So, while it hurt like crazy to push him away, she didn't think she could do anything else at the moment. She needed time and space to work on herself, to get her new medicine adjusted, so she could handle flying, to talk to her therapist about all her issues, and to find the well of strength, bravery, and determination inside her that she would need to be able to go back to him as an equal partner in the future.

Her tears blurred her vision too much to read the rest of his incoming texts, or to reply to tell him what she needed to do before they could possibly be together in the future. She knew if she didn't respond soon, he would just call her as soon as he could get somewhere private to talk. She didn't think she would be able to coherently explain everything to him as she blubbered into her pillow. So, she turned her phone off, not ready to talk to him or anyone else at the moment. She didn't know if she would be ready to talk again the next day, or if she would leave it off for a week or two, until she absolutely had to turn it back on to communicate with her family for the trip down to Kay's wedding.

Randi cried herself to sleep, still in her work uniform, opting to wallow in her misery until she was unable to shed another tear. She vowed to make sure she was truly at the rock bottom of her despair before she pulled up her big girl panties, climbed her way out of the hole, and ascended to the zenith of her dreams.

Chapter Seven

Tuesday, October 30, 2018

James was irritable and exhausted when he got on the plane to fly out
of Fargo and over to Bismarck, North Dakota, after a sleepless night,
unable to get a response from Randi. He thought they were doing
good in talking out what had been said when he spoke with her father
the day before. But then she said she didn't believe her dad would
actually say the things he'd heard the man say, and she wasn't sure she
could even be friends with him anymore, much less more than friends
like James wanted them to be.

He must have sent her two dozen more texts asking how to fix it
and what he could do to make up for his mistake of outing them to her
dad in the hour after she quit replying to him. He even left the arena
early, so he could go back to his hotel room and call her, only for his
calls to go straight to voicemail. He wasn't sure if she'd turned her
phone off or just blocked him, but either way he was distraught from
not being able to talk to her.

Instead of sitting with his brother at the front of the plane to listen
in while the writers talked over their future storylines, so he could
offer some input into the development of his character, James walked
to the back of the plane to pick a seat away from everyone else. He
didn't think he could get any more sleep in the secluded pod than he
had the night before, when his brief cat naps were interrupted by
nightmares about never being able to convince Randi to give him a
second chance, but it was worth a shot.

He stayed sitting up for take-off but started converting his pod to a
bed as soon as they were at cruising altitude. He'd just laid down
when Kay walked back to where he was and sat down in the seat
beside him.

"Are you okay, James?" Kay looked at him with concern written all over her expressive face.

"Yeah, I'm fine." James wasn't sure he wanted to tell Randi's sister how he'd screwed things up. "Just tired, didn't sleep well last night."

"Did you stay up too late talking to Randi?" Kay grinned at him.

Shit, she thinks I have a Skype sex hangover. I wish I could just agree with her, so I wouldn't have to admit how I fucked up yesterday. But if I do that and she talks to Randi later, then she could inadvertently make Randi think I was up all night with someone else since she broke up with me. Fuck!

Resigned to having to tell Kay the truth, James sat up, so they could talk like normal adults. "Not exactly," James admitted, running a hand through his hair as he tried to figure out how to tell her what happened. "I screwed up and Randi quit talking to me last night. I tossed and turned all night, and what little sleep I did get was plagued with nightmares about her never forgiving me."

"Oh!" Kay clutched a hand to her chest like she was startled at his revelation. "I'm sorry to hear that. How exactly did you screw things up?"

"I had Anthony call your dad yesterday to find out what was being done to keep her safe until that Mitch guy's arrested," James confessed, hanging his head in shame.

"Why would she get mad at you for that?" Kay looked confused at the cause of his disagreement with Randi.

"She's mad because I talked to ya'll's dad and she didn't even want him to know that we're friends," he sighed. "And I apparently made him realize that I wanna be a lot more than friends with her."

James still wasn't sure why Mr. Lee had gone from sounding like he was okay with James dating Randi to making Randi think he hated James. "When I talked to him, I thought things went well. I took his parting words as encouragement to keep pursuing something with Randi. But then he ended up giving her a lecture about me a few hours later and ordered her to make it clear to me that we'll only ever be just friends. I don't know what happened in the three hours between when I talked to him and when she did, but instead of talking things out, so we can figure it out and fix it, Randi just ghosted me."

"Ghosted you?" Kay looked at him quizzically.

"Yeah, she quit replying to texts and when I tried to call her it goes straight to voicemail," James replied, running his hand through his hair again, as if tugging on his hair would somehow give him clarity that he hadn't found all night. "I don't know if she turned her phone off or just blocked me. But either way, I'm worried about her and hate not having a way to know she's okay."

"Yeah." Kay drew the word out to multiple syllables, looking at him closely for a second before continuing. "Randi probably just needs a little time to figure things out and didn't want to lash out and say something she didn't really mean with you. Give her a day or two and then try reaching out again."

"Can you try calling her when we land?" James implored Kay. "Even if she doesn't wanna talk to me, I just need to know that she's okay."

"Yeah, I can do that," Kay agreed, standing to go back to her job of helping the parents with their kids' needs on the flight. "I'll call her from the gate while Anthony is finishing up his post flight duties, if you wanna meet me there."

"Thanks, Kay." James smiled sincerely at his friend's fiancée, even if it didn't quite reach his eyes.

"No problem," she replied with the slightest upturn of her lips. "I hope ya'll can work things out. I really do think you're perfect for each other."

James laid back down and caught a few winks of sleep on the short flight. All too soon he was awakened to the sound of Anthony's voice telling them all to prepare for landing. Being at the back of the plane allowed him extra time to gather his things when it was time to disembark, since he wouldn't push his way past the rest of the crew and families to exit the plane. He did take some time to help more than one of his coworkers' wives and children with their oversized suitcases, including Kay, Tia, and Maria, whom he followed off the plane.

They stopped to sit at the gate to wait for Anthony, and Kay dug through her purse for her phone. She turned off the airplane mode feature as she motioned for James to follow her a few feet away from her daughters before dialing Randi's number. She put it on speaker and held it in front of her. Unfortunately, James only heard one ring before it went to voicemail.

Leah Mae Wright

"Hey, Sis," Kay said into her phone to leave a message for Randi. "Give me a call when you get this. I need to talk to you about your schedule next week, so I can see you while I'm in Tulsa for court. Love you. Bye."

"Sorry," Kay apologized to James after she disconnected the call. "I'll let you know as soon as I hear from her."

"Thanks, Kay," James replied, earnestly. "I'll give her all the time she needs to forgive me and figure out what I can do to make things right, but I just need to know she's safe. Until that guy is caught, I'm gonna be worried about her."

"I know," Kay consoled, patting his forearm in a comforting gesture. "But I'm sure you guys will work it out."

"Work what out?" Anthony asked as he walked up to them.

"Just my sister going hermit because she's overwhelmed right now," Kay answered him before James could say a word. She took Anthony's hand in hers as she continued explaining. "And with them being in two different cities, James can't just barge into the bathroom, where she's probably figuring things out in a bubble bath, to pull her out of it like you do with me when I'm overwhelmed."

They all picked up their bags and made their way to the rental car counter before going back to their normally scheduled activities for the day. James managed to snag a ride with his brother, so he didn't have to get his own rental just to go to the hotel and arena. He slogged through his normal routine, barely conscious of what he was doing because his mind was consumed with thoughts of Randi.

He wondered if she would even watch him wrestle on the weekly live television program that night. Or if she would cut him out of her life completely and not see how off his game he was from not hearing back from her, even via text since the night before.

Not that she could completely cut him out of her life when they would be thrown together again at the wedding in just a few weeks. He would give her the time that Kay seemed to think she needed, but only until they were all in Heart's Destiny. He started formulating his plans to get back in her good graces. He would show her and her entire family that he was serious about her, no matter whether her father liked him or not.

I love her! And I know she loves me, too, even if she's not ready to admit it yet, James thought with a smile on his face. *And I'll make that clear, just as soon as we're in the same space again.*

~~~

Randi didn't bother turning her phone back on as she got up at three o'clock that afternoon and got ready to go to her therapy appointment. She'd originally scheduled her therapy sessions for Tuesday afternoons to have an excuse to not have to work on Tuesday nights, so she could watch James on the GWA's live weekly television show. But after crying herself to sleep the night before and staying in bed well past her normal morning wake up time, Randi was glad to have the day off to wallow, almost as much as she was glad to have the therapy session to help her figure out her feelings from the previous day's events. Maybe her therapist could help her decide whether or not she'd watch James on TV that night, too.

She took a quick shower, scrubbing her face free of the ruined makeup from the day before. She brushed her teeth and blow dried her hair, but she didn't bother reapplying makeup, knowing she would probably just ruin it again by crying through her therapy session. She made a couple of pieces of toast and grabbed a soda from the fridge to settle her stomach before she walked out the door.

She did take her phone off the charger and put it in her purse before she left the house. Even if she didn't turn it on because she didn't want to talk to anyone, it was a good idea to have it available in case she needed to call someone for an emergency before she got back home. Even if Mitch wasn't likely to attack her again, she could have a flat tire or minor fender bender that would require calling for help on the side of the road. She wasn't the reckless teenager her parents thought she was. She was a grown woman who knew how to take care of herself and was prepared for anything that might happen on her way to the therapist's office across town.

It only took about thirty minutes to get across the river from her little house in West Tulsa to the therapist's office on Utica close to Saint John's Hospital. She quickly parked in the lot designated for the
~~~

medical office building and made her way to the third-floor office, where she was greeted by a professionally dressed receptionist.

She briefly felt underdressed in her jeans and old college sweatshirt since even the other patients in the waiting room were dressed like they worked in a stuffy office setting. But when she looked around the room after checking in, she realized that it didn't matter what anyone there was wearing or what they did for a living, they were all there to deal with their own issues because nobody had a perfect life, even if they tried to present themselves as perfect in how they dressed.

She had to stop looking at people through the skewed lens of what they tried to project through social media or the superficial window dressing of their outward appearance. She didn't want to be like her parents and judge people as worthy or not worthy based on how they looked or the imperceptible masks they wore when interacting with others. She wanted to actually build connections with the real people they were deep inside, like she had with James in the last month. That went for family and friends, as well as lovers.

It wasn't long before she was called back to her therapist, Kelly's office. They made the usual small talk of casual greetings and enjoying the clear fall weather as they took their seats on either side of the desk.

"Have you thought anymore about your future career plans we were discussing last week?" Kelly leaned back in her chair with her notepad on her lap and pen in hand, ready to jot down notes about their session.

"Yes," Randi answered, tentatively smiling. "And the more I think about it, the more I think I wanna be a professional wrestler. I mean, it's the only job I've been able to find that really checks all my boxes, even ones I didn't realize I had until this weekend."

"More than just the being active and fun that we discussed last week?" Kelly was obviously trying to get Randi to explain in more detail, but she just nodded in response, not completely sure how to explain it. "What new boxes did you discover this weekend?"

"Like I told you last time, the only thing I really like about my current job is that I get to interact with different people every day," Randi explained. "Well, Saturday I was Skyping with James while he was signing autographs for fans and realized that wrestling would check that box, too. But not just the being able to interact with people.

It was a lot of positive feedback for him about how he actually impacts their lives by entertaining them each week. And it made me realize that I want that, too. That ability to make people happy, even if it's only by taking their mind off their problems for a little while when they're focused on my performance, instead of whatever else is going on in their lives."

"Do you not get that now with your current job?" Kelly moved her pen over the notepad to write out what Randi was saying.

"Maybe a little," Randi postulated in a low tone, not really sure a happy customer at the restaurant compared to the hundreds of happy wrestling fans she'd seen get James's autograph. "But even the best customer service in a restaurant can't make some customers happy, and I don't think whatever they're worried about goes away while they're eating. People really get into watching wrestling. Kind of like going to the movies, or a play, or even reading a book, where they're focused on the show or the story and disengage from their own problems for a while. I guess I could get that same sense of purpose from acting without having to learn to wrestle, but there aren't many local opportunities to make a living as an actress."

"Yes, we talked about the various obstacles of making a living in atypical jobs last week." Kelly flipped back on her notepad, referring to her earlier notes. "Have you come up with any solutions to the obstacles we identified last week for a wrestling career?"

"Well, you know I've been taking the antianxiety medication for a week now, and I think it's helping some." Randi thought back to her feelings as she'd lain in bed that morning. "I didn't freak out this morning when I thought about the people I care about being on a plane, but I'm still nervous when I think about flying myself. I know Dr. McShane said to message her after two weeks on it to let her know how it was working, but I'm thinking about sending her a message when I get home today to let her know how it's working now. Even if she doesn't wanna change anything until next week, I think it's still better to give her more information as I think about it than to wait another week to check in and risk forgetting something I'm feeling now."

"I agree, more information than necessary is definitely better than risking forgetting to relay something important," Kelly affirmed with a smile. "And the other obstacles?"

Leah Mae Wright

"I did some research on my computer about wrestling training," Randi reported, slightly deflated because she hadn't yet been successful in setting anything up. "Unfortunately, the only professional wrestling schools I could find were out of state. But I did email the local wrestling promotion to ask where their performers trained, or if any of them offered private training. I haven't heard back yet, but I'm hopeful that I'll hear something from them soon."

"Did you ask James about training you?" Kelly continued taking notes.

"No," Randi confessed, shifting in her chair, uncomfortable with what she was about to tell her therapist. "We kinda had a fight yesterday about my parental issues. That's really the biggest obstacle I'm facing for everything else in my life. And yesterday when I had the perfect opportunity to tell my dad about my future plans, I chickened out and couldn't even admit to being more than friends with James."

Randi knew that wasn't enough of an explanation for her therapist, so she went back and told Kelly all about the situation that really started with Kay and her ex-husband. Randi broke down the timeline from the night she met James and Kay met Anthony, detailing the events that led to Kay leaving town and working with the GWA. She told Kelly about Kay's house being broken into and everything being destroyed inside. She then told her about the night Mitch assaulted her at work and how it was being handled by the Tulsa Police Department, instead of the Sheriff's Department. She explained how James kept asking her for information about the case that she didn't have, since it wasn't in her father's jurisdiction. Finally, Randi told Kelly about James calling her father the day before to ask him about what was being done to keep her safe until Mitch was arrested, and how her dad had shown up at her house the night before, basically ordering her to put an end to anything other than friendship with James before he left.

"So, what exactly was your fight with James about when you spoke with him after your dad left?" Kelly inquired, still scribbling down notes.

"I didn't actually speak to James," Randi admitted, feeling embarrassed about fighting with him via text messages. "We texted until I couldn't read the texts through my tears anymore and turned my phone off."

Randi pulled her phone out of her purse and turned it on. Once it was through dinging with notifications about her missed calls and texts for the last twenty hours or so, she pulled up the text thread with James, scrolled back to when their conversation started about eight the previous evening, and handed her phone to Kelly, so she could just read Randi's humiliation, instead of her having to try to remember it and repeat it word for word.

"This doesn't seem like much of a fight between you and James." Kelly scrolled and read their messages from the previous night. "But I don't think you were really telling him everything you were feeling at the time either. Can you tell me more about what you were really mad at him for last night?"

Kelly handed Randi her phone back and Randi scrolled back through her messages with James to try to remember her feelings in the correct order.

"Obviously, my first message to him was sarcastic because I was mad about him calling Daddy," Randi admitted, pointing at the message on her phone screen. "He knew I don't tell my parents about anyone I'm dating, and I was mad that he didn't respect me enough to keep things just between us."

Kelly didn't say anything, just kept writing down notes, so Randi looked back at her phone to refer to the messages before trying to further explain her feelings at the time.

"I think part of it was that I was mad about my dad's reaction to James," Randi reasoned as she read over their conversation. "And especially how it seemed like we had two completely different conversations with my dad. From what James said in these texts, he had a nice long conversation with Daddy, and they got along great. But then when I talked to him, Daddy didn't mention any of that, he just told me to make sure James knows we'll only ever be friends, or he will for me if I can't."

Randi had to stop and grab a tissue from the box on Kelly's desk because her eyes were starting to fill up with unshed tears. She dabbed them away before they fell, trying to collect herself before she continued.

"I was confused, wondering which of us saw Daddy's real feelings about James and I dating," she confided, barely holding back a sob. "I was mad at James for telling Daddy things I should've been the one to tell him. I was mad at myself for not being able to stand up to Daddy and admit that I wanna be more than friends with James. I was mad at myself for not being able to tell him that I'm twenty-five and not fifteen."

"I should be strong enough to tell both my parents that I hate how they judge people based on looks or how they look down on people who don't meet their standards for what's proper, whether that's working at an unusual job, or if they say a curse word once in a while, or if they have tattoos. But I'm not strong enough to tell them any of that. And I sometimes hate myself for not even being able to say a curse word in my own head because I'm afraid they'll know I'm thinking it and will lecture me for it like I'm a rebellious teenager."

"Is that the worst they would do?" Randi wasn't sure exactly what she meant, so she tilted her head inquisitively at Kelly until she broke down her question better. "The worst punishment your parents would give you for saying a curse word or telling them any of the things you wish you could tell them is a lecture? They wouldn't beat you, or wash your mouth out with soap?"

"No, they'd never beat me for sure," Randi defended her parents, even though she wasn't sure they wouldn't wash her mouth out with soap for cussing. "They never even spanked me when I was a kid. The worst punishment I ever received was a month of no phone, no internet, and no extracurricular activities, after a three-hour lecture about how shameful my poetry was when I was a teenager. And the lecture was by far the worst of that punishment."

"What did you write about that they punished you for it?" Kelly looked appalled at the thought of being punished for writing poetry.

"I was fifteen and had just discovered the romance section in the library," Randi admitted sheepishly, hoping she didn't blush too much as she admitted to her teenage exploration of the sexual genre of reading material. "I knew better than to check any of those books out to take home to read, so I just read what I could when I finished with whatever homework I was doing in the library after school. We were also doing a unit on poetry in my English class in school that I really enjoyed. So, I took an empty spiral notebook from the desk where we stored our extra school supplies and filled it with my own poetry about the sex scenes I read in the books. When my parents found it, it didn't matter that I was not only still a virgin, but I also hadn't even kissed a boy yet. They lectured me about how disgusting the poems were, told me I should never say those vulgar words, much less write them down, and slut shamed me like I had given it up to every boy in school, all while making me watch my poetry notebook burn in the fireplace."

Randi noticed the brief widening of Kelly's eyes and slight drop of her jaw before she schooled her features to cover up her thoughts about what Randi had just said. *Maybe I'm not the only one who thinks it was an excessive punishment for a harmless way of exploring my sexuality as a teenager?*

"I know that was nothing compared to the trauma of living with abusive parents, but it was traumatic enough for me to still have issues ten years later," Randi sobbed, reaching for another tissue as a tear slipped down her cheek. "I know that's why I didn't lose my virginity until I was twenty. And why I don't tell my parents when I'm dating someone, so they don't figure out that I'm not still a virgin. And why I use words like sugar and fudge in place of curse words, even when I'm just thinking about cussing in my head. All because I don't want them to give me another of those lectures."

Randi didn't mention that she'd started working her way through some of her cussing issues with James. Since she'd only been successful at using foul language with him via text or whispering the words when they were having a sexual conversation and still used substitute words the rest of the time, she wasn't sure it really counted as being able to say them. And she really didn't want to talk to her therapist about the intimate details of her sex life any more than she wanted to talk to her parents about it. *Although maybe I should,* she pondered. *Since that same lecture from my parents caused my sexual hang-ups. Maybe next session? I think this is as deep as I'm able to go this session.*

They sat in silence for a few minutes while Randi wiped away the tears she couldn't hold back. It was a strange feeling, not being able to stop the flow of tears even as she sat there stoically, not feeling the need to wail dramatically like she had the night before. It was almost like she was coming to the end of her ability to release the pent-up emotions and only had a few tears left to release. She hoped she would feel better, maybe a little lighter, when the tears finally dried up.

"Okay, first, I want to make sure you know that words can absolutely be just as traumatic to our psyche as physical abuse is to the body," Kelly stated once Randi had stopped wiping her eyes. "So, I understand your feelings about a lecture from your parents being a traumatic event that you want to prevent from happening again."

Thank goodness, she understands me, Randi thought, hopeful that Kelly could help her figure out how to get past her fear of being lectured by her parents to be able to be her true self, even if she wasn't who they wanted her to be.

"But, unlike when you were a teenager, you don't have to stay and listen to their lectures as an adult," Kelly continued.

"So, I should just say whatever I'm thinking and leave if they start to lecture me about it?" Randi wasn't entirely comprehending such a simple solution.

"Ideally, yes," Kelly chuckled. "But it's probably not going to be that simple of a solution to implement. You know about the fight or flight response, right?"

"Yes," Randi nodded her head. "If a person is scared by something, they either respond by running away or trying to fight whatever's scaring them."

"Exactly," Kelly replied with a slight upturn of the corners of her mouth. "But it's actually possible that instead of responding by fighting or fleeing, they can also respond by freezing. I think that's what you did last night when your dad asked you about James. You were scared of getting a lecture from him, and instead of fighting with him by telling him what you want with James, or having a flight response and leaving the physical space where he was at the time, you froze, unable to say anything or move, until he said everything he wanted to say, and left you feeling like you'd barely survived a lecture."

"Oh my dog, you're right," Randi shrieked, covering her mouth with her hand at the realization. "And then I had both the fight and flight responses with James. First fighting with him, and then turning off my phone to run away from him when I couldn't keep fighting."

"And I think you were able to have those fight and flight responses with James because you knew you were safe to have them with him," Kelly remarked, pointing at Randi's phone. "And the texts he sent you after you turned off your phone are proof that you were right to feel safe with him to have those responses. I think they make it clear how much he cares about you and won't lecture you like your parents, even if you push him away or piss him off."

"You think he'll forgive me for losing it last night?" Randi scrolled down to see a couple dozen messages she hadn't read yet that all appeared to be groveling for her forgiveness, and begging her to answer her phone, or at least text him back to let him know she was okay.

"Definitely, even if you need to take a few more days to work up the courage to reply to him," Kelly affirmed with a smile. "In fact, that's what I want you to do for your homework this week."

"Work up the courage to reply to James?" Randi was confused about how that was her therapy homework.

"Sort of." Kelly bobbed her head to the side as she scribbled down another note. "Mostly I want you to practice saying the hard stuff to your parents, but also to James if you need to. You can either practice talking in a mirror, or to a stuffed animal if looking yourself in the eye is too hard at first. Imagine that stuffed animal is whoever you want to talk to, and practice staying to fight by saying the hard stuff, maybe even a real curse word too, not just your feelings, or telling them about your goals and dreams that they probably won't like. After you get it all out a few times without anyone around to lecture you about it, you might find it easier to say when you know you can walk away, instead of hearing a lecture from your parents, too."

"Okay, yeah, I can do that," Randi let out the breath she hadn't realized she'd been holding, feeling better about having a strategy to try.

"I already have you down for next Tuesday at four again." Kelly turned in her seat, referring to a calendar on her computer.

"Yes," Randi replied. "And the Tuesday after that. Then I'll be in Texas for my sister's wedding the week of Thanksgiving."

"We can do a telehealth appointment that week and we can book a standing appointment every Tuesday through December, if you want," Kelly offered as she clicked through her calendar.

"How hard is it to change them to telehealth appointments if I need to be out of town for any of the future sessions?" Randi pulled up her own calendar on her phone to put in the therapy times she had scheduled.

"It's booked the same way in my system," Kelly replied. "You'll just have to tell the person who calls to confirm your appointment on the Friday before that it needs to be a telehealth appointment, so they can confirm it as such on our system."

"Okay, then let's go ahead and book them," Randi decided, making notes on her calendar app for every Tuesday in December except for Christmas day. They both agreed to decide on the eighteenth of December if Randi needed to continue weekly appointments and pick a different day of the week during the holidays that fell on Tuesdays, or if she was ready to move to less frequent therapy sessions.

Once Randi had checked out and paid her co-pay for the appointment, she walked down to her car before pulling her phone back out of her purse to look at all the notifications she'd missed. Since her visual voicemail app allowed her to pick which messages she wanted to listen to without having to listen to all of the voicemail messages that had come in while her phone was off, Randi decided to listen to Kay's message while sitting in her car in the parking lot, in case it was important. She would wait to listen to the half-dozen voicemails from James when she got home.

"Hey, Sis. Give me a call when you get this. I need to talk to you about your schedule next week, so I can see you while I'm in Tulsa for court. Love you, Bye."

It wasn't an emergency call by any means, but Randi decided to go ahead and call Kay back anyway, even if it was only to find out if James had told her about the events of the day before. She pushed the call button beside her sister's name on the message screen and brought her phone to her ear as it rang.

"Hello," Kay chirped through the phone.

"Hey, sis, sorry I missed your call earlier," Randi greeted her sister, relaxing back into her seat to talk for a few minutes while sitting in the parking lot.

"No biggie, but give me a second to get out of the noisy classroom, so I can hear you while we talk."

Randi waited until the background noise died down before asking, "Why's the classroom area so noisy? I would think it would be quieter, so the kids could study."

"Yeah, normally it is," Kay chuckled. "But when a couple dozen kids get hyped up about tomorrow being Halloween, it's hard to keep them focused on their lessons, much less quiet as they discuss their costumes and whether or not they can trick-or-treat in the hotel after the company Halloween party."

"Yeah, I guess those are more important things to discuss than their schoolwork," Randi laughed.

"Exactly," Kay also laughed. "So, do you know your schedule for next week yet? We're going to get there Sunday evening, but we're going to stay at a hotel by the airport, so Mark can't find us before court Monday."

"I'm working three to eleven Sunday evening," Randi sighed. "Which means probably seven to three or eleven to seven on Monday, but I'm not sure yet. I know I'll be off on Tuesday because I specifically told them that I can't work Tuesdays, so I have a day that I can schedule doctor's appointments and stuff. I have my therapy sessions scheduled for every Tuesday at four for the next six weeks. And I have no clue what I'll be working the rest of the time you're in town."

"Oh, did you have another therapy session today?" Kay completely ignored the schedule discussion.

"Yeah, I'm sitting in the parking lot of my therapist's office where I just left there," Randi admitted, wondering how many questions Kay was going to ask her about the session.

"You think it's going to help you be able to fly down to the wedding?"

"I think the medication Dr. McShane prescribed last week is gonna help with that more than therapy," Randi confided. "But I think therapy is gonna help me deal with some other issues that medication can't really help with, so I'm gonna keep talking things through with Kelly and doing all the homework assignments she gives me, so I can live my best life."

"Awesome!" Kay exclaimed loudly, not quite shouting. "I'm so happy for you that you've found someone to talk to that you think will help you that way. I'm not going to ask any specifics about what you want to work through, because I hated it when people asked me about the sessions I did after my divorce. But I'm here for you if you ever wanna talk about it or need an assistant for any of your homework."

"Thanks, Sis." Randi was relieved to not have to get into details with Kay just yet. "My homework this week is to talk to a stuffed animal or to myself in a mirror, but I might give you a call if I work up to talking about my feelings with an actual person for my homework."

"Oh, I did that one back when I was in therapy," Kay giggled. "Only instead of a stuffed animal or myself in a mirror or even an actual person, I yelled at a picture of Mark to get out all my anger. It really helped."

"Mine isn't really about getting out anger, though," Randi admitted sheepishly. "It's more about being able to be myself and being able to tell people things I know they aren't gonna like hearing. Apparently, my fight or flight response is broken, and I freeze instead, so Kelly thinks that if I practice staying to fight when I'm afraid of an argument, then maybe eventually I won't freeze up and just do whatever I think other people expect me to do, instead of doing what I really wanna do in life."

"Oh…" Kay trailed off, drawing the word out to three or four syllables.

Randi wondered what her sister meant by the drawn-out word and waited for her to open up and ask whatever she really wanted to know. They sat there in quiet contemplation for a few minutes before Kay finally broke the silence.

"Is that what you did last night with James?" Kay's tone of voice was soft, alerting Randi to her wariness about asking the question.

"No, it's what I did with Daddy last night," Randi sighed. "I actually felt safe enough to have a normal fight and flight response with James, which is why we argued, and then I turned off my phone when I couldn't fight with him anymore."

"Oh-kay?" Kay elongated the word like it was a question. "That almost sounds like a good thing, feeling safe with him, I mean."

"Yeah, my therapist thought so, too," Randi confirmed, confused by why her eyes were watering again. "But I still feel like I need more time to figure out everything I'm feeling before I can explain it to him."

"I can definitely understand that." Kay sounded a little more upbeat than her last tentative statement. "But would it be okay with you if I told James that I talked to you, so he can maybe get a little more sleep tonight and not look like a zombie again tomorrow. I mean, I know tomorrow's Halloween, but I don't think he's planning to dress as a zombie for the party."

"Zombie James Bond would be too weird." Randi giggled at the mental image. "Yeah, you can tell him we talked. You can even tell him what we talked about if it keeps him from looking like a zombie any longer. But make sure he knows that it might be a few days before I'm ready to explain everything to him, so he doesn't worry or blow up my phone before I'm ready to talk to him."

"I will," Kay practically whispered. "In fact, I'll go see if I can find him now, so that maybe he'll be able to quit worrying about you a little bit and actually look more focused on what he's doing before he has to wrestle on the show tonight. The poor guy looked like he could barely put one foot in front of the other to walk off the plane this morning. He told me he didn't get much sleep and what little he did was broken up by nightmares about you."

"Yeah, definitely go talk to him right now," Randi commanded her sister, hating that she caused James's nightmares and needed to have Kay make things better for him while she couldn't. "I don't want him to risk getting injured in the ring because he's worried about me. Make sure he knows that I just need a little time to work on some issues on my own, but I'm most definitely not breaking up with him. We're not even on a break like Ross and Rachel, got it?"

"Yeah, I got it," Kay giggled. "Now, you go home so you can watch him on TV. And I'll go talk to him, so he can put on a good show for you tonight."

"Thanks, bye, Sis." Randi felt even better than she had after first leaving the therapist's office as her call with her sister ended.

"Bye, Sis," Kay replied before they both hung up their phones.

Randi put her phone back in her purse before putting on her seatbelt and starting her car to head for home.

~~~

James was just finishing up a third run through of the choreography for his match that night when he saw Kay running down the ramp from the stage to the ring out of the corner of his eye. Distracted by how fast her short legs were moving, even though she was wearing a pencil skirt and heels, he missed his cue and got clocked in the side of the head by Dion's elbow when he wasn't in the correct position to set
~~~

them up for a suplex. Thankfully, he only staggered from having his bell rung and wasn't knocked out by the blow to the temple.

"Fuck," James yelled, covering the side of his head, where he'd taken the hit, with his hand.

"Sorry, man," Dion started to apologize, but James cut him off from trying to take the blame for the botched move.

"No, that's all on me." James shook his head at his friend. "I got distracted and didn't get into the right position. Give me a minute for the bell to quit ringing between my ears and we'll try it again."

"We'll take more than a minute," Dion demanded, sitting on the second rope, and lifting the top rope to spread them apart for James to go through as he got out of the ring. "You need to go check in with Doc to make sure you don't have a concussion before we go again."

"I don't have a concussion," James told Dion as they both hopped down from the ring apron to the floor of the arena, where Kay was now standing and looking up at him with concern. "I just need to talk to Anthony's bride-to-be for a minute and then I'll be good to go."

"You do that, and I'll go get Doc." Dion's eye roll was implied as he started walking up the ramp to go find the athletic trainer they all called Doc. "It's better to be safe than sorry."

"You talked to Randi?" James directed his gaze at Kay, noticing the phone in her hand for the first time.

"Yes," Kay confirmed, still looking at him like she was worried. "Do you need to sit down or something? That looked like a bad blow."

"Naw, I'm fine," James drawled, hoping to reassure her with a small smile. "My head's a lot harder than Dion's elbow. I'm more concerned about Randi right now."

"Randi's fine," Kay asserted, finally returning his small smile with a slight upturn of the corners of her lips. "She turned her phone off last night and didn't turn it back on until a few minutes ago."

Thank fuck! James mentally exclaimed, elated that he could go get his phone out of his locker to text her again.

"But she needs you to give her a little time to do her therapy homework before she'll be ready to talk to you about everything." Kay's words stopped James in his tracks, but at least her expression appeared apologetic as she told him not to call or text Randi until Randi called or texted him first.

James wasn't sure if he could really hold himself back from reaching out to Randi like Kay was advising him. But after she explained about Randi talking through the events of the day before with her therapist, and that the therapist thought that her being able to have a proper fight or flight response with him when she just froze with her dad was because Randi knew, even if only subconsciously, that she was safe and secure in her relationship with James, he knew he would do whatever he could to keep her feeling safe and secure with him. Even giving her the time and space she needed, no matter how bad he wanted to hear her voice, so he could feel better.

"How long do you think she's gonna need?" James was hopeful it wouldn't be too long.

"I'm not sure," Kay sighed, the worried expression back on her face. "Hopefully, it won't be more than a day or two of talking to a teddy bear before she's ready to talk it all out with you."

"Talking to a teddy bear?" James's eyebrows drew together, showing how confused he was by Kay's statement.

"Yeah, that's her therapy homework," Kay giggled. "My therapist had me do something similar, only I yelled at a picture of my ex-husband, so I could get out all my anger at him. But Randi's therapist has her practicing what she's been too afraid to say to people with a stuffed animal. I think it's supposed to help her not be so afraid of getting a negative reaction when she's sharing something she feels vulnerable about, so she can eventually feel confident enough to stand up for herself to our parents. But I have a feeling she's also going to be practicing what she wants to say to you for the next couple of days, too."

"Okay, that makes more sense now." James wondered if she had a specific stuffed animal she had to use. "Does she already have a teddy bear that she's supposed to use for this homework?"

"I don't know if she still has any of her stuffed animals from when she was a kid or not," Kay shrugged. "But I'm sure she'll figure something out, even if she has to stop at the store on the way home from the therapist's office to get one."

"Would it be overstepping to send her one of my Slammin' Superstars?" James imagined Randi cuddling the stuffed version of his wrestling persona since he couldn't be there for her to cuddle at night.

"Are those the action figures I've seen at the merchandise tables around the arena?" Kay tilted her head like she was thinking.

"No, but I could send her one of those too," James grinned. *I'll send her a box full of every t-shirt and toy with my face on it, if it will get her to talk to me again sooner rather than later.* "The Slammin' Superstars are two-foot-tall stuffed wrestler shaped toys. I figured if she needs a stuffed animal, why not a stuffed James Dangerous?"

"I think she'd love that," Kay lightly chuckled.

"You don't think it would be too pushy?" James wanted to make sure he didn't overstep Randi's boundaries again. "To send it now instead of waiting for her to get back in contact with me first, I mean. 'Cause I don't wanna give her a reason to not wanna talk to me again."

"No, I don't think that's too pushy," Kay grinned up at him. "And it's not that she doesn't want to talk to you now. She's just trying to work through a lot of stuff in her head right now and wants to make sure she's got it at least partially figured out for herself before she shares everything with you. But she gave me specific instructions to make sure that you know that just because she needs a few days to herself, she's not breaking up with you. Ya'll aren't on a break like that couple on the old TV show **Friends** either. She still considers you to be together. I'm guessing she meant that as a couple, but she didn't clarify what labels ya'll might have for yourselves."

James couldn't contain the grin that spread across his face. They hadn't really labeled anything about their relationship, but he was glad that it sounded like they were on the same page as considering themselves a couple.

"Thanks, Kay." James leaned down and gave her a one-armed hug to show his appreciation. "Now, why don't you help me pick out the right size t-shirts to send her with the toys?"

"You're going to send her a whole bunch of James Dangerous merchandise, aren't you?" Kay returned his one-armed hug.

"Yeah, I was thinking one of everything with me on it," James admitted as they started walking up the ramp toward the backstage area.

"She wears a medium t-shirt, but prefers an extra-large to sleep in," Kay informed him. "But I'm not going to help you pick out everything because I have to get back to the classroom where I left

Anthony with all the kids, who are too hyped up about Halloween tomorrow and are probably driving him up a wall."

"Yeah, go rescue Anthony," James chuckled as they parted ways backstage.

Before he could make it out to the merchandise table to get everything to send to Randi, Dion and Doc caught up with him.

"I told you I'm fine," James argued as they walked up to him.

"I'll be the judge of that." Doc pointed toward the trainer's room. "After a quick exam to make sure you don't have a concussion."

James begrudgingly went to the trainer's room and hopped up on a massage table, so Doc could give him an exam that wasn't as quick as James would have preferred. In addition to examining the knot on the side of James's head, he shined a light in his eyes, had him follow his finger with his eyes, and asked him several questions to determine his cognitive state. Since the only symptom he was having was discomfort when the area around his temple was touched, and he wasn't having any visual or cognitive issues, Doc deemed him to not have a concussion without him having to do an ImPACT test, so James considered himself lucky to at least be allowed to skip that.

As soon as he left the trainer's room, he went straight to the merchandise table and got everything he wanted to send to Randi. He decided to go with two of each t-shirt design, one in a medium that she could wear with her jeans during the day and one in an extra-large that she could sleep in at night. He really liked the idea of her wearing his image to sleep, even if most of the shirts also had his brother on them. The jersey style shirt and "property of" shirt both just had his name on them, though, so he hoped she'd like and wear them the most.

He snagged one of the empty boxes from behind the merchandise table to box it all up. Then he found a member of the arena staff to direct him to the office where he could get a piece of paper to write her a note that he put in the box and someone to help him actually get the box shipped. After a trip back down to his locker to get his phone, so he had her address, and his wallet, so he could pay for the postage, the office clerk walked him over to their mail room, where he was able to get it sent off to Randi.

By the time he got all that done, he didn't have a chance to do another run through of the match with Dion. So, they talked it through while eating dinner in catering instead, with James reassuring Dion repeatedly that he wouldn't be distracted again when they were performing in front of the audience.

To keep from giving in to his intense urge to text Randi, James put his phone back in his locker when he changed into his ring gear for the show. His thumbs still felt twitchy to text her while he was watching the rest of the show on the backstage monitors, but he was able to hold himself back from actually doing it the rest of the night.

His singles match against Dion went off without a hitch, including a perfect transition from Dion putting James in a front facelock to James applying his own front facelock on Dion and converting it into a vertical suplex, right before James covered Dion for the pin. It was a pretty common sequence of moves, so James was still mentally kicking himself for botching it in rehearsals.

Instead of going back to the hotel and being tempted to call Randi, James went out to eat with the guys after the show. While part of him had missed the comradery of hanging out with his brother and friends after the shows since he'd started spending his nights in his room talking with Randi, sitting there listening to them rib him for the rookie mistake wasn't nearly as much fun as their normal nights out had been.

It all just made him miss Randi even more. So, when the rest of the guys left the diner to go to a club, probably to pick up a ring rat for the night (well, all of them but Dean since he'd developed a huge crush on the newest woman on the GWA roster), James went back to his hotel room and looked through the pictures of Randi he'd saved on his phone and the screen captures he'd taken from their Skype sessions on his laptop.

Even though he was as hard as a rock from looking at the racier pictures and sexual screen captures, he refused to jack off to her image on the screens when she wasn't actively participating on the other end of a Skype session. He doubted she would be masturbating to thoughts of him while she was working through her feelings, so he would abstain as well. He would probably be taking a few extra cold showers until she was ready to have another mutual masturbation session on Skype, but he didn't want to feel any kind of sexual pleasure without her. Not even just a little self-pleasure to release the pressure of excessive sperm production in his balls.

Damn, I hope she figures shit out soon, James mused as he stripped off his clothes to get in the first of those cold showers before going to bed. *My balls are gonna be as blue as my tux for Anthony's wedding, if I have to take too many of these ice-cold showers. I guess they'll be doubly blue, first from no fun times with Randi and then from trying to freeze them off in the shower.*

<div align="center">~~~</div>

Once Randi got home, she changed into a sports bra and workout shorts and pulled her hair up into a high ponytail. She pulled up her favorite spinning playlist on her phone before hopping on her indoor bike to work off some of her excess energy, since she'd mostly been a sloth all day.

After an hour of sweating it out with a mix of speed and hill climbing intervals, she got a quick shower. She put on her favorite soft flannel sleep pants with a crazy print of all different kinds of candy on them and a yellow oversized t-shirt. She reheated a bowl of chili in the microwave before settling on the sofa in the living room to watch James wrestle.

Amy joined her in watching the GWA's weekly television show, opting for a snack of popcorn, since she'd already eaten dinner while Randi was working out. As they watched the show, they speculated about which of the wrestlers would be at the wedding. They tried to figure out who Kay had told her was married and who was single, but they weren't sure they were right, since the wrestlers didn't all use their real names as even a part of their ring names, like James and Dean Dangerous.

"Even if my top pick is married, I'm still looking forward to meeting them all at the wedding," Amy confided between bites of popcorn. "And we know James's brother is single and he's my third top pick, so I'm okay with dancing with him at the wedding."

"Who are your other top picks?" Randi had no clue who her friend might be attracted to, since Amy hadn't mentioned anyone in particular as hoping he wasn't married.

"Surfer Josh is number one," Amy grinned, wiggling her eyebrows suggestively. "I really wanna know if he has tan lines under that speedo."

"Yeah, I think he's single," Randi grinned back at her bestie. "He was one of the guys who ate with James when they were in Tulsa, and I think all six of them were single."

"AAAAAWWWWWW!" Amy screamed into the throw pillow she picked up from her side of the couch. "I really hope he comes to the wedding then."

"Who's number two?" Randi was curious about who else outranked James's almost identical twin.

"Red," Amy replied with a dreamy look on her face.

"Yeah, I can pretty much guarantee Red doesn't have tan lines," Randi giggled. "I bet he's pasty white everywhere."

"Probably, bot dat sexy accent makes oehp fahr all 'is paleness and red 'air." Amy tried to mimic Red's Irish accent.

"I'm pretty sure he's single too, since he was also at the table with James when I waited on them at the Camelot. I'll ask Kay about them to be sure and maybe even figure out what their real names are for you before the wedding."

"Yeah, like I won't be too nervous to actually talk to them and completely forget their names, my name, and how to make words come out of my mouth when I'm actually in the same room with them," Amy scoffed with a self-deprecating laugh.

"Naw, you won't have to worry about that," Randi waved off Amy's nerves, laughing along with her friend. "Those guys were all over the top flirts, so I'm sure it won't matter if you can't speak, they'll still be flirting with you like crazy at the wedding. I just hope they don't end up fighting with all those hot Burleson boys Hazel and Susan sent pictures of in our group chat over who gets to dance with you."

"Oh, maybe I should just stick to the Burleson boys, so the Burleson girls have their choice of wrestlers?" Amy giggled.

"Naw, I'll just tell James to make sure they set up the ring somewhere close by, so we can just send them all there to fight over you," Randi suggested, enjoying a girl's night in with her best friend.

Overall, it was a better night than the night before. At least, until she saw the beginning of a black eye on James as he walked to the ring for his match on the live television show.

What the fudge? Randi covered her mouth with her hand in surprise at his appearance. She wanted to call him immediately to ask him what had happened but knew she couldn't since he was currently in the ring. *Plus, I'm not quite ready to talk to him about everything yet.* Instead, she grabbed her phone and sent her sister a text message.

Randi: Why does James have a black eye?

Kay: He took an elbow to the temple during rehearsals just before I talked to him.

Randi: But he's okay?

Kay: Yeah, he had to be cleared by the trainer before they'd let him back in the ring. No concussion, just a goose egg & a little bruising.

Randi: K, how'd the talk go?

Kay: Good, I relayed everything you wanted me to tell him. He's gonna wait to hear from you whenever you're ready to talk.

Randi: Thanks, Sis! {Smiling Face with Open Hands Emoji}

Relieved that James wasn't hurt, she put her phone back down on the coffee table in front of her and went back to watching him perform in the ring on her television. She still had to figure out what she wanted to say to him before she could reach out to him again, but she didn't think it would take her too long to do that. She'd get started by talking to one of the many pictures of him she'd saved on her phone or laptop as soon as the GWA show was over that night.

Chapter Eight

Randi had spent the rest of the previous week contemplating all the things she wanted to say to the various people in her life, planning for how to do her therapy homework more than actually doing it. Well, she thought about it when she couldn't find another way to distract herself anyway.

When she got off work on Wednesday at three in the afternoon, she went to a discount store to pick up a stuffed animal to use since she didn't have any from when she was a kid, having passed them on to her nieces years ago. But instead of immediately starting to try to sit and talk to the teddy bear when she got home, she did another workout before piddling around in the kitchen trying to figure out what she wanted to bake for a sweet snack.

When she couldn't find all the ingredients for either cookies or brownies in the pantry and fridge, she went to bed early instead. She got up Thursday morning and went to the store for the supplies and made a batch of chocolate chip cookies before going to trudge through the evening shift at work.

Friday morning, she ate cookies for breakfast while searching for jobs online. Then she worked from eleven in the morning to seven in the evening, focusing on her customers instead of her own issues. When she got home that night, she found the box James had sent her waiting on her bed, where Amy had carried it in for her. She opened the package to find a note on top of the box full of t-shirts and toys.

Angel,

Kay told me about your homework, and I thought these things might help you get through it. A stuffed version of me for you to talk to and the action figures of both me and Dean, so if you need to yell you can yell at his action figure instead of mine. Just please don't use them like voodoo dolls because we can't wrestle with broken bones.

I also put in every shirt I could find with my picture or name on it, so you have options to pick from to wear while doing your homework. I hope you'll wear them like armor, knowing that I'm on your side and will have your back if you need me standing behind you as you fight your battles. Or in the case of the oversized ones that I hope you'll sleep in, pretend they're me holding you while you rest.

I'm not trying to push past your boundaries, so I hope sending these things hasn't. But I do want you to know that I'm here for you whenever you're ready for me.

Love,

James

Randi cried for over an hour that night at his thoughtful words and gifts. She'd picked up her phone and started to call or text him at least two dozen times a day since then, but she'd chickened out on actually calling or texting him. She'd deleted every single message she started to send him because she didn't want to confuse him with her disjointed ramblings of all the things running through her head. And she didn't want to call him until she had some idea of what she was actually going to say when they spoke, so she didn't make things worse between them.

She'd tried to talk to the stuffed version of him over the weekend, but she felt silly doing it. So, she couldn't actually get everything she was thinking and feeling to come out sounding like coherent statements.

She wanted him to understand just how much she'd strayed from her normal life with him already. How it normally took six weeks or longer before she would feel comfortable enough with a date to even talk about the possibility of the relationship turning sexual. How the connection she felt between them that first night was such an anomaly for her. How even though she struggled to make herself say the dirty words, she couldn't stop herself from expressing her physical attraction to him and acting on her sexual desires with him.

She wanted to tell him about how off kilter it made her feel that they started their relationship at warp speed, but she was afraid that if she said that then he'd think she wanted him to slow things down. While she needed a break to figure out how to tell him everything she was thinking and feeling, she didn't think she really wanted to slow down with him.

If anything, she wanted to rush through fixing her anxiety issues, growing a backbone to be able to be her true self with her family, and training to become a professional wrestler, so she could travel with him twenty-four-seven and speed up their relationship even more. But she didn't want to come off as crazy clingy to him by telling him all that either.

Her experience might be somewhat limited, but she knew that most guys were turned off by clingy women. She didn't want James to know just how sticky she was feeling because she didn't want to take the chance of running him off.

She'd gotten to where she was so lost in her head worried about it, that even working the Monday morning breakfast shift, when she had more customers than she'd had in weeks, wasn't enough to distract her from her thoughts about James. So, when she took her thirty-minute lunch break at eleven, she pulled her phone out of her locker and opened a notes app to try to type out her thoughts, so she could arrange them in a more comprehensive way when she got home that afternoon.

She hoped to be able to come up with a script for what she should say to be able to call him.

About an hour after she got back on the floor from her lunch break, her family showed up for lunch. *Figures, I'd only get to see Kay with Mom, Daddy, Anthony, Tia, and Maria with her, and while I'm working with the boss watching like a hawk, so I can't ask her advice on what to say to James.*

After greetings were exchanged and Randi explained that she'd already taken her lunch break and couldn't eat with them, she noticed Kay smiled and waved at Mr. Brooks like they were old friends instead of former boss and employee.

"Stop, you're gonna get me fired too," Randi whispered as she grabbed Kay's hand and stopped her from continuing to wave.

"I wasn't fired from here," Kay denied without bothering to lower her voice. "I quit when he said I couldn't use my vacation time for a family emergency."

"That's not what he's telling everyone here." Randi leaned in so that only Kay could hear her. "He's telling everyone that you were fired when you didn't show up to work your normal shift without notifying him in advance, so he didn't have anyone in to replace you."

"Well, he's full of bull," Kay shrieked, obviously not realizing that the whole restaurant could hear her and that her statements were going to cause Randi more problems on the job. "I called him on Friday night and told him that I needed to use my vacation time, starting the following Monday for a family emergency. He told me that I couldn't use my vacation time, so I quit. He had the whole weekend to find someone to work when he knew I wouldn't be there."

"Baby," Anthony growly whispered, trying to get Kay's attention to shift to him from her anger at her former boss. "What do you recommend we order?"

"Anything you want, it's all good," Kay replied before turning back to Randi.

"I think he was trying to get you to focus on something else and quit making a scene, so I can keep my job," Randi pointed out, keeping her voice soft.

"Sorry, Sis, I wasn't thinking," Kay apologized, finally lowering her voice. "I just wanted to come here for lunch, so we could update you on court this morning. I didn't mean to make work difficult for you."

"Oh, yes, I need the scoop," Randi blurted, more worry filling her about the possibility of Mark wrecking Kay's happily ever after with Anthony.

"We won in court," Tia whisper-shouted, her smile beaming across the table at Randi. "Anthony's now our Dad and we don't have to see the old one ever again."

"Awesome," Randi exclaimed, feeling relieved of her momentary stress, and giving Tia a high five.

They quickly ordered their meals, so Randi wouldn't get in trouble for spending too much time at their table. But that didn't stop Mr. Brooks from pulling her aside, as she turned in their order in the kitchen, to reprimand her for causing a scene in the restaurant.

"I didn't cause a scene," Randi told her boss, raising her voice slightly, but she didn't think she was yelling like he was. "Kay almost did, but I diffused it by getting her to lower her voice and drop it."

"High-fiving the patrons at the table, where your sister was shouting disparaging remarks about me and the restaurant, isn't diffusing the situation," Mr. Brooks carped, his face turning beet red from his obvious anger.

"I didn't give my niece a high five because of what Kay was saying about you or quitting her job here," Randi defended, exasperated at having to explain her family issues to her boss. "Tia was excited about winning in court this morning and being adopted by Kay's fiancé. Believe me, nothing happy at that table had anything to do with you or the restaurant."

"Regardless of the reason, it's inappropriate to slap hands with patrons and cause a scene in the restaurant while you're working," Mr. Brooks growled. "If you can't maintain an appearance of professionalism, we might need to rethink your continued employment."

Fudgsicles! I can't lose this job until I have something else lined up to be able to pay my bills.

"I will be the utmost professional for the remainder of my time here," Randi promised, hoping it would be enough to keep her job at least for a little while longer.

"Yes, you will, or you'll be asked to leave. Now get back to work," Mr. Brooks ordered, turning on his heel to walk out of the kitchen before her.

It took all her self-control to finish out her shift without taking out all her pent-up frustrations with everything else in her life on her boss. Somehow, she maintained her professional appearance, even as she imagined pouring a pitcher of tea over his head or punching him in his smug face. Thankfully, once her family left, she only had to endure the restaurant for another hour before she was able to leave for the day.

As she walked by the schedule on the wall in the break room on her way to get her belongings from her locker to leave, she noticed that two of the four shifts she'd previously been scheduled to work that week were marked off. *So much for going back to full time this week.* Randi mentally noted the days she was no longer working.

She went straight home, showered, and changed into comfy sweats and one of the t-shirts James had sent her, before pulling up her laptop and transcribing her notes from her phone into some semblance of a script for what to say to him when they finally talked. When she thought she had it right, she tried to relax with a session of yoga to center herself before reviewing it again to make sure it was perfect.

Amy got home from work while she was sitting on the sofa reading over what she'd written for the umpteenth time. Still unsure of herself, she asked her friend's opinion, explaining how she wanted to open up to James about how she was falling for him, but she was scared by how she didn't feel their connection as strongly with them being so far apart, as she did the first night they met when their bond was palpable.

She explained about wanting to tell him that the safety she felt with him was more than just what her therapist had pointed out about her ability to have an appropriate fight or flight response with him. How she'd figured out in the past few days that the speed with which they moved to a physical relationship was because she'd felt safe with him that first day, in a way she hadn't ever felt safe with anyone else.

Randi also explained to Amy that she wanted to tell him about her hopes and dreams that she hadn't even been brave enough to type into her word processing program, where she was planning the script to talk to him, but she was afraid to be that vulnerable with anyone. If she couldn't even type out her deepest desires for fear of someone reading her dreams and ridiculing her for them, how was she ever going to be brave enough to say them out loud, much less achieve them?

"I think this is a good start." Amy pointed to the laptop that she sat on the coffee table in front of them. "But I don't think you should try to read this to him like a script. Maybe just have it open in front of you for reference, but actually have a conversation instead of reading a monologue."

"I'm just afraid that if I don't say it all at once, I won't say most of it," Randi admitted, wrapping her arms around her legs, where she'd pulled them up in front of her on the couch.

"Yeah, maybe not the first time you talk to him," Amy agreed with a sympathetic smile. "But even if you just get one point out each day, you guys will eventually talk it all out."

"Maybe I should practice saying it like my therapist recommended before I actually call him?"

"If that's what your therapist said to do, then yes, do that." Amy stood up from her position on the other side of the sofa. "I'm gonna go change and make dinner while you practice talking to James."

Randi got up off the sofa and followed Amy out of the living room, carrying her laptop and phone back to her bedroom, so she could practice her speaking points with the stuffed version of James that was laying on her bed. She giggled at the realization that she'd reverted to childhood by sleeping with the stuffed toy wrapped in her arms for the past three nights.

If the sleep shirts were his way of holding me at night, I hope he felt my arms around his voodoo doll, too.

She got situated with her laptop in front of her where she was sitting cross legged in the middle of her bed. She leaned back against the pillows keeping her propped up right next to the headboard, and held the two-foot-tall stuffed version of James in her lap. She looked down into his screen-printed fabric face as she tried to recite the monologue she'd written.

Yeah, Amy's right. That's not gonna work. I sound too stilted and fake.

She laid the toy face down across her lap, ran her fingers through her hair, fluffing it out to try and make herself feel like she was getting into character for a role. *If I think of it like I'm rehearsing for a play, maybe it'll be easier.*

When she looked down and realized that the movement of her body as she tried to shake out the nerves caused the toy to move, so it's face was over her crotch, she couldn't help but laugh. *Even the toy version of James likes oral sex! But the toy isn't nearly as good at it as the man.*

Her nerves about her therapy homework dissipated with her laughter, so she was much more relaxed as she picked up the toy and imagined only positive responses from James as she had a conversation with his stuffed mini doppelganger that she was calling "Little Jimmy."

It wasn't nearly as scary to think about actually telling him all her thoughts and feelings, when her mental version of him agreed with everything she said and was supportive of her whispered dream of traveling by his side and working in his chosen career.

What seemed like was only a few minutes, but was probably more like an hour later, Amy knocked on her bedroom door to let her know dinner was ready if she wanted to eat. Randi closed her laptop, made sure her phone was still in the pocket of her sweats, and went to the kitchen to eat with her best friend.

Amy talked briefly about work while they sat down to eat, but then switched to convincing Randi to go on another shopping trip with her the following weekend. They'd found a dress for Amy to wear to the wedding the weekend before, but now she wanted to make sure they both had new dresses that they would need for the rehearsal dinner and any other events the week of the wedding.

Knowing she couldn't budget in a bunch of new clothes at the moment, Randi redirected the conversation to discussing what they had in their closets that would work for the various activities they had planned, specifically pointing out that she had several dresses she wore to church that would work for most of the days. After planning out a schedule of what they would each wear for the nine days they would be in Texas, they finished cleaning up the kitchen after dinner and went to their separate rooms for the night.

It was only eight o'clock, so Randi knew she couldn't call James yet, as he would be at the arena working, even if he wasn't actually wrestling that night. She pulled out her phone and sent him a text message, before pulling up a new document on her laptop to start

Leah Mae Wright
typing out her thoughts about what she wanted to practice saying to
her parents.

                    Randi: Call me when you get to your hotel tonight. :)

James: It'll be after 1 a.m. your time when I get to the
           hotel tonight. You sure you want me to call & wake
           you up?

                        Randi: Where are you? City & Time Zone?

James: Reno, NV. Pacific.

                Randi: When will you be back in the Central Time Zone?

James: Going to Salt Lake City tomorrow, then Denver on
           Wednesday, both Mountain time. Thursday, Kansas
           City is Central time. Same for Friday in St. Louis and
           Saturday in Memphis. Then Eastern time for Atlanta
           on Sunday.

              Randi: It's crazy that you'll be in all four time zones in less
                            than a week. {Zany Face Emoji}

James: Now you know why I gave up wearing a watch &
           love that my cell phone changes the time for me based
           on GPS.

              Randi: Yeah, I bet all those changes would even confuse
                            an activity tracker watch.

James: Yep. So, do you still want me to call that late
           tonight? Or would you rather schedule a daytime call
           tomorrow? Or an 11 p.m. call Thursday?

**Randi: IDK Wish we could talk now while I feel ready.
Worried I might chicken out if we schedule another
day.**

**James: Then give me a minute to find someplace private
here & I'll call you now.**

Randi: I don't want to interrupt you at work.

**James: You're not interrupting, Angel. Just have to get
out of catering so the guys won't try to listen in.**

Randi didn't have a chance to type out a reply before her phone rang and James's name flashed on her phone screen.

"You're sure I'm not interrupting you at work?" Randi queried in lieu of a greeting when she answered the phone.

"Positive, Angel," James replied in his deep baritone voice that Randi almost felt vibrating in her ear more than heard. "I'm not wrestling tonight, so I don't have to sit with the guys to plan a match while eating dinner."

"Okay," Randi gave in, tentatively, feeling a few butterflies swirling around in her stomach as she realized she actually had to follow through with talking to him. "Before we discuss everything from last week, I wanna thank you for the gifts you sent me."

"You're welcome, Angel," James accepted, though his voice sounded a little clipped. "I was worried you'd be pissed that I sent them, since you hadn't let me send you any of the other things I'd suggested buying you in the past. But as soon as Kay said you needed a stuffed animal, I couldn't stop myself from sending you one."

"Yeah, well, that was mostly because I didn't want my parents to find out about you." Randi realized how bad that sounded, but she was unable to stop herself from finishing her statement. "And since that can of worms has already been opened, I'm willing to forgive you for overstepping that boundary, especially since being able to talk to a miniature version of you has helped me prepare for actually talking to you."

"I'm still sorry." James sounded a little down. "I really didn't mean to cross your boundaries. I'm just not used to being careful of them, but I promise I'll really try my best to get better at it."

"I think the reason I was fighting back about it so much was because everything is so different with you than what I'm used to from a boyfriend," Randi confided, cringing inside at using the boyfriend term, when they hadn't really labeled themselves as such. "So, I figured I should probably tell you more about just how different things are with you than with anyone I've dated in the past."

They had only briefly referred to either of their sexual histories in their past conversations, and Randi knew it was time for them to get into more detail, so he could understand where she was really coming from. She was glad that James was quietly waiting for her to direct the conversation, instead of interrupting her thinking time or trying to take over the discussion himself.

"I told you about the poetry I wrote in high school and how I didn't lose my virginity until I was twenty years old and had been in college for over two years," Randi began, willing herself not to shed a single tear as she spoke. "What I didn't tell you is that the punishment for that poetry didn't just cause me to limit my vocabulary. It made me repress my sexuality, like completely, for several years. In fact, I think I'm still repressing it some."

"Oh, Angel," James sighed, his deep voice washing over her like a hug from several states away.

"Like I said, it was the beginning of my junior year of college, and I was feeling a little bit of freedom being away from my family at OU. Leo was my assigned lab partner in biology and after a couple of weeks of working together, he asked me to lunch after class. After a month or so of going to lunch together after every biology class, we actually started going on dates at night. Movies, concerts, that kind of thing. It took another month of dating before we did more than kissing, and a couple of weeks of heavy petting before we went all the way. It was only the one time and then he backed off, no more dates, no more lunches, and he started missing class, so he wasn't even my lab partner anymore. As if I didn't already feel guilty for having sex because of my parents' opinions on sex outside of marriage, I started thinking there was something wrong with me because I'd enjoyed it, even though I was obviously bad at it, since he'd just used me to get what he wanted and then ghosted on me."

"Angel," James groaned through the phone. "He was an idiot. And you're not bad at sex."

"Thank you for saying that, but that's part of what I'm trying to tell you," Randi replied, not letting him continue interrupting her speech. "It's different with you. After that failed experiment in relationships, I spent the next couple of years where I only went on the occasional date. Like maybe one every two or three months. All first dates, and most of them not even ending with a goodbye kiss. The two that did kiss me at the end of the date, one was on the cheek and the other was on the forehead. There was no chemistry, no connection. I was twenty-three before I actually dated someone long enough to have sex again. That still took six weeks of dating to happen, and we broke up less than two weeks later. In the last two years, there have been three more guys that I've dated for at least six weeks before sleeping with them, and one that I only made wait for a month. But of all six of the guys I dated before you, only Billy thinks we were dating for more than two months. With the exception of Leo who ghosted me, I broke up with all of them, usually in the seventh or eighth week of dating, because I felt too guilty about having sex that I couldn't continue the relationship."

"Why does Billy think you dated longer then?" James interjected, interrupting her rant.

"Because he wasn't paying attention when I broke up with him." Randi giggled at the reminder of how James had taken care of her Billy problem the night they met. "Until you clarified it for him over a month after I'd broken it off. Thank you for that, too, by the way."

"No problem, Angel," James chuckled.

"My point is that you broke my pattern," Randi confessed, hoping he wouldn't take what she was about to say the wrong way. "If this were more like my normal life, we would just now be starting to talk about the relationship turning sexual and we'd break up around Thanksgiving."

"Fuck, no," James swore under his breath, but Randi still heard him.

"Don't freak out," Randi consoled, wanting to reassure him about their relationship being better than her normal. "I don't want us to follow my normal dating pattern."

"Good, because there's no way I'm letting you break up with me at Thanksgiving," James demanded gruffly. "Giving you space this last week has been tough enough, but I was able to bear it because I knew you weren't breaking things off between us. If I'd have thought that were the case, I'd have been camped out in your front yard until I convinced you to get back together."

"And I thank you again for giving me the space I needed." Randi tried to get their conversation back on track, so she could go over more of the points she'd outlined on her computer. "I've never felt as comfortable with someone as I instantly felt with you the day we met. It blindsided me, and I've struggled with how to deal with how fast things have moved between us. I needed this last week to really figure out what it all means, and where we go from here."

"And what did you figure out, Angel?" James's voice was softer than she'd ever heard it, alerting her to his trepidation at what she was about to tell him.

"That my therapist was just scratching the surface of how safe I feel with you, when she explained that I felt safe enough in our relationship to fight with you last week," Randi replied, her voice quivering a little as she admitted to her vulnerability with him. "The connection I felt when we first met was why I felt safe enough to share my sexual self with you from the first moment we were alone together. And even though it doesn't feel as strong when we're not in the same space, I still feel safe with you to step outside my comfort zone with our Skype sessions and intimate conversations."

"I'll always do everything I can to keep you safe, Angel," James promised reverently.

"I'm not just talking about my physical safety, ya know," Randi quipped, hoping he understood how hard this all was for her to talk about. "I trust you with my emotional safety, too."

"Um," James hummed into the phone like he was confused by her statement.

"I mean I trust you not to react badly to whatever I tell you," Randi clarified. "Like you're not gonna lecture me like my parents did or get mad at me for doing or saying something you don't agree with. Like last week when I was trying to fight with you, you just kept apologizing and trying to fix it, instead of yelling back at me or telling me how wrong I was for being upset."

"Angel, I would never…" James began, but Randi cut him off.

"I know you wouldn't. That's what I'm trying to tell you. I feel safe to be myself with you because I know you're not gonna make me feel bad for being me. That's the revelation I had this week. I should've felt that way with my parents my whole life, but I haven't. I've only partially felt that way with my sister and my best friend for the last few years, but I don't even feel safe enough with them to tell them everything about me and my hopes and dreams for the future. I've felt safe enough to share more with my therapist, but that's more because I know we have doctor-patient confidentiality than a connection with her. You're the only man I've ever felt safe enough to truly open up to, and I think the only reason I haven't completely told you everything about me is because the connection isn't as strong over the phone as it is in person."

"Then I'll quit wrestling and move to Tulsa, so we can be together in person all the time," James offered, as if that would solve all their problems.

"No," Randi exclaimed in response to his rash idea. "I don't want you to quit wrestling. I know you love your job, and I don't want you to give it up for me. I wanna try to work through my issues, so I can travel with you some of the time."

Or all the time, Randi thought but still couldn't make herself admit to him.

"Okay, I'll try to be patient and live with missing you constantly until you're ready to run away with me," James bantered, laughter apparent in his tone of voice.

They talked a few more minutes, with Randi telling him about how she was going to figure out what all she wanted to say to her parents the same way she'd figured out what to say to him. She explained that she had more to share with him, but they had plenty of time to talk about the rest of the things she wanted to tell him on their daily calls and texts. She also told him about wanting to save some of it for when they were actually together in person.

Although he'd written the L word in his note, she had no intention of saying it over the phone or even on a video chat. The first time she said it, she wanted to be in his arms.

~~~

Thursday, November 8, 2018

James felt better about his relationship with Randi than he had the previous week, even though he couldn't text with her while waiting backstage for his match that night because she was working. Their calls and texts on Tuesday and Wednesday had been almost back to normal, but he missed their sexy Skype sessions.

We'll get back to them eventually, he mentally promised himself as he watched the current match going on in the ring on the backstage monitor while seated beside his brother and a few of their friends, who also wrestled for the GWA. *But it's better for us to build our relationship on a strong foundation of friendship, than for it to be all about our sexual chemistry.*

He thought back over their conversations for the past couple of days, remembering her telling him more about her therapy sessions, and how her doctor had adjusted her medication to help her with her fear of flying. She'd admitted to being intrigued by the possibility of working with the GWA, so they could be together all the time. But she'd also admitted to thinking that, even if the medication helped her to be able to handle the daily flights, she wasn't sure she was qualified for any possible job openings the GWA might have available.

Maybe I can ask Rick what job openings there are and talk her into feeling qualified enough to interview with him?

As much as he wanted her to just travel with him as his girlfriend, and eventually his wife, letting him take care of her instead of Randi having to work, James knew that Randi was too independent for that to ever be a possibility. He tried to be as understanding as possible, realizing that she needed to work to feel like she had some control over her life because of her issues with her parents.

He didn't want to ever make her feel like he was trying to run her life like they had. They'd tried to dictate to her who she should be and
~~~

what she should do for a living, and she felt stifled by their overbearing ideals. But James liked her for who she was already and didn't want to change anything about her to be what he wanted, other than eventually changing her last name to be the same as his.

James didn't think the Lees were really bad parents, just extremely old fashioned and unyielding in their beliefs. His own parents weren't that much different in their thinking, with the exception of being more supportive of their kids in forging their own path in the world.

They'd preached abstinence until marriage to him and Dean when they were teenagers, though maybe not as strongly as Randi's parents had pushed the message. But David Hunter had also explained safe sex to his boys, and given them each a box of condoms on their sixteenth birthday to ensure they were prepared if they couldn't abstain.

When Randi had explained about part of her reasoning for not wanting to tell her parents about him being because she wanted to figure out how to make her parents like him before they met him and could see his bad boy appearance, James had told her about how his mother had reacted to her sons getting their first tattoos. Like Randi's parents, his parents had similar misconceptions about the type of people who adorned their body with art. Mandi Hunter hadn't been pleased when Dean told her over the phone that they'd been inked the first time.

She'd threatened to drag them to a doctor in San Antonio to have them lasered off, so her sons wouldn't turn into common criminals, even though they were both twenty-one and were in their junior year of college. When they came home for their Christmas break and showed her the way they'd used the tribal design on each of their left upper arms like a trellis to support the vines of flowers similar to the ones in her garden, she admitted that they weren't as bad as she'd imagined. When James pointed out the hidden names in the tattoo, where they used the flowers instead of a family tree to carry their loved ones with them wherever they might go in the world, she actually shed a tear and said she loved the artwork.

She might not have liked it as much when the one tattoo was extended to spread across his shoulders and into a full sleeve down each arm, incorporating several other symbols of things he enjoyed in life, but she didn't ever say another negative word about tattoos. At least not that James had been aware of, anyway.

Maybe when we're all in Texas for the wedding, Mom can talk to them about my tattoos and convince them I'm not a thug like Mr. Lee currently believes.

Or maybe Randi would figure out how to talk to her parents before then, and she could convince them he wasn't a bad guy, so they could spend more time together without having to sneak around, like he currently expected to have to do to see her the week of the wedding.

James was jolted out of his thoughts by a production assistant notifying him and Dean that they were next up in the ring. They were wrestling the new guys again that night, now that the Bama Boys were officially on the GWA roster. It wasn't a title match or even part of an ongoing feud for the storyline. Mason and Noah (who used the ring name Dixon) had been hired to expand the tag-team division and were rotating through wrestling with every other tag team in the company, so Rick could assess who they worked with best to develop their storylines for the following year. And even though the Dangerous Twins were currently in an ongoing feud with Dark Chocolate and Red (who in James's opinion really needed to come up with a tag-team name), they couldn't wrestle their biggest rivals every night or the fans would get bored before the end of the feud.

James really liked having new talent to work with, especially when they were as talented in the ring as the Bama Boys. While he thought their southern redneck gimmick was a bit too stereotypical to be taken seriously, it wasn't any worse than the biker gimmick he and his brother used, especially since they'd never been in a biker gang, so they were pretty much hypocritical, too.

Their match went off without a hitch, much like the one a few weeks before when they wrestled one another for the Bama Boys tryout match. After Dean pinned Dixon for the win, the Twins played up their heel personas by getting in some extra kicks while the referee's back was turned, and then taunted them as Dixon was helped backstage by Mason and the babyface wrestler, Tank, who ran in to save them from the Dangerous Twins' shady tactics.

As soon as they were back through the curtain to the backstage area, Rick gave them a nod of approval for their performance. James contemplated asking Rick about possible jobs for Randi with the GWA right then, but he knew his boss was still occupied with the rest of the show, since he was standing with the guys who were about to go out for the main event of the night.

James went to the locker room, took a shower, and changed into his light gray suit and white button-down shirt, opting to actually wear the suit coat since the temperature outside was in the low fifties. It wasn't quite cold enough for him to need a real coat, but James was starting to wish he'd kept some of the heavier winter suits he'd bought the previous month, instead of sending them to Texas for him to pick up on his Thanksgiving break.

The lighter weight summer suits he had with him weren't quite warm enough for the late-night trips from the arena to the hotel when the temperature started to dip lower. Not to mention the fact that the heavier shirts he bought with the new suits required cufflinks, and James had left his only pair of cufflinks at home when he'd switched to the lighter weight summer clothes last spring. He probably should have packed them and his heavy dress coat when he was home over the Labor Day break, but his hot-blooded nature had him feeling like it was too early during a late summer heat wave in Texas at the beginning of September.

He finished packing up his gear and was carrying everything out to the rental SUV with his brother, just as the final match of the night concluded. After storing their bags in the back of the vehicle, they walked back into the arena to see who all wanted to go for a late meal after the show.

While Dean walked back toward the locker room to talk to the other wrestlers, James made his way to Rick's temporary office space, where he was packing up his own gear to leave the arena for the night. It seemed to James like it might be the only time he could catch the boss, when he wasn't focused on twelve other tasks that day to be able to ask him about any job openings in the company.

"Hey, Boss," James got Rick's attention as he leaned against the doorway. He would've attempted to help Rick pack up but figured he'd be more in the way than actually helpful, since he didn't know Rick's usual system for organizing everything he carried around to every show.

"Hey, James, what's up?" Rick glanced up from the cord he was winding up only briefly to look at James.

"I just wanted to ask if there are any jobs you have open in the company." James felt oddly nervous about asking. "Not talent, but like personal assistant or someone to handle our social media or something like that?"

"Is this for someone in particular?" Rick put the cord into the side pocket of a messenger bag.

"Yeah, my, um, girlfriend," James sputtered, trying to keep a straight face while cursing himself in his head for using that term when he and Randi hadn't officially claimed those labels. "She's also Kay's sister, but she has issues with flying, so I don't think she'd wanna apply for the other flight attendant job."

"If she has issues with flying, how is she going to travel with us to do any other job?" Rick finished putting everything he needed to in the messenger bag and zipped it closed.

Shit, should I tell him about the meds she's trying to be able to fly? No, I can't disclose any of her medical stuff without her permission. Fuck!

"I think she's just a little too uncomfortable to try to work while in the air," James fibbed with a shrug, trying to portray the issue as less of a problem than it really was. "I haven't ever flown with her to know for sure, but I think she'll be fine, as long as I hold her hand during take-off and landing and if we hit any turbulence."

"I already have the camera crew sending pics to the team in New York for everyone's social media profiles." Rick picked up his stuff and started to walk out of the office area. "Does she have any teaching experience? We definitely need another teacher or two."

"Not that I know of." James shook his head, following his boss toward the exit where the rest of the crew congregated before leaving. "She's been working as a waitress at the same place where Kay worked before, and after Kay quit, her boss has been cutting her hours, like he's punishing Randi for Kay leaving. She's been applying to personal assistant and receptionist jobs for the last couple of weeks, but she's not having any luck getting called back for an interview."

"Kay's sister, huh?" Rick gave James a questioning look, stopping about twenty feet away from the rest of the crew. "I take it you're pretty serious about her, if you want her to work with us, so she can travel with you all the time."

"Well, I'm not planning a double wedding or anything," James denied sheepishly. "But I can see walking down the aisle with her in the next year or so."

"And like her sister, she's determined to pay her own way, and won't let you just swoop her out of her normal life and provide for her every want and need." Rick said it as a statement, not a question, but James nodded his head in agreement anyway.

"Alright, we can always use another production assistant or showrunner." Rick slapped his hand on James's shoulder. "When can she meet up with us to get started?"

"You mean when can we set up an interview?" James hoped Rick would understand the implication behind his question, knowing Randi wouldn't accept a job being handed to her without her even applying for it. "Or maybe when can she send you a résumé to apply on her own? I don't think she'll accept a job she doesn't think she got on her own merit without even applying or interviewing for it."

"Sure, we'll go with that," Rick chuckled. "Just give her my email address and tell her to send a résumé via email to apply for the production assistant position. I'll be watching for her name in my email. How does she spell it?"

"Randi, R-A-N-D-I, last name is Lee, same as Kay's," James answered his boss.

"Got it." Rick started walking toward the exit of the building again. "Oh, and make sure she knows to send it to me soon enough that I can schedule her *interview* while we're all in town for the wedding." The way Rick put special emphasis on the word "interview" gave James the impression that it would be just as staged as the wrestling matches in the GWA ring.

"Will do, thanks Boss." James smiled as they parted ways.

He caught up with his brother to go eat at a local diner with a few of the guys. As he sat there eating, he thought through how best to present the job opportunity to Randi. He couldn't call her until he finished eating and went back to his room at the hotel. But he knew it would probably take more than a single conversation to convince her to apply for the job, so he decided to go ahead and text her about it while he hung out with his fellow wrestlers, and would follow up later with their phone calls and more texts in the coming days.

> James: Have a job lead for you, GWA Production Assistant.

> Randi: As in television production? I'm not qualified for that. :(

> James: You wouldn't be producing the TV show. It's more of a go between from the writers & TV people to the talent, making sure we're ready to go on when it's time or that any props we need are in place, maybe fetching coffee or helping set up the merchandise tables, that kind of thing.

> Randi: Oh, okay, maybe I can do that once I'm sure I can fly without freaking out.

> James: You can definitely do it, Angel. Just email your résumé to Rick.Robertson@galacticwrestlingassociation.com with Production Assistant Job in the subject line. If you feel good enough about your flight down to the wedding, you can probably do an interview that week.

> Randi: Yeah, I think I'd rather bring a résumé with me & make sure I'm okay flying before I actually apply for the job.

Fuck! James silently cursed when he read Randi's response. *I don't wanna pressure her into anything she doesn't wanna do. But, fuck, I'm desperate enough to have her with me all the time that I'm not sure I'm gonna be able to stop myself from pushing beyond her boundaries again.*

Instead of risking pushing any further that night, he opted to change the subject with his next text.

> James: Since we're in the same time zone, can I call you in an hour when I get to my hotel room?

**Randi: Yeah, I just left work. Been texting from the
parking lot. An hour will give me time to get home &
changed out of my uniform. ;) {Bathtub Emoji}**

**James: Drive safe, Angel. Talk to you soon. {Smiling Face
with Heart Eyes Emoji}**

James pocketed his phone and dug into his meal. He wasn't sure
how he carried on a conversation with his brother and friends, when all
he could think about was how much of a chance he had at getting
Randi to repeat their video call while she was in her bathtub again.

Chapter Nine

Randi sat in her living room with her laptop in front of her on the coffee table, doing yet another online job search. She'd managed to cover her half of the rent and utilities for the month, even with her reduced hours at work, but she hadn't been able to add to her savings any, like she had in previous months. She'd also convinced Amy that she had more than enough dresses to wear to the various wedding events, so she hadn't had to dip into her savings account to get any more when they went shopping over the weekend.

But after the latest argument with her boss, when he tried to schedule her to work on the weekend, when she was supposed to be on an airplane to Texas, she no longer had a job to be able to cover her expenses. She needed to find a job fast if she didn't want to have to dip into her savings to cover her rent and utilities for December.

She still couldn't believe that Paul Brooks had ignored the vacation request that she'd put in almost a month in advance. It was bad enough that he'd cut her hours to punish her for Kay not giving him much notice about needing time off, but him firing her for wanting to use her vacation time, when she gave him a couple of days shy of a full month's notice, was ridiculous. Regardless of his idiocy, she'd worked her final shift at the Camelot Hotel restaurant, so she absolutely had to find another job as soon as possible.

She wasn't sure how much good it would do to send out résumés when she wouldn't be in town to go on interviews the next week, but she was still diligently searching for places to apply for work, even if she was only sending them to local Tulsa companies for the time being. James had been trying to convince her to apply for a production

204

assistant job with the GWA for the last week, but she just wasn't sure she could do it yet.

It wasn't that she lacked the ability to do the job. Not only had James given her a more thorough job description that made it sound like an easy job that would have her actively running all over the arena every night, but she'd also done a little internet research on the job description and thought it sounded right up her alley. The salary range she'd seen online was enticing as well. Even the lowest salary she'd seen online for production assistants was twice what she made as a waitress, and the highest was more than triple.

She just didn't want to apply for the job, only to then find out her medication wasn't enough to be able to fly without freaking out, making her have to withdraw her application. She knew if she did that, then even if she was able to finally find the right dosage of medication to be able to fly without fear, the negative first impression of withdrawing her application would prevent her from ever getting a job with the GWA in the future. And she wanted to work with James in the GWA way too much to take that risk.

Her doctor had already made two adjustments to her medication, trying to get her anxiety under control. She'd started out with the lowest dose, seven-and-a-half milligrams once a day. When Randi messaged her on October thirtieth, after only a week, Dr. McShane had her stay there for another week to see if Randi would have better results as it built up in her system some. When there was no more improvement the second week, when she messaged her on November sixth, Dr. McShane had increased her dosage to ten milligrams once a day.

Randi reported in again on Tuesday the thirteenth that she was no longer feeling even the slightest bit of anxiety when she thought about James, Kay, or her nieces being on a plane at the moment she was thinking of them, but she was still anxious about actually getting on a plane herself. Instead of going up to the next dosage size of pill once a day like Randi expected, Dr. McShane told her to go back to the seven-and-a-half-milligram pills, but take them twice a day instead of only once.

Randi was glad that she'd gotten another prescription called in that day, so she was able to get them picked up before she lost her job, since she wasn't sure how long her insurance would still be in effect, since it was provided by her workplace. With what was left of her first prescription and the new prescription, she had about five weeks' worth of medication if this dosage proved to be the most effective. And if she needed to go back to the ten-milligram dosage, but twice a day like she was taking the lower dose now, then she had a couple of weeks of those left over, too, if it took a while to get on a new health insurance plan through whatever new job she acquired.

As she thought about possibly needing them while she was in Texas, Randi decided to pack all of her medication bottles to take on her trip. She would take the ten milligram pills in case the doctor increased it again when she reported in on Tuesday about how her flight went over the weekend. And she would take all of the lowest dose pills in the hope that the new dosage schedule would be effective enough for her to actually apply for the GWA production assistant position.

If she emailed her résumé as soon as she got to the Burleson Ranch in Heart's Destiny on Saturday, then maybe she could interview with whoever was in charge of hiring on Monday or Tuesday when there weren't any specific wedding events she had to attend.

It would be a dream come true if I could start work immediately, and instead of flying home with my parents on Sunday the twenty-fifth, I could fly away with James on the twenty-sixth. Maybe I should go back to practicing telling my parents that I'm in love with James and wanna run away with him to be a professional wrestler, instead of continuing looking at jobs in Tulsa.

She'd been spending at least an hour a day trying to do just that, since she'd successfully transitioned from talking to her "Little Jimmy" doll to telling James more about her past and how she wanted things to be different with him. She was still holding back on using the L word or telling him about her dream of becoming a wrestler until she saw him in person. But she still considered her practice with what to say to James as successful.

Her practice with talking to her parents wasn't progressing nearly as well, though. She was still playing a role when she saw them, trying to appear to be the woman they wanted her to be, even though it felt more than a little fake. When her dad had asked about James at church, she just shrugged it off and said she hadn't talked to him much in the last couple of weeks. While that was technically true, since she'd gone almost a week without speaking to him while she was figuring out what to say to him, they were definitely back to daily conversations in the last ten days. So, it wasn't really as honest as her parents expected her to be.

She'd had a harder time looking at James's face while trying to imagine talking to her parents, so she'd switched to the teddy bear she'd bought instead. While that was easier to get the words out as she did her therapy homework each day, it wasn't proving to be as effective at helping her feel prepared to actually speak to her parents. When she told Kelly that at her last therapy session, they decided to have her switch to talking to a picture of her parents instead to see if that would be more effective.

It was a lot harder to get the words out when she could see their faces, but she was hopeful that it would get easier. And maybe, since their photograph couldn't talk back to her, she'd eventually feel strong enough to speak her mind to them when they could respond. It was probably going to take more than the couple of days she had before seeing them for their flight to be effective, though.

Just as she was closing out the job board on her laptop and bringing up a photo of her parents to get started on her next round of practice, her phone rang, distracting her from the task. As soon as she saw her sister's name on the screen, she swiped to answer the call.

"Hey, Sis, what's up?" Randi's tone of voice was so upbeat that she almost didn't recognize it as her own voice. *Maybe my meds are helping me not stress about more than just flying?*

"Hey, you sound awfully chipper this morning," Kay greeted her with a cheerful tone of her own.

"Of course, I'm chipper. I get to see you in two days, and I can't wait!"

"Wow, even knowing you have to fly to see me?" Kay sounded a little more tentative than before.

Randi thought for a second before responding, picturing herself on the plane from Tulsa to San Antonio and realizing that she was more nervous about talking to her parents on the flight than actually flying.

"Yeah, I think Dr. McShane's last adjustment to my medication might be working wonders on my airplane anxiety," Randi giggled with excitement. *Yes! If I'm this calm on the plane Saturday, I'll definitely be able to apply for that job with the GWA!*

"That's great!" Kay shouted in Randi's ear through the phone. "Does that mean you'll let me introduce you to my boss this weekend and recommend you for the other flight attendant job?"

"Yeah, I still don't think I'll be able to work while on a plane," Randi objected with a self-deprecating chuckle. "But James told me about a production assistant job with the GWA that I'm planning to apply for if my flight to Texas goes alright on Saturday."

"Oh, really?" Kay sounded curious about something, but she didn't actually ask a question for Randi to decipher what she wanted to know. "I haven't paid that much attention to all the different people and what they do, since most of my time at the arenas is spent with the girls and their schoolwork, so I didn't know about any other jobs with the company. Tell me about the job opening."

Randi briefly outlined the job details that James had given her before going over the more detailed job description she'd looked up online. Then she told her sister about the salary range she'd seen online, telling her that even though she didn't know the actual salary the GWA paid for production assistants, she'd be happy with the lowest in the range she'd seen.

When Kay told her how much she made as a flight attendant, and her salary was at the high end of the range Randi was looking at online for production assistants, Randi became a lot more hopeful to earn a similar rate of pay. Just the thought of possibly being able to get a job that paid more than three times what she was accustomed to earning made her giddy.

After another half hour of conversation, specifically planning to go to Destiny Dresses on Saturday as soon as Randi and Deanna got into town, so they could try on their dresses and shoes in case they needed any alterations before the wedding, the sisters disconnected their call. Randi pulled up her parents' picture again and started her homework.

"Mom, Dad, I'm not going back to Tulsa with you," Randi told their picture, being optimistic and practicing for telling them she was going to work in the GWA. "I've actually got a new job with the GWA, so I'll be flying out of San Antonio with them on Monday."

She imagined her parents' shocked faces and their questions about what job she would be doing with the wrestling company.

"Well, at first, I'm going to be a production assistant," she explained in response to her imagined parental questions. "But that's just a stepping stone, a foot in the door if you will. Eventually, I want to be a professional wrestler."

"You can't be a wrestler! Those outfits are too skimpy for my daughter to wear in public!"

"You'll just get hurt because you don't know how to fight for real, much less how to fake it!"

Randi envisioned her parents yelling at her in response to her statement. She slammed her laptop shut, so she couldn't see their faces anymore.

Yeah, I don't think this is gonna be enough for me to be able to talk to them next week, Randi worried as she tried to control her breathing, where she felt like she was going to hyperventilate from the imaginary lecture that had only barely started in her mind.

Once she got her momentary panic under control, she opened her laptop again and switched over to the document she'd started, where she was compiling everything she wanted to say to her parents, and started typing out their potential arguments against her dreams. Then she started brainstorming for how she should respond to each of them, changing the font color of her responses to a pretty purple as she typed them beside their arguments, so she had a visual delineation between them to help her remember them when she wasn't looking at the document.

She made notes about how the costumes worn by the women wrestlers on television were no worse than her short cheerleading skirts from high school and college, or the bathing suits she wore to the pool, lake, or river in the summer. She typed out how wrestling checked all her boxes for what she wanted in a career.

She switched over to the internet and searched out professional wrestler salaries and was shocked to see that there was a list of earnings for the GWA performers online. Since it wasn't an official company site, she wasn't sure if it was accurate or not, but she made note of the lowest estimated salary of a half-million dollars per year and the highest estimated salary of ten-million dollars per year. She quickly shut the browser window, not wanting to look through the list of names to see exactly how much they estimated that James made each year.

As much as she could see a future with him, she didn't think she really needed to know any of the details about his financial status until such time as they had a reason to combine their accounts. She loved James for who he was as a person, not how much money he made. So, unless they eventually started talking about marriage, there was no reason for her to know those details about him.

When she started to type out her response to the argument about her possibly getting hurt, she faltered for a moment. How could she argue about the risk of injuries in professional wrestling without knowing the statistics, or if she would learn to decrease her risk of injury during training? Or if she could even manage to figure out a way to get some training in the pseudo sport?

She'd heard back from the local promotion about the training they offered, but there was no way she could afford to shell out a thousand dollars a month for the classes. She really couldn't see budgeting that when she read the rest of the email that said it would take at least a year of training before she'd be ready to work on their shows. While twelve-thousand dollars for a year of training was way less expensive and only took a quarter of the time as her college degree, wrestling training wasn't covered by scholarships and grants like university tuition.

Randi remembered James mentioning that he and his brother were going to help Anthony with training Tia to wrestle. She wondered if they had ever trained anyone before, and if their training would be enough to prepare her for working in the ring. She started a new document with questions she wanted to ask James about what she would need to do to be able to wrestle for the GWA.

> Do I need to go to a specific wrestling school, or can you train me?
>
> How long will the training take to get me ring ready?
>
> Do I need any specific gear to get started or can I just wear my normal workout clothes?
>
> Is there anything I can start doing on my own now? Or do I have to wait to train until I can go to a wrestling school or travel with you?

Instead of opening up her parents' picture again, Randi opened a picture of James on her laptop and spent the rest of her afternoon practicing talking to him about her goal of becoming a professional wrestler. She wanted to wait to ask him in person, but the more she rehearsed talking to him, the more excited she got about the possibility. She wasn't sure she'd be able to wait two more days to bring it up with him when they were both in Texas.

She decided to expend some of her overly excited energy with another good spin workout to try and keep herself from texting him all her wrestling goals and questions about how to make it happen. It took all her willpower not to mention it when he texted her that he was at the arena in Oklahoma City, preparing for his last match before his Thanksgiving break.

Instead, they each complained about only being a couple hours apart geographically and not being able to see each other, even though they were in the same state that night. If she hadn't already spent the money on her airline ticket to Texas on Saturday, she would've been tempted to drive to Oklahoma City to hitch a ride with him on the GWA plane the next day instead. But she couldn't fathom wasting the money she'd already spent, much less the additional expense of gas in her car to get there. Not to mention how expensive it would be to park her car at the airport for an unknown length of time and having no idea of when or how she'd be able to go pick it back up.

Randi told James about the appointment she had Saturday afternoon to try on her dress for the wedding, and he made plans to try on his tuxedo at the same time. With plans shored up for when they would finally get to see each other again, their conversation turned back to everything they'd each done and seen that day and her plans to spend the next day packing for the trip while he was already traveling to Texas.

When he had to quit texting to go wrestle, Randi was relieved that she hadn't broken down and talked about training to wrestle in their text conversation. Now she just had to get through their phone call when he got to his hotel room after the show and the Skype session they planned for the next night without saying any of the things she wanted to tell him face to face.

Surely, I can do that, right?

Leah Mae Wright

~ ~ ~

James was excited to introduce his GWA family to his parents, grandparents, and the rest of his extended family and friends in Heart's Destiny, Texas. It was too bad that their little town didn't have a big enough airport for the corporate jet to be able to land there, so the GWA crew had to caravan from the airport in San Antonio to the small town about an hour southwest of the city. Since it was the other flight crew that flew them into San Antonio and not the one Anthony and Kay were on, James and Dean led the way for everyone going to Anthony and Kay's wedding.

Since they'd taken Dean's truck to the airport when they left town at the end of their Labor Day break, he was behind the wheel on their way home that afternoon. With them always traveling together for work, they traded off who would leave their vehicle at the airport while they were working. James would drive them back to the airport when their Thanksgiving break was over and then home for their Christmas break in a month.

Or maybe I'll just give Dean my keys to drive himself home, if I can convince Randi to let me come stay with her for my Christmas break instead of coming home? James contemplated how things would be changing with his travel schedule, so he could spend more time with his girlfriend. *Guess I'd better tell the rest of my family about her tonight, too, since they'll be meeting her tomorrow.*

He had a smile on his face the whole ride from the airport, thinking about how much his parents and grandparents were going to love Randi when they met her. He wished he could pick her up at the airport the next day, but she'd already informed him that her father had scheduled a rental car to take them all to the Burleson Ranch. Once they got there, Randi and Deanna would be riding with Kay to go try on their wedding attire.

James had already confirmed with Anthony that he and Dean would meet him at Benny's Formalwear at the same time. Dean was slightly irritated at having to drive himself there, but James wanted to make sure he had his own vehicle, so he could show Randi around town after the appointment, and they could be alone. There wasn't anything else wedding related that they had to do that afternoon, unless she wanted to go back into San Antonio to pick up any party supplies they might need for the bachelor and bachelorette party that night.

They hadn't figured out how they were going to get Randi's luggage out of her father's rental car for her to be able to stay with James, but he was still hopeful it would happen. He thought it might be easier for her to sneak out of the bed and breakfast to be with him, so he specifically told her about hiring the crew to help his mom get all the rooms finished at the plantation house, making room for her family to be able to stay there. But as of their talk the night before, she was still expecting to stay with the Burlesons on the ranch.

Fuck, I wish she was ready to just tell them that she's staying with me instead.

He couldn't ruminate on that thought for long, though, because they'd just pulled off the highway and onto Walker Road and only had a couple more miles before they would turn into the main entrance to the bed and breakfast on the family homestead. Instead of going on down to Rogers Road and going in the back way to where their cabins were located southwest of the rest of the older family homes to drop off their stuff first thing, Dean pulled into the main drive that circled through the parklike setting of the bed and breakfast.

He pulled off to the side of the drive and pointed out the parking area for the B and B to the left of the original building. Once everyone seemed to know where they were going, Dean veered right to follow the road that led through the property to the house they grew up in, where their parents still lived. Instead of following the road on around past their grandparents' house and back to the two cabins James and Dean had built the year before, Dean parked at their parents' house, so they could walk over to the original building that had been converted into the bed and breakfast and introduce everyone to their mom.

As they walked up toward the backside of the house that had once been their second or third great-grandparents' home, before his parents added on to it to combine it with another set of great-grandparents' former home to convert the two expanded houses into one, making the bed and breakfast, James noticed that the work crew he'd hired hadn't just cleared any overgrowth on the path back to the plantation house in the middle of the property. They'd cut a wide swath through the trees and paved a road back to the massive mansion that could now be seen from a mile away.

"Shit, I hope they didn't get any ideas about clear cutting back to our places like that," Dean complained, as they stood there staring at the house that they'd had to fight through briars and brambles to get to as teenagers.

"Naw, the road still turns into gravel once we pass Meemaw and PopPop's house," James pointed out to his brother before turning toward the back entrance to the bed and breakfast.

"Maybe not yet, but now that they've done this," Dean replied, waving his hand at the new road to the plantation house. "How long do you think it'll take them to realize they can do the same thing to be able to see our houses too? Maybe we should've built farther south, so we can maintain some privacy when we're home."

"I'm sure this is just because of expanding the business and needing to be able to point out the other building for guests who are staying in those rooms," James reassured his brother, opening the back door to the original B and B building, motioning to his brother to precede him inside. "They won't clear cut to our houses until we give 'em grandkids that they wanna see running from house to house."

"What's this about grandkids?" Their mother, Mandi Hunter, chimed in from beside the main desk in the lobby, excitement lighting her eyes.

"Just that you're not gonna clear-cut the woods between here and our houses for another ten years or so when we finally give you grandkids," Dean replied, bending to kiss their mother on the cheek.

"You'd better be joking about waiting ten more years before giving me grandkids!" Mandi chided, playfully swatting at Dean.

James thought about telling his mother that he was thinking closer to five years for having kids, but he wasn't sure she'd be much happier with that timeline, so he kept his mouth shut on the subject. He just bent to kiss her other cheek and was grateful for the arrival of his boss and the rest of the GWA crew that would be checking in for their rooms, so he could change the subject by making introductions.

It took over an hour to get everyone organized and assigned to the rooms on the second and third floors of the plantation house. Since they'd gotten all fifty of them ready in time, and everyone from the GWA was there for the wedding, they would all be staying in the new rooms, so they would just have to go downstairs for the various holiday and wedding events that were being held in the building. As they'd only been able to install the ramps to the entrances and hadn't been able to get the new elevator installed at the plantation house in time for the wedding, having the GWA crew stay there also freed up the already ADA compliant building for any older or physically impaired guests to stay in the rooms with elevator access.

Mandi explained that she'd hired a few additional staff members to be able to take care of such a large group of guests. She'd moved the main breakfast portion of the bed and breakfast to the plantation house as well, since the majority of the rooms were now in that building and there were wheelchair ramps on all the entrances so physically impaired guests could get to the first floor where the dining room and ballroom were located. They'd have more of a continental breakfast at the smaller building for anyone who didn't want to go to the plantation house for the breakfast buffet.

She had brochures made to inform everyone about the various eateries around town for lunches and dinners. She also informed everyone that in addition to the rehearsal dinner and dinner at the reception after the wedding that the Burlesons were having catered, they were also hosting Thanksgiving dinner in the ballroom at the plantation house for everyone who was there for the wedding instead of going home to spend Thanksgiving with their families.

Once the keys to the rooms were all distributed, James and Dean hopped on their mother's golf cart to drive over to the plantation house to see all the improvements for themselves, while the rest of the GWA drove over to the other parking lot that had been paved for guests attending functions or staying in the rooms in the plantation house. When they arrived, it took them a minute to sit and gawk at the impressive changes to the mansion from the last time they'd seen it, allowing their boss time to park and walk over to where they were getting off the golf cart.

"You didn't tell me this place was on par with the Biltmore house." Rick nodded at the mansion as he approached them with his daughter at his side and suitcases in both hands.

"Naw, only about half the size of the Biltmore," Dean quipped with a chuckle. "Although our great, great, great, great," he paused to turn to James before continuing, "was that enough greats for the grandpa who built this place?"

James nodded, even though he wasn't quite sure if it was their fourth or fifth great-grandfather who had built the building. While winter wasn't really cold in Heart's Destiny, he still didn't want to take off his shirt to consult his family-tree tattoo to count the generations to make sure they were exactly right in estimating that it was their fourth-great-grandpa who first helped found the town.

"Grandpa William was the first Hunter in the area," Dean continued, turning back to face Rick. "And he probably thought he was building the largest family home in the US when he built this place a few years before Vanderbilt surpassed him with the Biltmore."

"Well, it's still impressive," Rick praised as the rest of the GWA started gathering around them. "I'm not sure how your mom managed to get fifty rooms in here, when the Biltmore only has thirty-five, though."

"Strategic planning and much smaller rooms," James told his boss as he reached out to help one of the kids with a big suitcase. "When we were talking about what furniture she needed for all the rooms last month, she told me that she was putting bunk beds in the smaller rooms, so she could make them more like the family suites you mentioned. So instead of fifty rooms, it's more like twenty family suites and ten regular rooms."

"And the ten regular rooms are the ones she'd already finished before we surprised her with hiring the construction crew she needed to finish out the rest," Dean added, as he too assisted someone with carrying their luggage toward the main entrance of the stately mansion turned hotel.

Once they entered the foyer, they carried everyone's bags up the stairs to their rooms before showing them around the lower level. A few of the kids grumbled about having to go up and down so many stairs, but when their parents started explaining that elevators weren't commonplace in Texas a hundred-and-forty-five years ago, when the original home was built, they quickly quit complaining. He didn't have time to mention the new elevator that was being installed on the end of the building by the parking lot before they started asking a million questions about what it was like to live there so long ago, like they expected James and Dean to know firsthand, instead of just knowing the few stories they'd heard from their family members about their ancestors.

After a tour of the ballroom, living room, library, parlors, dining room, and kitchen on the lower level, James and Dean left their friends, coworkers, and their families to settle into their rooms for the evening. Dean planned to meet with some of the single guys later to go to Tully's Roadhouse for a pregame of the bachelor party, but it had to be later in the evening as both of the Hunters were expected to have dinner with their parents and grandparents that first night in town.

They took the golf cart back up to the original B and B building and walked back over to Dean's truck, so they could go to their cabins and unpack their bags for a while. James texted Randi throughout the afternoon as he aired out and cleaned his home. It wasn't that it was dirty per se, just that it was dusty and stuffy from being closed up for the last ten weeks.

He thought it was a bit strange to be talking to her about what she was packing as he was unpacking his bags. But when she asked him what she should pack to wear for her potential interview and job with the GWA, in case she was able to fly comfortably and start work immediately at the end of the holiday break, any strange feelings he had about their current conversation were replaced with a soul-deep longing for that to be the outcome of their time in town for the holiday and wedding.

Just her talking about the possibility eased his trepidation about her not having already sent her résumé to Rick. When she told him that she was putting her laptop in her carry-on, so she could send the email as soon as she knew she was okay to fly, James was ecstatic at how certain she seemed that she would not only be able to fly to the wedding without anxiety, but also that she would be ready to tackle flying daily with the GWA immediately.

He wanted to start their planned Skype session immediately, too, but he had to wait until after he went to his grandparents' house for dinner with his family first. He almost felt like he floated through the rest of the afternoon as he went through his normal grooming rituals on autopilot before driving over to his grandparents' house for dinner. James felt high on life knowing Randi would soon be in his arms again.

When he arrived at Meemaw and PopPop's house, he knew better than to stop to knock on the door before walking inside. If he was visiting their place in New York City that they'd bought back when they were regularly there for business, he would've had to ring the bell. But they never locked the doors on their house in Heart's Destiny and expected their family to make themselves at home.

He walked straight to the kitchen, where he found Meemaw standing at the stove stirring a pot of stew. "Hey, Meemaw," James greeted her over the sound of his stomach growling at the delicious aroma that he'd missed while traveling for work. He bent to kiss the top of her head as he came up beside her. "Where is everybody? Surely, I'm not the first one here for dinner."

"You are, actually," Meemaw replied as she put the serving spoon down on the spoon rest that had been on her stove for as long as James could remember and turned to give him a hug. James returned her hug as she continued. "Your dad and PopPop are probably still over at the stables. Your mom said she had a few things to finish up but should be here shortly. And I have no idea where your brother is, but he'd better hurry up and get here. I was ready to eat an hour ago, so I'm putting dinner on the table at six, whether everyone's here or not."

"I'm here, Meemaw," Dean announced as he walked into the kitchen. He took his turn hugging Meemaw before she put them both to work setting the table.

It wasn't more than a couple of minutes before everyone else arrived and moved to the dinner table. Once they were all seated, PopPop said grace and they all started ladling up bowlfuls of stew and slathering butter on rolls. It was mostly small talk at first, talking about how great the plantation house looked, and catching up on the town gossip.

"So, um, I," James stuttered, not really sure how to transition from town gossip to his own romantic revelations. He cleared his throat before starting over. "I wanted to give you all a heads up that you'll be meeting my girlfriend this weekend."

"Really?" His mother, Mandi, arched her eyebrow as she looked at him. "Is she one of the women who checked into the B and B today?"

"No," James adamantly denied, looking around the table at everyone else before turning to look directly at his mother to finish answering her question. "She won't be in town until tomorrow."

"And who is she?" Meemaw drew his attention back around to her with her question. "How did you meet her?"

"Her name is Randi," James answered, unconsciously smiling as he said her name. "She's Kay's sister and I met her the same day Anthony met Kay."

"But not exactly the same way," Dean chuckled. "Randi was our waitress at lunch, but James was too shy to talk to her then. He had to have Anthony text him to come to the hotel bar that night to meet her when he met Kay."

"I wasn't too shy to talk to her," James objected to his brother's assessment of the day he met Randi. "I could see she was overwhelmed by you and the rest of the guys' merciless flirting, and I didn't wanna make it worse for her. And it's a good thing I didn't say much at lunch because that was what caught her attention, making her tell her sister about wishing she could've met me without ya'll around, which is what Anthony overheard that led to him connecting the dots to formally introduce us."

"So, it was love at second sight instead of first?" Mandi was obviously fighting to keep her joy contained to only slightly grinning.

James smiled and shook his head at his mother. "No, I think we both felt it the first time our eyes met, but it was a missed opportunity to connect at lunch. And we exchanged numbers within a minute of seeing each other the second time that day, so we didn't take a chance on missing the connection again."

"How does dating work when you're in a different city every day?" PopPop looked confused as everyone resumed eating. "Does she travel with you some? Or do you take time off to go back to where she lives to take her out?"

"We've only really been able to go out in person that one night," James admitted, knowing his family would question his belief that their phone calls and Skype sessions counted as dates. "But we've talked, texted, and Skyped almost daily for the last seven weeks, so we've had a lot of virtual dates."

"Virtual dates?" His dad, David, questioned with a quizzical expression on his face. "Kind of hard to woo a woman over the phone, isn't it?"

"Maybe not with calls and texts, but they've been doing a lot more than wooing on Skype," Dean smirked.

James looked at his brother incredulously, shocked that he was talking about Skype sex with their parents and grandparents.

"And how do you know what they do on Skype?" David interrogated Dean with a raised eyebrow of his own.

"Yeah," James wondered aloud, staring at Dean. "You've only seen me Skype with her one time, and that was at the fan expo when all we did was talk and I showed her around the arena."

"I may have only been in the same room with you when you've Skyped with her the one time." Dean pointed his spoon at James. "But the walls are thin in some of the hotels we've stayed in, and I can hear you."

"Stop right there," Meemaw demanded, holding up her hand to Dean. "I don't want to hear the details about their dates from you, virtual or otherwise."

James could feel himself blushing at the thought of his brother overhearing him commanding Randi's pleasure during one of their sexy Skype sessions, and the blush only deepened at the thought of Dean repeating any of the dirty things he'd said to her in front of their parents and grandparents. He hoped his beard covered most of it when Meemaw turned to him and studied his face.

"I don't think I want to hear them from you either, James." Her face brightened with a little grin. "But I do want you to tell us more about Randi. What's she like?"

"She's awesome," James gushed, trying to think of all the ways he wanted to describe her to his family. "She's smart and funny. She has a ton of energy and can't stand sitting still without something to keep her mind occupied. She's compassionate and always trying to find ways to help or take care of the people she cares about. She's creative and radiant. Like she has this inner glow that lights up any room she walks into and draws people to her like a magnet. And she makes me feel like, I, I can't even describe the way she makes me feel when she smiles at me."

"Yep, he's clearly gone for her," PopPop chortled. "Guess we need to go through the family jewels to give him a selection of engagement rings to pick from."

Before James could think of what to say in response to his grandpa's statement, his brother killed the potentially life-changing moment.

"And he didn't even describe her for you to know how smokin' hot she is." Dean wagged his eyebrows suggestively and grinned at their grandfather.

"Well, that was just a given," PopPop chuckled, leaning over to put his arm around Meemaw. "We Hunter men are only attracted to the hottest chicks." He pecked her cheek with a kiss to prove his point.

"Is that so?" Mandi looked over at David.

"Absolutely," David replied to his wife, giving her a chaste kiss on the lips as well.

James just laughed and went back to eating his stew. *Only my family would deflect from Dean's inappropriate comment about my hot girlfriend by complementing their wives.*

"So, when do we get to meet her?" Mandi inquired once everyone was back to eating their dinner.

"I'm not sure," James shrugged after swallowing a mouthful of stew. "As soon as she gets to town tomorrow, we're all supposed to meet up at Benny's and Destiny Dresses to try on our clothes for the wedding. Then we have to get the stuff together for the bachelor and bachelorette party tomorrow night, and I'm not sure how much time we'll have in between to do more than grab a quick bite to eat. So, probably Sunday morning at church."

"Oh, are you not going to the cookout tomorrow afternoon?" Meemaw looked surprised that he wasn't attending a cookout he hadn't even heard about.

"What cookout?" James wondered what Meemaw was talking about since everyone else at the table looked as confused about the event she was referring to as James felt.

"Mom, are you sure you don't have the date wrong for the cookout?" David looked at his mother with concern. "I know the Burlesons were talking about doing them with some planned trail rides on the days there weren't other wedding events scheduled to keep the out-of-town guests fed and entertained, but I don't think Saturday was one of those days."

"Yes, Saturday is gonna be one of those days." Meemaw wiped her mouth with her napkin before placing it on the table beside her bowl and getting up to walk across the room. She plucked a piece of paper out from under a magnet on the refrigerator before walking back to the table and handing it to her son, David. "I wrote down the schedule

Leah Mae Wright

Hazel gave me, so I wouldn't miss anything this week. But she specifically asked us to come to the cookout on Saturday, so all the parents can meet all the grandparents before going to the bachelor and bachelorette party and leaving their kids for a sleepover in the bunkhouse."

"You're going to a sleepover in the Burlesons' bunkhouse?" David looked at Meemaw like she had two heads. "With all the kids who checked in with their parents today at the B and B?"

"Yes, and Hazel's new granddaughters and Kay's brother's kids," Meemaw confirmed, going back to her seat to resume eating.

"Us and a few other people from around town," PopPop agreed with a smile. "The Bensons, the Deeres, and Marie Milton that I know of for sure."

"And Hazel and Bob, and Jon and Susan, of course," Meemaw added. "And Kay's parents, or I guess that would be Kay and Randi's parents." She smiled at James with the addition of the Lees to the grandparent party. "Hazel said she has a few other people on standby to watch the kids too, if there are more kids than she's currently expecting. But it's mostly us older folks who would rather play with grandbabies than go to a bachelor or bachelorette party."

"I wonder why she didn't ask us?" Mandi looked between Meemaw, PopPop, and David.

"Probably because you have so much other stuff you're doing for the wedding that she figured your plate was full this weekend." PopPop smiled at his daughter-in-law.

"I guess," Mandi sighed. "But she should've at least told me about it, so I could've told everyone when they checked in today."

"Maybe she posted it in the group chat to invite the wrestlers' wives?" Dean shrugged one shoulder. "But since none of the guys are included in that chat, we just didn't hear about it?"

"No," Mandi disagreed, looking concerned. "I'm in that chat group and it hasn't been mentioned in there. Nobody's really posted there for a couple of weeks now, since Kay picked the dresses and stuff, and we finalized the plans for everything. Maybe I should call Hazel and find out what the plan is, so I can share it with all our out-of-town guests?"

"That's probably a good idea," James agreed, nodding at his mother. "And I'll check in with Anthony to find out if those of us without kids are supposed to be there for the cookout, too."

They quickly finished eating before reaching out to the Burlesons. Dean helped clean up from dinner while Mandi went into the other room to call Hazel and James stepped out onto the porch to text Anthony.

> **James: Just heard from Meemaw about a cookout tomorrow afternoon & kids slumber party in ya'll's bunkhouse tomorrow night. Wanted to check if the cookout was just so the out-of-town parents can get to know the grandparents who're babysitting the kids during the bachelor/bachelorette party or if those of us without kids are supposed to be there too.**

> **Anthony: This is the first I've heard about either of those things. Hadn't even registered that everyone would need childcare for the party you'd already told me about.**

> **James: Still too new to the Dad thing that you didn't think about childcare for your girls?**

> **Anthony: No, figured they'd stay with either my parents or Kay's, but didn't think about all the GWA kids.**

> **James: Well, might want to ask your mom then & let me know if you want me to spread the word with the crew at the B&B.**

> **Anthony: Yeah, thanks for the heads up. I'll let you know when I find out anything.**

James walked back into the house to catch the tail end of his mother's conversation with Hazel.

"Yes, okay, I'll spread the word. See you tomorrow at noon."
When she saw him enter the room, she turned to James and explained
the situation. "Everyone's invited to the cookout. They're planning to
start the grill around noon outside the south bunkhouse. They'll be
doing trail rides and kids games all afternoon and evening, so it
doesn't matter what time you stop by after the tux fitting, you'll be
able to eat before the bachelor and bachelorette party. They're going
to do the same thing, the cookout and games, but not the sleepover or
bounce house, on Monday, Tuesday, and Wednesday too, so everyone
has that option for food and entertainment if they need it, but none of
them are mandatory events for anyone."

"Good to know." James wondered how the cookout would impact
his alone time with Randi the next day. "Anthony didn't know about
the cookout or the kids' sleepover, so he was no help in firming up my
plans for tomorrow."

"Well, if you still need to go pick up the decorations and stuff for
the party, why don't you do that right after your tux fitting and then
come to the cookout after," Mandi suggested, winding her arm through
her sons to lead him back into the kitchen where the rest of the family
was still gathered. "If we have everyone meet there for the evening,
then ya'll can all leave for the party together."

James wasn't so sure that Randi or any of the other women would
want to go out for the night after getting sweaty and grubby at a
cookout, but he didn't argue with his mother. They pitched in with the
rest of the family that was cleaning up after dinner, laughing and
chatting as a family for a little while. Until James absolutely couldn't
wait a moment longer to head back to his cabin to Skype with Randi.

*Fuck, I hope she has an easy flight tomorrow, so she'll send her
résumé to Rick and do her interview in a couple more days. It would
be so, fucking, awesome if this is our last night to need to Skype to see
each other because we'll be together all the time while working
together.*

~~~

Randi was more excited than nervous as she finished up washing every
article of clothing she owned except for the ratty old t-shirt and shorts
~~~

she wore to pack on Friday. She was having absolutely no panic attack symptoms when she thought about flying, so she wanted to be prepared to actually get the job with the GWA and start immediately without having to go home to Tulsa to pick up anything she would want with her on her travels.

As soon as James had texted her that he was home, she'd inundated him with questions about the company dress code, how he did laundry while traveling, and how she would have to pack her toiletries to get through security when they carried all their luggage on board the private plane. He'd been patient with her in answering all her questions, even before she told him that she thought her medication was working well enough that she would be able to apply for the production assistant job after her flight to San Antonio.

After that, even his texts seemed as excited about her possibly starting work with the GWA at the end of their Thanksgiving break as she was feeling. He got really specific in breaking down the particulars, including how he stocked up on the travel size bottles of everything with a shopping trip about once a month and had his clothing laundered through the hotel concierges every three or four days.

It was good to know that she only had to pack a week's worth of clothing instead of her entire closet, since she was only allowed two checked bags on her commercial flight to San Antonio. That was still a lot since she had to pack a week's worth of professional outfits, plus a week's worth of casual and workout clothes, and a week's worth of sleepwear and underthings. Thankfully, she'd already planned to pack most of that for the week in Texas. But after her afternoon texting with James, she decided to swap out some of the dresses she'd planned to wear to the wedding events with skirts, slacks, and dressy tops that she could mix and match to make more than one outfit with each piece.

She finished packing most of her things while James was having dinner with his family. She waited to pack her toiletries, knowing she would need them the next morning. She didn't run out and buy the travel-sized bottles, since she could pack her full-sized products in her checked luggage for the commercial flight. She didn't want to jinx herself out of the job by buying the small bottles before she knew she'd need them.

I can pick them up in Texas next week if I get the job, she decided as she settled in her bed waiting for James to finish his family dinner to Skype with her. She had her laptop open, so she pulled up a picture of her parents and did her therapy homework while she waited for him.

"Mom, Dad, I'm a grown woman, not a teenager anymore," she appealed to her parents' picture on her computer screen. "It's my decision who I date and what I wanna do with my life, not yours. I love you and know that you only want what you think is best for me. But what you think is best for me, and what's actually best for me, are two different things. So, I'm respectfully asking you to please show your love for me by accepting me as I am, and not lecturing me about doing things you don't agree with, or who I date."

She ran through her speech a few times, wondering if she needed to add on the specifics about dating James and pursuing a career as a professional wrestler, or if it was enough as it was without specifics. It was always when she got into the specifics of wanting to be with James and her job plans that she heard their negative comments in her head, so she decided to just get comfortable with the script for a while. Depending on how things went with her flight and potential job interview, she might even be able to get at least that much out with James at her side sometime in the next week while actually talking to her parents instead of just to their picture.

Randi repeated the words so many times that she no longer needed to look at the document on her computer to remember them word for word. Just as she was thinking about switching to practice some of the more detailed conversations she'd scripted out, her computer chimed with the notification that James was calling her on Skype. She switched apps on her computer to accept his call faster than she even realized was possible.

"Hi," Randi barely breathed out the word as soon as James appeared on her computer screen, suddenly feeling a little self-conscious about her sloppy attire when he was dressed to kill in a burgundy button-down and jeans.

"Good evening, Angel," James greeted her, smiling at her through the screen. "All packed for your flight tomorrow?"

"Mostly," she replied, smiling back at him. "Just have a few things I'm still using tonight and in the morning that I'll pack when I'm done with them."

"Still feel like you're gonna be able to fly without a panic attack?" James tilted his head like he was studying her through the screen.

"Yeah," Randi crowed, smiling wider. "I mean, even thinking about getting on a plane used to cause me to feel like I was on the brink of a panic attack. But I'm not feeling my heart racing, or feeling even slightly nauseated at the thought now. And you can see that my jittery leg is as still as a stone, when it's normally bouncing like crazy when I'm worried or nervous. So, I think my meds are working, but I won't know for sure until I get on the plane in the morning."

"Fuck, I can't wait to see you tomorrow," he growled while letting his eyes wander up and down her body. "It's gonna take every ounce of self-control I have to not ravish you the instant we're in the same room."

Randi giggled at the mental image of him carrying her out of the bridal shop before she could even look at the dress she was supposed to try on the next day, so he could take her off somewhere more private to fuck her brains out.

"You think that's funny, Angel?" James's deep voice sent tingles across her whole body. "Let's see if you're still laughing when I throw you over my shoulder and tell everyone we'll see them at the wedding, but I need a whole week alone with you first. And then I'll carry you out to my truck and back to my house, so I can spend the whole fucking week balls-deep inside you."

"You wouldn't!" Randi squealed, shocked yet still aroused by his declaration.

"Hell, yeah, I would," James shouted back. "As bad as I've missed you, it's gonna take an act of God to keep my hands to myself while we get through all these wedding events with everyone around."

"James…" Randi drew his name out to be several syllables, incredulous at his potential lack of control.

"I don't think Anthony and Kay realize what a bad idea it is to have us scheduled to try on our wedding clothes the first time we see each other after seven weeks apart," James warned, looking at her lasciviously. "If I can finagle it where we're sharing a dressing room, it'll take a couple of hours before we get changed into them, and the whole town will hear you screaming my name the whole time."

Randi wasn't sure how to respond to his wild statements. Based on the way her nipples tightened and her pussy flooded, she knew she was more turned on by the thought of being overheard while having sex with James than she wanted to admit. But she was also mortified at the thought of who all might be at the bridal shop to overhear them.

"Yeah, that's only happening if you can guarantee that the only people who hear us are strangers and I'll never have to meet them," Randi finally averred, shaking her head at his outrageous declarations. "So, there will be no public displays this week when my whole family could be lurking around."

"What about public displays the following week, when we'll be in Florida and the only family member in the same city will be my twin?" James wagged his eyebrows at her suggestively.

"Yeah, I've read books about women who are into the whole twin thing, but I've never had that fantasy," Randi quipped with a slight grin. "In fact, I don't think I even want your brother to catch us in flagrante delicto, so you'll have to make sure he's on the other side of the building if we ever try to have a quickie at work."

Holy sugar, no, shit, I can think holy shit with James, Randi thought not realizing her facial expression was giving away her mental musings to James. *Holy shit! I'm thinking about sneaking off to fuck him in some random arena when we're both supposed to be working. I wonder how many places we could find, like under the bleachers before the fans arrive, or in a janitor's closet, or, oh the best idea yet, the showers in the locker room while everyone else is eating dinner.*

"Fuck, Angel," James groaned as he pressed one hand over the bulge in his jeans. "I hope that sexy expression is from thinking about us sneaking off to fuck in an arena somewhere and not that twins fantasy."

"Oh, it's definitely not the twins fantasy," Randi affirmed with a giggle. "I was thinking about all the potential places we could find to *fuck* in an arena." She was still lowering her voice to whisper the dirty words, but it felt good to Randi to be able to say them to James without shame, nonetheless.

"Yeah, and where all did you think would be good places?" James stroked his cock through his jeans.

"The showers in the locker room while everyone else is off eating dinner," Randi started listing her ideas, her voice sounding breathier than normal. "Or maybe under the bleachers before anyone arrives for the show."

She really liked the idea of having sex somewhere where there was the possibility of being caught, but it was still a very low probability. It wasn't that she wanted to flaunt her body or have an audience to validate her feelings of attractiveness.

She wasn't a pin-up model by any stretch of the imagination, but she didn't have body image issues either. She considered herself to be an average, girl-next-door type with an athletic body. Maybe not as sexy as a supermodel but attractive, nonetheless. Even though she couldn't ever see her abs ripple like James's, she knew they were there, under the thin layer of body fat that covered her flat midsection in preparation for protecting any future children she would have, because she felt them when she did her workouts regularly.

She thought her subconscious reason for being turned on by the thought of being seen while engaging in a carnal act had something to do with her wanting to overcome the guilt and shame she felt for enjoying sex. Like if other people wanted to watch her, them enjoying watching her would make her feel validated, like she would no longer have a reason to be ashamed of her sexuality. *Maybe that's something else I should talk to Kelly about?*

"Fuck, yes, Angel," James crooned, bringing her back to the moment with him.

Maybe that's why I don't feel that shame with him, she thought. *All these Skype sessions where we watch each other have shown me that I'm not the only one who likes sex. And it's not only okay to like it, but it's actually supposed to be enjoyable with him.*

"We both need to lose some clothing if we're gonna talk about all the things we can do in semi-public places once you start this new job," James advised, starting to unbutton his shirt. "I wanna see your pretty pussy when I tell you all my ideas for where I can eat you out."

"Then I need to see your *cock*," Randi whispered as she slipped her shorts down her legs. "So, I can tell you where I've imagined *sucking you off*."

It only took a few seconds for them to both be completely nude, which still surprised Randi as being possible, even after so many sexy Skype sessions between them.

"I wanna lick every inch of you while we're under the ring," James growled in that gravelly voice that made Randi quiver with need. "Maybe sneak under there before anyone arrives for rehearsals and see how quiet you can be when I make you come while the guys are wrestling three feet above us."

"Or maybe I'll just hide under the ring and catch you standing near the opening of the ring apron, so I can *suck* your *cock* while you try not to let the guys figure out what's going on," Randi purred, loving the way his eyes darkened with lust at her idea.

Randi instinctually started touching herself the way she knew James wanted her to, before he even had the chance to give her directions, like he usually did during their virtual sex sessions. She'd come a long way from the first time when he had to talk her into taking off her clothes while they were on a video chat. He'd eased her into their mutual masturbation sessions by stripping for her first and then giving her gentle directions on how and where to touch herself as she removed her clothing for him.

Now, after over a dozen of these video encounters, she didn't need him to tell her to start by lightly trailing a fingertip in swirls around her breasts. She did it because she knew he liked to watch as her nipples hardened before she even gave them the lightest touch.

I wonder if he realizes that my nipples are hard because of that hungry look on his face, more than from me touching myself? She moved her other hand down to touch her sex. *Or that all this wetness is because of watching him stroke his cock?*

"Fuck, Angel," James moaned through her computer as she pushed two fingers inside her center. "I can't think about anything but what I'm seeing when you play with your pussy like that. I want so bad to lick up all that cream you're making while you finger-fuck yourself for me."

"I wish it was your fingers instead of mine," Randi confessed, pumping her fingers in and out to give him a show. "Or better yet, your big, hard, *cock*. My little fingers are a poor substitute for how you fill me up."

"You'll get my cock tomorrow, Angel," James promised, squeezing his shaft in a tight grip as his hand moved roughly up and down his length. "Just as soon as I can get you alone."

Randi pushed her thumb down on her clit, rubbing it in circles to give her the friction she needed to come, since her fingers weren't long enough to reach the spot inside that James had so deftly found their first night together. She pinched her nipple with her other hand, knowing he liked to see her alternate plucking them, so they stood out even more than just from her normal level of arousal.

James continued telling Randi how he wanted to fuck her as soon as she got to town the next day. He described his ideas for taking her from behind in the bridal shop dressing room, for her riding him in his truck on a back road just outside of town, and for tying her to his bed in his cabin and teasing her for hours before finally sinking inside her again. Each scene he described was more erotic than the last, and each one took her over the edge to orgasmlandia.

His words were more responsible for her orgasms than her hands on her own body. Especially when his voice deepened as he commanded her to, "Come for me now, Angel."

She'd never been multi-orgasmic before meeting James. She'd just been happy to figure out how to get one on her own when she was between sexual partners or when her previous partners hadn't gotten the job done. But not only had James given her three the night they met, but he'd also realized that the key to her repeats was all in her head when he wasn't the one physically touching her. All his dirty talk had been strategic to tap into that mental aspect of her sexuality to give her multiple O's every single time they virtually fucked.

This round of cybersex was no different than all the others with how he took her over with his words, even if the scenes he described were all new. He talked her through orgasm after orgasm, finally going over with her when she reached the peak for the fifth (Or sixth? Or seventh?) time. Randi wasn't sure because she was so blissed out that she lost count of how many times she came. She collapsed back into her pillows, feeling like she was floating away in another realm, unable to move or even think, much less speak.

"You okay, Angel?" she vaguely heard James asking her. Somehow, she managed to summon the energy to lift her thumb, hoping her hand gesture appeared to James as the thumbs up she intended it to be as she drifted off to dreamland.

She didn't hear him talking about how they should've saved the monster orgasms that wiped her out for when he was with her and able to take care of her afterwards. She also didn't hear him trying to coax her to move her computer off the bed, so she wouldn't accidentally kick it off and break it in her sleep. Nor did she hear his "Goodnight,

Angel," when he realized she was lightly snoring and not going to respond to him the rest of the night.

Which was probably good, so she didn't think he was being creepy for watching her sleep for a couple of hours before he finally disconnected the video chat to catch a few z's of his own.

Chapter Ten

Saturday, November 17, 2018

Randi was surprised at how calm she was as she sat in the backseat of her parents' car with Amy and Deanna on their way to the airport. She would've said it was because she'd taken her medication before they got there to pick her and Amy up that morning, but she'd only taken it maybe five minutes before they arrived. So, she didn't think it had really had time to digest yet, much less be at its most effective point in her system.

The conversation in the car varied from the initial excitement about the trip and the upcoming wedding to whether or not any of them had issues with getting so much time off work to go away for the whole week. Randi shifted in her seat with the topic change, uncomfortable because she hadn't mentioned her recent change in employment status to anyone yet.

"I didn't mention who's wedding I'm attending, so it wasn't as big a deal as I was afraid of," Deanna confided with a conspiratorial smile.

"Oh, that's right, you were worried about the conflict with you working for a competitor of the Burlesons," Randi's mother, Mary Lee exclaimed, turning in her seat to look back at Deanna. "So, does that mean you're going to be staying in Tulsa where you currently work and not looking at jobs with the Burlesons this week?"

"Well, I'm not in dire need of another job now," Deanna shrugged. "But if the Burlesons want to offer me something with better pay and benefits, I'd definitely have to consider it."

"What about you, Amy?" Randi's father, Charles Lee, looked back at them in the rearview mirror for a moment.

Leah Mae Wright

"We were already closed most of the week for Thanksgiving, so I just had to take vacation time on Monday and Tuesday," Amy replied with a smile. "So, it wasn't a big deal."

"Good," Charles grinned, shifting his gaze to his youngest daughter. "Randi?"

"No," Randi squeaked, unable to meet her father's gaze in the rearview mirror. "No problems getting the time off." *I have all the time off I want, since I don't have a job anymore.*

"So, which of the charities did you all pick from the list Kay sent us?" Mary effectively changed the subject for Randi when she didn't even realize how much her daughter appreciated it.

She was referring to the list of their favorite charities that Kay and Anthony had put together and sent out to everyone, asking that in lieu of wedding gifts, everyone should donate to one of them instead. Randi wasn't sure if Kay had always had a list of favorite charities or if the list was brought about by Anthony's influence on her, but she liked knowing that her sister had such a giving heart that she would rather take care of others than receive a bunch of gifts herself. Almost as much as Randi loved the warm, fuzzy feeling she got when she made her donation, even though it wasn't as much as she would've liked to have given.

"I picked Saint Jude," Randi announced, smiling up at her mother.

"Me, too." Amy bobbed her head with a smile at Randi.

"Great minds," Deanna chuckled with a wide grin of her own. "We all think alike."

Before anyone could ask where her parents had donated, they were pulling into a parking space at the airport. Soon, they'd unloaded all their luggage from the huge trunk in the Lincoln Town Car that her parents had owned since it was new in 2011. Since that was the last year they were made, Randi figured her picky father would have to finally switch to an SUV when it came time to replace his favorite car.

They made their way through the airport to the check-in counter, where they turned over the majority of their luggage. Then waited in an exceptionally long line to get through security before walking what seemed like another mile to the gate, where they had to sit and wait to be able to board the plane. Even through all the walking and waiting, Randi didn't feel nervous, which she counted as her first win of the day.

Then Deanna stirred up a bout of butterflies in her stomach by asking, "Randi, what do you think about the hot groomsmen we get to walk down the aisle with?"

That you can ogle Dean all you want, but you'd better keep even your eyes off of James, Randi mentally warned, hoping she wasn't broadcasting her thoughts to everyone around them that could see her face, especially her ever-watchful father.

"They seem nice enough," Randi fibbed, trying to appear nonchalant. "At least what little I've talked to them while coordinating the bachelor and bachelorette party for tonight."

Please buy that line of bull sugar! Randi mentally kicked herself for still not being able to think a curse word while in her parents' presence. *I guess I can only think of bad words when I'm looking at Little Jimmy or James's picture or video chatting with him. I wonder if his presence this week will override my inability to think them with my parents around?*

She tried to keep from blushing as she thought about the way her practicing talking to James had turned to her practicing thinking dirty words that she wanted to be able to say to him when they were alone. And how that had all led to her finally being able to say them as more than a whisper the night before in their sexy Skype session. *Nope, don't think about that now! Just be glad you didn't break your computer when you fell asleep after, while it was still in kicking range.*

"Oh, you've talked to them?" Deanna looked more interested than Randi wanted her to be. "When I asked for a number to be able to help coordinate the parties, Kay told me that she wasn't allowed to give out their numbers because of their celebrity status."

"Yeah, I actually met James and got his number the same night that Kay met Anthony," Randi admitted, looking down at her hands that were fidgeting in her lap, instead of looking up to see who all was paying attention to their conversation. "I don't have Dean's number, but James put his phone on speaker a couple of times when Dean was there, so he could tell me about what all he'd set up with one of their high school friends for the party."

"Oh, so they've set it all up?" Deanna's voice sounded sharp. "Kay told me you were handling everything."

"Yeah, they're the ones who know everyone there," Randi shrugged, finally lifting her gaze to Deanna. *Please stop asking all these questions,* she tried to project with her eyes to Deanna. "All I really did was tell them what I've seen at the other bachelorette parties I've attended and confirm that we'd be there today, so they could book the club for tonight."

"So, were the guys going to pick up the party supplies too, or just book the venue?" Amy looked quizzically at Randi. "I mean, I can't picture the Dangerous Twins going shopping for bachelorette party sashes, much less the penis straws or party games like at Kathy's bachelorette party."

Randi was torn between laughing at the mental image of James and Dean going shopping for bachelorette party supplies while dressed in their ring gear, or dying of embarrassment because her best friend had just mentioned penis straws in front of her parents. Forget fight, flight, or freeze, she couldn't do any of those things at the moment. Instead, her jaw dropped to the floor in shock at the same time a bark of laughter escaped her throat and her entire face felt like it had turned fire engine red.

"What on earth is so funny?" Mary looked back and forth between the three of them when Randi couldn't stop laughing, and both Amy and Deanna joined her with the giggles.

Randi couldn't catch her breath from laughing so hard, which she considered a good thing, since it prevented her from having to try to answer her mother.

"Men-mental pic-picture," Deanna stuttered out through her own laughter. "How, how about, ha, try, ha-ha, trying on the tiaras?"

"Oh," Amy snorted, flapping her hands like that would stop her from laughing, so she could talk. "Oh, yes, ha-ha, while wear, hehe, wearing their wrestling tights."

"It's like back when they were in high school and got the giggles at slumber parties," Charles chuckled.

Randi's shock at her dad joining them in their bout of laughter helped her get hers a little more under control, but she still didn't want to be the one to explain to her mom what was so funny. Surprisingly, it was her father who finally explained things to his wife.

"The two young men that Anthony has standing up with him at the wedding are professional wrestlers," Charles told Mary.

"Yes, I know that," Mary huffed, not understanding why that mattered.

"The girls are picturing them going shopping while dressed like they belong in a biker gang because that's what they wear when they wrestle." Charles smiled at his wife.

"Technically, they take off the leather jackets to wrestle." Amy clarified now that she'd finally gotten her laughter under control. She waggled her eyebrows as she continued. "So, we were really picturing them in their spandex pants and wrestling boots with all their upper body muscles and tattoos on display."

"Don't forget the sexy long hair and beards," Deanna added, fanning herself like she was overheated by thoughts of Randi's boyfriend and his brother. "While they're both gorgeous as all get out, they would definitely stand out in the bachelorette party section of Party City."

"Oh, yes," Mary giggled, lightly blushing as her gaze skimmed over the younger women. "That would be a funny thing to imagine seeing." When her eyes landed on Randi, she asked, "And you've been talking to James for the last few weeks?"

Fudgsicles! Randi wished a sinkhole would swallow her right at that moment, so she didn't have to answer her mother. *You can do this. They aren't gonna lecture you in the middle of a crowded airport. You can tell them that you've been Skype dating him for the past seven weeks without telling them what you do on those sexy Skype sessions.*

"Yeah, uh, yes," Randi squeaked out.

Before she could elaborate on the status of her relationship with James, the overhead speaker blared with the gate attendant announcing it was time for them to board their plane.

Talk about saved by the bell, ur, blare, Randi thought as she stood and gathered her purse and carry-on bag to go wait in line to board the plane. Once they were seated on the aircraft, Randi couldn't have continued the conversation with her mother, even if she wanted to, because they were seated on opposite sides of the plane. Randi took the window seat on one side of the row they were all assigned, with Amy beside her and Deanna in the aisle seat. Charles and Mary were across the aisle in the aisle seat and middle seat respectfully. The only way they could've been farther apart on the same row would've been for her mother to be in the other window seat.

Surprisingly, Randi relaxed as she watched out the window to see the ground crew as they finished up loading the luggage on the plane. She switched her phone to airplane mode and hoped she'd still be able to listen to music on it once they were in the air, since she hadn't thought to bring a book to read on the trip. Unfortunately, she was disappointed to find out that she couldn't, since her music was stored in the cloud and not actually downloaded to her device.

While she had a momentary feeling of her stomach dropping as they took off, she didn't have any other signs of anxiety on the flight. She even found watching out the window at the clouds and ground below them relaxing, which boggled her mind considering she'd been so nervous just thinking about flying previously.

They had an hour layover in Dallas, which she used to pull her laptop out of her carry-on, set up a Wi-Fi hotspot with her phone, and send her résumé to the email address James had given her for the person in charge of hiring for the GWA, while everyone else was off looking for snacks and restrooms.

"Whatcha working on?" Deanna sat down next to Randi at the gate where their next plane would be boarding soon.

"Just have to send a quick email," Randi explained as she finished typing her cover letter as the body of the email message.

"Is that your résumé?" Deanna leaned in to look at Randi's screen over her shoulder. "Are you applying for a new job?"

"Shuh!" Randi hissed at Deanna while looking around to make sure her parents weren't close by to hear their conversation. "Yes, but I don't wanna talk about it around my parents."

"Oh, sorry," Deanna half-heartedly apologized, sitting back in her seat, and looking around like she was making sure they weren't close by like Randi had just done. "And I'm sorry for whatever I did or said earlier that pissed you off, too."

"I'm not pi, peeved at you." Randi hit send on her message, feeling a little surprised that she almost said pissed while in the same building as her parents. "I'm sorry if I sounded like it earlier. I just don't like to talk about guys around my parents, either."

"Oh," Deanna breathed out the word, just before her eyes widened and she blurted, "OH!" again. The second time was a lot louder than the first and her mouth comically made an oversized O shape for a beat longer than it took to actually say the word. She looked around again before asking, "So, your talks with James have been about more than just the bachelor and bachelorette party then?"

Randi visually scanned the area to make sure her parents weren't close by before answering. "Yeah, we've kinda been seeing each other over Skype for the past few weeks." Randi looked back at her computer to make sure the email had been sent before closing her laptop and turning off the hotspot on her phone.

"Lucky girl!" Deanna's jealousy showed in her fake smile.

"Who's a lucky girl?" Mary took the seat on the other side of Deanna.

Oh my Dog! Where'd she come from? And was she close enough to hear me tell Deanna about seeing James?

"Kay," Deanna replied with a wistful sigh. "Not only has she found the man of her dreams, who's adopting her daughters, but Randi just told me about the house he's planning to build for her. I hope I'm lucky enough to find a man like him, who'll treat me like a queen and build me a castle."

Randi couldn't believe how easily the lie rolled off Deanna's tongue, but she was grateful for Deanna's quick thinking and ability to cover for her with her mother.

"Oh, yes, Kay is definitely living the fairy-tale romance." Mary graced them with a beaming smile. "But I think the castle is more for Maria than Kay. Every time Kay's mentioned the area where they're building, she's said she pictured something a little more rustic to blend in with the woodland environment around it, but Maria keeps drawing pictures of castles. So, her favorite woodland chalet design has ended up with some stone turrets to turn it into Maria's dream castle."

Randi finished putting her laptop away and excused herself for her own bathroom break while the conversation continued without her. By the time she made it back to the gate, so had the rest of their party, and they were all standing to board the next plane.

Perfect timing! She released the tension in her shoulders as she took her place in line with them. Luckily for her, they had the same seating arrangement as on the previous flight. Randi sat back and relaxed for the next flight, hopeful she'd get to the Burleson Ranch and quickly receive a response from her email to schedule an interview in the next few days.

~ ~ ~

James had spent his morning finishing up his laundry and making sure his home was prepared for when Randi arrived, before going over to the plantation house to have breakfast with his coworkers who were staying at the bed and breakfast. Since her plane wouldn't be arriving in San Antonio until around noon, and then it would take another hour for her to get to Heart's Destiny, he had a lot of time to kill before he actually got to see her.

Since at least part of the day would be spent on the ranch and possibly on the back of a horse, he'd opted to wear jeans and a Henley with his cowboy boots. The boots were quite the departure from the biker boots he wore with his gimmick wear, his wrestling boots he wore in the ring, and especially from the dress shoes he wore most of the time with the suits and business casual attire he wore for traveling. So, James fully expected to be ribbed for wearing them when the rest of the crew first saw him that morning.

"Dude, where's your cowboy hat?" Surfer Josh Parker started the ribbing as soon as James walked into the dining room of the plantation house and got in line behind him for the breakfast buffet.

"And shouldn't you be wearing a western shirt and huge belt buckle to go with those boots?" Brent Crockett mocked from his place in line ahead of Josh, waving a hand up and down like he was trying to point out the inconsistencies in James's attire.

"Don't forget the piece of straw he should be chewing on to pull off the cowboy gimmick," Jeff Evans added from his seat at the table with his wife and kids.

"Laugh all ye want, boyos," Liam Connery, aka Red, defended James as he walked up to get in line behind him, sporting his own cowboy boots that looked brand new. "I'm wit James ahn makin' sure I'm wearin' de right footwear fahr de tasks o' de day."

"Where did you find a pair of cowboy boots?" Dark Chocolate Dion Davis probed Red as he joined them in the line.

"Dean took me shoppin' dis mornin'," Red replied as they moved forward to start filling their plates with bacon, scrambled eggs, and fried potatoes.

"And why do you sound like you're fresh off the boat from Ireland this morning?" Josh looked back at Red from his place at the beginning of the line where he was almost finished filling his breakfast plate. "You don't normally sound that Irish, even when you're doing promos."

"De ladies like de accent," Red grinned. "I'm practicin' fahr when we meet Anthony's sisters and cousins."

"You won't have too long to practice before meeting them," Dean pointed out as he finally joined them to eat. "We're all supposed to go to the ranch around noon for a cookout. They're setting up a bounce house for the kids, along with a bunch of games and horseback riding all afternoon."

"Yeah, your mom's been trying to catch everyone this morning to make sure we all knew about it," Jeff's wife, Jana told them, pointing at James and Dean when they sat down at the next table over from where the family was sitting for breakfast. "She said they're setting up a sleepover for all our kids for tonight, too."

"I can't believe they thought to arrange babysitting for all of us to be able to go to the party tonight," one of the other women at the table with Jeff and Jana mentioned.

James had tried to pay attention the day before when everyone was introducing themselves to his mother, so he'd know all of the women's names to be able to introduce them to Randi, but he must have missed hearing hers. He wondered if the Burlesons would've name tags at the cookout to help ease the confusion of so many people interacting for the first time this week. He hoped they thought of some way to introduce so many new people. Then he wouldn't look like an idiot when he didn't know the names of some of his coworkers' wives.

There was more general small talk as they all ate breakfast. While his coworkers and their families went back to their rooms to get ready to go to the cookout, James checked in with his mom to make sure she didn't need him to do anything to help her that morning. When she didn't need him to do anything at the B and B, he decided to head over to Anthony's house.

He told his mother that he was going on over there to see if they needed help setting up for the cookout, but he was really heading over there because he knew that was where Randi would be going as soon as she arrived in town. *Maybe she can ride with me from the ranch to the fittings?*

It was a bit strange to be able to just drive straight through the gate at the Burleson Ranch instead of having to stop and put in a code like normal. But when he stopped and thought about how they'd have to give the code to so many people this week for all the activities they were having there, he decided it made more sense that they just left the gate closest to the houses open when they expected a bunch of people to be coming through it.

James pulled into the driveway at the house that Anthony had told him about moving into until he could build a bigger one on the south side of the ranch. Instead of pulling around to park by the garage, he pulled off to the side of the driveway in front of the house. Knowing he would be leaving to go to the fitting appointment a little after one o'clock since their appointment was at one-thirty, he didn't want to take a chance on getting blocked in by parking at the back of the house.

When he walked up to the front door, he contemplated walking in like he would've done as a kid going to his best friend's house. If he was going to the one next door, where Anthony's parents lived, he probably would've just walked in like back when they were kids. But since he wasn't sure how Kay would feel about him just walking into her new home like he lived there, James actually stopped on the porch, knocked on the door, and waited for someone to open it before going inside.

"James!" Tia shouted as she opened the front door. "Can you check with the amusement vendors to find out if we can do some wrestling training in the bounce house? Daddy said he doesn't know if adults are allowed to get in it or if it's just for kids. And Mom's been keeping him busy getting ready for everyone to arrive today, so he hasn't had a chance to go with me to find out. But since you're here, maybe we can get in some training time before the rest of the kids get here and we have to stop so the little kids can bounce."

"I'm not exactly dressed for your wrestling lessons, Squirt." James ruffled the girl's hair as he walked into the house. "And I don't think bounce houses are rated for someone my size to take bumps in them, so I don't think they'd let me in it to train with you, either."

"Sorry, Princess." Anthony walked down the stairs into the foyer where James and Tia were standing. "We can't have him busting the bounce house before anyone else even gets here to get in it with you and your sister."

"Well, then we need to come up with another way for me to keep up with my training when we're home for two whole weeks," Tia declared, her lips turning up in a sort of half smile. "Daddy, can we maybe add a training room to the house plans? And ask Mr. Rick where to buy a wrestling ring to put up in it, so I can keep up my training, even when you and Mom aren't working?"

"Maybe we should've had him bring a ring crew to town this week," James chuckled at the puppy dog eyes Tia was giving Anthony. *He's only been legally her dad for a little over a week, but I think he was wrapped around her finger from the moment he met her momma.*

"Yeah, and where would we have a ring set up around here?" Anthony shook his head.

"The bunkhouse where we're having our sleepover tonight," Tia answered without a moment's hesitation.

"Nope, no room after all the stuff we've carried down there for tonight," Anthony disagreed, ruffling her hair.

"That was actually why I came early," James admitted, running a hand through his hair, and wishing he'd put it up, so it wouldn't keep falling down in his eyes. He thought it looked best down, but not if he was constantly knotting it up by running his hand through it to keep it out of his eyes. And he wanted to look his best the first time he met Randi's parents. "Wanted to see if you needed any help getting set up for the cookout and stuff."

"I think most of it's done." Anthony motioned toward the door. "I'd just come back to the house to get this one off her tablet to take her down to where we've got everything set up and pick up a jacket for Kay."

James finally noticed the jacket in Anthony's hand as they made their way out of the house. Anthony and Tia went to get on the four-wheeler that James hadn't noticed on his way into the house. James looked around and realized that the area around the houses was deserted and assumed that everyone was already down at the south bunkhouse for the festivities.

Leah Mae Wright

"You think someone should stay up here to direct everyone down to the bunkhouse?" James walked past their four-wheeler to go to his truck.

"Naw, we've put up signs on Rogers directing everyone to the south gate." Anthony made sure Tia's helmet was on properly before putting on his own. "But I guess if you came from your south gate to our north gate, then you'd have maybe only caught the backside of the one by the gate and wouldn't have realized you were going the wrong way. Hope Dean doesn't lead anyone else that same way."

"I'll send him a text to make sure," James offered as he got in his truck. He sent the quick text to his brother before starting his vehicle and following Anthony and Tia down to the south bunkhouse.

He was shocked to see how they'd turned a pasture into a parking lot and had the old training paddocks set up with a bunch of different activities for the kids. There was a six-foot-long barbeque smoker set up beside the bunkhouse and James's mouth watered at the unmistakable smell of brisket coming from it. Next to it was a more traditional grill that Anthony's dad, Bob, was loading up with burgers.

There were Burlesons standing around in clusters around the different things set up to occupy the kids, as well as fluttering around going in and out of the bunkhouse. Apparently, that's where the rest of the cooking was taking place for the day, with Anthony's mom, Hazel, directing traffic for the various side dishes and desserts.

James made the rounds greeting old friends who felt more like family from how close they'd been raised together. Tia had made a beeline for the bounce house and was disappointed to learn that it was only for kids under sixty inches tall. She barely made the cutoff at fifty-nine-and-three-quarters inches tall. There were a couple of the older boys who traveled with the GWA that wouldn't even be able to get in the bounce house.

When the guys started arriving, Tia convinced Dion to kneel beside the opening to the bounce house and act as her ring post, so she could practice planchas and other aerial wrestling moves for a little bit. As the other kids got there, some of them joined in, which made the wrestlers all laugh at how Dion got stuck with a half dozen kids all climbing on him.

Of course, everyone else joined in on the laughter when Kay realized that she was the only adult there who was small enough to get in and bounce with the kids, even going so far as to climb on Dion's shoulders to jump in like her daughters. Once more people started arriving, she spent quite a few minutes in there coaxing some of the smaller kids to join in on the festivities, finally giving Dion a reprieve.

James ended up playing a couple of rounds of horseshoes with the Burleson cousins and his coworkers that he introduced them to. Not too long into their game, one of Anthony's aunts walked over and handed out those old-fashioned stickers that said "Hello, my name is…" with a space to write in their individual names.

Thank fuck, I wasn't the only one who thought these were needed! He wrote his name in the space and slapped it on his shirt right over his heart.

He'd just finished his third game of horseshoes when high pitched squealing drew his attention to the newest arrivals at the cookout. Randi was a vision in a long bohemian style skirt with an abstract blue swirl pattern and a white blouse with an elastic neckline that looked like it could be worn off her shoulders. He guessed that she was only wearing it with her shoulders covered because she was with her parents, who looked completely out of place for a cookout on the ranch in their Sunday best.

Without consciously thinking or acknowledging the people speaking around him, James's feet carried him in her direction. He extended his arms, as if he was going to greet her with a hug, but he dropped them to his sides again as soon as her father stepped in between them.

Fuck, what was I thinking? I can't just scoop her up into my arms with everyone around. But I can take the bull by the horns and introduce myself to Randi's parents.

"Good afternoon, Mr. Lee." James extended his hand to Randi's father. While the older man probably looked intimidating to most people, especially if he was in his uniform, James was a couple of inches taller and a lot more muscular than Charles, so he wasn't nearly as intimidated by his scowl since his gun wasn't on his hip. "I'm James Hunter."

"Nice to meet you, James." Charles Lee shook James's hand with a good strong grip.

James didn't back down from the show of strength, tightening his own grip in the handshake. But showing that he wasn't going to be afraid of Randi's father was only part of meeting her parents. He also had to show his charming side to her mother if he had any hope of convincing them that he was good enough for their daughter, so he turned to her as soon as Mr. Lee released his grip.

"Mrs. Lee." James smiled at the older woman with Randi's striking green eyes. When she extended her hand toward him, he gently lifted it to his lips, instead of shaking it like he had with her husband. After a soft brush of his lips across the back of her hand, he smiled at her once more. "I see where Randi gets her wise, all-seeing eyes."

"Oh, aren't you a charmer," Mrs. Lee grinned as he released her hand and took a step back from her. "You can call me Mary and my husband is Charles. No need for formalities with our daughter's friends."

"Thank you, Mary," James acknowledged her friendly gesture as Randi finally stepped around her father and back into his line of sight. James turned toward her instinctually, but somehow restrained himself from reaching out to take her in his arms like he wanted. "It's good to see you again, Angel."

"Her name is Randi," Charles bellowed, but James ignored him and just smiled at his girl.

Before anyone could say anything more, Kay, Tia, and Maria were pushing James aside, so they could greet their family with hugs and squeals of delight. It didn't take long for Kay to whistle for everyone's attention, so she could introduce her parents, sister, and two friends to the whole crowd at once. Then Anthony's aunt was there passing out more name tags for them.

Hazel and Bob came over to greet the Lees, and then Kay was rounding up the wedding party to go for the dress and tux fittings. At least the ones who had come in from out of town in the last two days, since apparently, they'd already picked up the dresses for Kay, Tia, and Maria. Since he couldn't get close to Randi to offer her a ride to the bridal shop and formalwear store, he extended the offer of a ride to the group as a whole.

Instead of getting any alone time with Randi like he wanted, he ended up with Anthony and Dean in his truck and Kay drove Randi, Deanna, and Amy in her SUV. Even his plan to get Randi alone after the fitting to go get the party supplies they'd need for that night was thwarted when Anthony explained that his sisters had taken Kay to San Antonio to get them a couple of days before.

He was contemplating his chances of getting her alone in a dressing room as he parked beside Kay in front of the stores on Appaloosa Avenue. Opening Randi's car door was the closest he would get to her that afternoon, though, because as soon as they all went in the main entrance to Destiny Dresses, the guys were all directed to go through a side door to Benny's Formalwear, where the men's dressing rooms were located on the opposite side of the building from the women's changing area.

He was handed a garment bag and directed to a dressing room to change. When he opened the garment bag to pull out the tuxedo, he also found a separate bag with a matching pair of Oxford dress shoes.

"Dude, are we really going to Elvis's wedding in these blue suede shoes?" Dean hollered from the other dressing room. "I mean, I know you liked to rock out back in the day, Anthony, but I didn't know you thought of yourself as the king of rock-n-roll."

"Naw," Anthony replied with a chuckle. "Ya'll are the Elvis impersonators at our wedding, my shoes are Navy issued dress whites."

"Does that mean we get to officiate like in a Vegas wedding?" Dean chuckled.

James just shook his head at his brother and friend and changed out of his jeans and cowboy boots into the tuxedo. He didn't put the shoes on because they wouldn't fit over his thick white socks that he had on to wear with the boots.

"Um, what are our options for socks?" James stepped out of the dressing room carrying the shoes in his hand. "I don't think my white tube socks are gonna work."

"Kay!" Anthony yelled for his bride-to-be to come over from the women's side of the conjoined stores. "Baby, I need you to decide which of these socks look best with the guys' shoes."

"What?" Kay hollered back as she poked her head through the doorway between the two stores.

"Actually, we may need bigger shoes, too," Dean interjected as he came out of the dressing room wearing the shoes without socks. "These are a little tight without socks and I don't know that I can wear them enough to stretch them out before the wedding."

"Seriously?" Anthony looked down at Dean's feet. "I thought you were both a size thirteen."

"We were back in high school," James replied to his friend. "But our feet had another growth spurt in college, at least a little one. Now a thirteen and a half is a perfect fit in most shoes, but I usually get a fourteen because it's so hard to find half sizes."

"They're definitely not going to stretch out." Benny pointed to Dean's feet for him to take off the shoes. He walked over to the computer on the back counter as he continued speaking. "Take those off and put them back in the bags and I'll order the correct size for a rush delivery."

"Thanks, Mr. Benson." James turned back to his dressing room to grab the shoe bag to put his in while Dean took his off on his way back to his own dressing room for the other shoe bag.

"We still need to figure out the sock issue, though," Anthony pointed out, motioning for Kay to come all the way into the menswear store.

"Okay, give me a minute." Kay held up a hand to Anthony. "Once I see how the bridesmaids' dresses look, I'll be right over to help you pick out socks."

"Do you need to see how we look side by side with the ladies?" Dean wagged his brows suggestively.

"No, I already know that the tuxes and dresses match, and I don't have time for you to flirt," Kay scolded, shaking a finger at Dean. "We have to hurry and get back to the cookout and all our other guests."

Resigned to not even getting to see Randi in her bridesmaid's dress, James looked at the display of men's dress socks to see what the options were for he and his brother. They mostly ranged from several shades of tan to gray to black. The only blue option was a navy blue that was a lot darker than the royal blue of the tuxedos and shoes, but it was his pick for the best option.

A few minutes later, Kay came back to look at the same display and quickly picked out the navy socks. She had James and Dean move around in the tuxedos a little bit to make sure they didn't need any alterations to be able to dance at the wedding without risking ripping a seam. Once she approved of the tuxes and socks and confirmed that the correct size shoes would be in the store on Tuesday, she kissed

Anthony on the cheek and motioned over her shoulder at the women's side of the store to indicate she was going back to the bridesmaids. "We'll see you guys back at the ranch."

James went back to the dressing room to change back into his casual clothes. He tucked the correct size navy socks into the bag with his tux as he hung everything back up. He felt a little weird when he went to pay for the tux, dress shirt, socks, and shoes, only to find out that it had all already been covered by Anthony. It wasn't like it was a rental that Anthony was covering for his groomsmen to return after the wedding. He'd actually bought their tuxedos and accessories. James pulled his phone out and made a second donation to another of the charities on their list in the amount he'd expected to spend on the formalwear for the wedding, wanting to ease his guilty conscience for having his friend cover his tab for the wedding attire.

~~~

After the fastest fitting for formalwear that Randi could ever believe was possible, Kay drove the girls over to a western wear store named Boots & Britches because Amy and Deanna both complained about not bringing appropriate clothing for going horseback riding. Randi was glad that she'd talked to James while she was packing, so she had her boots and jeans in her suitcase. But she had to wait to change into them once they were back on the ranch after their friends finished shopping.

As they were browsing through the store, Randi wished she would have gone over to the menswear side of the bridal shop to catch a ride back to the ranch with James and the guys, instead of tagging along with the ladies. It wasn't that she didn't want to spend time with her sister and friends. She just wanted to spend some time with James more, even if it was in the presence of others, when they couldn't do more than stare at each other from across the field of people and activities back on the ranch.

"You seriously don't need to find some boots and jeans?" Deanna gave Randi a strange look as she stood there watching her friends looking through the rack of jeans for their sizes.

"No, I packed them," Randi confirmed.
~~~

Leah Mae Wright

"I can't believe I forgot to pack mine," Amy sighed, shaking her head as she shuffled through the rack until she pulled out a pair of jeans in the size she wanted. "Between the mention of the trail rides in the group chat and Randi and I planning what we were going to bring and specifically saying we needed boots and jeans to ride horses, I should've remembered them when I was packing."

"I guess I missed that post in the group chat," Deanna shrugged, finally pulling a pair of jeans from the rack.

"Eh, at least we were able to get here to get what you need before the store closes." Kay led the way as they walked through the store to the wall of boots at the back.

Of course, they each have to try on a half a dozen different styles of boots when we're in a rush, Randi thought, getting more and more impatient each minute they took to dawdle in the store. Her phone buzzed, so she pulled it out of her purse to see that James was as impatient to see her again as she was to see him.

> **James: Where are you? Just got to the ranch & can't find you.**

> **Randi: Amy & Deanna forgot to pack for horseback riding, so we're at Boots & Britches. Hopefully, they won't take too much longer. {Face with Rolling Eyes Emoji}**

> **James: K. I'll let Anthony know since he's freaked out that ya'll left before we did & aren't here yet.**

> **Randi: Was he the only one worried? {Thinking Face Emoji}**

> **James: Nope. {Relieved Face Emoji} Now hurry home, I need to at least get my eyes on you even if that's all I can get on you in this crowd.**

> **Randi: See you soon! {Smiling Face with Heart-Eyes Emoji}**

"Kay, text your man and let him know you're okay," Randi directed her sister as she tucked her phone back in her purse. "James said he's worried because we left first and didn't get back to the ranch before them."

"Wow, he keeps you on a short leash," Deanna criticized as she walked across the room in yet another pair of boots.

"He's probably not really that worried if he didn't text Kay himself," Amy pointed out, putting the lid on the box of boots she'd just taken off.

"No, he's probably freaked out and doesn't want to take a chance on me trying to read his text while driving and getting in an accident," Kay corrected Amy's assumption as she typed on her phone.

"Like I said, short leash," Deanna grumbled as she sat back down to take off the boots she was trying on. "I couldn't stand to be with a guy who had to keep such close tabs on me like that."

"You say that now, but I bet you'll change your tune if you fall in love with someone who's suffered a loss like Anthony and needs to know where you are, so he doesn't worry about losing you, too," Kay teasingly admonished her BFF, still texting on her phone.

"What kind of loss are you talking about that would justify being that clingy?" Deanna's condescending tone indicated she doubted the validity of Kay's justification of Anthony's feelings. Not that she noticed she was irritating the other women while boxing up the boots she'd just taken off.

Kay looked up from her phone with an unusual expression, like she wasn't quite sure she should tell them. She seemed to be deep in thought for a moment before shaking her head like she was debating in her mind whether or not to share Anthony's history with her sister and friends.

"I don't think anyone will bring it up this week, but just in case, I guess ya'll need to know," Kay finally voiced her decision. She took a deep breath and put her phone back in the back pocket of her jeans before explaining. "Back when he was a teenager, Anthony's high school sweetheart and their unborn baby were killed in a car accident."

"Oh, Dog," Randi gasped, her hand flying up to cover her mouth to keep her from expressing her shock at his loss.

"He was on a Navy base in Florida and supposed to marry her the next week when he came home on leave," Kay continued. "He'd have married her before he enlisted, but he had to wait until she turned eighteen. Then she died on her eighteenth birthday, so instead of getting married on his leave, he buried his family. Now he worries about the girls and I if we get in a car with anyone but him behind the wheel. And because I understand where his anxiety is coming from, I don't mind checking in with him to let him know exactly where I am and when I'll be home. He's not trying to be a controlling asshole like my ex. He's just trying to ease his anxiety. And since I don't want to lose him to a heart attack from his excessive worrying, I usually tell him before I make extra pit stops when I go to town without him."

"Sorry, guess we didn't give you a chance to tell him when we asked about places to get boots and jeans on the way home," Amy apologized. "He's okay with your texts now, though, right?"

"Yeah, he's fine now," Kay smiled at Randi's bestie. "But ya'll need to hurry because I was serious about needing to get back to the ranch and the rest of the guests."

Randi was a little irritated at Deanna for not apologizing to Kay, as well as for her "short leash" comments, but she didn't say anything as they finally settled on the boots they wanted and rushed up to the checkout counter. Randi understood Anthony's anxiety issues after such a tragic loss, especially since she'd been dealing with her own anxiety issues recently.

Since she was learning more about her own issues stemming from a fear of how other people would react to her if they knew the real person underneath the façade she put on for the world to see, Deanna's negative comments about Anthony and Kay's relationship dynamics set her on edge. While she knew the comments weren't directed at her in any way, Randi didn't want to risk being the next person Deanna commented negatively about by lowering her guard around her sister's best friend at any point that week, when they'd be around each other.

Randi was learning a lot about herself in her therapy sessions. In addition to realizing that her hesitation to have sex before her previous boyfriends had pushed her into it was because she felt guilty about wanting to be a sexual person, and that she'd pushed James to be rougher than she was really ready for that first night, so she'd feel like she had no choice to ease her guilt, she'd also realized how she'd cut herself off from people for the last few years because of her trust issues.

While her therapist hadn't figured out a way to help ease her guilty feelings about sex that had been drilled into her as a teenager, Randi was working on various strategies with her therapist to try to reach out and connect with new friends to help her overcome some of her other trust issues. It was working really well with James, but hearing negative comments like Deanna had made earlier, made Randi leery of trying to make friends with too many new people.

So, instead of being the outgoing person she wanted to be, she quietly observed everyone at the cookout when they got back to the ranch. She'd managed to snag her suitcases from her parents' rental car to change clothes in the bunkhouse, so she could participate in the horseback riding and various activities like riding four-wheelers and playing corn hole with her nieces and the other kids. But she mostly just listened to the adult conversations around her without making many comments.

She paid attention to the women around her, mostly trying to see who made any snide remarks and who was almost always positive and inclusive, so she could figure out who she might like to become friends with, or who to avoid in the future if she got the opportunity to be around them. She was glad that everyone seemed to be wearing the name tags they'd been given on arrival, so she was able to sort of keep track of who was related to Anthony and who was there from the GWA. For the most part, they all seemed to be friendly and outgoing, making her think that she might be able to be more herself with them in the future.

At least when I'm not trying to avoid negative comments or lectures from my parents.

As much as James had said he'd missed her and would have a hard time keeping his hands off her when they finally got to see each other, Randi was surprised that he seemed to be keeping his distance at the cookout. He was hanging out with the guys mostly, not coming close enough to speak to her all afternoon. When she took her turn on a trail ride, he and one of his friends joined the group, but they brought up the rear where Randi was up front, right behind Tia and Maria, who were first and second in line behind their new grandfather. It was like James tried to maintain about a twenty-foot distance between them, close enough to watch her constantly, but not close enough to talk or touch.

Leah Mae Wright

She'd been tempted several times to pull out her phone to text him, wanting to be closer to him while they ate barbeque, or to take a chance to sneak away on a four-wheeler together. But since nobody else had a phone out, she figured it would not only be considered rude, but would also be very obvious that they were texting each other, if they were the only two people with phones out under the scrutiny of so many prying eyes.

After a long, tiring day, Randi was grateful for the announcement by one of Anthony's sisters that it was time for the ladies to leave to go get ready for the bachelorette party, even though she was embarrassed that she'd forgotten to confirm that someone had gotten the party supplies. Since her parents were staying at the bunkhouse that night with all the kids, Randi put her suitcases in Kay's Jeep to go to her house to get ready for the party.

She wished she could've put her things in James's truck, so she could go get ready for the party with him at his house, instead of with her sister and their friends at Kay's new home. She ended up changing in Tia's room and sharing the mirror in the Jack and Jill bathroom with Amy and Deanna to touch up their hair and makeup for the evening, while Kay and Anthony were getting ready together in the master bedroom and bathroom.

She took a little longer than her friends, who apparently convinced Anthony to show them to their rooms in his parents' house next door, while she finished up with those things she could only do once everyone else was out of the bathroom. Instead of having him make a second trip to the other house to help her with her things, Randi left most of her stuff in Tia's room. If she didn't end up going home with James after the party, she could crash in Tia's bed for the night, since her niece would be sleeping in the bunkhouse with all the other kids and the multitude of grandparents that had shown up for babysitting duty at the cookout.

I probably shouldn't ask Kay to bring my bags to the party, so I can take them with me to James's house later. Randi made her way down the stairs to go with her sister to the party. *While I'm sure she wouldn't mind, it'll be a lot easier to sneak me back in here early in the morning than it would be to carry all my luggage in when Mom and Dad could show up any minute.*

Chapter Eleven

When he arrived at Tully's Roadhouse for the joint bachelor and bachelorette party, James was surprised to see that not only had Anthony's sisters stepped up to get the party supplies earlier in the week, but they'd also arranged for the bar to be decorated with a banner that read, "Congratulations Anthony and Kay," and enough streamers and balloons that if they'd been outside, they'd have been able to be seen from outer space. The rustic country bar was covered in so much bridal white it was almost unrecognizable as a dive bar, looking nearly like a dignified reception hall.

"When did Charlotte and Becky have time to do all this?" James prodded his brother, who had walked into the bar just ahead of him.

"They didn't," a gruff voice bellowed from behind the bar. James turned to see who was speaking and recognized Leo Walker, a fellow descendant of one of the founders of their small town, who he remembered as being a year or two older than him and his brother. "They suckered my brothers and cousins into hanging this shit up. I still can't believe they were able to sweet talk Uncle Tully into letting them turn the bar into a bridal shop."

"Are they gonna all be here tonight?" James posed the question to Leo, since he didn't see any of Leo's brothers or cousins in the main room of the bar. Most of the youngest generation of Walkers worked for Leo's father, Wyatt Walker at Walker Construction, with the exception of Leo, who worked for his uncle at the bar, and his older brother Luke, who had his own garage in town. But James wanted to make sure he bought their other brother, Landon, and their cousins, Aiden, Dalton, Hayden, and Hudson, an extra round of beer in thanks for all their hard work on the bed and breakfast in the last month.

Leah Mae Wright

"Yeah, they're in back playin' pool." Leo lifted his chin in the direction of the doorway to the back room, where all the pool tables were located.

"Cool, we'll probably end up splitting the party, so we can play a few games while the girls do all their bachelorette party stuff out here," Dean announced, leaning against the bar. "Why don't we start with a couple of pitchers for the guys who are already here and in the back?"

Of course, you wanna split the party on gender lines, so I don't get to spend any more time with Randi tonight than I got to earlier at the cookout, James grumbled in his head, beginning to wonder if the universe was against him getting alone time with his girl.

"We can do that," Leo replied, grabbing two pitchers from under the bar. "Any preference for brand?"

"Naw, just whatever's most popular with the rest of the guys," Dean decided.

"Ya'll wanna open a tab for the party or pay as you go?"

"We'll open a tab." Dean pulled his card out of his wallet and handed it to Leo.

"Actually, Dean will cover the tab for the guys, and I'll cover the tab for the ladies," James corrected his brother, taking out his own card to hand to Leo to open the ladies' tab, even though they hadn't arrived yet.

They hadn't discussed how they would split the cost of all the drinks for the night, but James didn't want his brother covering all of it. Nor did he want to risk Randi thinking she would have to cover the cost for the women's portion of the party. He knew she must be stressing about costs for everything with how her boss had been messing with her hours at work the last few weeks. And while he knew it would be a sure thing for her to get the job with the GWA, he wasn't one-hundred percent sure she believed that yet. Besides, even if she started work with the GWA as soon as they went back on the road after the holiday break, she wouldn't have that income immediately to feel comfortable paying for the bar tab that night.

Once Leo handed them each a pitcher of beer and a stack of plastic cups to take to the back, they headed into the poolhall portion of the bar. In addition to Leo's brothers and cousins already being back there, Anthony's older brothers were all there, too. James sat his pitcher and stack of cups down on the closest bar height table to the pool table where the majority of the guys were congregating.

"Heard ya'll were coming to town for the wedding." James nodded to the Burlesons, who were normally stationed out of town with the Navy, as he walked up to the pool table where Josh and Jake Burleson were standing with Aiden, Dalton, Haydon, and Hudson Walker. "But wasn't sure when you'd actually get here."

"Got in last night." Jake shook hands with James.

"Couldn't miss our little brother's bachelor party," Josh quipped, taking his turn with the handshake greetings.

James momentarily wondered why neither of the Burleson twins explained why they hadn't been at the barbeque earlier. Then again, with so many people there, he supposed he could've easily missed them since he was so focused on watching Randi all afternoon.

Bobby Burleson and Luke Walker walked back to the table carrying pool cues from where they'd been on the other side of the room picking them out. Landon Walker wasn't far behind them. They finished exchanging greetings and handshakes, then James thanked the Walkers for all their hard work at the bed and breakfast before pointing out the first two pitchers of beer for everyone. Since two pitchers wasn't enough for all eleven of them to get a full cup, James went back up to the front of the bar to get a few more.

While he was standing at the bar waiting for Leo to fill a tray with beer pitchers, more people started arriving for the party. Several of the GWA guys, a few of their wives, and several of Anthony's cousins, plus his two sisters.

"Hey, where's the happy couple?" Rick walked up to the bar beside James.

"I think they're gonna be the last to arrive," James replied to his boss. "Anthony's brothers and a few of our other friends are already in the back playin' pool, though."

"Oh, good, the guys are separating off to the other room, so we can play our pin the dick on the dude game without our brothers in the room," Anthony's cousin Jen chuckled, pushing her brother JJ toward the back of the bar.

"Seriously, girls actually play those games at bachelorette parties?" Justin Burleson followed his brother and sister back toward the pool room.

Leah Mae Wright

"Only when our brothers and cousins aren't around," Becky Burleson answered him as she stopped beside James at the bar. She pointed at the tray in front of James where Leo was putting another pitcher. "That's going back with the guys, right? I'm assuming you know better than to order beer for the ladies."

"I just opened a tab for you ladies," James conceded, holding his hands up in surrender. "I wouldn't make the mistake of trying to guess what to order for ya'll."

"Aw, that's so sweet that you're covering our drinks all night," Becky cooed, leaning in to give him a hug of thanks. Unfortunately, that was the exact moment that Randi walked into the bar with Anthony, Kay, and the other two women who had come to town with her family.

"Just doing my part as co-best man." James lightly tapped her back with one hand to return the hug, before quickly releasing her and raising his hands again to show Randi he wasn't into Becky. "Dean's covering half too, so why don't you go back and thank him with all the hugs." *Hopefully, he won't be too rude with brushing her off, since the woman he's crushing on isn't here to see the brotherly show of affection.*

"Will do," Becky grinned as she released her hold on James and bounced away toward the back without putting in an order for drinks for the women.

"Randi," James shouted over the increasing noise of the bar filling up with party goers.

She'd stopped to put her purse down at a table across the room from where he was standing at the bar, so he motioned for her to come to the bar.

When she didn't move toward him, focusing on taking off her jacket and hanging it on the back of the chair in front of her instead of him, James shouted again, "Angel, I need you over here for co-hosting duties, so we can get this party started."

It wasn't really his main reason for wanting to speak with her at that exact moment, but he'd use having her act as the point person for the bachelorette party to get her close to him. Once he introduced her to Leo, then he'd make sure she didn't have any reason to feel jealous of Becky for a friendly hug.

"What are my co-hosting duties?" Randi arched an eyebrow at him when she finally got to the bar area.

James hated that she stopped walking toward him when she was still far enough away from him that he couldn't reach out and touch her. He took a step towards her, so he could clasp her hand in his to gently pull her closer to the bar. She was acting skittish, so he resisted the urge to wrap his arms around her and kiss her senseless, but it was only because he thought she wouldn't want him to in front of everyone who was mingling around them and figuring out what was happening for the party.

"Leo," James called out, turning toward the bartender. "This is my girl, ur, Randi. If you're not sure if someone's here for the bachelorette party, ask her. She can sign on my card to pay the ladies' tab tonight, too."

"Your girl, huh?" Randi looked up at him questioningly.

"Yeah, my girl," James beamed, unable to resist hauling her in close and leaning down to kiss her. He kept it chaste in deference to the fact that they were surrounded by people, but he hoped she recognized it as him claiming her in front of their friends and family. She looked a little dazed when they parted lips, so he thought she understood his intention for the kiss.

"Nice to meet you, Randi," Leo greeted her as he put the last pitcher of beer that would fit on the tray in front of James.

"This is Leo Walker," James introduced the bartender before turning back to him and saying, "Don't even think about hitting on her."

"Nice to meet you too, Leo," Randi giggled lightly. "But I don't know what he's talking about for signing on his card." She pointed at James with her thumb.

"Just that I had Dad add you to my accounts at the bank, so if he can't get my signature for whatever reason tonight, yours will work to pay my half of our bar tab," James admitted, keeping his arm around her shoulders. "We've ordered beer for the guys, but I figured you'd have a better idea of what to order for the ladies to drink."

"Oh, uh, okay," Randi sputtered, looking like she was confused by his statement, but he didn't want to explain further because the bar was not the right location to talk to her about combining their accounts as they progressed to the next phase of their relationship.

"How about I go ahead and take these to the back for the guys?" Rick asked from behind James. James was surprised by hearing his boss, having forgotten that he was there the instant he saw Randi walk in the door. "And you can help Randi get the ladies started with their drinks."

"Oh, uh, yeah, thanks, Boss," James stammered, passing the tray of beer to Rick. He turned back to Randi before asking, "So, Angel, what do you think we should order for the ladies?"

"I'm not sure." Randi shook her head before turning to look around the bar. When her gaze finally landed on Kay, who was sitting on Anthony's lap at a table at the back of the room, just outside the doorway to the poolhall, she shouted, "Kay, what are we drinking tonight?"

"I want sangria," Kay yelled back. "But I don't know what everyone else wants!"

A few of the ladies who were clustered around looked up from their conversations, but nobody else replied as to what they wanted to drink. "Fine, let's get a few pitchers of sangria to start," Randi decided, throwing her hands up in exasperation at the lack of input from the rest of the women at the party. "If they want anything else, they can come order it themselves."

"Coming right up," Leo smiled. "And Melissa should be here soon to keep the rounds coming to the tables, so you won't have to come back to the bar."

"Thanks, man." James was curious as to why the waitress wasn't already there, but not curious enough to ask.

"So, um, it looks like we're segregating the party." Randi looked up at James as she motioned around the room. "Ladies in this room and gentlemen in the back room?"

"Yeah, Anthony's cousins were talking about bachelorette party games they didn't want their brothers and male cousins around for," James confirmed, pulling her in for a loose embrace while they waited for Leo to fix up the pitchers of sangria. "But as soon as ya'll are done with the dick-themed games, I hope we can co-mingle again. Maybe see which one of us is better at pool?"

"I think that can be arranged," Randi cooed, wrapping her arms around his waist, and leaning her head against his chest. "Or maybe we can get that jukebox going and practice dancing for the wedding?"

"We can definitely do that," James agreed, loving how she felt pressed against him. They swayed together there in an intimate embrace for several minutes, completely ignoring the party going on around them.

As much as he longed to take her home to spend the whole night making love to her, James knew he had to control himself for a little while longer. He knew that being there for her sister at the various wedding events was important to Randi, so he would just enjoy being able to be close with her while her parents weren't around at this one. He'd wait to unleash his lust with her for a few hours once they left the bar and got back to his cabin where they could be alone.

But, damn, it's gonna be an uncomfortable few hours with my dick pressing against my zipper, wanting to get out to her, every time I even get a glimpse of her from across the crowded room.

He helped her distribute the pitchers of sangria to the tables the women had claimed before dragging Anthony away from his bride-to-be and back to the pool tables with the rest of the guys. He only had one beer, just enough to toast his best friend at the beginning of the night. Then he switched to drinking bottled water, wanting to maintain a clear head to be safe driving Randi home for the night.

Home. Fuck! Is it too soon to ask her to move in with me? I want my place to be her home, too. But, if she doesn't wanna leave Tulsa permanently, maybe I'll just plan to leave some of my stuff at her place after Christmas, and we'll both call Tulsa home.

<div align="center">~~~</div>

Randi quickly recovered from her instant bout of jealousy at seeing Anthony's sister hugging James when she walked into the bar for the party. Not just because of the way he introduced her as "his girl" to the bartender and publicly claimed her as his with that hard, but chaste, kiss in front of most of the wedding guests. The evidence of how much he wanted her had been pressed into her belly while they waited for the first round of sangria, and again later in the evening when they danced for real once the girls were through with their games for the night.

Leah Mae Wright

The tight jeans that James was wearing made it obvious to anyone who looked when he was aroused that night. And Randi was definitely looking every chance she got. The bulge behind his zipper only grew when James was looking at Randi. And it quickly deflated as soon as anyone else spoke to him and took his attention away from the laser focus he seemed to have on her.

After the first round of sangria, one of Anthony's sisters had ordered a round of blow job shots, which led to several rounds of shots with even more raunchy names. Five rounds of liquid courage later, Randi was a lot more open to getting to know the ladies around her. She found she really liked the family her sister was marrying into, both Anthony's biological relatives and the coworkers that Kay said felt like family.

Dog, I hope I'm not too drunk to remember all this in the morning.

They laughed and joked around as they played a few games. Randi felt pretty good about being the person who knew the bride best and was completely unapologetic for pinning the dick on the dude's navel during the blindfolded game. "The dude on that poster is way too short to be life sized," she'd told the girls when they all laughed at her high placement. "I put the dick at the height where I felt James's earlier, so if we're supposed to be aiming for Kay's groom, it probably should be even higher since Anthony is so tall."

Her comments led to a barrage of "you go girl" and other similar comments about her and James, as well as a few grossed-out comments from the women related to Anthony, who didn't want to imagine the dude in the game as Kay's groom. Eventually, the conversation changed to the women comparing notes about the single men in the back room playing pool, and deciding that they wanted to go hang out with the guys, instead of playing more bachelorette party games.

Once the couples started pairing off, Randi spent the rest of the night glued to James, either beside him when they played pool, on his lap while they visited with the rest of the people at the party, or in his arms when they danced. At the end of the night, she insisted on signing the receipt for James's portion of the tab, not really believing that he'd added her to his accounts to make it a legal transaction, and hoping she wouldn't end up in jail for credit card theft by trying to prove it. After being reassured by Anthony's brother, the chief of police in their small town, that he wouldn't arrest her if James's card was declined because of her signature, she signed the receipt.

I can't wait to see his face on Monday, when the bank or the bar calls him to come sign the receipt himself, because there's no way they'll accept my signature when they don't have it on file for his accounts.

The ground spun slightly as they walked out of the bar, but it mostly stopped when James wrapped his arm around her to walk her to his big blue truck. Ever the gentleman, he opened the passenger door for her, helped her get in the jacked-up Dodge Ram, and even fastened her seatbelt for her, before kissing her on the forehead, shutting her door, and going around to the driver's side to get in and start the vehicle. She was a little sleepy on the drive back to his cabin, but she somehow managed to stay awake to watch him confidently navigate the roads around town and pull off onto a gravel road on his family's land.

The sight of the majestic log home that he drove up to revived her slightly. When he told her that he had a cabin on his family's property, she expected something small like a hunting cabin. When he said it was a three bedroom, she imagined something more like her parents' cabin in River's End, Oklahoma. Before seeing James's home, she considered the cabin her parents owned to be large for a log home at almost three-thousand square feet with four bedrooms and three bathrooms. But the outside of James's cabin looked like it was more than twice the size of her parents' cabin.

"That's not a cabin," Randi blurted as they pulled around to the garage entry on the side of the home. "That's a log mansion!"

"Maybe if I'd have finished out the basement level." James reached up to hit the garage door opener on his visor. The center door of the three garage doors opened for him to pull into what appeared to be a six-car garage at minimum. "But the second floor is only built out over the garage, kitchen, dining room, and den with lofts to look down at the gym and great room, so it's only about seventy-five-hundred square feet of livable space, including the garage. I think a mansion has to be at least ten-thousand square feet."

Randi could only gape at him as he shut off the truck and pushed the button to close the garage door. When he opened his door to get out of the truck, she saw a couple of older model sports cars parked to the left of where he'd parked the truck.

She was so focused on looking at the classic muscle cars that had obviously been refurbished from their original nineteen-sixties paint jobs to the gleaming yellow and red beauties that looked like brand-new versions of the older body styles, that she didn't realize James had walked around the truck to open her door for her. He reached across her to unbuckle her seatbelt before she checked back into the present moment.

"Ready to go in, Angel?" James offered her a hand to help her down from the tall truck.

Randi took James's hand to get out of the vehicle. She was still a little wobbly on her feet, so she leaned heavily against him as he walked her into his home. They walked in through the largest laundry room Randi had ever seen. In addition to the washer and dryer, there was a folding table built into the cabinets on one wall. The other side of the room was all cabinets with a bench built into one section with storage for shoes and coats. *I guess it's a combination of the laundry room and a mud room?*

They stepped out of that room and into the spacious open floor plan of the central portion of the house. To her right was the kitchen with gleaming stainless-steel appliances and more rustic wood cabinets with granite countertops along two walls and making up the central island. There was a doorway on the third wall, the one that shared space with the doorway to the laundry room, that Randi assumed was a pantry, just before what appeared to be the bottom of a staircase in the corner. There was no fourth wall where the kitchen opened up into the dining room, which appeared to be a round room. Randi assumed that the dining room area would appear similar to a castle turret from the outside of the house.

Just past the dining room was the space that James had described as the great room. It was an open space that encompassed the foyer of the formal entryway on the right and a living room sectioned off with sofas and chairs to encourage a large group of people to sit around and talk on the left. In between the foyer section and the living room section of the great room was a large fireplace that backed up into the main staircase in the area that Randi would assume was the very center of the house.

James pointed out the downstairs bathroom off the foyer before showing her through a doorway off the living area to what he called the den. Randi would've called it his man cave as that was where he had a huge television set up with more seating and a built-in bar.

Just past the den, the space opened up to a home gym almost as big as his garage. It was a truly professional setup that put Randi's spin bike in the corner of her living room to shame. There were several cardio machines along the wall on the left side of the room and several weight machines along the wall on the right side of the room. The wall at the end of the room had racks of free weights and four different types of weight benches. The center of the room was open, and Randi could imagine it would be a fabulous space for doing yoga, Pilates, or aerobic dance workouts. In the corner right next to the wall separating that room from the bar was a smaller spiral staircase, making the third set of stairs that she'd seen inside the home.

"Wow, this place is amazing!" Randi exclaimed, looking up at James in awe.

"I'm glad you like it." James pulled her into his arms and kissed the top of her head. "The bedrooms are all upstairs."

"Yes, that's what I really wanna see." Randi ran her hands up his chest to wrap her arms around his neck. "Unless you have some ideas for creative ways to use the gym equipment before we go to bed."

She pulled his head down as she pushed up onto her tiptoes to bring their lips together. Randi was tired of waiting to finally get naked with James. It had been too long since he'd been inside her. And while the orgasms she'd gotten during their sexy Skype sessions were a hundred times better than any she'd had before she met James, the ones she'd experienced on their one night together were a thousand times better than those.

She desperately wanted that out-of-this-world experience again as soon as possible. But even with the evidence that he wanted her as bad as she wanted him pressing into her belly, James pulled back, keeping the kiss mostly chaste when she tried to deepen it.

"Oh, Angel," James sighed as he took a step back from her. "As much as I desperately wanna fuck you against every surface in this whole house, I can't tonight."

"Yeah, you can." Randi stepped into him and reached out to cop a feel of his cock through his jeans.

"No, Angel, I can't," James argued, pulling her hand away from his crotch. "Not when you're too tipsy to remember it in the morning."

"I'm not tipsy," Randi disagreed before finally realizing how much she was slurring her words. *I passed tipsy with the third round of shots. And drunk when we switched back to sangria after the, um, fifth? Or sixth? Or seventh? Shit, I don't know how many rounds of shots we had. But when we went to play pool, I switched to water, so my drunk would wear off before we got here because I wanted to be able to remember our first time in your bed.*

"Well, you'll have to remember our first time in my bed being tomorrow morning when you've sobered up." James took her hand and led her back through the house to the main stairs.

Shit, did I say all that out loud?

"Yes, Angel, you did," James laughed as he aimed her at the staircase.

She swayed as the room tilted and missed putting her foot on the bottom step.

"Ya know what, let's not take a chance on you falling down those stairs or breaking an ankle in those sexy as fuck shoes." James scooped her up into his arms. He carried her, bridal style, up the stairs.

There was a small landing around the top of the stairs but only half walls surrounding the area, so she could see down to the first floor. There were walkways that led to rooms on either side of the house, but James didn't show her where they led. He just walked down the one leading back over the kitchen and dining room areas where the walls transitioned to going all the way to the ceiling. They went down a long hallway, passing what she assumed was the top of the staircase leading down to the kitchen before he carried her through a set of double doors to enter the master suite.

The bedroom and ensuite bathroom covered the same square footage as the garage below it. He passed a sitting area that had French doors leading out to a balcony on the back of the house and headed straight to a rustic California king-sized four-poster bed. James gently laid Randi on the navy-blue comforter covering the bed before disappearing through the leftmost of the three doorways off a short hallway in the opposite corner from where they'd entered the room.

She looked around the room while he was distracted with whatever he was doing, wherever he went. Where there had been family pictures on the walls in the living room downstairs and wrestling memorabilia on the walls in the den and gym areas, the walls in his bedroom were surprisingly bare.

The outer walls were all dark wood to match the vaulted ceiling, so she imagined they would be harder to hang things on. But the tan walls that surrounded the rock fireplace, which separated the bathroom, closet, and sitting room from the rest of the space, and the far wall that separated the master suite from the hallway and secondary staircase could really use some artwork. Randi didn't have time to decide what she would like to see hanging on those walls because he returned too quickly. He had a t-shirt in hand, so she assumed that doorway led to his closet.

"This will probably swallow you whole, but I figured it'd be comfortable for you to sleep in." James handed the t-shirt to Randi. "You need some help getting ready for bed?"

"No, I think I can do it." Randi smiled up at him.

"The bathroom is right over there." James pointed to the center door of the three doors off that short hallway, indicating it led to the restroom. "I don't have any of your girly stuff for removing your makeup or whatever, but there are towels and washcloths in the cabinet between the sinks. And since I buy in bulk to keep from having to shop too often, there's probably an unopened toothbrush or two in the third drawer down from there."

"Okay, thanks." Randi smiled at him as she took the soft gray shirt and went into the bathroom, passing that third doorway that she could now see was another glass door into the sitting room. She quickly found a washcloth and toothbrush right where he'd told her they would be. She went to the sink to the right of the cabinet to wash her face and brush her teeth, since it appeared to be the one he usually used. She put her new toothbrush in the holder beside his when she was done.

She took a moment in the water closet to empty her bladder before stripping out of her bohemian blue skirt and white peasant top. She unwound the straps of her shoes that went up her legs before taking them off. She removed her strapless bra, but left her panties on, before putting on the t-shirt he'd given her to sleep in. He was right about it being way too big for her. The shoulder seams fell halfway to her elbows and the hem was just above her knees.

I look like a kid playing dress-up. She giggled as she folded her clothes. She tucked her bra into her shirt before stacking them up on the counter beside the sink that nobody would be using that night. She pulled her brush out of her purse and ran it through her hair. She pulled her phone and charger out of her purse when she put the brush back. She left her purse with her clothing and padded back out to the bedroom in her bare feet.

James was walking back into the room carrying a glass of water and a bottle of over-the-counter pain relievers when she stepped out of the bathroom.

"Thought you might want these to stave off a hangover." James lifted the items up to show her.

"Thanks." Randi wasn't quite sure why she felt self-conscious as his eyes wandered down her body and back up to her face. "Um, where can I plug in my phone?"

He crossed the room and sat the water and headache pills on the bedside table before reaching for her phone. She handed it over quickly and he reached behind the bedside table to plug in the charger, setting the phone down on the table once it was charging.

"Take those," he commanded as he kissed the top of her head and disappeared into the closet again.

Randi opened the pill bottle and took out two, swallowing them down with half the glass of water.

James reappeared with a bundle of cotton wadded up in his hand, so Randi couldn't determine what article of clothing he was taking into the bathroom with him to change into.

"Get in bed, Angel," James ordered, lifting his chin to motion toward the bed as he walked by to go to the restroom. "I'll be right back."

While James was going through his bedtime routine, Randi pulled the comforter down and slipped into the bed. The sheets and pillowcases were also navy-blue to match the comforter and smelled like sandalwood and mint, which she thought had to be from James's bodywash. Randi nestled down in the bed, enjoying the smell of James that surrounded her. She'd enjoyed that smell more than a few times that night, every time he held her in his arms.

When James came out of the bathroom, he stood beside the bed for a few minutes just looking down at Randi. She took a moment to appreciate his bare chest and the tent he was making in his dark gray pajama pants before bringing her gaze back up to his face. She wasn't sure why he was so intently staring at her, but she was starting to feel uncomfortable under the scrutiny.

"Did I steal your favorite side of the bed?" She giggled at the thought of how they could share his favorite side of the bed.

"No, Angel." James looked at her reverently.

"Then why are you just standing there staring at me?"

"Just trying to memorize every detail of how you look in my bed, Angel." James's deep voice caused a wet spot in Randi's panties.

Finally, he walked around the bed and got in from the other side. He picked up a tablet from the other bedside table and used it to turn off the lights in his smart home. Once he returned it to the table beside the bed, he rolled onto his side in the middle of the bed and pulled Randi into his arms.

She snuggled in, resting her head on his upper arm, and pressing her palms into his chest as his arms encircled her. She'd never actually spent the night with any of her previous boyfriends, so she wasn't sure if she'd be able to sleep on her side cuddled up to him all night.

"Goodnight, Angel," James whispered into her hair.

"Goodnight, James," Randi whispered back as her eyes fluttered closed. "You're a much better cuddler than Little Jimmy."

"Who's little Jimmy?" She barely registered James's question.

"That's what I've been calling your stuffed doppelganger," Randi thought she said before drifting off to sleep feeling surrounded by James.

~~~

Sunday, November 18, 2018

Randi woke Sunday morning to the blaring of her phone alarm where she'd set it to remind her to take her medication at six in the morning. When she tried to move to locate her phone to turn off the alarm, she
~~~

found rolling over impossible. She'd apparently rolled onto her back at some point in the night, with James rolling with her to lay half on his stomach on top of her. His right arm and leg were draped over her body, effectively pinning her to the mattress. While it wasn't uncomfortable to be under him in the bed, not being able to move to turn off the alarm was painful for her already pounding head.

"James," Randi whispered in his ear since their heads were so close together on the pillow. "I need to get up and turn that alarm off and take my medicine."

"Okay, Angel," James slurred, but he didn't move.

"James," Randi implored again, a little louder, when he didn't move off of her.

"Mmm," James moaned in his sleep.

"I kinda need you to get off me so I can get up," Randi giggled as she brought her free hand up to push on his shoulder.

His morning wood poked into her thigh as he started to roll in his half-awake state. He didn't get very far before he was pressing back into her.

"Humping my leg like a dog isn't exactly what I was expecting from you this morning," Randi laughed, finally getting her right arm up from where it had been trapped under James, so she could use both hands to push against his chest and shoulder to try to move him enough that she could wiggle out from under him.

"Huh?" James finally lifted his head and slightly opened his eyes. "Sorry," he mumbled when he awoke enough to roll off of her.

Randi quickly rolled to the edge of the bed, so she could silence her alarm. She grabbed the water glass from the bedside table on her way to the bathroom. She refilled it from the tap to take her medicine, which she got out of her purse, before brushing her teeth and making a quick stop in the water closet.

She took the half-full water glass back to the bedroom and took two more headache pills to help get rid of any residual hangover she had from the night before. James had rolled onto his back and covered his eyes with his forearm. She wasn't sure if he'd gone back to sleep or not since she couldn't see his eyes. She could see the tent he was making of the sheet and comforter, though, so she decided it was time to get up for the day whether he wanted to go back to sleep or not.

She crawled back under the covers and rolled over to lay her head on his left shoulder. His arm came up around her, pulling her in close, like he was ready to go back to sleep while cuddling. *Yeah, not happening, Jimmy.* Randi ran her hand across his chest, enjoying the feel of her fingers twining with the perfect amount of hair scattered across his pecs. She followed the happy trail of hair down his eight pack abs until she hit the waistband of his pajama pants.

She was tempted to push those pants out of her way and play with his morning wood, but the sight of words hidden in his tattoo right in front of her eyes distracted her from her initial plan to wake him up. She pushed up on her elbow to look more closely at the design on his shoulder and down his arm.

From the pictures she'd seen online and watching him wrestle shirtless on television, she thought it was a tribal design with various colors peeking through the dark lines. Since he hadn't taken his shirt off their first night together and she hadn't looked closely at his tats when he was nude for their video calls, she hadn't figured out exactly what the design was yet, even though she'd seen him shirtless several times in their seven-week long relationship.

The bold black lines that she'd thought were a tribal design were actually more like vines weaving through a trellis. The colorful designs that she couldn't make out clearly on television or in the pictures on her computer were actually flowers, at least on his shoulder and bicep. As she looked farther down his arm, there were still flowers, but they were interspersed with other things hidden around them. There were musical notes, a set of drums, a mini wrestling ring, a luchador's mask, and even a pair of wrestling boots with surprisingly detailed laces for such a small design.

The words she first noticed when her eyes were less than an inch away from the tattoo were less noticeable as she pushed up to a seated position to continue exploring his arm. It seemed they started on his bicep and only went up to his shoulder, and were names written in pairs around the petals of the flowers. As she worked her way back up his arm from the wrist where the last of the flowers disguised his other items of interest, she realized that the vines of flowers were a family tree of sorts.

James was written on one flower with space left after it that she assumed was reserved for his future wife. She assumed the flowers on the vine below there would be where he tattooed his children and grandchildren's names. She ran a finger around the tattoo, finding Dean written on a flower on his triceps, in a similar manner to his own. The vines going up from James and Dean's names converged into a flower with the names David and Mandi.

There were two vines branching off from the flower containing his parents' names, one going up to a flower with the names Donald and Joan and the other going up to a flower with the names Richard and Patricia.

I wonder if that's the Rick and Patty I met yesterday at the cookout? They didn't mention their last name, but they were about the right age to be James's grandparents.

There wasn't a vine up from Donald and Joan's flower, so Randi trailed up one from Richard and Patricia to find another flower with the names Joseph and Margaret. Above that one she found a flower with the names James and Elizabeth.

I wonder if he was named after his great-great-grandfather and not just James Dean?

The vine off of that flower led to William Jr. and Emily on his deltoid. She couldn't trace it any farther because the vines led back across his shoulders and upper back.

"Having fun, Angel?" James lowered his other arm from across his eyes and looked up at her.

"Just exploring the secrets of your tattoos," she admitted, smiling down at him. "Are there names on the other arm, too?"

"Yes and no." James rolled toward her, so she could see his other arm to trace the vines coming back down the other side. "You've been looking at the family tree. The other side is more quotes and song lyrics that I like, with only the occasional name given if I knew who to credit for the quote when I had the tat done."

Randi was surprised to see the mix of quotes and lyrics that James had tattooed on his body. He had quotes from Walt Disney, Albert Einstein, and Dr. Seuss mixed with bible verses and rock-n-roll lyrics weaved around the flowers, vines, and various items tattooed down his right arm.

"Are you about done tracing my tats?" James queried after Randi had spent a few minutes running her fingers over the colorful designs on his arms.

"Yeah, for now anyway." Randi trailed her hands back up his arms and across his shoulders. She slid her palms down his chest and looked into his blue-gray eyes, wondering if the bluer appearance was because of the fact that he was laying on the navy-blue sheets.

"Good, because I have better ideas for what we can do this morning," James growled, his arms coming around her, so he could roll them to where she was straddling him on the bed, and he was laying on his back.

He weaved his fingers through her hair, bringing her face down to his for a passionate kiss. His other hand massaged down her back, stopping just above her butt to press her down into him as he rocked his hips to tease her with his erection. Their ten-inch height difference meant that only the head was trapped between their bodies while their lips were lined up for the kiss, but even the first couple of inches of him pressing against her mound was enough to get her worked up quickly.

Can we still call this dry-humping when I'm so wet, I'm soaking through my panties and maybe his pajama pants?

She started to feel embarrassed about the damp spot she felt in her panties from being so turned on so fast, but the feeling was fleeting. James invading her mouth with his tongue overrode all her thoughts.

She'd thought her intense orgasms during their virtual sex sessions were primarily mental from the vivid imagery of James's words more than based on her own physical touch. But the way James was turning off her brain with his possessive kissing and touching left her with no doubt that the most intense orgasms she would ever have were because of James causing them.

There was a mental component of them when he wasn't physically present with her, but the mental part wasn't necessary when he was the one touching her. And if he ever combined his physical presence with the mental aspect of sex, Randi wasn't sure she would survive the seismic activity within her own body.

"Fuck, Angel," James groaned as they broke off the kiss to take a breath. "I need you so fucking bad."

He started to trail kisses down her neck, but Randi pulled back to sit up on top of him before he could cause too much beard burn on her neck for her to be able to cover with the little bit of makeup she had in her purse. She grabbed the hem of his shirt that she was wearing and pulled it up and off over her head.

"Too many clothes between us," Randi teasingly complained, grinding her sex against his erection to prove her point. She didn't have a chance to back away any further to be able to remove her panties because James pulled her hips forward onto his abs and her torso down to him, so he could get his mouth on her breasts.

First, he trailed open mouthed kisses across her cleavage before licking down between the globes, then across the right mound to flick the tip of his tongue across her nipple. He latched on and suckled gently, grazing her with his teeth before soothing the abrasion by swirling his tongue around the taut tip. He moved to give the other side equal treatment at the same time he worked his pajama pants down to free his rock-hard member.

James released her nipple from his mouth and flipped her to her back on the side of the bed where he'd gotten in it the night before. He pushed up onto his knees between her legs and made quick work of removing her light blue satin panties, resting her feet on his chest to slide them down her legs.

"As pretty as these little panties are, I like the sight of you bare for me even better," he murmured as he tossed the panties to the floor.

"You need to finish losing those pants, too." Randi pointed at the pajama pants that were still around his thighs.

James pushed off the bed and dropped his pants the rest of the way to the floor. He reached out, opened the drawer in the bedside table, and pulled out a strip of condoms. He ripped one of the condoms off the strip before tossing the rest on the bed. He sheathed himself quickly before crawling back onto the bed. Instead of positioning himself to enter her as she expected, he pushed back and let his lower legs hang off the end of the bed as he lowered his head between her thighs.

Randi impatiently waited for James to get started with the second time she'd ever received oral sex. The first time had been the night she met James. She'd enjoyed it the first time, even though the position had felt precarious at the time on top of a boulder in Chandler Park. She hadn't felt embarrassed with the cover of darkness they had in the middle of the night alone in the park.

But even though laying on her back in the bed was a lot more comfortable position, the light streaming in the triangular shaped windows above the bed and the floor to ceiling windows on the back of his house between the bedroom door and the sitting room heightened her feelings of vulnerability and felt like a spotlight on her shameful behavior. She felt herself blush from head to toe as he spent a moment looking closely at the most private part of her body.

She hadn't felt that exposed on their video calls, even when she was completely naked and had the lights on in the room, because she'd never moved the camera that close to her most intimate areas. Looking down at his face and seeing how James was closely examining her, she felt overwhelmed and afraid of what he must be thinking about her. Just as she was starting to spiral through all the derogatory terms that she knew society would label her with if anyone knew what she was doing right then, James lifted his eyes to lock with hers.

"Focus on me, Angel," James commanded, his breath tickling across her lower lips. "Don't be embarrassed about anything we do together. We're not doing anything to be ashamed of."

"I'm not," Randi softly protested. "Not really. I'm more self-conscious about how close you're examining me and how awkward I feel being on display for you."

"Don't lie to me, Angel," James barked, pushing up onto his hands like he was doing a yoga cobra pose. "You've been on display for me a dozen times on video and haven't tensed up and turned beet red from being self-conscious of me seeing you before."

"Yeah, but you didn't get that close of a look on any of those video chats," Randi argued, pushing up onto her elbows, so she was closer to eye to eye with James.

James didn't respond, just raised an eyebrow at her.

"Fine, yes, I was also thinking about how I'd be labeled a slut if anyone knew what we're doing," she admitted with a huff. "But it was mostly that you haven't gotten that good of a look down there before, since the camera is always an arm's length away from me when we Skype and it was dark in the park the first time you, uh, you know."

"Oh, Angel," James chuckled. "It wasn't that dark in the park. The moonlight was bright enough to give me a very good view when I ate your pussy that night. And no matter what anyone else thinks or says, enjoying sex doesn't make you a slut. Not that I would care if it did, since I'd be wearing that same label right beside you."

"No, you wouldn't," Randi disagreed, shaking her head. "Men get praised for their virility while women get degraded for even acknowledging our sexuality."

"Angel," James drawled, pushing up to sit back on his heels, his erect and latex-covered penis standing at attention between them. "I can't change societal norms any more than I can change weather patterns, but I can and will change the voices in your head by praising you constantly for sharing your sexuality with me. You are gorgeous, inside and out. And as much as my inner caveman wants to keep you hidden away from the prying eyes of other men, it's not because it's wrong for you to show off your sexy body. It's purely because I wanna keep you all to myself. But if you need me to take you to a sex club and show you off, so you can hear the praise of a room full of people to help drown out the voices in your head that are telling you sex is wrong, I'll do it, if that's what you need."

"No, I don't need that," Randi protested, sitting up and reaching for James. "I just need you. I don't feel like anything we do is wrong when I look in your eyes and feel our connection."

"Then don't take your eyes off mine, Angel," James commanded, pulling her into his arms and slowly sliding inside her one agonizing inch at a time. "Fuck, you feel so good, so perfect."

He pulled her legs up and she instinctively wrapped them around his waist as her arms went around his neck. She weaved her fingers through his long dark hair, just as he did the same with one of his hands through her blonde tresses. His other hand cupped her butt, where he was using his grip on her to control how she moved on him.

"No, Jimmy, you're perfect," Randi purred as he finally filled her completely. She may have told him she wanted rough and rowdy sex the night they met, but she was glad that he took his time to ease inside her to allow her body to adjust to the size of his invasion before he upped the pace of his powerful strokes.

He brought their foreheads together, so they were looking deep into each other's eyes as they made love. Even if they got a little rougher and their pillow talk turned dirty, Randi couldn't think of being with James as anything other than making love. He may have gotten her to call it fucking in texts, but that was never how she'd classify the intimate joining of their bodies.

"So tight, so wet, so fucking good," James praised her as he moved his hand from her hair to her hip, gripping her hipbones in both hands, so he could bounce her up and down in rhythm with his powerful thrusts up into her body. "Your pussy is my version of heaven, Angel."

"Oh, James," Randi panted, her body tightening in preparation for an explosive climax. "So, good, so close."

He shifted his grip on her hips, so he could stroke his thumb over her clitoris. The pressure was perfect, causing her to pull his hair harder than she realized and dig her nails into his scalp and the back of his neck.

"That's it, Angel," James growled, still looking deep into her eyes. "Come now. Come on my cock!"

His words were the last piece of the puzzle that she needed to push her over the edge. Between the intensity of their connected gazes, the pressure of his thumb on her clit, and the exquisite way he stretched her open to reach that secret spot inside her that no one else had ever found, she'd been guaranteed an amazing orgasm. But combined with his commanding tone and dirty words, she couldn't think of a word strong enough to describe the magnitude of what she was feeling.

In addition to the rippling spasms of her channel, the feeling of coming apart around him, and the explosion of light she saw around them, as if their auras were consummating their relationship, she had the oddest sensation of wetting the bed, even though she knew she'd already emptied her bladder that morning. She wasn't sure what exactly was happening in her body, only that she couldn't stop it and she loved the way it felt.

"Fuck, yes, Angel," James shouted, continuing to push her buttons both inside and out. "Squirt all over me, Randi. Don't. Fucking. Stop." He punctuated his last statement with a deep, powerful plunge into her body after each word.

"Yes, James, oh fuck, yes," Randi exclaimed as the waves of pleasure overtook her.

Randi wasn't sure if one orgasm lasted for ten minutes, or if she had ten orgasms with one rolling into the next repeatedly. James finally joined her on the rocket ship to outer space where they floated weightlessly in each other's arms. Even through the most extreme orgasmic experience of her life, they never broke eye contact. James kept his focus on her as much as she kept her focus on him. Their bond of togetherness was the most profound part of the whole encounter.

Instead of collapsing on the bed as Randi expected in her out-of-breath state, James picked her up and carried her into the bathroom. He gently placed her on the bench inside his massive shower and went to take care of the condom before joining her in the cavernous space. The whole shower was tiled to match the rustic wood look of the whole house, including the bench she was seated on, save for the plethora of stainless-steel shower heads and the glass doors that James just stepped through.

He went to a panel on the opposite end of the shower that was as big as her entire bathroom back home. After a few swipes across the screen, warm water sprayed out from the two rain shower heads that came from the ceiling and four of the eight body jets that were positioned around the walls.

"Wow!" Randi breathed out the word, in awe of the way the little room filled with water and steam. "But what's up with being stingy and hogging the body jets at your end of the shower?"

"Not being stingy, Angel." James walked toward her with purpose. "Just warming up the room without risking drowning while I eat my breakfast."

James dropped to his knees when he reached her, placing his hands on her knees, and spreading her legs. "Someone sidetracked me when I planned to eat my fill earlier and I didn't get to spend near enough time with my head between your legs, Angel."

Randi leaned back against the tile wall of the shower as James lowered his head. Somehow, he still maintained eye contact with her, even though she was in a mostly seated position as he took his first long slow lick through her folds.

"Since I'm not gonna be able to talk for the next few minutes," James murmured between teasing licks through her slit and up to her clit. "I'm gonna need you to keep the dirty talk going by telling me what you like while I eat your pussy, Angel."

"I'm gonna need you to do more than tease me, Jimmy," Randi instructed, weaving her fingers through his hair to guide his face back to her sex.

He pushed his nose into her clit as he teased her opening with his tongue, and Randi couldn't help but laugh at him using his nose as if it was a sexual organ. "Not with your nose, silly," she giggled, not able to remember ever laughing during sex with anyone before him. She rather liked feeling playful during their intimate moments. It was hard to be self-conscious or ashamed when they were having so much fun together.

"Then tell me what you want me to do, Angel." James's warm breath blew across her most sensitive spot in a very tantalizing way.

"I want you to suck my clit," Randi directed, quivering with need. "Fu-fuck me with your fingers and tongue."

"As you wish," James quoted one of her favorite movies before devouring her like a man possessed with the need to taste every hidden crevice of her vagina.

He sucked on her clit while impaling her on first one, then two, and finally three of his long, thick fingers.

"Yes, yes, yes, James, fuck yes," Randi cried out as she went over the edge the first time in the shower. She continued repeating his name as he extended her high for a few moments before bringing her back down by softening his suckling and stroking.

He slowly pulled his fingers from her body, moving them to trace circles around her overly sensitized nub. He fucked her with his tongue, licking deep inside her as he increased the pressure of his fingertip against her pink pearl.

He hardened the tip of his tongue as he curled it up to rub across her G-spot at the same time he used two fingers to caress her distended clitoris, moving back and forth on both sides at once. The combination of having both of her buttons stimulated at the same time sent her into a screaming climax. She clutched his tongue tightly in her sheath as her inner walls contracted around his oral probe.

She wasn't sure her cries of pleasure were coherent enough to be understood as his name and words of love as she felt herself squirting again. *Dog, I hope he likes the taste of that as much as I love the feeling!*

"Holy, wow!" Randi floated back down into her body.

James responded by chuckling lightly while lapping up the juices that hadn't been shot down his throat during her pulsating ejaculation. He continued giving her open-mouthed kisses as he moved up her body. He only slowed for a single suckle of each nipple before moving up the column of her throat and claiming her lips in a passionate kiss.

She tasted herself on his lips and tongue and was surprised to not be turned off by the tangy sweet taste. She savored it as their tongues entwined, exploring each other's mouths as their hands explored each other's bodies for several long moments.

"Fuck, Angel," James growled as they broke the kiss, and he brought their foreheads together once more. "You are fucking amazing. I always thought they used special effects in the squirting videos I've seen. I never knew it was really possible, but now I'm looking forward to making you squirt every time."

He stood, pulling her up with him to go turn on the rest of the jets, kissing the whole way over to the other side of the shower. They continued making out as they washed each other in the shower, whispering sweet nothings and kissing each newly cleaned area once the bubbles from his ocean scented bodywash were rinsed away. Randi luxuriated in the feel of him giving her a scalp massage as he washed and conditioned her hair. Their height difference made it difficult for her to return the favor, so he sat on the bench to make it easier for her to reciprocate the scalp massage while washing and conditioning his long locks.

Just as she was about to take her turn washing the lower half of his body and planning to spend some time on her knees to assure his cock's cleanliness with her mouth, an alarm blared from the bedroom.

"Fuck," James shouted as she started to soap up his engorged shaft.

"What's the alarm for?" Randi attempted to at least give him a good hand job before he jumped out of the shower to go turn it off.

"It's eight o'clock," James groaned as he disentangled himself from her grasp and turned to rinse off with the closest body jet in the shower. "That's the time Anthony told Rick that the parents all needed to go to the ranch to pick up their kids this morning after the sleepover. I set the alarm for that time, so we could maybe sneak you back to their house while your folks are still down at the bunkhouse."

"Oh, yeah," was all Randi could get past her lips as she quickly rinsed herself off while James stepped out of the shower.

He grabbed a towel and started drying himself off as he went into the bedroom to shut off the alarm. He was back before she was completely done, which was good since she had no idea how to shut off his fancy shower. He finished drying himself off and wrapped the towel around his waist before grabbing a second towel from the cabinet and walking back toward the shower door.

"I don't know how to turn this off," Randi informed him when she realized he was standing there holding the towel open, waiting for her to finish, so he could wrap it around her.

He reached in and swiped the screen to life before pointing out a button that said, "all off," and pushing it to turn off all the jets of water spraying in the massive shower. She stepped into his embrace with the oversized navy-blue towel and pushed up onto her tiptoes to give him a peck of a kiss.

"Thank you." Randi took over drying herself off. His confused expression prompted her to explain why she was thankful for him. "For being so thoughtful and trying to keep things from being awkward with my parents this morning."

"No problem, Angel." James smiled down at her before moving over to the sink to brush his teeth and comb his hair.

They made quick work of getting dressed, even though she had to put on her clothes from the day before, since James's clothes were way too big for her to wear without looking suspicious as she entered the ranch. James actually put on a suit and tie, getting dressed for church, even though they didn't have to be there until ten that morning.

When they exited the Hunters' Homestead, as James called his family's land, they turned right to go to the north gate onto the Burleson Ranch instead of going to the south gate that she'd used the day before when she arrived with her parents. There wasn't anyone around when they pulled into the driveway beside Kay's new home with Anthony, but she still didn't want to take any chances on getting caught sneaking in. So, she only gave James a quick kiss goodbye before hustling out of his truck and up to the front door. James drove off as she was opening the door that her sister apparently left unlocked.

Leah Mae Wright

Can't do that back home in Tulsa. Randi walked in and went straight up the stairs to Tia's room where she'd left her suitcases. She quickly stripped out of the clothes she'd worn to travel down there and out to the bachelorette party the night before. She swapped undergarments before going into the Jack and Jill bathroom to blow dry her hair and put on her makeup.

She was almost fully put together and ready to go to church when Tia walked into the room. Luckily, she was already mostly in the nicest dress she'd brought with her, and it was just her niece and not Kay's fiancé or anyone else in the family. After a quick fib about borrowing Tia's bedroom for the night since she didn't know where she was supposed to sleep in the house next door, Randi helped Tia pick a dress for church and they made their way back downstairs to meet up with the rest of the family.

Even though Kay and Anthony obviously knew where she'd really spent the night, they went along with her lie. Anthony even sold it to the rest of their family members when he helped her take her things next door to his parents' house. Not that she was going to be able to stay there the next night. She found out that her parents were in Anthony's old room, across the hall from his sisters' old rooms where Amy and Deanna were bunking for the duration of their stay. Anthony's brothers, Jake and Josh, were in their old rooms on the third floor. With Randi's brother David taking over the other bedroom on that floor with his wife, Diana, and using the game room attached through the Jack and Jill bathroom for their two-year-old son, Davy, and infant daughter, Danica, there weren't any other bedrooms available for Randi.

Fudge! I should've just gone in and got my bags to take back to James's house this morning.

She didn't get a chance to voice her desire to stay with James before she was being ushered out of the house, directed to follow Anthony, who was carrying her suitcases across the way to his sister Charlotte's house. Charlotte welcomed her with a bear hug before instructing Anthony to put Randi's things in the guest bedroom.

Charlotte made sure she had everything she needed, including the gate code in case it was closed when she came back late from any excursions she had planned for later in the week.

This might not be too bad, Randi thought as she got in the car to ride with Charlotte to the church. *She certainly isn't trying to keep an eye on me like Mom and Dad would if I was staying in the same house as them. Maybe James and I can sneak in a few more overnight dates this week?*

Chapter Twelve

James made his way to Kara's Kakes after dropping Randi off at her sister's house. He knew Kara only opened from six to nine on Sunday mornings, so she could make it to church on time. But he hoped that he wasn't too late to get a dozen donuts for breakfast, since he missed eating earlier at the B and B, and didn't want to risk the guys ribbing him about what he was doing instead of being there for breakfast in front of his mother.

"Cutting it close, James," Kara looked at the clock as he walked into her shop at five minutes before nine.

"Sorry, Kara," James apologized, smiling sheepishly at the brunette baker, who was a couple of years older than him. He remembered seeing her around school, but she was a couple of grades ahead of him, so he hadn't paid as much attention to her as he had the girls in his classes. "Just need a dozen donuts. Whatever you have left."

"No preference?" Kara arched an eyebrow at him as she pulled out a bakery box and tongs before opening the door on the back of the display case built into the counter.

"Nothing with messy filling." James looked down at his suit and tie and realized he didn't want to risk dripping jelly filling on his Sunday best before church. *I don't wanna give Randi's folks another reason to think I'm not worthy of her.*

Kara filled the box quickly with a mix of glazed donuts, both yeast and cake, and some with chocolate, caramel, and white icing, while James looked around at the rest of the display cases of baked goods.

While he was there, he also picked up a German chocolate cake to take as his contribution to the potluck dinner after the service. Since it was also going to be Anthony and Kay's wedding shower, he wasn't a hundred percent certain that they were doing the normal potluck after church. But if he didn't need the cake for the potluck, he'd take it to Thanksgiving instead. Either way, it would be eaten within a few days, and he wasn't at risk of showing up empty handed for an event he needed to contribute toward.

Damn, I should've thought to ask Randi about what I needed to bring today. Fuck, I probably should've fed her before taking her back to the ranch, too. Maybe I can catch her at church early and share my donuts?

"Thanks, Kara. See ya at church." James waved goodbye to the baker after swiping his card to pay for his purchases.

He put his bakery boxes in the passenger seat as he got into his truck. He backed out of the space on Longhorn Lane and took a left on Mustang Lane to head over to Rogers Road, where he made another left to go to the church at the corner of Rogers and Walker Roads. He parked near the entrance to the parking lot, leaving the close parking for the elderly parishioners and those who couldn't handle walking as far to enter the building.

There weren't many cars there yet and none that he recognized as the Burlesons' vehicles or the large sedan that Randi's father had rented. He opened his donut box and ate one of each kind that there was more than one of in the box. He wanted to save a variety for Randi to pick from if he got the chance to offer them to her.

When she hadn't shown up within fifteen minutes of him arriving, James pulled out his phone and texted her.

James: I'm already at the church. I have donuts for breakfast if you want some before going in. {Doughnut Emoji}

He sat there waiting as a few more cars trickled into the lot, but Randi didn't respond to his text. She also didn't exit any of the vehicles that had recently arrived at the church. After another fifteen minutes of waiting, a caravan of Burleson vehicles pulled into the church, along with the Lees' rental car. James started to grab his bakery boxes to go meet Randi when she got out of the car, but he stopped when he realized how weird it would look for him to bring her a box of seven donuts when there were way more than seven people around her.

Leah Mae Wright

Am I ever gonna outgrow my awkward teenager stage when it comes to dating and interacting with my girlfriend's family? Shit, should I take the cake? Naw, I'll come back out and get it if I need it after the service.

He watched Randi get out of Charlotte's car as he walked across the parking lot to where everyone was congregating before walking into the church. He wished he'd been faster to get there, so he could've opened her car door and helped her out of the car. It was more than just the gentlemanly manners his parents had instilled in him since childhood that fueled that desire. Most of it was that he wanted an excuse to touch her, even if it was just holding her hand to help her out of the car.

He greeted Bob and Hazel Burleson first, as they were the closest to him in the crowd that was gathering on the sidewalk leading up to the front of the church. Randi somehow ended up on the opposite side of the crowd, at least fifteen feet away from him, like she'd been most of the day before at the cookout. He'd followed her around like a puppy the day before, staying close enough to wherever she was to keep her in his sights, but far enough away that he wouldn't draw the attention of her overprotective father. Looked like he'd be doing the same thing at church.

"Where are the rest of your family?" Hazel gave him a motherly hug in greeting.

"Not sure, ma'am." James gently returned her hug. "I didn't go to the B and B this morning. I grabbed some donuts in town before I headed here."

"Are donuts on your normal training diet?" Josh Burleson quipped. Josh was the Navy SEAL in the Burleson clan, so he would be the one who most understood how James had to maintain a training diet for wrestling.

"Yeah, my training diet isn't as strict as I'm sure yours is." James smiled at the Burleson who was closest to he and his brother in size.

"Or maybe you've just missed Kara's bakery goodness as much as we have," Jake Burleson interjected as he slapped a hand on his twin brother's back and grinned at them.

James looked back and forth between the fraternal twins, noticing their differences as he tried to decipher which one of them had more of an interest in the baker than her bakery goods. Josh was an inch taller than Jake, even with James at six-foot-four. He also had lighter hair and eyes than his brother, a sandy brown just a shade darker than blond and hazel eyes. Brown eyed, dark brown-haired Jake was significantly smaller than Josh, not carrying near as much muscle on his six-foot-three frame, but that was probably because he spent most of his time behind a computer, working in naval intelligence tracking down terrorists via their cyber trails.

"Yeah, not much of a chance to get donuts that good as we rush through the continental breakfast while checking out of a hotel," James admitted, still not sure which of the brothers looked more focused on Kara. "Most places don't do the full buffet breakfast like Ma at the B and B either."

They made more small talk about how James supplemented his road diet with protein shakes for breakfast most mornings while driving to the airport, then ate an early lunch as soon as he checked into the hotel, a late second lunch after his workout, and then dinner in catering while at the arena followed by a final meal each day after the show. As the rest of the GWA crew started arriving, the Burlesons learned that James wasn't the only one who ate five or more meals a day. While most of them were shocked at how much food the wrestlers ate each day, once they started explaining training schedules it became abundantly clear that it took a lot of fuel to maintain their muscle mass with their extremely high activity levels.

Soon, everyone was ushered into the church. Instead of going to their usual seats, most of the congregation from town ceded the right side of the church to all the out-of-town guests and the Burlesons. James sat with his coworkers instead of his family, a couple of pews back from where Randi was seated with her family.

James couldn't focus on the pastor as he preached his sermon that morning. His focus was solely directed at the woman of his dreams, sitting two rows up and three people down, so he had a decent view of her profile for the rest of the morning. She sang along with every song, not even needing the hymnal like he did to know the words. With as many other voices as were around them, he couldn't tell if she was really as off key as she'd told him she was when singing. Not that it mattered, especially since he was probably off key too, since Dean wasn't right beside him to harmonize with to find the right notes for the songs.

Leah Mae Wright

Finally, when the last prayer to dismiss the service was over, Pastor Harrison made an announcement, "In lieu of our usual potluck, the Burleson family would like to invite everyone to join them in the fellowship hall for a wedding shower for Anthony and Kay."

It took a few minutes for everyone to exit the chapel and make their way over to the fellowship hall. While only about half of the townsfolk who normally stayed for the potluck attended the wedding shower, the place was still packed with all the extra out-of-town guests. Hazel took over directing traffic to get everyone in the room and seated, specifically pulling the wedding party aside to sit at the head table with the bride and groom's immediate families.

Kay was seated on Randi's left, with Anthony on her left. *Of course, they're seated so he can hold her left hand with his right while they eat, just like they do every day in catering,* James realized, chuckling lightly as he approached the table.

Anthony's father, Bob, was seated to the left of his son, with his wife, Hazel on his left. Mary Lee was seated beside Hazel, with Charles to her left. Next to Charles was the other bridesmaid, Deanna. That left two seats open between the bridesmaids for him and Dean.

Finally, James mentally cheered as he was directed to sit beside Randi. *Even if I still can't touch her, I'll at least be able to smell her lightly floral, lightly fruity perfume.*

He was surprised that he didn't smell her normal scent when he took his seat, but he liked the fact that she still smelled like his bodywash instead. *Guess that wasn't perfume she was wearing before. Shit, is it gonna give us away that we smell alike today?*

He fidgeted in his seat, aching to reach over and hold her hand or put his arm around her shoulders on the back of her chair, and missed the speech Hazel gave thanking the caterers and explaining what the order of events for the party was going to be. He tried to pay attention to what was going on around him, but he pretty much lost the fight with himself to stay engaged in the party and only saw or heard Randi as the party went on around them.

He followed her lead when it came time to go through the line for food. The conversation over the meal was more small talk, but he tried to pay attention since Randi's parents were seated on the other side of the round table from where he and Randi sat.

"Oh, that's going to be fun to read at the end of the party," Kay chuckled as Hazel passed a piece of paper and pen to Mary Lee who was sitting beside her.

"What exactly do I do now?" Mary asked Hazel as she took the items.

"Just write out the next sentence in Anthony and Kay's love story," Hazel directed. "Then pass it to the next person. Everyone but Anthony and Kay get to write a sentence and then we'll read the whole thing at the end of the party."

Mary wrote on the paper then handed it to Charles, who wrote something and passed it on to Deanna.

"Oh, yeah, that's definitely gonna be an interesting read at the end," Randi giggled beside him. "I'm sure it won't be anywhere close to accurate for your actual love story."

"Hopefully, it won't be any more embarrassing than the newlywed game questions," Kay replied to her sister.

Dean handed the paper and pen to James, who looked down at what was already written.

> Anthony and Kay met at the Camelot Hotel. The hotel is a replica of a fairy-tale castle. She saw him as her knight in shining armor. He rescued her from the evil dragon (AKA her ex). A noble and brave knight, Anthony valiantly fought the dragon, defeating him in the most widely seen jousting match in Tulsa history.

James thought for a moment about what to write for his part before adding to the previous statements.

> Sir Anthony protected Queen Kay and Princesses Tia and Maria from the wrath of the defeated dragon's family by flying them away to his own kingdom.

"Oh, those aren't embarrassing," Hazel insisted, smiling at Kay as James passed the pen and paper to Randi.

"Wait, you're not supposed to know them." Kay pointed an accusatory finger at Hazel. "You're playing the game and it won't be

Leah Mae Wright

fair if you and Bob already know the questions to synchronize your answers."

James watched as Randi added the next line to the paper, reading over her shoulder.

The new royal family went off on a new adventure, joining the traveling circus known as the Galactic Wrestling Association.

James chuckled at what he knew would be added to the story from the lunatics he worked with when they realized that the GWA was included in the story.

"No, I don't know them," Hazel replied with a grin. "But I made sure Susan knows to keep them appropriate for the venue when I put her in charge of the game."

"I thought there were four couples on the newlywed game." Deanna arched an eyebrow questioningly. "Don't you need another couple to play?"

"Oh, that's right, Dee!" Mary looked around the table. "It was four couples. Who else can we get to play?"

"Maybe David and Diana?" Charles turned in his chair to look at a couple at the next table over.

"Nope, not happening." The guy shook his head adamantly. James wasn't sure who he was, since he hadn't met him the day before at the cookout.

"Maybe some of your married friends from work?" Bob suggested to Anthony.

"Yeah, I'm not sure any of them will wanna be put on the spot at the last minute." Anthony looked at Kay as if he was hopeful she might have some ideas.

"Why don't we have Randi and James play?" Hazel prompted, looking first at Mary Lee, then across the table at James and Randi. "Ya'll have known each other the same amount of time as Anthony and Kay, so you should be evenly matched in the game, like we are with the Lees."

Yeah, so much for keeping us a secret from her folks, James thought as he looked over at Randi. He'd follow her lead on whether or not he was willing to participate in the game. She looked up at him with wide eyes, like a deer frozen in the headlights of an oncoming vehicle.

Fuck! How am I gonna make this easiest on her? James's first thought was that he should refuse, so her parents wouldn't know how close they'd gotten already in their relationship. But if she was really going to interview for a job with the GWA in a couple of days and start work the next week, surely her parents would figure out that they were closer than they already knew.

As he quickly weighed his options for how to respond, he couldn't deny his inner caveman, who wanted nothing more than to publicly claim Randi as his woman. "I'm game if you are, Angel." James gave her what he hoped was a reassuring smile.

"Yes!" Dean exclaimed loudly beside James. "If your answers are anything like your promos, this is gonna be hilarious."

James wasn't sure if it was his reassuring smile or Dean's exclamation that snapped Randi back to life from her temporarily frozen state, but he was glad when she winked at him before speaking.

"Hey, don't knock his promos," Randi giggled slightly. "At least I know if any of these questions are about dessert, his answer will be chocolate cream pie."

Dean barked out a laugh before slapping James on the back and saying, "I really like your girl, bro. You should put a ring on her finger ASAP."

Plannin' on it, James agreed in his head, but he didn't get a chance to say.

"I'm clearly missing the joke." Charles glared at James and Dean.

James wasn't sure if Dean didn't notice Charles's glare or just chose to ignore it as he proceeded to explain about the chocolate cream pie promo that James would apparently never live down. His voice kept getting louder as he went through the story, eventually leading to Dion coming over to the table to introduce himself to the people he hadn't previously met.

Surprisingly, after more ribbing from his coworkers than he really wanted to endure in front of Randi's parents, James noticed that even Charles was smiling at him. Though Charles probably wouldn't have been smiling had he realized that Randi had reached under the table to hold James's hand as they finished their meal.

Damn, she's a lefty, James realized, noticing that Randi ate left-handed. *Guess that means we can hold hands while we eat too, like Anthony and Kay. So many strange parallels between the four of us.*

When they were finished eating, Hazel stood to direct traffic again. She looked around the room, presumably looking for where the love story was in the crowd, so she could keep track of it to be able to read the whole thing at the end of the party.

"Alright, everyone, make sure you've entered your guesses in the how-many-Kisses-for-the-Missus game while we clear the dishes and get set up for the newlywed game," she announced.

Apparently, the catering service included a staff that cleared the tables and took the dishes to the kitchen for washing. It was the first time James realized that, instead of eating off of paper plates like they usually did for the church potlucks, they were using stoneware plates, glass cups, and real silverware. *Like I've noticed much more than Randi in that red dress and heels since she arrived at the church this morning.*

"I need to go put in my guess before we start the newlywed game," Randi declared to the table at large.

"Me, too," James agreed, standing, and pulling out her chair for her. "Maybe we can strategize together for both games."

He couldn't get enough of looking at her in that red dress as they walked across the room. It wasn't like it was a slinky dress that hugged all her curves or something that was too short or low cut to be too revealing for their surroundings. It was pretty prim and proper other than the vibrant color. The flared skirt went below her knees to about mid-calf and the scalloped neckline barely showed a flash of her collarbone. The bodice was fitted, but it wasn't exceptionally tight. It had three-quarter-length sleeves and a bow tied at the right hip in the front.

How the fuck can a dress with a bow be that sexy? It looks like a dress one of her nieces would wear, for fucks sake.

Regardless of the fact that it wasn't a revealing dress, James was glad for the length of his dark gray suit coat that helped him hide the evidence of how much he liked seeing it on Randi. He also liked the feel of the soft material beneath his hand where he rested it on her low back to escort her over to the table where they were supposed to guess how many Hershey's Kisses were in the glass jar.

"How many do you think are in there?" Randi inquired as they approached the table. "I wanna say that size canister holds a five-pound bag of flour or sugar, but I don't know what the equivalent is for Hershey's Kisses."

"Maybe we can google it?"

"Yeah, I would, but I've misplaced my phone," Randi sighed, picking up the canister like she was trying to count the Kisses she could see.

Fuck, I bet it's still plugged in on my bedside table, James thought as he pulled out his phone to search for how many Kisses were in a pound.

"Did you get it off the charger this morning?" James typed *How many Hershey's Kisses in a one pound bag?* in the Google search bar on his phone.

"Nope." Randi looked up at him with recognition dawning on her face. "Guess I need to sneak back to your place to pick it up after this, huh?"

"Guess so." James smiled down at her and tried not to think about what else they could sneak off and do that evening. "Okay, there are a hundred Hershey's Kisses in a one-pound bag. How heavy does that jar feel?"

"It's not as heavy as my flour canister at home." Randi bounced her hand holding the jar like she was trying to weigh it. "Maybe three or four pounds, but definitely not five."

She handed the jar to James like she wanted him to verify her weight estimation. Since he didn't ever lift weights that low in the gym, he wasn't sure he could accurately estimate, so he just agreed with her. In the end they put their guesses in at three-hundred-and-twenty-five and three-hundred-and-fifty pieces, with James guessing the lower number because he wasn't sure how much of the weight the container would account for in the total weight of the jar plus the candy.

Once they finished putting their guesses in the box beside the jar of candy, they walked back to the front of the room, where they found four pairs of chairs set up for the newlywed game. Anthony and Kay were already seated in the chairs closest to the podium, where Anthony's Aunt Susan was standing with note cards in front of her that James assumed contained the questions for the game. Bob and Hazel

Leah Mae Wright

Burleson were in the next set of chairs with Charles and Mary Lee in the third set. That left the last set for James and Randi. James took the right chair, so he could hold Randi's hand if she got brave enough to let him when everyone in the room could see.

One of Anthony's other aunts handed out cards and markers for them to write their answers on before Susan called for everyone's attention to start the game. James looked out at the crowd of people that included his family sitting front and center to watch him play with Randi as his partner, and he felt guilty for not introducing her to them personally at the cookout the day before. He knew that they'd met her, having seen her talk to his parents and grandparents briefly from across the crowd, but he still should've personally introduced her to them as his girlfriend. The only reason he hadn't was his attempt at trying to maintain her boundaries while her parents were around.

He couldn't waste time worrying about that though, as the ladies were asked to follow one of the other women out of the room while the men answered the first round of questions for the game. Once the ladies were out of the room, where they couldn't see what the men were writing, the men were instructed to write down their answers to the first three questions.

"Question one," Susan announced. "What did your wife wear on your first date?"

James uncapped his marker and wrote on the first card.

Jeans and a pink t-shirt.

"Question two. When did you know your wife was *The One*?"

James had to think for a moment before he wrote on the next card. *I can't exactly write "I claimed her as mine the first time we fucked" on a card that will be seen by her parents. But I was actually thinking it before that, so that's not the right answer anyway. I probably shouldn't write that "I knew I'd spend my life giving her everything she ever wanted the first time she looked me in the eye and asked me to fulfill one of her fantasies" either.*

The tentative expression on Randi's face the first night they met flashed before his eyes as James remembered how nervous she was to share that fantasy with him, like she expected him to reject her for the request. That was honestly the moment he knew she was it for him.

But both of those moments were on the night we met, and the question only asked when, not what was happening at the time.

James quickly wrote his final answer on the card for the second question.

The night we met.

Once he turned over his card to indicate he was finished with his answer, Susan spoke again. "Last question. When and where was your first kiss?"

Well, fuck, can't exactly keep it platonic for her parents with this answer, James inwardly groused, chuckling lightly as he wrote his answer on the third card.

On top of a boulder in Chandler Park in the early morning hours of September 30th.

Once everyone had finished writing their answers and the guys were instructed to place all three cards face down on their lap with the last one on bottom and the first one on top, the ladies were led back into the room. Randi looked uneasy as she took her seat beside him, so he reached over and squeezed her hand, hoping it would help quell her nerves. She squeezed his back as they smiled at each other, and Susan started asking the ladies the same questions that she'd already asked the men.

"Jeans and a t-shirt," Kay answered in response to the first question. "But the color of the shirt will depend on what he's claiming as our first date. Purple when we went to the fun park with the girls or baby blue the night we met and went to eat at the diner."

"Jeans and a light blue t-shirt," Anthony grinned as he flipped up his first card. "I think the diner counts as our first date." He punctuated his statement with a peck of a kiss to Kay's lips.

"Five points for our soon-to-be-weds," Susan announced with a chuckle. "Hazel, what did you wear on your first date with Bob?"

"Oh, goodness," Hazel sighed. "I think I wore a dress, but I don't remember the color."

"It was a pale blue dress," Bob told her as he flipped up his card.

"I think that's a match since they both said a dress?" Susan turned to the audience for their feedback. After a few shouts of "yes" and "that's a match" Susan awarded them their five points and went on to ask Mary, "Mary, what did you wear on your first date with Charles?"

"A yellow dress," Mary replied. She leaned in and kissed Charles on the cheek when he turned up his card and read it aloud, "A pretty yellow dress."

"Five points for the Lees." Susan turned to look toward James and Randi. "Let's keep the correct answer streak going. Randi, what did you wear on your first date with James?"

"Well, we haven't really been on an official date," Randi admitted, biting her lip as she looked up at him. "But I was wearing jeans and a light pink t-shirt the night we met. If Anthony and Kay count that night as their first date, then I guess that was ours too, even though we ate at a different diner."

"That's what I counted as our first date," James agreed, flipping up his card to reveal his matching answer.

"Five points for the dating duo," Susan announced. "This is looking like it'll be a close game. Now back to Kay. When did Anthony say that he knew you were *The One*?"

"I'm not sure if he's going to say the night we met or whatever night it was when he started dreaming about me over a year before we actually met." Kay looked at Anthony. "But since he didn't know who I was all those times he dreamt about me, I'm going to say the night we met, because that's the first time he actually knew my name."

"Well, I got a little more specific," Anthony grinned as he flipped up his card. "I said it was when you walked in the bar and climbed the barstool beside me like a ladder, but that was the night we met."

Several people around the room laughed at Anthony's descriptive response, but Susan accepted the answer, awarding them another five points.

"Hazel, when did Bob say that he knew you were *The One*?" Susan moved down the line of contestants to keep the game flowing while Anthony and Kay made out.

"The first time he saw me when I was only fifteen," Hazel answered confidently.

Bob flipped up his card and elaborated, "The first time I saw her at a picnic right outside this church and it was a long five years to have to wait for her to be old enough to go on a date with me."

Bob and Hazel shared a chaste kiss as Susan awarded them another five points.

"Mary, when did Charles say that he knew you were *The One*?"

"Oh goodness, I'm not sure." Mary turned to look at Charles. "Maybe the night we met when he first saw me in my nursing uniform while he was guarding a prisoner in the emergency room where I worked at the time?"

Charles hung his head as he flipped up his card to show it to his wife.

"When I saw her carrying a sleepy two-year-old Kay across the grocery store parking lot," Mary read aloud from his card. "When was that? I don't remember you going grocery shopping with me when Kay was two."

"It was a few days before we actually met," Charles confessed, looking slightly embarrassed. "I was on patrol and saw you going into Warehouse Market one night after work. You were wearing your nurse's uniform that night, too. And it helped me recognize you a few days later when we were both in the ER at Saint John's."

"Sorry, just because she was wearing the same outfit, it was two different nights, so no points for the Lees this round," Susan cajoled before turning to Randi. "Randi, when did James say that he knew you were *The One*?"

"Is this really applicable since we're not married?" Randi motioned back and forth between them. "I mean, I don't really know that he's even had that thought about me."

"Yes, it's applicable," James barked a little gruffer than he intended. "I wrote down an answer, so you just have to guess what I wrote, not contemplate whether or not you've gotten to that point with me yet."

She studied his face intently as she thought about her answer. James knew she still had some reservations about them, but he hoped she knew he was all in with her already.

"During our Skype call when he introduced me to his fans as his girlfriend," Randi finally stated.

James wasn't sure whether he should be dejected that she thought it took him almost a month to know she was it for him, or thrilled that she'd just claimed to be his girlfriend in front of both their families. He decided to go with the latter as he flipped up his card and shook his head. "No, Angel, the night we met."

"Really?" Randi looked shocked by his answer.

"Yes, really." James took her hand and pulled it to his lips, so he could kiss each of her knuckles before twining their fingers and resting their joined hands on his thigh.

"Alright, moving on to the final question the men have already answered." Susan brought them back to the game, not mentioning their lack of points for that question. "Kay, when and where was your first kiss with Anthony?"

"In the parking lot of the Camelot Hotel the night we met," Kay answered, squealing when Anthony flipped up his card that said the exact same thing.

"It was unforgettable," Anthony bragged as they kissed again and were awarded another five points.

"Hazel, when and where was your first kiss with Bob?"

"On my front porch at the end of our first date." Hazel looked at her husband expectantly.

"That was the second kiss." Bob shook his head, holding up his answer card. "The first one was in the truck before we left the movie theater parking lot on our first date."

After declaring that the place was required to match and not just the date, the Burlesons were not awarded any points for the third question.

"Mary, when and where was your first kiss with Charles?"

"On my front porch at the end of our first date," Mary replied, lightly laughing. "My Charles didn't try to sneak it in any earlier like Bob did with Hazel."

"As a man of the law, I would never steal anything, even an early kiss," Charles quipped, flipping his card up to show his matching answer to his wife's.

"Five points for the Lees. Randi, when and where was your first kiss with James?"

James couldn't quite make out what Charles said under his breath, but to his ears, it sounded like he was suggesting the answer should be "never." *Fuck, I hope Randi didn't hear that!*

"The night we met," Randi admitted, sheepishly.

Shit, so she did hear her fucking father.

Before James could figure out how to comfort her and diffuse the situation with Charles, Susan spoke again, asking, "And where was it?"

"While sitting on top of one of the big rocks at Chandler Park," Randi softly answered, looking down at her lap, so only James could see that she was lightly blushing as she spoke.

"One of the many moments that night when I realized we were meant for each other," James declared, flipping his card over with his right hand while squeezing her hand again with his left. When she looked up at him, looking surprised by his statement, he dropped the card and cupped her face with his hand, leaning over to kiss her as Susan awarded them five more points.

James didn't try to keep the kiss chaste, even though they were technically in a church in front of a mixed audience that wouldn't all feel comfortable observing the public display of affection. When Randi reached up with the hand not holding his to drag him closer by his hair, he forgot where he was and speared his tongue into her mouth. When their passion ignited, the kiss could only be described as a claiming. It was James's bold declaration to all who witnessed it that Randi was his and he was hers.

"Ya'll can examine each other's tonsils when the game is over, after you leave the church," James heard a loud male voice declare, reminding him of where he was and who all was around.

He slowly backed away from Randi's delicious mouth, winking at her as Anthony grabbed his arm and hauled him up out of his chair.

"Time for us to leave the room, so the ladies can answer the next round of questions." Anthony pulled James out the door behind Bob and Charles.

As soon as they were out in the hallway, Bob slapped James on the shoulder. "I'm guessing after that kiss, we'll be planning your wedding next."

"Uh, we, we're not quite there yet," James stammered, realizing that Randi's father was staring daggers through him.

"Am I going to need to go home and get my shotgun to move things along, son?" Charles glared at James, his hand seeming to go instinctually to his hip where he normally carried his police issued weapon.

"No, sir," James replied, his mouth forming the words without his conscious thought. When he saw Charles's lips turn up into the slightest smile, James relaxed and smiled back at the older man. "At least not for me. Maybe for your daughter."

Charles barked out the most unexpected roar of laughter. "Yeah, well, she always was my most stubborn child, so you're probably right about that one. I don't know where she got those bothersome traits, like keeping things close to the vest and stubbornly refusing to let anyone see her as anything but strong and independent." He shook his head when he quit speaking, but he was still smiling.

Maybe he's not as unaccepting of Randi and I together as we thought.

James thought he might be jokingly admitting to being the parent she got those traits from, but he wasn't sure enough about that to joke back with Charles. Anthony, on the other hand, didn't seem to have any qualms about messing with his future father-in-law.

"I don't know if it's nature or nurture, but those seem to be common family traits that both of your daughters got from you, Charles." Anthony grinned from ear to ear.

"Yeah, well, don't tell their mother that," Charles chuckled as the door opened and they were gestured back to the other room. "I have to keep her thinking that those things are all hereditary from her side of the family."

<div align="center">~~~</div>

Randi struggled to compose herself after the very church-inappropriate kiss that James gave her before he had to leave the room. *Sugar, we're in the middle of a game! I have to get it together, like yesterday!* After a couple of deep breaths, she was able to pick up the cards and marker from beneath her chair to get started answering the questions that Anthony's aunt was asking.

"Ladies, if your husband was a Disney character, who would he be?"

Randi thought for a minute, remembering back to when she and Kay had compared their guys to Prince Charming and almost writing that on her card. But knowing that her sister would surely use that answer, she wanted to be different. *With his long hair and beard, I'll go with the furriest prince.* She quickly wrote on the first card.

The Beast

"Next question," Susan announced when they'd all finished writing. "What is your husband's dream job?"

Oh, that's an easy one! Randi thought as she wrote her next answer on the next card in her stack.

Wrestler

"What color are your husband's eyes?"

He says they're gray, but I think they're magical color changing eyes. Randi giggled as she wrote on her next card.

Gray, Brown, Blue, Green

All of the Above

But he says they're gray.

"Final question, ladies," Susan continued once Randi had finally quit writing.

Oops, guess my long answer held up the game.

"This one is the bonus question worth twenty-five points at the end of the game. Do you have a couple's song and, if so, what is it?"

We've talked about music and have several songs we both like, but we don't have a couple's song. Randi thought for a few minutes to remember the song lyrics he had tattooed on his arm, thinking maybe she could write one of them down as their song. *But he wouldn't know that's where I'd go with this question.*

Finally, she wrote her answer, feeling guilty for delaying the game when the other three contestants had already finished writing their answers.

We don't have a couple's song.

But he likes **Heart-Shaped Box** *by Nirvana so much
that he has a tattoo of a line of lyrics from it.
"Forever in debt to your priceless advice."*

Once she finally got through writing it all out, they were instructed to stack their cards face down in their laps in the reverse order of how they were asked. So, the bonus question was on bottom of the stack and the card on top was the first question they were asked. Then the men were invited back into the room.

When the guys were all seated, Susan explained that the next three questions were worth ten points each and that the final bonus question was worth twenty-five points.

"We'll start with you, Anthony," Susan went on. "If you were a Disney character, which character would Kay say you were?"

"Prince Charming," Anthony answered, chuckling, and giving Kay a lascivious look.

Yeah, I don't wanna know how many times they've role-played that, Randi thought, rolling her eyes as Kay flipped up her card to show that was the correct answer and kissed her fiancé.

They were awarded their ten points and Susan moved down the line to ask Bob the same question.

"As often as she feeds me spaghetti, I'm gonna say the Tramp," Bob smiled, looking at his wife with hearts in his eyes.

"The Tramp," Hazel agreed as she flipped up her card with the same answer. "Even though you don't just steal kisses when I make spaghetti."

They stole a kiss while Susan awarded them their ten points.

"Charles, if you were a Disney character, which character would Mary say you were?"

Randi inwardly cringed when her father smugly answered, "Why, Prince Charming, of course."

"Nope, my daughters got the princes, I got Woody from *Toy Story*," Mary teased, flipping up her card.

"What?" Charles had confusion written all over his face. "Why Woody?"

"Because he wears a badge," Mary shrugged before pecking him on the cheek. "Just like you."

Randi couldn't help the giggle that escaped at the weirdness of her parents, not catching all of Susan's statement about them not getting any points for that question.

"James, if you were a Disney character, which character would Randi say you were?"

James scratched his chin while looking at her intently before answering. "I'm assuming she'd say I was one of the princes." He turned to look at her mother over his shoulder to tell her, "Thanks, Mary, for giving me that hint." Then he turned back to Randi and grinned. "But I'm obviously the fuzziest prince, so I'm gonna say the Beast."

"You are definitely a fuzzy Beast," Randi giggled as she flipped up her card that confirmed his correct answer.

They were awarded ten points before Susan went back to Anthony and Kay to ask the next question.

"Anthony, what would Kay say is your dream job?"

"The one I have, a pilot," Anthony answered with a grin at Kay.

Kay flipped her card over to show the same answer and they kissed again as they were awarded another ten points.

"Bob, what would Hazel say is your dream job?"

"A cowboy, like the first Burleson who settled here," Bob replied with a wistful smile.

"I said a cowboy, but I didn't mention your many generations of ancestors who held that job before you." Hazel flipped up her card.

"I think we just need the profession to match, not the explanation," Susan chuckled. "Ten points for the Burlesons. Charles, what would Mary say is your dream job?"

"Being Sheriff," Charles replied with a smile.

Randi was glad her dad was working at his dream job. *Now if I can only convince him to be happy for me pursuing my dream job.*

Mary flipped her card up and Susan awarded them ten points for the matching answers.

"James, what would Randi say is your dream job?"

"Randi knows I'm living my dream as a professional wrestler." James smiled down at Randi.

Leah Mae Wright

"I just put wrestler. Did I need to specify the professional part?" Randi flipped up her card.

"Naw, the professional part is implied by it being a job," one of the guys that Randi recognized as being with the GWA said from the middle of the room. "Amateur wrestlers can't get paid for their matches."

"I think wrestler is sufficient to match," Susan agreed in her official capacity as the game show hostess. "Ten points for the dating duo. Now for the last of our ten-point questions. Anthony, what color did Kay say your eyes are?"

"Brown," Anthony replied quickly.

"Dark chocolate brown, actually," Kay retorted as she flipped up her card.

"Ten points for the soon-to-be-weds," Susan announced before turning toward the next couple in line. "Bob, what color did Hazel say your eyes are?"

"Brown," Bob gave the same answer as his son.

"Yep, but I agree with Kay. They both have that dark chocolate quality to them." Hazel flipped up her card.

They were awarded the ten points before Susan posed the same question to Randi's father. Her parents both answered "blue" and were awarded the ten points for the question.

"James, what color did Randi say your eyes are?"

"I hope she said gray, since her description of my 'magic color changing eyes' isn't actually a color," James chuckled.

Randi flipped up her card and let him read it aloud. "Gray, brown, blue, green. All of the above. But he says they're gray." They both chuckled at her answer before he turned to face Susan. "Since she put gray on there twice, I'm assuming we can count it as a match, since she only listed the other colors once?"

"Ten points for the dating duo," Susan announced with a little laugh along with them. "Finally, the bonus question, worth twenty-five points. Anthony, do you and Kay have a song, and if so, what is it?"

"I'd have to say the one I wrote for her." Anthony smiled down at Kay.

"You never told me the name of it," Kay lifted one shoulder as she flipped up her card. "So, I wrote the line from it that I thought should be the name, *More Than You'll Ever Know*."

"That's the perfect name for it," Anthony agreed, kissing Kay.

"Is that the one you said you'd record for us to play at the wedding?" Hazel queried over the top of Susan awarding them the twenty-five points.

"Yeah, Ma, that's the one," Anthony informed her when he finally came up for a breath from his lip lock with Kay.

"You need your band to back you up on the recording?" James leaned over to ask Anthony.

"Naw, it's acoustic, but you're welcome to run the board for the recording if you want," Anthony replied.

That settled, Susan redirected everyone back to the game going on, asking Bob about he and Hazel's song.

"*Feels So Right* by Alabama," Bob answered.

"Oh, Bob," Hazel sighed, as she flipped up her card. "Our wedding song was *There's No Way* by Alabama."

"Well, yeah, but only because you wouldn't let me play *Feels So Right* in front of your parents," Bob replied with a shrug of his shoulders.

"Oh my gosh," one of the Burlesons' daughters blurted from the front row.

Randi giggled at first, glad it wasn't her parents that were discussing a sexual song in front of everyone in the church. But she stifled the giggles quickly when Susan moved to ask her parents about their song, and she realized that it was still a possibility.

"*Islands in the Stream* by Kenny Rogers and Dolly Parton," Charles announced, making Randi want to sink into the floor remembering the lines that specifically mention "making love" in the song her father named.

"No, Charles." Mary shook her head, turning over her card. "Our wedding song was *A Long and Lasting Love* by Crystal Gayle."

"Yeah, but the first song we danced to was *Islands in the Stream*, so I've always thought of it as our song," Charles explained.

Thankfully, Susan moved them along, so Randi didn't have to think long about her parents and sexual music.

"James, do you and Randi have a couple's song and, if so, what is it?"

"We don't have one yet," James answered, looking sad at the admission. "I can't even claim the first song we danced to, since I don't know the names of the current country stuff that was playing last night."

"That was **Strip It Down** by Luke Bryan," Kay announced, not at all helpfully in Randi's opinion.

"Yeah, well, we can discuss the possibility of that being our song later, but it's not what I wrote down." Randi turned over her final card, showing it to James.

We don't have a couple's song.

But he likes **Heart-Shaped Box** *by Nirvana so much that he has a tattoo of a line of lyrics from it.*
"Forever in debt to your priceless advice."

"Yeah, we're definitely not choosing **Heart-Shaped Box** as our couple's song," James laughed. "That's the only line in that song I like, and I got the tattoo in reference to some advice from my PopPop more than the song."

"Ya'll can decide on your couple's song later." Susan kept them from getting off track while playing the game. "I'm awarding you the twenty-five points since you both said you don't have one. Our final point totals are thirty points for the Lees, forty points for the Burlesons, sixty-five points for the dating duo, and a perfect score of seventy points for the soon-to-be-weds. It seems our young couples know each other better than their parents. Well, at least the ladies' parents. We'll have to come up with new questions and get David & Mandi and Rick & Patty to participate at the next wedding."

Next wedding? Surely, she's not referring to James and I as if we're engaged! Although she was nervous about how her parents would perceive Susan's statement, she wasn't freaking out as much as she thought she would about potentially marrying James someday. In fact, the more she thought about it, the more she could see it as a real possibility. She smiled up at him as she envisioned their wedding. *Him in that black James Bond tux and me in a sexy satin sheath style white dress. Sleeveless with a deep V-neckline, both front and back, maybe with lace over the satin.*

She was so lost in thought about the perfect wedding dress to look her best at the altar beside James that she almost missed her father's response to Susan's mention of the next wedding.

"At least give Mary and I a couple of months to reminisce first, so we have a chance to compete against James's parents and grandparents," Charles chuckled.

What the what? My Daddy didn't just joke about playing this game at a wedding shower for James and I, no way. I must still be in bed dreaming. None of this is real. And since it's just a dream, I can practice telling my parents about wanting to be with James and becoming a professional wrestler.

"Don't worry, Daddy, you'll have at least a year to reminisce with Mom before James and I will be setting a wedding date," Randi told her dream father. "That is if he can stand dating me while also training me to wrestle. I won't consider a proposal until I'm able to contribute equally to our household by working alongside him in the ring."

"Oh, and you think that will take a year, huh?" James chuckled, slinging his arm across her shoulders. "I think I can have you ring ready in a quarter of that time, Angel."

"You want to be a professional wrestler?" Her dream father appeared in front of her.

"Yes, it's my dream job," Randi replied. "Wrestling checks all the boxes I've been going over with my therapist for my perfect job."

Randi finally registered what James had said and turned her head to look up at him. "You're really willing to train me?"

"Of course, Angel." James pulled her in for a hug and kissed the top of her head. "We can get started whenever you're ready."

"Thank you, Jimmy." Randi wrapped her arms around his waist to return the hug. "Now I just have to interview and get that production assistant job, so we can travel together to be able to train more than when you're off for holidays."

"You sent Rick your résumé, right?" James pulled back to look down into her eyes.

"Yes, yesterday afternoon," Randi confirmed.

"Is that what you were doing on your computer in the airport in Dallas?" The dream version of Randi's mother posed the question.

"Yes, Mom," Randi replied to her dream parent. "I wanna work with the GWA, so James and I can be together. I applied for a production assistant job to start with, but I plan on transitioning to the talent roster once I learn all I need to be a wrestler."

"Well, you always were the performer in the family." Dream Mary smiled at Randi.

Yep, definitely a dream version of my mother.

"You were first in line for every play all through school," Dream Mary continued. "Between the acting bug and your athletic endeavors of gymnastics and cheerleading, I can see how wrestling would be right up your alley."

"You'll make sure our baby girl is safe in the ring?" Her dream father turned to question James. "You won't let her get hurt?"

"Absolutely, sir," James answered. "Randi's wellbeing is my utmost concern."

"Very well." Dream Charles pulled Randi away from James's side to wrap her in a bear hug. "I'm proud of you, baby girl. I can't wait to watch you achieve all your goals."

"Oh, let me in on these hugs," Dream Mary squealed, putting one arm around Randi and the other around Charles. Randi embraced both her parents, positively certain she'd wake up from the dream any moment.

She didn't realize that their family group hug drowned out the reading of the guest written love story that had passed around the room during the shower. She also didn't hear the announcement of the winner of the how-many-Kisses-for-the-Missus game or the number of candy pieces in the jar.

Randi was too busy relishing the affection and support of her parents that she feared wasn't real. It wasn't until Tia burst into their bubble that she started questioning her own sanity and the events of the last few minutes of the wedding shower.

Chapter Thirteen

Randi awoke to her phone ringing on the bedside table in the guest room at Anthony's sister Charlotte's house. At first, she thought it was her medication alarm, but when she sat up and looked at the screen through eyes which were still blurry from sleep, she realized it was way too early for that. Seeing her sister was calling at almost four in the morning, Randi quickly swiped the screen to answer the call, worried that something was seriously wrong for her sister to be calling so early.

"Hello," Randi croaked as soon as she got the phone to her ear, suddenly wide awake. "What's wrong?"

"Nothing's wrong, well, not really wrong," Kay stammered, sounding nervous. "It's normal, but still kind of an emergency. Do you have any feminine pads or tampons with you?"

"Yeah, why?" Randi was confused why her older sister would be calling her for a tampon.

"Tia got her first period, and I don't have any here." Kay sounded slightly panicked. "And there's no place open this early in town to get what she needs immediately. Can you bring over some supplies for her and I'll replace them for you once the store opens?"

"Yeah, no problem." Randi jumped out of bed and grabbed the supplies from her suitcase. "I'll be right there."

"Thanks, Sis, you're a lifesaver," Kay expressed her gratitude just before they disconnected the call.

Randi pulled on a pair of yoga pants over her panties, figuring the oversized t-shirt she slept in was adequate coverage for her upper body to run a couple hundred yards over to Kay's house. She did put on socks and tennis shoes first, not wanting to take a chance on what she might step in on the ranch.

Less than five minutes later, she was walking into Kay's front door and handing over the goods. Instead of going back to Charlotte's house and going back to bed when Kay ran upstairs to tend to Tia, Randi wanted to wait to talk to her sister after she was finished helping her daughter.

"Got any coffee?" Randi inquired as Kay turned to go back up the stairs.

"Not made," Kay replied.

"That's fine, I'll put on a pot while you take care of Tia." Randi pointed down the hallway in the direction of Kay's kitchen. "Meet me in the kitchen when you're done? I need some sisterly advice."

"Yeah, sure." Kay continued up the stairs. "I'll be down in a bit."

Randi walked down the hall and into her sister's aqua and pink kitchen, shaking her head at the room that didn't reflect Kay's style nearly as much as the living room and dining room. She quickly found the coffee in the pantry and set a pot to brew. She poured herself a cup, adding plenty of cream and sugar to make it drinkable.

Randi didn't often drink coffee, preferring to get her caffeine from soda instead, but it seemed an appropriate drink for so early in the morning. She would need the wake-up juice to clear the cobwebs from her head, so she could figure out how much of the previous day had been real and how much had been her made-up delusion.

That's what she'd determined most of the day before had to have been—a delusion based on her not realizing that she shouldn't have imbibed at the bachelorette party while taking anxiolytic medication. Now she wanted to rehash the events of the day before with someone who could tell her what parts were real and what parts were her delirium.

Not that she would give Kay many of the details of her private time with James to confirm their validity. She would wait to confirm them with him later that day when they went on the date that she was pretty sure she'd really set with him, when he'd dropped her and Tia back at the ranch after their evening of wrestling training on the mats in his home gym. *Well, if Kay confirms that Tia and I actually went with James to train after the wedding shower yesterday, then I'll assume the date was real, too.*

She was contemplating whether or not she'd needed to go back to James's house to get her phone, or if losing her phone that morning was part of her hallucination, when Kay walked into the kitchen. Her outfit was similar to Randi's, yoga pants and an oversized t-shirt, but her shirt was a plain navy-blue, whereas Randi's was heather gray and said "Property of James Dangerous" on the front.

Donuts! I probably shouldn't have worn this shirt out of my borrowed bedroom. I'll have to make this a quick chat with Kay, so I can go back and change before Mom or Dad pop over here.

"So, what's up, Sis?" Kay poured herself a cup of coffee and took a seat beside Randi at the kitchen table.

"I think I screwed up by drinking at your bachelorette party," Randi blurted, taking a sip of her coffee, and lightly wincing at the taste. "I'm not sure I should have also taken my anxiety medicine that night. Like maybe mixing them caused me to have some hallucinations yesterday."

"What did your doctor say about drinking while you're on it?"

"She didn't say anything about it," Randi admitted, already wondering if she needed to call her doctor's office to report the strange effects of the day before. "And when I read the paper about it when I got the first prescription, it said that one of the side effects could be dizziness and alcohol could make that worse, but since I haven't had any issues with dizziness on it, I didn't think I needed to worry about any other issues with having a few drinks Saturday night."

"Well, if you didn't see any risk of hallucinations as a side effect in the medication paperwork, maybe that wasn't the cause?" Kay tilted her head as if she was contemplating her own thoughts on the side effect possibilities. "Describe them to me, so I can try to help you figure out why you had them."

"It's not like I saw a pink elephant in the room that I know was a hallucination," Randi began. "It's more like I felt like I was dreaming when I was talking to Mom and Dad after the newlywed game. They weren't acting the way I expected them to about James and I dating. I remember thinking I must still be asleep and dreaming, so I decided to practice talking to the dream versions of them like my therapist has had me talking to their picture. But their reaction to my goal of becoming a wrestler and traveling the world with James was also off from what I expected. So, I'm not sure if anything yesterday was real, or if I dreamed most of the day."

"Ya'll were huddled up off to the side of the room talking while we were reading the paper from the pass-the-love-story game, so I don't know exactly what was said." Kay tilted her head once more, like she was thinking hard while watching Randi's face intently.

Randi felt like she was under a microscope as her sister observed her so carefully, but she maintained eye contact to make sure Kay could read anything she needed to help her figure things out.

"But after you and Tia left with James to go pick up your phone and go through your first wrestling lesson," Kay stated, smiling at her sister, "Mom mentioned how much she liked your future mother-in-law and Dad spent some time talking to Rick about how your schedule would work to allow you training time while traveling and working as a PA. So, I think you might have actually told them about your career plans and how you feel about James. I don't think their reaction was just your imagination."

"It's just such a complete flip from three weeks ago, when Dad found out I'd been talking to James, and basically ordered me to keep him in the friend zone," Randi confided, still not quite believing that the events of the day before weren't her fanciful delusions of the way she wanted them to react. "Not to mention how they normally have strong negative opinions about guys with long hair, beards, tattoos, and jobs they don't think are suitable for women. It's hard to believe they'd flip their opinions that fast."

"Yeah, well, Daddy probably ran a background check on James since he first heard his name three weeks ago," Kay chuckled. "Between that, all the interaction they've had with my future in-laws the past month, which probably included some firsthand accounts about James, and Anthony, the girls, and I talking him up to Mom and Dad, they were bound to come around on their opinions of James."

"You've been talking him up to them?" Randi was surprised since she hadn't ever asked Kay to do that, thinking it would be too little too late after not mentioning him to her parents in the first few weeks of dating him.

"Of course. I could tell how close ya'll were getting, so I wanted to make sure Mom and Dad liked him before they got down here. I didn't want them to fight with my future mother-in-law and her friends over their matchmaking schemes this week."

"Matchmaking schemes?" Randi wasn't sure how they might have included her and James.

"Oh, yeah, I think there's something in the water here in Heart's Destiny," Kay laughed. "I'm not sure if it's everyone in Mom and Dad's generation, or just the women, but I'm sure the women are ready to marry off their adult children and become grandparents. They cornered me the other day to ask about the single people coming to town for the wedding to figure out who they could match up with their kids. James's mom even came over to Hazel's to ask me about you. And they're trying to convince Deanna to come to work for Burleson Oil, so they can match her with Anthony's cousin JJ. I wouldn't be surprised if they don't try to recruit Amy, too."

"Seriously?" Randi chuckled, shocked at the thought that the fifty-somethings of the town were so serious about matchmaking for their children.

"Oh yeah, this whole town is wedding and baby crazy," Kay confirmed before finishing off her cup of coffee.

"Speaking of baby crazy…" Randi trailed off, suddenly realizing that her older sister should've had the supplies Tia needed that morning, since she'd been traveling in and out of Heart's Destiny for the last six weeks. Surely, she'd needed them herself in that time. "Is there a reason you haven't needed feminine supplies in the last six weeks?"

Kay's mouth opened as if she was going to speak, but she just closed it quickly as the color drained from her face.

"I would think you'd have bought all new supplies for your period if you hadn't brought them with you the first time you left Tulsa," Randi continued, trying to lead her sister to confirm her suspicion. "Have you not had a period since you moved here?"

"No, no, no," Kay chanted. "It's not possible." She grabbed her phone, which she'd laid on the table beside her, and scrolled over to her calendar. "Fuck, shit, damn."

"Whoa, Sis, calm down," Randi comforted, putting a hand on Kay's shoulder, hoping it would help ground her sister. "When was your last period?"

"I finished it on the fourth of October," Kay admitted, counting days on her calendar. "I should've had it again the week before we went to court. I vaguely remember thinking it was just late because I was so stressed then, but I haven't thought about it since."

"Okay, well, winning in court only lifted one major stressor off your plate." Randi hoped she was being a calming voice for her sister. "With your travel schedule and the wedding, it could still just be that you skipped it because of stress."

"No, I'm never late, and good stress, like my wedding and the job I love, wouldn't stop it altogether," Kay denied, tears starting to stream down her face.

"It's okay. We'll get a test to make sure before we freak out, okay?" Randi rubbed her hands down from Kay's shoulders to her elbows trying to calm her sister down.

"I can't go buy a test here!" Kay screeched. "I wouldn't even make it home from the store before the gossip grapevine would have spread the news back to everyone on the ranch."

"It's not that big a deal." Randi continued, trying to soothe her sister. "Everyone knows how much you and Anthony love each other, so nobody is gonna be shocked you got knocked up before the wedding."

"Oh, no, they'll probably all think I've cheated on him," Kay trembled, her eyes wide with fear.

"No way. You guys are practically glued together, there's no way you were with anyone else since you met him."

"I haven't, I wouldn't, couldn't," Kay sobbed. "But it's not supposed to be pos-possible for him."

Kay stuttered through the story of how Anthony had been injured when he was in the Navy. Though Randi only caught every other word as Kay cried through the whole explanation, she got the gist of it as being that Anthony had supposedly been exposed to enough radiation to sterilize him.

Sugar! No wonder she's freaked out, Randi realized as she pulled her sister into her arms. *Even if I can't fix it for her, I can give her a shoulder to cry on.*

"Yeah, well, doctors can be wrong," Randi cajoled, hugging her crying sister, and not even caring that her tears were soaking through her sleep shirt. "They're just *practicing* medicine after all. They haven't perfected it. So, maybe set him an appointment for a sperm count test at the same time that you go in and confirm a possible pregnancy."

"I don't even know where the doctor's office is here," Kay sniffled, her sobs starting to ease off. "Anthony introduced me to a doctor at church yesterday, but I can't even remember his name. How have I lived here for over a month without switching to a local doctor?"

"It just hasn't been your number one priority," Randi reassured her sister. "Hello, it probably hasn't even been in the top one hundred on your priorities list lately. But it'll be okay. Now that we know finding a doctor needs to be moved to the top of the priority list, we can look one up online and see how soon you can get in for an appointment. And if they can't see you today or tomorrow, then I'll pick up a home test for you while I'm in San Antonio tonight. That might confirm that it was just stress and not as big a rush to see a doctor."

"You really think it could be stress?" Kay pulled out of Randi's embrace to look her sister in the eyes again.

"Yeah, definitely," Randi affirmed. "I mean, that's the most likely scenario with Anthony's accident and all."

"You're right," Kay declared, wiping her face with the hem of her shirt. "I don't need to freak out yet. But how are you gonna get a test without telling James?"

"I'll just tell him I need to stop at a drug store for tampons," Randi shrugged. "I guarantee he won't wanna come in with me for that, so I can easily hide a test or two in the bottom of the bag."

"Thank you." Kay hugged Randi again. "I don't know what I would do without you here right now."

"No problem," Randi replied. "That's what sisters are for."

~ ~ ~

James floated through his morning, relieved that not only had Randi been able to tell her parents about wanting to be with him and what she wanted to do for her future career, but also that they'd had such a positive reaction to the revelations of the previous day. He wished she would have come back to his house to spend the night, but he understood her desire not to flaunt the sexual part of their relationship in front of her old-fashioned parents. Besides, she would be sharing his bed soon enough, when they left Heart's Destiny, Texas, the next Monday to fly out for the GWA show in Tampa, Florida.

Maybe we can even squeeze in some beach banging before we have to go to the arena, he mused as he got ready for the day. He dressed for the activities he'd planned for his daytime date with Randi, jeans and a Henley with hiking boots, so he could take her to the rocky outcropping on the south side of the homestead for a picnic lunch before going to San Antonio to walk around the RiverWalk and have dinner.

He had breakfast at the plantation house with the rest of the GWA crew. But when they all started getting ready to go to the Burleson Ranch for another day of horseback riding and barbeque, James went to the kitchen to have his mother's staff help him stock a cooler with drinks and a picnic basket with snacks for the day. Then he went to the ranch to pick up Randi for their date.

She was a vision in her tight jeans and turquoise sweater when she answered the door at Charlotte's house. She was wearing cowboy boots instead of hiking boots, but the sexiness factor of how she was wearing them over the bottom of her jeans was worth any lack of traction she'd have on their short hike. *Fucking hell, I'll carry her across any slippery spots if I need to. If I can walk with my dick as hard as steel from the sight of her, that is.*

She had her golden hair twisted up in some kind of braided version of a bun that he'd never seen before. As much as he loved the way her hair normally flowed down her back in waves, having her neck exposed with her hair up was tempting him to spend the first hour of their date nibbling her nape. If he kept any possible marks on the back of her neck, she could easily let her hair down to cover them when her family was around.

"Are we going?" Randi looked up at him with a slight grin. "Or are you just gonna stand there staring at me all day?"

"Sorry, Angel." James took a step back, so she could exit the house. "The sight of you just took my breath away, and I needed a minute to take in the vision that you are before I could even think to inhale again, much less remember what we're supposed to be doing."

He wanted to swing her up into his arms and kiss her senseless right then, but he was a little worried he'd forget where they were and take it too far in the middle of the Burleson houses, where they could be interrupted any second. Instead, he offered her his arm as he escorted her to his truck, opening the passenger door and helping her inside before walking around the vehicle to get behind the wheel.

"So, where all are we going today?" Randi inquired as he turned on the truck and pulled out of the driveway.

"First, I wanna show you more of the homestead," James answered, waggling his eyebrows at her suggestively. "I figured we'd have a picnic lunch, and you can compare our natural boulders to the ones your grandfather moved in Chandler Park."

"Comparing boulders, huh?" Randi giggled. "Are they as private as the park was, so I can compare their comfort level against my back? Or are we just comparing their appearance?"

"They're more private than the park was, Angel," James assured her, pulling through the gate to leave the ranch. "And we can compare them however you want. At least for the next five or six hours before we need to leave for San Antonio, so you can see the RiverWalk before our dinner reservations."

"You made reservations for dinner?" Randi looked concerned. "Do I need to go back and grab a change of clothes right quick, so we don't have to come back to the ranch before going to San Antonio?"

"Naw, we're dressed just fine for where I'm taking you tonight," James reassured her, slowing down to make the turn back into his family's land. He went on to tell her all about the RiverWalk in San Antonio and the restaurant where he planned to take her for dinner as he weaved his way through the property.

She told him about the interview she'd set up with Rick for Wednesday and expressed her concern about whether or not Rick witnessing her speech to her parents the day before might have a negative impact on her job prospects with the GWA. He tried to positively reassure her that there would be no negative fallout from her speaking her mind to her parents, but he wasn't sure he adequately convinced her.

When the road beneath the tires turned from gravel into dirt, James stopped for a moment to switch the truck into four-wheel drive. Randi squealed with excitement as the trail got rougher, telling him about how long it had been since she'd been off roading with her high school friends through a creek in Oklahoma.

Leah Mae Wright

They were having so much fun muddin' as Randi called it that James almost hated that he had to turn away from the creek bed to go farther southwest to the rocky outcropping that he wanted to show her. Her exclamation of "Oh, James," when she first saw the rock formation made it all worth it though.

"It's amazing how much this is like Chandler!" Randi squealed with delight as they got out of the truck once he parked.

"There aren't any maintained trails though." James took her hand and guided her through the tall grass that surrounded the boulders. "Maybe this wasn't such a good idea. I should've cleared some of this out, so we could watch for snakes better before I brought you here."

"Well, we don't have to walk through it." Randi squeezed his hand and pulled him to a stop before they made it to the first boulder. "It's special enough that you showed it to me. We can have that picnic in your truck instead, and plan another hike here when we're prepared to clear the brush to do it."

"You're amazing, Angel!" James scooped her up in his arms to carry her back to the truck. He didn't want to take any extra chances that she'd be the one to step too close to a snake hidden in the overgrowth and get bitten before they'd really started their date.

She giggled up at him when he sat her in the bed of the truck. He stepped up on the bumper to join her before backtracking to get the blanket and picnic supplies out of the cab. Eventually, they laid the blanket out in the bed of the truck, relaxing on it as they talked their way through lunch.

She finally asked him about the cars she'd seen in his garage the other night, and he told her about bonding with his dad and PopPop while fixing them up together while he was in high school. She talked about building similar bonds with her mother and sister in the kitchen learning to cook. More and more shared memories of their lives deepened their bond as they ate sandwiches and sipped sweet tea.

"I didn't know what kind of fruit you might prefer, so I brought several options." James pulled out containers of grapes, strawberries, and one that contained a mix of diced peaches, pears, pineapple, and cherries.

"You don't happen to have a fork in there for the mixed fruit, do you?" Randi opened the container. "This is a bit juicy to be a finger food like the others."

"Nope, but I'll feed it to you if you don't wanna get your fingers too sticky from the juice." James dipped his thumb and forefinger into the container to pick up a chunk of fruit to hold it up to Randi's lips.

The way she closed her lips over his fingers instead of just biting the fruit made his cock twitch in his suddenly too tight jeans. When she swirled her tongue around his digits to take the fruit and lick off the juice, James imagined how her mouth would feel on his rock-hard dick.

"Keep that up, Angel, and I'm gonna be feeding you something else," James moaned, pressing his free hand over the front of his pants to make sure she knew what he meant.

"Then maybe you should be the one eating this pineapple," Randi suggested, smiling at him as she released his fingers from her luscious lips. "I hear it makes certain things taste better, but I don't know how fast it works."

"Is that why you taste so sweet, Angel?" James grabbed a piece of pineapple from the container and ate it himself. "You eat a lot of pineapple?"

"I do like pineapple." Randi plucked a grape from the other container and put it to his lips. "But I don't eat it daily or anything."

James tried to tease her with his tongue on her fingers as he consumed the grape, but he almost choked on the fruit that he hadn't chewed before accidentally swallowing. He tried to cover his embarrassment by feeding her a strawberry next, but he still saw concern in her eyes as she took the fruit between her teeth.

She chewed and swallowed before saying, "I'm ready to move on from the fruit course. Think I can have some of that eggplant in your pants now?"

All traces of embarrassment about being a grown man and choking on a grape disintegrated. James quickly closed up the fruit containers and placed them back in the cooler with the drinks. "Absolutely, Angel, but you've gotta tell me exactly what you wanna do first. Using the dirtiest words you can think of, not calling my cock an eggplant."

"I wanna be on my knees with you looming over me," Randi purred in that throaty, sexy voice he loved hearing her use. "I want you to pull my hair to push my face toward your cock, ordering me to unfasten your jeans and take your dick out to play. I wanna lick and suck your cock until you lose control and fuck my face. I want your dick so far down my throat that I can't even taste it when you come."

"Fuck, Angel," James groaned, afraid he might come in his pants from her dirty description alone.

"Or maybe you'll use my hair to pull me off your dick, so you can yank my pants down and bend me over the tailgate to fuck me from behind," Randi continued, causing James to lose all semblance of control.

He pushed up from his seated position to sit on the side of the truck, grabbing her by the hair to do everything she'd just told him she wanted.

"Lift your sweater, Angel," James ordered as he pulled her up to her knees between his legs. "I wanna watch your tits bouncing out of your bra while you suck my cock."

She did as instructed, pulling the front of her sweater over her head, so it was bunched up on the back of her neck, and unfastening the front clasp of her bra before he got both hands back in her hair. He was wrecking her fancy up-do, but he didn't care. He just continued barking out the orders required to fulfill the fantasy she'd described.

The first swipe of her tongue across the head of his cock was exquisite. She was tentative at first, licking him like a lollipop a few times before she sucked just the head of his cock into her mouth. She swirled her tongue around the head a few times before releasing him from her mouth to lick his full length again.

He was beginning to wonder if she was just teasing him to get him to take over control and get rougher, or if she was really inexperienced at giving blow jobs. But when she enveloped him in her hot, wet mouth and sucked him to the back of her throat, he was afraid he would be the one who came off as the most inexperienced of the two of them by coming too soon like a teenage virgin. The way her throat closed down around him felt so fucking good, he wasn't sure if he'd be able to hold back long enough to do everything she wanted before exploding down her throat.

He tried not to get too rough with his hands in her hair, not wanting to hurt her by pulling too hard. He mostly just dug his fingers into the twisted-up braids as he let her control how she bobbed up and down his shaft. But the deeper she took him, the harder it was for him to maintain his loose grip on her head.

"Fuck, Angel," he shouted as he took control, holding her head still as he thrust between her lips. "You. Are. Too. Fucking. Good. At. Sucking. Cock!" He punctuated each word with a plunge of his steel rod into her mouth.

Just as he felt his balls tightening in preparation for a blistering orgasm, James pulled her off his cock with a forceful tug of her hair. He pulled her up, so he could get her voluptuous mounds in his mouth. While he alternated licking and sucking on her taut pink tips, he made quick work of unfastening her jeans and shoving them down to her knees.

He continued tasting her tits while he grabbed his wallet from his back pocket, thankful that his own jeans had only been opened, not pushed down yet, so he could reach the condom in his wallet swiftly. He lightly bit her diamond-hard nipples as he sheathed himself in the latex.

As much as he wanted to do just as she'd described, bending her over the tailgate to impale her on his cock from behind, he knew he had to make sure she was ready to take him first. He dropped his wallet and the condom wrapper in the bed of his truck to free up his hand, so he could finger her perfect pink pussy.

"Damn, Angel, you're soaked," James rasped, loving how wet she'd gotten from sucking his cock and him sucking her titties. "Did you get this wet from sucking my cock?"

"Yes, Jimmy," Randi panted out through lips swollen from his rough usage of her mouth.

"Or was it from me sucking and biting your nipples?" James added a second finger to make sure she was stretched open enough to take all of him immediately. Usually, he liked working his way into her a slow inch at a time, but he wanted to give her the rough fuck from behind that she asked for, so he had to make sure she was ready for all of him at once.

"Both, Jimmy," Randi moaned his name breathlessly. "I get wet from everything you do to me."

"Then bend over, Angel," James demanded, his voice an octave deeper than normal. "Grab hold of the tailgate and don't let go."

As soon as she was on her knees with both hands gripping the top of the tailgate of his truck, James moved in behind her on his own knees. He gripped her hip with one hand and his condom-covered cock with the other.

He had an intense urge to strip off the condom, wanting nothing but her surrounding him. But although he trusted that they were both clean, he didn't know her birth control status to know if it was truly safe to go bareback. So, he kept his cock covered, deciding to talk to her about that possibility at a later date, not wanting to delay being inside her a moment longer to have the discussion right then.

He lined up his cock with her soaking wet slit and impaled her with one hard shove into her still almost too tight channel.

"Fuck, yes, James," Randi shouted as he bottomed out inside her. "Take me just like that. Hard and deep with every thrust."

He pulled out and slapped her ass, telling her, "I'm in charge now, Angel. I'll fuck you however I want because you're mine. Instead of giving me orders, I want you to be a good girl, telling me who you belong to by screaming my name every time I make you come."

"Yes, Jimmy," Randi shouted as James speared her with his cock. "I'm yours, James, only yours."

James slid his hands up from her hips to grab her bouncing breasts as he pounded into her. He kneaded and squeezed them, using them like handles to control her movement back and forth as he ravished her quivering pussy with his cock.

"Fuck, Angel, I love how your cunt tightens around my cock when you come," James rasped over Randi's cries of passion. "It's like you're trying to milk my cum out of me."

"Yes, James, come with me," Randi shouted as the walls of her pussy spasmed around him.

"No, not yet, Angel." James shoved in her to the hilt and held still inside her to enjoy the feel of her contracting around his cock. "I wanna make you come a dozen more times first."

As the waves of her release started to slow around him, James pulled back, leaving only his head inside her before burrowing back in deep. He reined in the power of his thrusts, hoping to keep her from being too sore later from the hard impact of his hips slamming into hers every time. He kept a steady rhythm as he delved between her thighs, moving one hand down, so he could brush a finger over her clit to ease her over the edge the second time.

"James, James, James," Randi chanted his name repeatedly as she came apart in his arms.

He clamped an arm around her waist, holding her up when she seemed like she was about to collapse from the intensity of her orgasm. He held still inside her, gently massaging her back with his free hand while she recovered.

"I don't think I can handle a dozen that intense." Randi finally started coming back to him from whatever other plane of existence she'd floated off to when she came.

"Well, let's just aim for one more then, Angel," James chuckled before starting to move again.

When he realized how wet his hand was from her squirting on it when he was rubbing her clit, James decided to use her excessive arousal to tease her asshole open a little. She'd said she was open to anal exploration when they'd discussed positions and kinks the night they met, but he hadn't yet pushed her to try anything back there yet. Now he wanted to find out just how open she was to the backdoor action he wanted to try.

He trailed his slick, slippery finger between her cheeks to probe her rosette. She sucked in a breath, but she didn't protest, so he pushed through the tight ring of muscle to his first knuckle. He pumped his finger in and out of her super tight asshole in an alternating rhythm with his thrusting cock. In with his cock, out with his finger, in with his finger, out with his cock.

Randi moaned lightly as he pushed his finger deeper into her ass, but the way she was pushing back against him like she was begging for more indicated to him that it wasn't a moan of protest.

"You like that, Angel?" James wanted to make sure before he pushed for more.

"Yes, James," Randi purred. "It feels better than I ever imagined."

"It's sexy as fuck to see, too," James admitted, struggling to maintain control as he probed her with a second finger. He sped up his movements once they were both buried as far as they could be in her puckered little hole. He held his cock still deep in her pussy as he scissored his fingers in her ass, wanting desperately to open her up enough to one day be able to replace his fingers with his dick.

"I can't believe it feels this good without lube," Randi sighed out.

"Oh, there's plenty of lube, Angel," James chuckled. "I'm using your cum as lube from when you squirted all over my hand. And once I get you opened up enough to take a third finger in your ass, we're both gonna come from how fucking awesome it's gonna feel with me filling both your holes."

Randi whimpered as she rocked her hips against his, telling him without words that she was ready to be fucked in both holes at once. James wasted no time in penetrating her anus with a third cum soaked finger. He twined them together in her ass, trying to stiffen them, so they'd feel more like a cock fucking her in the ass at the same time he was fucking her with his cock in her cunt. While his thrusts weren't as hard as Randi had wanted, the fact that James was plowing into both holes at once more than made up for it in the intensity of the sensations in both their bodies.

"Oh, James, yes," Randi shouted as she clamped down on him like a vise, both her pussy on his cock and her ass on his fingers. She repeatedly shouted his name as she came, triggering his own explosive climax.

"Fuck, yes, Randi," James shouted, shoving his cock and fingers in as deep as they could go and holding himself there as his orgasm ripped through him. His cock felt like a roman candle, shooting off almost a dozen times before he finally felt spent. He shouted her name with each burst of cum into the condom, unsure how the latex tube could possibly hold it all.

Though his legs were quivering and felt too weak to hold him up, James wouldn't allow himself to collapse on top of Randi. Instead, he pulled her back into his arms, falling back to the bed of the truck and cradling her to his chest while they recovered.

Once he caught his breath, James reached into the picnic basket to get out the package of wet wipes that the B and B staff recommended he pack to be able to clean up after eating. He started with his hands, but then moved on to intimately cleaning Randi from their afternoon adventure. He disposed of the condom and cleaned himself last. Randi helped him finish packing everything up, so they could go on to their next activity for the day.

It took a little over an hour to get to the San Antonio RiverWalk, partially because they had to stop at a rest area on the highway into the city to dispose of the small trash bag they'd filled from their picnic, and partly because Randi asked him to make an extra stop just before they got downtown. James was worried when she pointed out the chain drugstore and asked him to pull in for a minute.

"Is everything okay?" James signaled to pull into the parking lot and tried not to look too concerned.

"Yeah, just need to grab some tampons." Randi smiled at him.

"Oh, um, okay," James stuttered, barely able to focus to park his truck. *Fuck, was I too rough and now she's feeling like she's starting her period because of it?* "Are you cramping like it's starting? From, uh, earlier. Did I make it worse for you by being too rough, ya know when we were…?"

His voice trailed off as Randi exclaimed, "No!" She reached over to put a hand on his forearm reassuringly. "Everything earlier was perfect. But I'm kinda irregular and like to have them on hand, just in case, even though I don't always have a period every month. And I donated the package I had with me this morning to my niece's first cycle. This is just a restocking trip in case I need them."

"Whew," James breathed out, relieved he hadn't hurt her. Only to instantly worry about why her cycle was irregular. "The irregular thing, though, is that normal? Like your doctor knows about it, and there's nothing to worry about?"

"Yes, it's perfectly normal," Randi confirmed, squeezing his arm where her hand still rested. "And my doctor knows all about it."

"Okay, good." James was still a little flustered, but he was somewhat comforted by her positive attitude.

She leaned over and kissed him on the cheek before taking off her seatbelt and saying, "I'll be right back."

She jumped down out of his truck before James could get his wits about him to go open her door for her. *Probably didn't want me following her around the store to the tampon aisle anyway,* he decided as he sat there waiting for her to get what she needed and return to the truck.

Randi returned to his truck with a bag that was way fuller than James had expected for just a small package of tampons. She dropped it in the floorboard at her feet and buckled up before he put the truck in reverse and backed out of the parking space. Once he was back on the road and headed toward downtown, James stole a glance down at the bag.

Leah Mae Wright

He clearly saw the tampons on top, along with a couple bags of candy. But the words *"pregnancy test"* that showed through the side of the white bag under those things were what caught his eye.

Holy Shit, he inwardly cursed as he quickly looked back at the road. It took everything he had in him to maintain his focus on driving them safely to their destination.

Why is she trying to hide that at the bottom of the bag? Should I ask her about it? Or should I wait until she's ready to tell me I'm gonna be a father?

Holy fuck, I'm gonna be a father!

Maybe. She hasn't taken the test yet, so maybe not. That's probably why she didn't mention it. She's not sure because of her irregular periods, so she wants to wait to talk to me about it.

She probably thinks I'll freak out since we both said we wanted to wait another five years or so to have kids. So, she doesn't wanna risk me having a bad reaction, in case it's a false alarm.

Not that I'd have a bad reaction. At least I don't think.

Fuck, I might be a father! Yeah, it's a surprise, but I'm not upset about it. Hell, I'll be thrilled to have a baby with Randi.

A little girl with her blonde hair and vibrant green eyes will have me wrapped around her finger just like her mama.

Who am I kidding? I'll be wrapped around the kid's finger no matter what the gender or which one of us they look most like. A healthy baby is all that matters.

Or babies. I know twins are supposedly only hereditary on the woman's side of the family, but wouldn't it be awesome for our babies to have a built-in best friend like Dean and I.

I probably shouldn't mention that to Randi when we talk about it later, though. She's probably already freaked out enough, and doesn't need to be scared anymore by the thought of carrying two babies my size in her tiny little tummy.

Damn, I can't wait for her to take the test and tell me about it. I wonder when she's planning on taking the test? Hopefully, it won't be too long, like tonight or tomorrow morning at the latest.

The rest of the afternoon and evening flew by in a blur for James. All through their walk around the river in downtown San Antonio, he was lost in thought about their possible baby. Thoughts of the baby bled over to his constant need to touch her as well, like he always wanted to have a hand on Randi.

They'd mostly held hands as they walked around, but James found himself wrapping his arms around Randi often, too. Mostly that had been an arm around her shoulders, or a hand on the small of her back, as they walked. But he'd even caught himself with his hands lingering on her flat belly as he hugged her from behind while they looked out over the river while standing on one of the bridges.

They maintained their normal level of conversation throughout the date. She elaborated more about her decision to pursue wrestling as a career, and he managed to school his features as he adjusted his training plans for her in his head based on her potentially delicate condition.

James couldn't comment on the taste of his steak dinner, but he'd always remember the way Randi looked as they sat riverside to eat it. He didn't know if it was the twinkle lights strung over the patio seating, or his imagination of her pregnancy glow, but she was ravishing. Sparkling like her personality.

All too soon, the night was over. James dropped Randi off at Charlotte's house, giving her a passionate goodnight kiss on the porch, without ever mentioning what he'd seen in her drugstore bag.

He sent her a quick text as he fell into his way too empty bed, wishing she was there with him.

James: Goodnight, Angel. Sweet dreams! {Face Blowing a Kiss Emoji}

Randi: Goodnight, Jimmy. But my dreams won't be sweet. They'll be dirty because I'll be dreaming about you. {Kissing Face with Closed Eyes Emoji}

Chapter Fourteen

Randi texted her sister first thing after Charlotte left the house to go to work, thinking the privacy of the guest bathroom where she was staying would be the best place for Kay to take the pregnancy test she'd bought for her the day before.

> **Randi: Hey, Sis, thought you might want to come see me
> at Charlotte's this morning.**

> **Kay: Can't. We're all meeting at Hazel's for breakfast
> with both families. Meet me there.**

> **Randi: But I have something you need to do privately, not
> at your future in-laws' house.**

> **Kay: I know. But I can't get away to do it now. Just come
> over for breakfast and we'll figure out when & where
> we can sneak off alone.**

> **Randi: Fine, see you in a few.**

Randi knew that she should leave the test hidden in her suitcase, so there was no chance of anyone seeing it but her and Kay. But since she had plans for later in the day with James and her telehealth appointment with her therapist, she didn't know when she'd get a chance to pass the test on to Kay if she didn't do it that morning. So, common sense be darned, she put the box in her purse as she got ready to leave for the day.

It was a short walk from the house she was staying in over to Bob and Hazel Burleson's huge house that looked like it belonged in a movie about the Civil War Era. She still couldn't comprehend how everyone left their doors unlocked on the ranch, but she chalked it up to a difference between living in a city like Tulsa and living in a small town like Heart's Destiny. The fact that the chief of police lived on the ranch probably had something to do with it, too.

As much as it pained her not to knock and wait for someone to answer the door, she did as she'd been instructed the first day she'd arrived and walked right into the stately home. She followed the sound of voices to the dining room where she found three huge tables set up for breakfast. There were enough seats around the tables to feed an army, but with all the Lees in addition to the Burlesons and their extended families, the room was still almost full, even with several people missing because of having to go to work, like Charlotte.

Kay motioned her over to where she'd saved Randi a seat next to hers. Randi hugged her sister as she reached her side, whispering in her ear, "It's in my purse if we can sneak off for a moment this morning."

"Thanks, Sis," Kay whispered back, releasing Randi from the hug, so she could sit down in the chair beside her.

After a few minutes of small talk with her sister, nieces, Anthony, and his brothers sitting closest to them, Randi was instructed to go to the kitchen to fill her plate at the breakfast buffet set up in there. She filled her plate with scrambled eggs, bacon, and toast and chose a glass of orange juice to wash it all down with before returning to her seat.

It was another hour plus of small talk before she got the brilliant idea to ask Kay to show her to a restroom, so she could wash up after eating. *Sugar, I should've thought of that before eating.*

"Oh, yeah, right this way," Kay agreed, grabbing Randi's hand, and pulling her out of the room.

Randi made sure to grab her purse, so she could pass the test on to her sister, even if Kay probably wouldn't be able to take it right then. As soon as they were alone in the bathroom by the Burlesons' family room, Randi locked the door and dug through her purse to get the test for her sister.

Leah Mae Wright

"I know you probably wanna wait to take this, but I'm gonna spend the day with James," Randi explained softly, holding the box out to her sister. "So, you should probably take this with you to take when you can today."

"Crap, I didn't bring my purse with me to be able to hide it." Kay looked around the bathroom, like she was trying to figure out where she could hide it for later. "If I take it now, can you keep it hidden for me for a little while?"

"You want me to put your used pee stick back in my purse?" Randi whisper-shouted at her sister. "That's like seriously gross."

"Please, Sis, I'll wrap it in toilet paper and put it back in the box, so it won't contaminate anything in your purse," Kay pleaded, looking up at Randi with big doe eyes. "I couldn't get us an appointment with the doctor until next Wednesday, and I'm not sure how to tell Anthony yet."

Randi understood her sister's precarious position with her fiancé. Reluctantly, she agreed. "Fine, I'll hide it for you for a couple of days if it's positive. But you'd better hurry and pee on the thing or someone's gonna come looking for us."

Kay went into the water closet and did her business. She came back out carrying the stick that she laid on a few squares of toilet paper on the vanity while she washed her hands. Nerves over waiting for the three minutes to be up caused Randi to have to pee in sympathy, so she took a turn in the water closet as well. By the time she finished washing her hands, Kay was picking up the test and looking at the results.

"Well?" Randi was unable to read Kay's blank expression. When Kay just stared at the test without saying a word, Randi leaned in close to check the results for herself. *I guess it's pretty definitive when the test says the word "pregnant" in the little display window.* Randi put an arm around her sister's shoulders to comfort her. "Are you okay, Sis?"

Randi wasn't sure if it was her words or the physical contact that shook Kay out of her obviously shocked state, but she was glad when her sister nodded her head. "Yes, I'm, I'm gonna be a mom again. To a little boy this time, with brown hair and blue eyes."

"Whoa, how do you know all that from that test?" Randi wasn't sure where her sister had conjured the description of her unborn child.

"Not from the test," Kay giggled, looking up at Randi with watery eyes. "From Anthony's dreams. He's been dreaming about our family for over a year. That's how he knew we were meant to be together the day we met. He described our other kids to me the day before we went to court from his dream about Tia's sixteenth birthday. The youngest was a two or three-year-old boy with brown hair and blue eyes. On Tia's sixteenth birthday, this baby will be about two and a half, so I know he is who Anthony saw in his dreams."

"Wow," Randi breathed out the word, in awe at the possibility of Anthony's dreams becoming reality.

They both jumped as there was a loud knock at the door before they heard a loud female voice. "Everything okay in there?"

"Yeah, we'll be out in a minute," Randi replied as Kay wrapped the test stick in toilet paper and shoved it back in the box. Randi wished she had a bag to put the box in before she stuck it in her purse, but she tried not to cringe too bad when she had to put it back in with just the box and toilet paper keeping Kay's urine off her things.

They left the restroom, going back to the dining room to join the rest of the family, chatting about their plans for the day. Randi didn't even think about the fact that she hadn't seen the test instructions go back in the box as one of Anthony's female cousins went into the restroom they'd just vacated. Not that she would have opened the box to verify they hadn't been left behind in the bathroom had she thought about them.

<div style="text-align:center">~~~</div>

Jen Burleson picked up the paper that either Kay or her sister had dropped in the restroom, planning to return it to them at the table in case it was important. When she looked down to see what it was, her jaw dropped. "Pregnancy test instructions," she read aloud from the paper.

Knowing that her cousin Anthony had been sterilized by his accident right before he left the Navy, she assumed it was Randi who'd taken a pregnancy test that morning because Kay couldn't possibly be pregnant.

Since she'd only just met Kay's sister, she wasn't sure what to do with the information in her hand. She didn't think she knew her well enough to convince her to go off somewhere private, so she could give them back to her, but she also didn't want to embarrass her by giving the paper to her in front of the whole family either.

She thought briefly about possibly trying to pass it to her via her boyfriend, James Hunter, since she'd known him since they were kids. Based on their behavior at the wedding events over the weekend, Jen assumed he was the father of Randi's baby. But she wasn't sure if they'd talked about it or not, and she didn't want to get in the middle of their relationship if they hadn't. Since she was taking the test with her sister instead of James, Jen decided talking to him about it was probably a bad idea.

Assuming that Randi had taken the test that morning, Jen contemplated just throwing the instructions in the trashcan. But then Jen wondered if her knock on the door had interrupted Randi before she actually peed on the stick, leaving her still needing the instructions. Not to mention if she threw it away in her aunt and uncle's house, someone else in the family would find it and wonder who in the family might be knocked up.

Not wanting to risk anyone thinking it might be her in the family way, Jen folded the paper up and stuffed it in her pocket before doing her business in the bathroom. She'd talk to her sister later and get her opinion about what she should do, knowing Julie would keep the pregnancy gossip to herself.

~~~

James knew he wasn't acting like himself as he showed Randi around Heart's Destiny. He'd driven around at first, showing her the schools and rodeo arena before stopping at Kara's Kakes to introduce her to the lady responsible for the donuts she and Tia had devoured when they were at his house on Sunday to start their wrestling training. Instead of walking around the center of town to introduce her to the rest of the people closest to him, like his dad at the bank or his childhood friend Nick, who owned the Book Nook, he drove between destinations, even when they were only a block apart. Not to mention
~~~

the fact that he'd driven his 1972 yellow Barracuda instead of his truck, so she would have an easier time getting in and out of the vehicle at every stop.

Fuck, I should've thought of the safety of the lap belt across her belly, James mentally berated himself as he watched her unbuckle her seatbelt when they got to the Burger Barn for lunch. *I need to spend some time researching the safest cars for pregnant women to ride in, so I can buy something safer while I'm home this week.*

"Why are you acting so weird?" Randi gave him a quizzical look as he took her hand to help her out of the car.

"I'm not acting weird," James denied, smiling down at her. He kissed the top of her head as he wrapped his arm around her shoulders to lead her into the restaurant. "I'm just enjoying spending the day with you, Angel."

"Yeah, I'm enjoying spending the day with you, too." Randi snaked her arm around his waist as they walked. "But you're still acting weird with all the door opening and helping me in and out of the car, like I'm not capable of sitting down or standing up without assistance."

Fuck, I don't mean to treat her like she's made of glass, but I don't know how to stop wanting to take care of her and our baby to the point that I'm being stupid about it.

"I know you're more than capable, Angel." James opened the door to the restaurant and directed her through it in front of him. "I just wanna take care of you and," James coughed to stop himself from saying *"our baby"* at the end of that sentence. He covered his almost faux pas by saying, "and treat you like the queen you are to me."

Dumbass, she's gonna think I'm stealing the lines Anthony says to Kay with the queen shit. I should've stuck to my own pet name for her or some variation, like saying I wanna worship her like the goddess she is to me.

Thankfully, he didn't have to worry about her commenting on his asinine lines because Tom and Tiffany Taylor, the proprietors of the Burger Barn, diverted her attention from what he'd said. James thought the couple was about ten years younger than his parents, so somewhere in their mid-forties. But he would always remember them as they'd been in their late twenties, when they'd first opened the closest thing Heart's Destiny had to a fast-food place. He wasn't quite ten years old at the time, but he remembered having his first non-homemade burger there with his great-grandparents, who were Meemaw's parents, Grandpa and Grandma Sloan, before they passed away.

"I just couldn't believe it when you and James played the newlywed game the other day," Tiffany gushed, coming around the counter to pull Randi into a hug. "The whole town's been abuzz with the news about Anthony and Kay, but nobody told us that James had also found his lady love that night in Tulsa."

"Oh, um, yeah," Randi sputtered, looking awkward as she returned Tiffany's hug. "We've been a little more private than my sister and Anthony."

"Only because you weren't in town for the last couple of months." Tiffany released Randi and moved back behind the counter. "There's no such thing as privacy in Heart's Destiny. Gossip goes up on our town page online before it's even finished happening."

Oh, Fuck! James saw the color drain from Randi's face and knew she was worried about what was being said about them, or if anyone knew she'd bought a pregnancy test the day before. James pulled Randi into his side, hoping to keep her upright while he figured out how to diffuse the situation.

"Geez, Tiff, way to freak the girl out before she even knows your name." Tom stepped up to the counter from his usual place back in the kitchen. "Don't listen to my wife, Randi. Most things stay private between couples here. The only gossip that goes up online is who's dating and who's not, maybe some speculation about pending baby announcements when one of the wanna-be grandmas in town thinks their daughter or daughter-in-law has gained a few pounds after eating a big meal. But the only thing they've posted about ya'll is that you're dating, and that you trounced your parents in the newlywed game. I'm Tom Taylor, by the way, and this is my usually more reserved wife, Tiffany."

"Nice to meet you." Randi's voice still sounded a little shaky to James. "Sorry if I look freaked out. I'm just not used to the way things work in a small town. And after breakfast with my whole family, and almost all of the Burlesons this morning, I was afraid you were gonna tell me they've already started planning our wedding, when we've just started dating."

Hmm, James pondered. *I wonder if that's all she's worried about. Or did she take the test this morning? And now she's wondering who all is speculating about our pending baby announcement.*

The conversation changed to ordering their burgers as a few more people came into the restaurant, so James let the subject drop without broaching it with Randi. As much as he wanted to ask her about the test results, knowing that she needed to think things through before mentioning them, so she could keep her anxiety at bay, made it clear to him that he needed to wait until she was ready to talk to him about it.

They had a nice lunch, only interrupted a few times by people stopping by their table to say "hi" or welcome Randi to town. When Randi mentioned needing someplace private to do her telehealth appointment at four o'clock, James decided to take her back to his cabin. He spent that hour in his home gym, while she was upstairs talking to her therapist, so she was able to keep it private, even from him.

He briefly wondered how she was going to work her sessions into her schedule once she started working with the GWA, but he dropped that train of thought when he veered off on a tangent, trying to figure out how they were both going to work around having a baby. He had to slow down the speed of the treadmill when he almost fell off the end from thinking about how they'd need to rewrite the storylines, so he could take off for paternity leave when the baby was born.

How long was Tank off work when his wife had the twins? Was it longer because they had twins? Or do all pregnant ladies have to stop flying at a specific time in their pregnancy?

James pulled his phone out of his pocket and started doing some online searches to try and figure out when he and Randi's baby was due, when she'd have to quit flying, and how long most people took for maternity and paternity leave when they had a baby. He quickly cleared his screen and shoved his phone back in his pocket when Randi walked into the room after her therapy session.

"Can we do my next wrestling lesson now?" Randi looked excited about the training when she reached the front of his treadmill. "Or do you have other plans for us for tonight?"

Fuck, I should've looked up training guidelines for pregnant women, so I'd know what we could safely do, James thought as he stopped the treadmill. *Maybe we can work on mat work, and I can switch it up from teaching her submission holds to gently making love to her?*

He looked her up and down, acknowledging in his head how bad he'd wanted to peel those yoga pants down her legs all day. He'd changed into loose athletic shorts to work out when they got back to his house and just the thought of peeling those sexy tights down her legs was making him tent them.

"Yeah, Angel," James finally answered her as he stepped down off the treadmill and walked over to the cabinet where he stored the extra thick mats he put down for when he practiced at home. He adjusted himself in his shorts, trying to keep his plan from being too obvious before they got started. "But I think you got the bumps down the other day, so I think we'll work on some submissions today."

"Submissions?" Randi arched an eyebrow inquisitively. "You mean I'll get to learn how to make you tap out?"

"Oh, I'll be tapping something," James quipped as he laid out the six-inch thick mats. Since they weren't bumping on them, he decided not to tape them together. One would be wide enough for them to use it like a bed and he had no intention of getting so rowdy that they might slip in between them and hit the floor if they separated. "But I don't know that I'll be tapping out."

Randi giggled at the suggestive look he gave her as he toed off his shoes and laid down on the center mat. She kicked off her shoes and socks before joining him on the mat. He instructed her how to get into the position to put him in an armbar and loved the feel of her wrapping her legs around his arm as she attempted the move for the first time. Even though she mostly had the positioning correct, she wasn't strong enough to make it painful for him.

"Is this right?" Randi tried to crank down on his arm.

"Yeah, Angel." James appreciated the feel of her pussy pushed up against his triceps and the swell of her breast under his palm.

"Then why aren't you tapping out?" Randi squeezed her thighs around his upper arm and made James wish they were practicing naked.

James flexed his fingers enough to tweak her nipple through her t-shirt. "Because I don't want you to let go," he finally retorted as he started to massage her tit. He rolled to reach across her with his other hand, so he could play with both of her boobs at once.

"Why do I think this isn't really how this move is supposed to work?" Randi's giggle shifted to a moan of pleasure as he caressed her perky peaks just the way he knew she liked.

He rolled up onto his knees, pinning her shoulders to the mat, since she hadn't let go of his arm with her legs. Looming over her as he was, allowed him to watch her facial expression change as he kneaded her breasts. She went from playful but serious about training to melting under his touch.

"Seems like it's going exactly the way we both want it to, Angel," James observed aloud as Randi released her hold on his arm to wrap her long sexy legs around his waist. "And if we get rid of some of these unnecessary clothes, it'll be even better."

Randi skimmed her palms up his arms, across his shoulders, and linked them together behind his neck. She didn't have to pull very hard to get him moving down toward her, so their lips could lock and cease all attempts at talking.

James had just thought his dick was hard earlier. As soon as he tasted her, it lengthened and thickened almost to the point of pain. Instead of standing at attention for her, it poked straight out toward her, acting like a divining rod aiming at the wet heat of her pussy. He'd never felt such an extreme need for a woman as he did for Randi. It was so overwhelming and intense that he hoped he'd be able to control his rougher impulses to keep things gentle until he knew what else was safe while she was expecting their baby.

Not that Randi was keeping anything gentle as she dug her fingernails into his upper back and shoulders. *Fuck yes, I hope she leaves marks.* James moaned, backing off just enough to push her shirt up but not releasing her mouth from his claiming kiss.

Randi started pulling at his shirt as well, leading him to break the kiss, so they could both remove the barriers between them to get skin on skin. James pulled his t-shirt off with one hand, grasping the material covering his upper back as Randi crossed her arms at the front hem of hers to whip it off over her head. James stripped off his shorts and boxer briefs in one fell swoop, while Randi removed her bra.

"Fuck, I don't think I'll ever get enough of seeing your beautiful body." James reached for the waistband of her leggings, so he could drag them down her legs, taking her panties with them. He was glad they'd both already removed their shoes, so they weren't a hindrance in getting naked quickly.

"Ditto," Randi agreed as she reclined back on the mat. James crawled over the top of her, holding most of his weight off of her by holding himself up on his forearms, which were resting on the mat on either side of her head. "But I wanna do more than just see your hot bod."

Randi ran her hands over his chest and shoulders for a second before moving down to trail them across his abs, moving closer and closer to his excessively engorged cock.

"Hands above your head, Angel," James commanded, knowing he was too close to the edge to be able to last if she got her hands on his dick.

"But I wanna touch you, Jimmy," Randi purred in that breathy tone that almost made him come without her even touching him.

"You can touch me later," James assured her, starting to lavish her with open-mouthed kisses to her neck and collarbone as she moved her arms above her head. "Right now, I wanna worship you like the goddess you are deserves."

He trailed his tongue over every inch of her exposed skin, paying special attention to anyplace she seemed to especially enjoy. He took his time, making sure he didn't leave any part of her unloved. He made her come multiple times with his mouth and fingers, soaking the mat beneath them with a mix of her arousal and the precum leaking out of his cock while he cherished his woman.

Just as he started to move into place, so he could finally fill her, James paused, remembering that his wallet and all of his condoms were upstairs in his bedroom. "Fuck, Angel," he swore, starting to push up off of her to go get the prophylactics. "Condoms are all upstairs. I'll be right back."

"We don't need them," Randi protested, reaching for him, and pulling him back down on top of her. "I'm clean and safe, so as long as you're clean too, I don't want anything between us."

"I'm clean and I've never done it without a condom," James confessed. He didn't mention his realization that they wouldn't need a condom if she was already pregnant as he notched the head of his cock against the hood of her cleft. He was too busy enjoying the feel of sliding into her tight wet sheath with nothing to block the sensations between them.

He claimed her mouth with his, mimicking with his tongue the way he was slowly sliding in and out of her pussy with his cock. It wasn't their normal fast paced fucking. It was slow, sensual lovemaking, connecting them in a way they hadn't experienced before.

Their hands roamed each other's bodies with reverence as they told each other without words how they felt. The only sounds in the room were their impassioned moans of pleasure, which were mostly felt more than heard, and the soft sloshing of the wetness between them lubricating their movements.

As much as James had feared he'd lose control of his primal instinct to rut into her like a wild animal, he found that he needed this deeper sacred connection with Randi much more.

Who knew slow and sensual could be so erotic and amazing? Fuck, this might be my new favorite way to make love to Randi.

When her inner walls began to flutter around him, James knew he wouldn't be able to hold back his own climax much longer. Randi turned her head, breaking their kiss to suck in a deep breath as her body bared down on him in what could only be described as a full-body orgasmic spasm.

It was glorious to watch her break apart in his arms. It was wonderful to hear her chanting his name repeatedly as she came on his cock. But the most magnificent feeling was when he joined her in the throes of ecstasy during their simultaneous climax.

"Randi, Angel," James shouted both her name and his pet name for her over and over as their gazes locked and waves of pleasure flowed over them both.

I love you, he thought, wanting to tell her immediately. But since he knew it was considered to be a dick move to say those three little words for the first time while still buried inside his woman, he held them back for the time being.

He should have said it the night before during their romantic dinner overlooking the river, but he'd been distracted by his thoughts about potentially becoming a father. Now he would need to plan another romantic moment to express his feelings of undying love for her. It wouldn't be that night as they sat at his dining room table eating pizza while wearing their workout clothes.

Leah Mae Wright

With everything going on the next few days for Thanksgiving and the wedding, I may have to wait to plan another romantic date on Sunday, when we can finally get some more alone time.

~~~

Wednesday, November 21, 2018

Randi decided on Wednesday morning that not having her own vehicle in Heart's Destiny sucked. She was scheduled to meet Rick Robertson at the bed and breakfast for her interview at ten a.m., but she hadn't thought about not having her own means of transportation to get to the interview when she scheduled it. She knew she could call James to come and get her and take her, but she also knew he had other plans that day to keep him too busy to chauffeur her around. He had to go pick up the correct shoes for the wedding and then he was helping Anthony record the song he wanted played at the wedding for Kay. Besides, she didn't want him to think that meant he could stay and observe her interview.

Dog, I hope it's just a one-on-one interview and not out in the open in front of all the other guests of the B and B, Randi worried as she finished dressing in her most professional-looking outfit. She'd taken extra time with her hair and makeup that morning, wanting to look her best for the professional meeting. She knew Rick had already seen her normal daily self in several more casual, unprofessional settings, but she wanted to present herself as confident and qualified for the job during the interview.

She'd thought about just walking over to the bed and breakfast, thinking it was just across one road from the Burleson Ranch and within walking distance. But after James drove her around his family's property, showing her that the plantation house where she was supposed to meet Rick was actually about five miles away from Charlotte's house on the ranch where she was staying, she decided trying to walk the winding gravel road through the Hunters' property in heels was not her best option.

So, once she made sure she had everything she might need in her messenger bag, Randi walked over to her sister's house to ask Kay to
~~~

give her a ride. As nervous as she was for the interview, she forgot that she'd been told to just walk on in and stopped on the porch to knock on the front door.

"Come on in, it's open," she heard a feminine voice yell from somewhere in the house.

"I'll never get used to these unlocked doors here," Randi mumbled to herself as she walked into her sister's home. "Kay?" she shouted, trying to figure out where in the house to go to find her sister, so she could ask her for a ride.

"In the kitchen," Kay yelled back.

Randi walked down the central hall through the house to get to the kitchen. She was immediately greeted by her niece, Maria, barreling into her and hugging her around the waist.

"Aunt Randi, are you gonna help us make pies for Thanksgiving?" Maria inquired as Randi returned her jubilant hug.

"Um, not right now." Randi looked down into Maria's blue-green eyes. "I have a meeting to go to first, but then I'm planning to come back and bake with ya'll."

And hopefully, having all her grandchildren in the room while we're all baking together will keep Mom from lecturing me about my interview this morning.

"Is this your interview with Rick?" Kay inquired from her spot by the kitchen island where she was kneading dough of some sort.

"Yeah, I was just coming to ask you to run me over there for it, since I don't have my car here," Randi replied to her sister.

"Oh, um, I can't exactly leave right now," Kay sputtered, continuing to beat up the floury lump in front of her. "But you're welcome to take my Jeep to go. The keys are on the hook by the back door."

"Oh, yeah, okay, thanks," Randi stumbled through saying, flustered by the possibility of driving her sister's new vehicle. The last time she'd borrowed her sister's car, she'd gotten in an accident, so she hadn't expected Kay to ever trust her with another of her cars.

"I'm assuming James showed you how to get to the B and B?" Kay questioned at Randi's flummoxed response to her offer of the use of her brand-new SUV.

"Yeah, I know how to get there," Randi replied, deciding to confess her confusion to her sister. "I'm just surprised that you trust me to drive your brand-new Jeep after what happened the last time I borrowed your car."

"Yeah, well, that was a long time ago," Kay shrugged before shaking her head at her sister. "I'm sure your driving has improved a lot since you were sixteen. And the traffic here is nothing like Tulsa, so I'm pretty sure you'll make it safely to your interview and back without any issues."

Randi fought back the tears that were welling up in her eyes. She hadn't realized just how much baggage she was still carrying around from her teenage years. But the last few moments unburdened her of at least one old bag she hadn't realized she'd lugged with her into adulthood. If her sister could forgive her for a teenage mistake, maybe her parents could finally see her as an adult, too. They'd seemed to be acting like it the last few days, but Randi was still leery of trusting their new attitudes to not revert to past negative opinions.

"Thanks, Sis, that means a lot," Randi choked out. "I'd give you a hug to show you how much I appreciate your faith in me, but I don't wanna get flour on my clothes before the interview."

"Well, change into something appropriate for being covered in flour before you come back to bake this afternoon," Kay smiled.

"Definitely," Randi replied before saying her goodbyes to her sister and nieces and heading out the back door to find Kay's silver Jeep Cherokee.

She had to move the seat back and adjust the mirrors to be able to drive the vehicle after her much shorter sister. She appreciated the sweet ride of the SUV as she made her way off of the ranch and over to the Hunters' property to the plantation house, which housed several rooms for the bed and breakfast, as well as the ballroom, where they'd have Thanksgiving, the rehearsal dinner, and the wedding reception in the next three days.

James had driven by the plantation house a few times in the last few days that she'd been spending most of her time with him, but he hadn't stopped, so she could go in and see the inside of the massive building.

Randi was in awe at the structure as she parked in the nearby parking lot to walk toward the front of the building. James and his family may have called it the plantation house, but to Randi it more closely resembled one of the regal homes owned by British royalty like she'd seen on a television travel show. It dwarfed the home of

Anthony's parents, which she thought looked more like a southern plantation house, appearing at least four times the size of the Burlesons' home.

She couldn't dwell on the appearance of the building, though, because of the nervous flutters in her belly from thinking about the interview, which was the reason she was there right then. She barely registered all the ornate features of the stately home turned event space, as she was directed to the library where she was meeting with Rick Robertson.

She was fifteen minutes early for the interview, but Rick was already in the library waiting for her when she walked into the room. After brief introductions, they sat across from each other at a desk, which had probably been in the building since the eighteen-hundreds when the place was built, to begin the interview.

It didn't follow the normal interview flow that Randi had been expecting. Instead of asking her about her qualifications, or why she wanted to work with the GWA, Rick began by explaining the duties of the job. He pointed out that it wasn't a job with set hours like she thought it would be. Instead, she'd be traveling on the same schedule as the performers and would have similar flexibility in her day to spend sightseeing or training as soon as they got off the plane in a new city each day. She'd possibly have to take notes in a meeting on the plane, but most of her work would be in the evenings. She would have to be in the arena by four each afternoon to make sure everything was set up for that evening's show and would coordinate with the writing staff to make sure each of the nightly performances flowed smoothly. It would be a lot of making sure any props were in place and directing the talent to their allotted match and promo times and locations.

He quoted her a salary that exceeded the range she'd seen online for production assistants. She wasn't sure she completely covered her shock at hearing the large dollar amount, but if Rick noticed her surprised face, he didn't mention it. He just kept going over the benefits and holiday breaks, like her jaw hadn't dropped to the floor at the salary.

"Any questions?" Rick finally asked after his long monologue about the job.

"Shouldn't you be asking me questions?" Randi still wasn't sure why he hadn't asked about her in any way. "Like about my work experience or qualifications for the job?"

"Between your very detailed résumé, observing you at the wedding events so far, and the personal recommendations of more than one of my current employees, I believe I have all those answers already." Rick leaned back in his chair with a smile. "So, my only question for you is, are you ready to start work on Monday?"

"Yes, sir, absolutely!" Randi exclaimed. She probably answered a little too fast, but she didn't want to take any chances on him changing his mind and rescinding the job offer.

"Perfect." Rick reached into the bag she hadn't noticed on the floor by his feet and pulled out a tablet computer. "All our HR forms are online, so you can fill them out on here. It's pretty self-explanatory, but just take a picture of your driver's license and social security card when you get to that part of the paperwork."

Randi took the tablet when he handed it to her across the desk and quickly got started filling out the various forms.

"Oh, one other thing," Rick interjected as she got her wallet out to take the pictures he'd mentioned of her documents. "I know you and James are dating. And while I don't want any specifics about your relationship, I do need to know if you want to share a hotel room with him, or if you want your own, so I can add you to our bookings for next week."

Randi felt herself blush at the question. *Sugar, Fudge, Drums! I should've talked to James about that before this interview. I know he says we're together, and we've certainly been banging like bunnies all week, but he's also been taking me back to the ranch every night instead of having me stay with him. So, I don't know if he wants to share a hotel room on the road or not.*

"Uh, I don't know," Randi finally stuttered, hating that she was probably turning beet red in front of her new boss. "James and I haven't really talked about the possibility of sharing a hotel room, so maybe just book my own for now, with the option of sharing later?"

"We can do that." Rick gave her a sly smile. "I'll add you to our booking list and you can always make the change yourself when you arrive at the hotel. Just let me know if it ends up a permanent change, so I can adjust how the rooms are booked in the future."

After only a few more minutes of small talk while Randi finished filling out the human resources paperwork, Rick excused himself to take his daughter to the Alamo for the afternoon while Randi went back to the ranch.

She went straight back to Charlotte's house to change out of her dress slacks, silk blouse, and blazer and into jeans and a t-shirt to go to her sister's house to bake the day away. She was looking forward to spending the day with her family, but secretly hoped she'd also get to see James if he came home with Anthony from the recording studio.

Too excited to wait to see if she'd get the chance to tell him her good news about the job in person, she sent him a quick text after parking in her sister's driveway.

Randi: Good news! I got the job!!! {Victory Hand Emoji}

James: That's awesome, Angel! So proud of you.

Randi: Any chance you can come home with Anthony when ya'll are done in the studio? I'll be there baking. Thought we could share a piece of pie to celebrate. {Pie Emoji} {Clinking Glasses Emoji}

James: Absolutely. See you in a couple of hours. {Face Blowing a Kiss Emoji}

Chapter Fifteen

Thursday, November 22, 2018, Thanksgiving Day

Randi laid in bed for a while after she woke up on Thanksgiving. She flipped on the television in the guest room where she was staying to watch the big parade while she was getting ready for the day. But she didn't pay attention to most of it because she was too lost in her own thoughts about the events of the evening before.

James had come to dinner at Anthony and Kay's house after he and Anthony were finished in the recording studio, but so had all of her immediate family. She'd been nervous enough when it was just the women in her family making pies, cakes, and cookies all afternoon to have plenty to serve the whole town and all the out-of-town wedding guests for Thanksgiving, worried about the questions her mother and sister-in-law would have for her about her relationship with James. Having her father and brother there for what seemed like a pre-Thanksgiving family only dinner that she'd inadvertently invited James to attend was more nerve-racking than even her twice a day medication could handle.

It wasn't that they'd behaved badly or treated James like he was unwelcome, like she still half expected them to do. In fact, they'd all treated James like he was already one of the family. It was strange sitting around the table with everyone coupled up—her mom and dad, Kay and Anthony, David and Diana, and her and James—minus the kids of course. Though the way Tia and Maria had taken over the care and feeding of David and Diana's kids, toddler Davy and baby Danica, as soon as David brought them in the house, they almost seemed like their own unit at one end of the table, too.

When James had proposed a toast to congratulate her for getting her new job, her parents had even sounded happy and proud of her for pursuing her dreams, offering their own congratulations. She'd been sure they'd have presented her with a list of objections to her new career path, but they hadn't said anything but positive comments about her job, training to wrestle, and how much they liked her new boss from the conversations they'd had with him over the past few days. The only slightly negative reaction from her parents was when her alarm went off for her to take her evening dose of medication, and that was more surprise that she was on medication than actually objecting to it.

It was still slightly unbelievable to her that they were responding so wonderfully to the changes she was making in her life. She'd talked to her therapist on Tuesday about how they'd reacted at the wedding shower and her fear that it was only because they were surrounded by a room full of strangers at the time. Kelly reminded her that if their attitudes changed when it was just the three of them in the room, then she could get up and walk out now that she was an adult. She'd also tried to steer Randi toward believing her parents' positive reactions weren't just for show.

Randi was trying to believe it was all really happening the way she'd hoped and prayed for, but she still felt a little like a kid starting to question their belief in Santa Claus as she saw her parents in a new light. That's why she took an extra hour to lay in bed going over every moment of the last few days, just to try to reinforce the positive vibes with everyone around her.

Just as she was finally ready to get up and get in the shower to get ready for the town-wide holiday celebration, a news report broke into the parade coverage that caught her eye.

"Heiress Brooklyn Barns was kidnapped overnight from her family estate in Macon, Georgia," the reporter announced as a photo of a young blonde woman appeared on the screen. "She's five-foot-three and approximately one-hundred-and-twenty pounds, with blonde hair and blue eyes."

Randi flopped back down to sit on the edge of the bed as she watched the news report, her heart going out to the young woman.

"Brooklyn is the daughter of Bradley Stanton Barns the third and the late Madeline Ashbury-Barns," the reporter continued as the images of the missing woman and her family flashed on the screen. "She's scheduled to be married to Clayton Donaldson on Saturday,

December first, at which time she will inherit the Ashbury estate, including Ashbury Enterprises, a multinational conglomerate currently run by her father."

The photo on the screen switched to an image of the beautiful young woman in a floor-length blue dress, looking like she was going to a formal dance, or possibly a charity event, and being escorted by a man who looked to be in his fifties, but it wasn't the same man that was in the pictures that appeared to be her father. *Geez, I hope that's not her fiancé,* Randi thought as she continued watching the report.

"Local authorities have no comment at this time, but her father believes the kidnapping is linked to a business rival, who is attempting to disrupt the operations of Ashbury Enterprises," the reporter continued. "Please contact the Macon Police Department at the number on the bottom of the screen if you have any information about kidnapped heiress Brooklyn Brielle Barns."

Randi said a quick prayer for the young lady's safety before going to the restroom to take a shower and get ready for the Thanksgiving celebration. After her shower, she opened her suitcase to get out her undergarments and found the instructions for a pregnancy test laying on top of her clothes.

What the fudge? Where'd that come from?

Randi dug down into the bottom of the bag where she'd stashed Kay's pregnancy test the day before and verified that it was indeed the same brand.

Sugar! I bet Kay left the instructions in the bathroom and whoever found them thinks they're mine! For Dog's sake, Randi, grow up. If ever there was a right time to think the real curse words, having your new boyfriend's gossipy small town thinking you're knocked up is probably it. If you can whisper them or text them to James, you can think them in your own head. Shit, Damn, Fuck! This is so not good!

Randi shoved the instruction sheet into the shopping bag she'd put the test box in and wrapped it up as small as possible to put in her purse. *Kay's taking this thing back today and clearing up any confusion about who's knocked up as soon as fucking possible!*

She quickly dressed and finished putting on her makeup and fixing her hair. It may have been a futile attempt to show everyone that she wasn't pregnant, but she dressed in the most figure-hugging dress she'd brought with her, a navy-blue sweater dress with a brown pleather belt that cinched it in over her slim waist. She paired the knee length dress with a pair of brown boots to match the belt. The boots came up over her calves to just below the knee and added four inches to her height.

While going up from her normal five-foot-six to five-foot-ten wouldn't put her at eye level with any of the men in her family, the Burleson family, or the GWA wrestlers, she would tower over pretty much all of the women. *I just hope the extra height is intimidating enough to keep whoever found that instruction sheet and thinks it's mine from sharing her suspicion with everyone today.*

Not that she really knew how to intimidate anyone to possibly prevent the rumors she knew would be spreading throughout the holiday celebration. It was more a case of trying to make herself feel strong enough to withstand anything that might be said about her.

Stand tall and strong. Be proud of who you are. Randi recited the mantra her therapist had given her at one of her earlier appointments in her head. After a few cleansing breaths and rounds of the words filling her head, she was finally ready to go face the crowd.

Charlotte was in her living room watching an update on the missing woman from Georgia when Randi emerged from her temporary room.

"Did they find her?" Randi had switched off the television in her room and hadn't seen the most recent reports.

"No," Charlotte replied, shaking her head. "This was just an interview with her father and fiancé, saying they suspect foul play because her phone and all her stuff was left in her room."

"But you don't think that, do you?" Randi could read Charlotte's disbelief loud and clear based on the skeptical expression on her face.

"After seeing the fiancé," Charlotte scoffed, clicking the television off with the remote in her hand. "No, I don't. I think she was being pressured to marry one of her dad's friends and took off to escape, leaving her phone behind, so they couldn't track her down."

"So that old guy in the first pictures I saw was actually her fiancé?" Randi shuddered at the thought of having to marry someone her father's age.

"Yeah, but instead of admitting that she didn't want to marry the old coot, they're saying she was kidnapped by a business rival," Charlotte accused, gathering her things so they could go to the bed and breakfast for Thanksgiving.

"Yeah, I saw that earlier, but the pictures that were being shown didn't identify which one was her father and which one was her fiancé. So, I didn't think about the possibility of her actually being a runaway bride, instead of a kidnapping victim like they reported."

"I don't know for sure that she ran away," Charlotte backtracked from her earlier statement, as they walked out the door. "I'm just guessing based on what I would do if I were in her shoes."

"Now that I'm really thinking about it, I agree with you." Randi walked with Charlotte toward her car, too focused on their conversation to remember that she was supposed to be riding with her parents to the event.

When Charlotte's sister and a couple of her female cousins appeared beside them at the car, obviously planning to ride with Charlotte, Randi reversed directions. "See ya'll there," she waved as she turned to walk toward the Burleson house where her parents were parked. If Charlotte had been going alone, she probably would've just gotten a ride with her. But since she suspected it was one of the female cousins who'd been next in the restroom after she and Kay had gone for Kay to take the test, Randi didn't want to risk the possible questions they'd have in the car when it would feel like four against one.

Not that the inquisition was much better in the car with her parents, Amy, and Deanna. Apparently, while Randi had spent most of her time on Monday and Tuesday with James and then her mother, sister, and sister-in-law on Wednesday, Amy and Deanna had spent all three days hanging out with the Burlesons and a few of the wrestlers and their wives. Apparently, they had a lot of questions about the gossip they'd overheard.

Randi confirmed that she was dating James and had gotten a job with the GWA, but she refuted the wedding rumors and speculation about her future sleeping arrangements while traveling for her new job. She felt a little uncomfortable telling them that she would have her own hotel room, and wouldn't be sharing James's room, because she wasn't one-hundred percent sure that would be true for long. But since her parents were in the car, she wasn't about to mention that, nor the fact that they didn't have to share a bedroom to have sex.

Thankfully, neither of her friends brought up the pregnancy rumor that she feared the Burleson cousins would be sharing soon. *But that's probably only because the Burlesons know that Amy is my best friend and Deanna is Kay's, so they probably didn't feel comfortable speculating which one of us is knocked up with the two of them.*

Randi was glad it was a short trip to the plantation house, hoping to find Kay quickly to pass the test on to her and get it out of her purse. As soon as they walked in the building, they were directed to go the opposite direction than she'd gone the day before for her interview to find the ballroom where everyone was gathering for Thanksgiving dinner. Randi saw Kay across the room, unloading the boxes of pies, cakes, and cookies they'd baked the day before onto a long table against the wall. She made a beeline for her sister, needing to lighten her load both physically and metaphorically.

"Hey, Sis, let me help you with that," Randi offered as soon as she reached her sister's side.

"Oh, thanks." Kay pointed to another box pushed under the table on the floor. "You can unload that one while I finish this one."

Randi pulled the box out from under the table and put her purse where it had just been sitting before starting to unload the baked goods.

"Um, I have something I need to give you privately," Randi whispered, hoping her sister would know what she meant.

"Oh?" Kay looked up at Randi inquisitively.

Randi gave her sister a pointed look, trying to convey the message without words.

"Oh!" Kay exclaimed, her mouth forming an O as realization dawned.

"I have reason to believe someone thinks it's mine," Randi whispered, leaning close to her sister as she put a cake on the table. "So, you need to clear up any rumors ASAP."

"Why would you think someone suspects it's yours?" Kay whispered back, her eyes wide in shock at the assumption.

"Because when I opened my suitcase this morning, the instructions were laying on top of my things, and I didn't put them there," Randi hissed, praying that the noise of other conversations in the room was enough to cover her whispered conversation with her sister. "I don't know if they dug through any of my other stuff to find it and see the results, but I'm sure the rumor mill is gonna be running rampant about me today. So, I hope you've figured out how to tell Anthony in time to keep Mom, Dad, and James from getting the wrong idea about my condition."

"Oh, shit, Randi!" Kay whisper-shouted, looking mortified. "I'm so sorry. I wouldn't have asked you to hide the test for me if I'd have thought it would cause rumors about you like that. I'll fix it, I promise. I don't know how yet, but I'll figure out something."

"Thanks, but can we start by getting it out of my purse and into yours?" Randi arched an eyebrow at her sister as they continued putting out the desserts.

"I should've had you hide it at our house yesterday," Kay belatedly suggested, looking around like she was trying to figure out where they could go to make the switch. "If anyone catches us with it today, it'll just make the situation worse."

"Yeah, well, I didn't know it was compromised until this morning, so I didn't think about it yesterday." Randi snapped her mouth shut as Mary Lee and Hazel Burleson walked toward them.

"Oh, these desserts look fabulous," Hazel gushed as she reached the table where Randi and Kay were finishing putting them out. "I can't wait to get a taste. But first, we have to get everyone to take their seats, so we can say grace before they start lining up for the buffet."

Hazel ushered them away from the dessert table to the other side of the room where they'd already corralled their family to sit for the meal. James's mother stepped up to a podium where they had a microphone set up, so she could be heard over the crowd noise as she asked for everyone to take a seat.

James was stopped by his grandmother one table over from where Randi was sitting as he was walking in her direction. Randi was disappointed that he didn't come sit beside her, but she understood when he sat down with his grandparents instead.

Soon, the church pastor replaced Mandi Hunter at the podium and said a prayer of thanks for all in attendance, ending with good wishes for the rest of the world. After a hearty "amen" was echoed in unison by a majority of the room, Pastor Harrison directed the elderly and the parents with small children to line up first for the buffet.

Apparently, Mandi Hunter ran the facility like a well-oiled machine, as it didn't take long before everyone in the room, including the staff who had pitched in to help when they technically had the day off, had a plateful of food and had taken their seats to enjoy the meal.

The vast room filling with a din of the conversations going on at each individual table made it hard for Randi to keep up with everything being discussed around her.

She did catch her father filling Anthony and Kay in on the arrests and court appearances of the Fox brothers. She'd received a call from Officer Dennis the week before, informing her that Mitch had been arrested, but she hadn't heard the news that her dad was telling everyone about him pleading guilty, so Randi wouldn't have to appear in court to testify against him.

Thank goodness, she thought, realizing that having to go back to Tulsa to testify could've posed an issue with her new job.

As the meal went on with mostly pleasant conversation, other than the brief mention of the Fox brothers and their legal issues, Randi started to relax. She quit focusing on keeping her purse—or more specifically Kay's pregnancy test—tucked between her feet under the table, so nobody could snoop through it, and just enjoyed interacting with her family and friends, both new and old.

After the main meal was finished, people started swapping seats, so they could move around the room and speak to more and more of the other people in attendance who hadn't originally sat at their dinner table. James took her by the hand and escorted her around the room to make sure she was introduced to what felt like the whole town and everyone who worked with the GWA. She was having such a good time getting to know his family and friends that she didn't even think about the fact that she left her purse unattended under her original seat.

Randi was enjoying a conversation with James, his cousin, Ashley Myers, and their grandmother, Joan Myers, when she heard her niece shout from across the room. "That's Aunt Randi's purse!"

Fuck! Shit! Damn! Randi thought as she felt the room spin around her from whipping her head around to see who was holding the ticking time bomb, aka her purse with Kay's positive pregnancy test inside.

"Oh, well, then let's take it to her, so it doesn't get lost with everyone playing musical chairs." The woman holding her bag held it out to Maria.

Randi had met so many people that week that she couldn't remember exactly who the woman was, but she knew it wasn't one of Anthony's siblings or cousins. She let out a breath that she hadn't realized she'd been holding when the woman handed the purse to

Maria, who started walking toward her. She was relieved that it didn't appear that the woman had snooped in her bag to catch a glimpse of the test tucked inside.

Her relief was short lived, however, when Maria tripped about halfway across the room and the contents of her handbag spilled out, scattering on the floor. She jumped to her feet and ran toward her niece, as did her sister. Kay went straight to her daughter, Maria, who was crying from her scraped knees. Whereas Randi was frantically searching the floor with her eyes for the bag containing the test.

Both of the Lee sisters were trying to soothe Maria with their words, as Kay scooped her daughter into her arms, and Randi started stuffing all her belongings back into her purse. Unfortunately, while most things like her wallet, hairbrush, lipstick, phone, and keys were close to the purse and easily shoved back into her handbag, the plastic shopping bag the test was in had glided across the glossy hardwood floor and under one of the nearby tables. And Randi wasn't the first to see it, much less reach it.

"Fuck! Shit! Damn!" was rapidly becoming Randi's new mantra as she repeated the words over and over again in her head. She couldn't stop the train wreck in the ballroom as the middle-aged gentleman who was sitting at the table the test had ended up under reached down and picked it up, holding it up in the air for all the world to see.

"Thanks," she barked at the man, trying to quickly grab it from his hand to shove it back in her purse.

Unfortunately, he didn't release his hold on the plastic bag as Randi pulled it from the other side. When the bag split, the wadded-up paper instructions fluttered to the floor and the box containing the test went flying over Randi's head.

She heard the thud of the box hitting someone and whipped around so fast to see where it went that she lost her balance. Her mortification at seeing James holding the test box to his chest was only amplified by her falling into him and smashing the box between them.

James immediately wrapped her in his arms, steadying her and keeping her from falling further. Randi buried her face in his chest, praying the makeup she'd put on that morning was enough to disguise the heat she felt infusing her cheeks.

"It's okay, Angel," James tried to comfort her, his deep voice rumbling through her. "I've got you."

Randi wasn't so sure of that as the crowd noise around them went from a hushed whisper to a cacophony of voices sharing her supposed news with those not close enough to see what flew out of her purse. *No, no, no, this can't be happening!* Randi screamed repeatedly in her head, trying to drown out the noise around her.

She wasn't sure if the roar of the crowd had actually died down, or if James holding her made her feel safe to hide inside her own head for a while, but she was comforted by only hearing the strong beat of his heart under his navy-blue button-down shirt. *We're actually dressed to match today, and we didn't plan it in advance,* Randi thought, trying to center herself by focusing only on what she could see and feel, her and James, as if the rest of the world disappeared around them.

She wasn't sure how long she floated there in her own realm, ignoring the voices of the people around them, just breathing in the soothing, ocean fresh scent of James's bodywash, but it wasn't nearly long enough. James's declaration that "of course, we're getting married" shattered her bubble of solitude.

"No," Randi shouted as she pushed out of James's arms. "We are most definitely not getting married!"

She barely registered that her father was saying something to her as she grabbed the crushed box and shoved it in her purse before storming out of the room. She ignored everyone who called after her or tried to stop her from leaving. She didn't bother trying to find her sister in the crowd to clear up the confusion, knowing that Kay was focused on taking care of Maria's injured knees. She didn't even bother trying to find someone to drive her back to the Burleson Ranch. She just took off walking, not caring that she was embarking on a five-mile walk in four-inch heels.

She knew that anyone who followed her from the plantation house would expect her to go toward the main entrance of the bed and breakfast on Walker Road, so the majority of the walk would be on paved roads. When he didn't find her by going that way, she knew James would take the gravel road back to his house to try to find her. Since those were the only two options for leaving the area in a vehicle, Randi opted to elude them by cutting through the woods where they wouldn't think to look for her.

When her phone started ringing in her purse, Randi pulled it out and declined James's call. She started to turn it off, but being unsure of her ability to maintain a walking course through the woods headed due west to get to the Burleson Ranch, she turned on the Do-Not-Disturb feature instead, so all her calls would go to voicemail, but she could still use her phone. Then she opened her map app and set it for walking directions to her sister's address. The app may have been confused by her walking where it didn't show there was a road, but she could clearly see the dot indicating her sister's house on the map to maintain her course.

Her extreme flight response, combined with her ingenuity in using her phone's features, ended up saving her a lot of steps, even though they were more difficult steps through the rougher terrain. But the fact that the shortest distance between two points is a straight line cut the five-mile winding route between the two locations down to only about a mile and a half.

She'd be pulling sticker burrs out of her sweater dress all night, but she made it to the relative safety of Charlotte's guest bedroom in only about thirty minutes. She hadn't seen anyone out and about when she crossed Rogers Road or once she got onto the ranch. So, she counted her lucky stars and locked herself in the room. She'd have her meltdown in private and then corner her sister the next morning to convince her to clear up the mess.

Maybe I'll get lucky, and she'll have already fixed it by the time I'm supposed to meet her to go Black Friday shopping in the morning. Randi prayed for such a speedy solution as she stripped off her clothes and slipped into the bathtub to soak away her stressful day.

~~~

James felt like Randi had just ripped his heart from his chest when she shouted she wouldn't marry him and stormed out of the room. It wasn't that he intended his statement to be a proposal. He knew she wasn't ready for that yet. He'd only been trying to stop her father's rant by making his future intentions clear. He knew he'd never be able to change Charles Lee's beliefs about premarital sex, but he thought at least knowing that James wanted to marry Randi would make it seem like less of a crime, so Charles would tone down his lecture, and at least, lower his voice.
~~~

When Randi reached her breaking point and followed her therapist's advice to leave the room when her father was yelling, he tried to follow her immediately, wanting to be there for her to lean on while she processed her feelings. He also knew they needed to talk about everything without an audience, but he was stopped by her father and brother both getting in his face.

"I think you've done more than enough to upset my daughter," Charles Lee barked, grabbing James's arm as he tried to walk past the older man.

"Sir, with all due respect, I don't think I'm the reason Randi's upset right now," James softly argued, pointedly looking down at his arm where Charles had grabbed him.

"So, you're not the one who knocked my sister up?" David Lee pushed past his father to stand toe to toe with James. "Because I'm sure that's why she's upset right now."

James sized up Randi's older brother, trying to be understanding of the man's heightened emotions, as he assessed his potential need to defend himself and determined the best way to diffuse the situation. Like Randi's father, her brother was a couple of inches shorter than James. Where Charles probably came close to the same weight as James, his waistline having thickened with age, David was a lot thinner. With a good fifty pounds of muscle advantage over David, James was more worried about accidentally hurting Randi's brother than any damage the other man could inflict on him if he decided to try to defend his sister's honor with his fists.

James took a moment to take a deep breath as the two men continued to bellow about how he'd disgraced their family. He simply stood there, letting them rant and rave, biding his time until they'd exhausted their arguments, so he could finally speak his piece with them. He felt his brother step up behind him and hoped Dean wouldn't lose his temper along with the Lees.

When they finally seemed to stop yelling over one another, James took advantage of the momentary silence to speak up. "First of all," he asserted, holding up a hand to stop them from interrupting him when both Charles and David opened their mouths, as if they were about to yell over him once again. "All we saw was a box for a pregnancy test, not the actual test to know if Randi's even taken it yet, much less whether or not it's positive. Second of all, she was embarrassed by everyone seeing the box, but she wasn't shaking mad while I was holding her, not until you started yelling at her."

"Now, just hold on right there," Charles shouted, his grip tightening around James's forearm.

"No!" James snapped, yanking his arm out of Randi's father's grasp, and pointing a finger in the man's face. "You back the fuck off! The woman I love is so traumatized by you yelling at her when she was a teenager that she doesn't feel safe to be herself around you. She can't tell you about her hopes and dreams, or how she really feels about anything. Hell, she doesn't even tell you when she's dating someone, so she can avoid being lectured about how she shouldn't see anyone you don't deem appropriate. The only reason she's managed to tell you about dating me, or wanting to learn to wrestle, is because she's been practicing talking to your picture for the last month on the advice of her therapist. And at the first sign of something going on between us that you don't like, instead of letting your adult daughter have the space and time she needs to make her own decisions about her life, or the opportunity to discuss things with me, her partner, you're traumatizing her again by yelling at her in front of God and everybody. So, if you wanna yell and scream at the person to blame for upsetting Randi today, go do it in a fucking mirror! And get out of my way, because I don't care if she's pregnant or not pregnant, or if she wants to marry me or live in sin for the rest of our lives, I'm gonna go mend my Angel's broken wings, so I can be the man to watch her fly to her greatest heights and achieve all her dreams."

"Damn, that was a hell of a promo," James heard someone say as he pushed his way past the Lees, who both looked to be in shock at his outburst, to go look for Randi.

Fuck, I hope the assholes I work with didn't record that, he thought as he exited the ballroom and ran toward the front door of the plantation house. *Randi will be pissed at me for cursing out her father. Hell, I'll probably hear a lecture from my own folks for losing my temper in front of the whole town like that.*

He didn't have time to dwell on the potential fallout from his exchange with Charles and David Lee at the moment. He had to focus on finding Randi and making sure she was okay. He looked up the paved drive that went north towards the original bed and breakfast, but he didn't see any sign of Randi or anyone else heading away from the plantation house.

He pulled out his phone and tried to call her, only to be sent to voicemail after two rings. He hung up and redialed, but knew she'd turned her phone off when his second call went straight to voicemail without even ringing.

"Angel," he cooed when the phone indicated he could leave a message, hoping she'd find his message soothing. "I know you're upset and need space to figure things out on your own. But I need to know you're okay. Fuck, I know you're not okay right now. I mean I need to know you're somewhere safe and not in a car with a stranger headed out of town, or hurt in a ditch somewhere between here and the Burlesons' place. I hate the thought of you trying to walk all the way back there. If you call and tell me where you are, I'll come give you a ride without saying a word, so you can have your space. Or if you're already somewhere safe, just text me to let me know. Please. I, uh, just need to know you're safe."

James hung up, kicking himself for almost saying *"I love you"* to her for the first time on a voicemail. He knew it would be useless to try calling her again and he didn't want to take a chance on those three little words slipping out before he could say them to her face to face, so he pocketed his phone while he thought about which direction she might have gone.

He jogged to the parking lot where he'd parked his truck, clicking the unlock button as soon as he got close, so he could jump into the vehicle as soon as he reached it. He drove the mile back up to the older B and B building, but he didn't see Randi anywhere. It was another quarter mile to the exit onto Walker Road, but he wasn't optimistic that she'd made it that far in the few minutes he'd been delayed in leaving after her, especially since she was wearing heels that took her to only half a foot shorter than him.

Damn, that outfit is sexy as hell, but it's totally inappropriate for walking five miles back to the Burlesons'. James pulled down close enough to Walker Road that he could look to see if Randi was walking on it toward the ranch. When he didn't see her, he turned around and went back through his family's land to the gravel road that led back to his place. *She must have gone there thinking it's closer than the ranch, and easier to get to in those killer heels.*

Leah Mae Wright

When he got to his house, he slammed the truck in park, not even bothering to turn it off before he was running in to look for Randi. "Fuck, where the hell is she?" he screamed after he tore through the whole place and couldn't find her.

He ran back to his truck and followed the maze of trails through the property, searching to see if she'd maybe tried to go down by the creek or over by the rocks where they'd had their picnic a few days before. After searching everywhere he'd taken her on the property that week, James took the side exit onto Rogers Road and looked for her on the Burleson Ranch next.

With no luck at finding her on any of the trails he knew about there, he retraced his steps back to the north gate onto Rogers, heading north to Walker and then east back to the bed and breakfast. After a couple of hours of searching with no luck, he went back to the plantation house to see if she'd come back to the party.

He found that most of the guests had departed, leaving just his family and the GWA crew there enjoying what was left on the dessert table. He started to ask if anyone had seen Randi come back earlier, but he didn't get the chance. His eyes locked with his mom's and the shake of her head told him all he needed to know. *Randi didn't come back here after that fiasco.*

"Hey, you okay?" Dean walked up to James, flanked by Rick and Dion.

"I, uh, I don't know," James admitted, not sure what to do to make the situation better for Randi when he couldn't even find her. He felt completely shattered by her running away from everyone, including him. He wanted to be her rock to lean on, her person she could count on to always be there for her. She was the love of his life and he wanted to be the same for her, but he didn't know if she would let him.

"Were you able to catch up with her and talk at all?" Rick guided him to a table where they all sat down.

"No, I can't find her," James sighed, hanging his head, and feeling defeated. "I drove all over looking for her, but saw no sign of her. I know she's doing what her therapist recommended, the walking away when her parents started lecturing part anyway. But I wish she'd let me be there for her while she's working through her feelings. I thought we'd gotten a lot closer the last few days, but it doesn't feel like it now when she's shutting me out, too."

"When you caught the test, were you able to see if it was positive?" Dion inquired. "Or hell, even tell if she'd taken it?"

"No," James informed his friends, shaking his head. *Fuck, has she taken it? Or did she open it and then chicken out of actually taking it when she read the directions?*

"So, what exactly has been going on with ya'll?" Dean looked concerned. "What was all that about with the test and then the altercation with her dad?"

"She's had issues with her parents since she was a teenager," James confided, trying to be vague, so he didn't share more than Randi would be comfortable with. "In addition to her anxiety about flying, she's internalized a particularly brutal lecture they gave her when she was fifteen, and the thought of telling them something that will lead to another of those lectures triggers her anxiety."

"Yeah, that's why ya'll went almost a week without speaking last month, right, because she didn't wanna tell them about dating you." Dean reminded James of his first misstep in his relationship with Randi.

"Yeah, when I talked to her dad, he showed up at her house that night and basically ordered her to friend-zone me," James explained, shaking his head, worried that Randi would go into hiding for another week. "It took a couple of therapy sessions and a week of hibernation for her to work up the courage to talk to me again. And I get it, I mean, especially then because the situation was all my fault. It takes her some extra time to think about things on her own before she's ready to share her feelings with anyone. That's why I was waiting her out on the test thing."

"You knew about the test before today?" Dean looked at his brother with a surprised expression.

"I knew she bought the test Monday night while we were in San Antonio, but she didn't mention it. I just saw it through the bag where she was trying to hide it under other things. Knowing how she has to think things through, I've been waiting for her to be ready to talk to me about it. In fact, now that I'm really thinking about it, I don't think she's taken the test yet."

"Really?" Dion raised an eyebrow in suspicion.

"Really," James replied. "If she'd taken it, she wouldn't be carrying it around in her purse. I think she bought it in case she didn't start her period this week. She probably opened it to read the instructions to know when would be best to take it. Then shoved it in her purse because it was either the wrong time to take it, or her period actually started, and she didn't need to take it after all."

"You're probably right," Rick nodded. "Especially since a couple of tampons also spilled out of her purse."

"Yeah, she bought those the same time she bought the test, and she's obviously had to open the package since they were loose in her bag and not still in the box." James felt a little down at the realization that Randi probably wasn't pregnant.

Guess I want kids with her sooner than the five years we talked about. Hopefully, we'll actually get a chance to revisit that talk soon. If she doesn't completely cut things off with me after today.

"So, if her freak out today wasn't pregnancy hormones," Dean contemplated. "It was all because of how her dad reacted to seeing the test?"

"Yeah," James confirmed his brother's theory, nodding his head at his brother. "I mean she was blushing pretty hard trying to keep everyone from seeing the test, but I'm sure that embarrassment would've been no big deal if her dad hadn't started in. The way she was relaxing in my arms, I figured she just needed a minute to know I was there for her. And then we'd put it back in her purse and go back to visiting with everyone, so we could discuss it together later."

"But then her dad started in with the slut shaming." Dion shook his head in disgust. "I wouldn't have even realized what was going on if he hadn't started preaching about the sins of the flesh and how disgraceful he finds premarital sex."

"Yeah, that's when she started shaking." James hated the memory of Randi shaking with fear, or anger, or both. "And I probably made it worse, instead of better, when I said what I did about us getting married eventually. But I thought knowing my intentions would make it seem like less of an issue, so he'd tone it down."

Rick chuckled and shook his head at James. "You're obviously not a father yet. I dread the day Britney starts dating because I fear I'll probably yell at every boy who comes around acting like he wants to kiss her. And I might end up in jail if any of them try to justify wanting to have sex with her where I can hear it, even when she's grown."

"So, if Randi were your daughter, you'd have behaved the same way Charles did today?" James arched an eyebrow at his boss, shocked at the thought.

"No," Rick backtracked, smirking at James. "I wouldn't do anything in front of an audience. I'd wait until I caught you alone, so I wouldn't be the prime suspect when the authorities found your body."

"I think I'll go warn Cooper to keep Connor and Cody away from Britney." Dion feigned standing up to find their fellow wrestler.

"Like I haven't already warned Cooper's boys," Rick laughed. "I did that as soon as they became teenagers. And I think Anthony's already talked to them about Tia, too."

"Damn, all these overprotective dads with daughters are making me glad I'm still single," Dean chuckled. "I'm not ready to join your ranks anytime soon."

"Naw, we're firmly in the ranks of the bad boys trying to lure the pretty girls away from their overprotective daddies," Dion quipped, slapping a hand on Dean's shoulder.

"Anyway, back to James and his overprotective daddy issues." Rick brought their conversation back to the previous topic. "You think she ran because of her dad yelling at you? Or because of what you said about getting married?"

"I honestly don't know," James admitted, wishing he'd hear back from Randi soon, so he could ask her that. "She started shaking when he started hollering, but I don't know if she even realized that he was mostly yelling at me and not her. Like I told him, she was traumatized by a similar rant when she was a teenager, so she could've been reliving that the whole time, for all I know. That's just one of the things she and I need to talk about. But I can't talk to her if I can't find her."

"Have you tried her phone?" Dean suggested.

"Yeah, it's going straight to voicemail," James replied. "When did Anthony leave? Maybe I should call him and see if any of his family, or Kay's family, have had any luck locating her. When I searched the ranch, I didn't go in any of the buildings, but maybe she's safely in her room at Charlotte's."

"They left about fifteen minutes before you got back," Rick informed him. "If she's at any of the houses on the ranch, they should've had time to locate her by now."

James pulled his phone out of his pocket and dialed Anthony.

"Hey, James," Anthony greeted him through the phone.

"Hey, um, I just wanted to see if any of ya'll have found Randi," James stammered, saying a silent prayer that she was safely ensconced in one of the guest bedrooms there.

"She's not here at our place." Anthony sounded concerned. "I thought you'd caught up with her, since neither one of you came back for dessert."

"No, I drove all over looking for her, but didn't find her," James told his friend, sounding desperate to his own ears. "I even went in and searched my whole house in case she went there to hide from her dad, since he doesn't know where it is. But when I drove through the ranch, I didn't wanna snoop through any of the houses."

"Give me a minute to message the family and see if anyone else has located her." James heard clicking in his ear where Anthony had apparently stayed on the call but switched screens on his phone to text them.

"You still there?" Anthony came back on the line a few minutes later.

"Yeah, I'm here," James replied.

"Charlotte said her bedroom door is locked and she can hear the TV on," Anthony told him. "She said that they'd turned off all the televisions before leaving this morning, so Charlotte thinks she's there, but not answering when she knocks on the door."

"If she's not answering, why would she turn the TV on?" James was confused and slightly worried that Randi may have turned on the television to make them think she was there and then snuck out somewhere else to really be alone.

"Apparently, they were both really interested in the story about that missing heiress in Georgia, so Charlotte thinks Randi has the TV on to get the latest updates," Anthony explained.

James remembered how Randi hadn't been the only one talking about the missing woman during Thanksgiving dinner. *Maybe,* he thought. *She was certainly interested in the events of the case, so maybe following the latest news is helping take her mind off of the mess here this afternoon.* James hoped Charlotte was right in thinking Randi was there but just wanted to be alone.

"You think she'd be okay with me coming over to check on her?" James hoped his friend might have some insight since he was marrying Randi's sister.

"Who? Charlotte or Randi?" Anthony sounded confused by James's question.

"Randi," James declared. "I know Charlotte won't mind me stopping by, unless I damage her guest bedroom door to get in there to see Randi."

"Yeah, he wants to go check on Randi," Anthony informed someone there with him of James's idea to talk to Randi. "Yeah, okay."

There was the distinct sound of a smacking kiss before Anthony came back on the line. "Kay's gonna go over to Charlotte's to make sure Randi is okay. She said it's probably best if you give her a little space and talk to her after the rehearsal tomorrow, instead of going over there now."

"Okay," James sighed, dejected. "Have Kay message me to confirm that Randi's there, please. I know she needs her space, and I wanna respect her boundaries and give it to her, but I need to know she's safe and not injured from walking all the way back to the ranch."

"Will do," Anthony agreed before they disconnected the call.

"He thinks she's at Charlotte's," James told the expectant faces surrounding him. "Kay's gonna confirm that, but I'm supposed to give her space. At least until after the rehearsal tomorrow night."

"You gonna be able to stay away from her that long?" Dean knew his brother too well.

"Yeah, I'll just head home and hit the weights to expend some of this pent-up frustration," James decided.

"Or you could come to my place and hit the heavy bag," Dean suggested, giving James a sympathetic smile. "You know actually hitting something helps get it all out better than anything."

"Yeah, sounds good, bro," James agreed, lifting his chin toward Dion before adding, "Wanna join us?"

"Sure," Dion replied to James before turning to Dean and asking, "We rounding up the rest of the guys to make it a pain party?"

"Sounds like a plan," Dean smirked.

"You guys are nuts," Rick proclaimed, grinning at the guys, knowing that what they called a "pain party" was actually a brutally tough workout, followed by sparring with very few punches pulled. "I'm going to go drag my daughter away from the cookies and see if we can't get a Kids Against Maturity game going before bedtime."

"Have a good night," James told his boss as they all got up and dispersed for their various evening activities.

He made sure to go by and tell his family good night before actually leaving the plantation house. His mother tried to ask him about Randi and the earlier incident, but he told her he'd have to fill her in later, once he actually spoke to Randi.

James went home and changed into workout clothes from his jeans and button down before going to his brother's house. Once he got home, he contemplated staying in for the night, instead of going to hang out with Dean and the guys, knowing he wouldn't be good company until he'd heard from Randi.

As he was pulling up his text screen to message Dean about his change in plans, his phone buzzed with a message from Anthony.

Anthony: Kay has confirmed Randi is safe & sound at Charlotte's. They're having some sisterly bonding time tonight & going Black Friday shopping in a few hours.

James: Thanks. Any idea what time I can see her tomorrow?

Anthony: They're going to SA @ 12a.m. w/ plans to be home by 8a.m. They'll sleep all morning since they aren't sleeping tonight. Not sure what time they'll wake up, but Kay & I are going to the courthouse at 4p.m. for the marriage license & the rehearsal is at 5p.m. at the church. After that?

James: K. Thanks. See ya tomorrow.

Anthony: Kay did say to tell you that Randi's fine, just needs some time to think things through. But ya'll are good.

We're good? James wondered what that cryptic message meant, but he didn't bother asking, knowing Anthony wouldn't have any specific information about what Randi and Kay were talking about overnight.

Knowing she was safe and spending time with her sister, James felt better. With less to worry about, he didn't have a valid reason to stay home and mope when he'd told his brother he'd be over at his house for a workout. So, James grabbed his keys, wallet, and phone and went to see how hard the guys would push him through a workout.

Hopefully, it won't be so bad that we have trouble walking down the aisle for Anthony's wedding Saturday.

Chapter Sixteen

Randi wasn't sure what she was thinking when she agreed to go Black Friday shopping at midnight with her sister, Amy, Deanna, Diana, and all four of the twenty-something-year-old Burleson women. After the incident at Thanksgiving dinner, she'd planned to hide out until it was time to meet up with all the women who were planning to leave at four in the morning for the annual shopping extravaganza. Her sister showing up at Charlotte's house to verify she was alive for James, however, changed her plans.

She'd only opened the bedroom door for Kay, so she could give her sister back her pee stick. But once Kay was in the guest bedroom with Randi, she refused to leave. They talked for a few minutes, trying to come up with a way to clear up the confusion before they were interrupted by Charlotte.

The next thing Randi knew, Charlotte's house was overrun with women wanting to make sure Randi was okay. Since Kay wasn't ready to announce her pregnancy yet, Randi wasn't sure what to tell them, so she went with "I'm fine, just embarrassed, and I really don't wanna talk about it."

Luckily, they let the subject drop and started talking about where all they wanted to go for the best Black Friday deals. When they realized several of the stores they wanted to visit were opening at midnight, they revised their plans.

Randi was surprised her mother hadn't decided to tag along with the younger women, so she could grill her about the contents of the box that started the fiasco on Thanksgiving. But she was glad that the older generation was still planning to go shopping at four, so she could avoid her parents until the rehearsal.

Kay better tell Anthony about the baby before then, so I can make sure everyone knows I'm not the one knocked up, Randi inwardly fumed as she sat in the front seat of her sister's Jeep. She would've told her sister that out loud, but she couldn't with Amy, Deanna, and Diana in the back seat. The Burleson women were all in Charlotte's car ahead of them on the highway going into San Antonio.

"This is so fun," Diana chirped happily from the back of the vehicle. "I haven't gone Black Friday shopping since we moved to Wichita."

"Why not?" Kay arched an eyebrow at their sister-in-law through the rearview mirror. "You used to love going with us in Tulsa."

"Yeah, but it's not the same without friends and family going with," Diana replied. "David went with me the first year we were there, but he didn't want to get up early, so we missed most of the good deals by going at lunchtime. And he didn't like the idea of me going alone while he was home with the kids, so I just skipped it."

"I didn't think he had a problem with taking care of the kids on his own?" Randi questioned, unsure what the problem was with her big brother.

"Oh, no, it wasn't that. He didn't think it was safe for me to be by myself in a crazy mob scene of shoppers like he saw on the news."

"Ah, so he inherited Daddy's crazy overprotective gene," Kay laughed.

"I know you used to complain about that when we were in high school," Deanna commented, shaking her head. "But I didn't realize how bad that crazy overprotective thing really was until I saw how your dad laid into James yesterday."

Randi wasn't sure exactly what Deanna was talking about, having hidden in her head in James's arms and not comprehending what all was being said. She'd registered her father yelling and knew it was about the pregnancy test that had been in her purse, so she assumed he was giving her a lecture about saving herself for marriage, repenting for the sins of having sex before marriage, and having impure thoughts, the way he'd done when she was a teenager. It wasn't until James mentioned marriage that she snapped out of her trancelike state and embraced the flight portion of her fight, flight, or freeze response to the situation.

"I, um," Randi stuttered, trying to work up the courage to ask her friends what all her father had yelled, since Kay hadn't been able to tell her earlier because she'd taken Maria to the restroom to clean up her scraped knees when it all went down. "I kinda zoned out and didn't really hear what Daddy was saying." She turned in her seat to look directly at Deanna before asking, "Did you say he laid into James? He wasn't yelling at me?"

"Oh, yeah, it was all about James," Deanna divulged, bobbing her head in an exaggerated nod. "Well, all about how James disgraced his family name by deflowering his daughter, ur, you. He was going on about how a real man doesn't give-in to the sins of the flesh and would wait until marriage to procreate."

"Don't forget how he accused James of being a man-whore," Amy added.

"No way!" Kay shouted. "Our dad wouldn't use the term man-whore."

"No, he didn't say it exactly that way," Amy amended, giggling. "But I can't stop laughing at the way he said it that basically meant man-whore to be able to repeat it word for word."

Diana and Deanna joined Amy in laughter for a moment before they finally mimicked, in unison, using the deepest voices they could manage, "I won't have my daughter defiled by a promiscuous deviant, who has probably spread his seed far and wide while traveling with a modernized version of a vaudevillian sideshow."

"Yeah, that sounds more like Daddy," Kay laughed along with the ladies in the back of the SUV.

"James must have realized that you thought your dad was yelling at you," Diana asserted once their laughter had died down. "Now that I know that was your perception, the way James put Charles in his place makes a lot more sense."

"James did what?" Randi squealed.

"Damn, I missed all the good stuff while cleaning up Maria's knees in the bathroom," Kay pouted before Diana could explain her statement.

"He didn't yell nearly as loud as Charles, or even David, but he definitely raised his voice enough to make his reprimand clear," Diana affirmed.

"Wait, David was yelling too?" Randi didn't remember even seeing her brother in the general vicinity when she fled the scene.

"Yeah, he stepped up to James after you left," Diana confirmed. "I was a little worried they'd start throwing punches for a second."

"Me, too, especially when Charles grabbed James's arm to stop him from going after you," Deanna interjected.

"Naw, I knew James was too much of a gentle giant to let it come to blows," Amy disagreed, shaking her head. "He was already trying to diffuse the situation by declaring his intention to marry you eventually, but your dad ignored that statement when you said you were definitely not getting married."

"Is that what he said?" Deanna asked Amy. "He wasn't speaking loud enough for me to hear what he was saying, but his body language and facial expressions were clear that he was trying to calm Charles down while also comforting Randi."

"Yeah, he didn't respond to any of the insults, or whatever you want to call the things Charles was saying, but he did say that nothing he and Randi did together was defiling because he had every intention of them getting married, but only once Randi's ready, not when her father threatens them with a shotgun wedding," Amy replied.

Randi felt horrible for misunderstanding what James had said and lashing out that she wouldn't marry him before running away. She would have to think of a way to apologize to him quickly. so she could do it the instant she saw him next.

"Okay, now that that part's clear," Kay redirected the conversation as she flipped on her blinker and followed Charlotte onto the exit ramp from the highway. "Go back to what James said to reprimand Daddy for making a scene and causing Randi to leave the party early."

"When Randi left, James started to follow her," Diana stated. "Charles grabbed his arm and stopped him from going after her, saying that James had already upset her enough. That's when David stepped up into James's face, too. James just stood there letting them both shout and scream and act a fool for several minutes."

"I couldn't understand half of what they were saying, since they kept shouting over each other." Deanna pouted at missing the finer points of the altercation.

"It was a bunch of BS about how despicable they considered James for knocking up Randi, but also insisting he man up and marry her immediately." Amy gave them an abbreviated overview. "I think Charles even said something about a double wedding this weekend."

"Maybe it's a good thing I didn't hear all of it," Kay groaned, shaking her head.

"Anyway, when there was a brief second when David and Charles both stopped ranting to take a breath at the same time, James held up his free hand to indicate that they should shut up, so he could speak. He pointed out that we'd only seen a box for a pregnancy test, not the actual test to know if Randi had even taken it, or if it was positive, pretty much shutting down their push for a shotgun wedding. Instead of commenting on any of the other stuff they'd said about him, he pointed out that he wasn't the one to upset Randi. He said she was embarrassed by everyone seeing the box, but she didn't start shaking in his arms until Charles started yelling at her. That's what confused me when it happened because I only heard Charles yelling at James."

"But James knows me better than anyone, so he recognized that I thought Daddy was yelling at me," Randi sighed, in awe at just how well James knew her after such a short time.

"Yeah, that's what I think," Diana agreed, reaching up to squeeze Randi's shoulder. "Anyway, Charles shouted at James to hold on, and I could see him digging his fingers into James's arm. I was worried James would punch him right then, but instead he pulled out of Charles's grasp and pointed a finger in his face."

"Oh, yeah, I clearly heard James then, even from across the room," Deanna smirked. "I couldn't believe he told your dad to back the fuck off."

"Yeah, David stepped back then," Diana chuckled. "I think that's the only time I've seen fear in my husband's eyes."

"I can't say I blame him, that would have scared me too," Kay remarked with wide eyes. "We've never seen anyone stand up to Daddy like that. So, was that it? Is that when they let James leave?"

"Oh, no!" Diana exclaimed, shaking her head. "I don't remember it word for word, but he said something about the woman he loves being so traumatized from being yelled at as a teenager that she doesn't feel safe being herself around Charles. He said something about Randi not telling Charles about her hopes and dreams or who she dates, so she can avoid another traumatic lecture. He said something about it taking therapy and a month of practicing what to say for Randi to be able to tell him about dating James or wanting to become a wrestler."

"So much for doctor patient confidentiality," Deanna snorted.

"James isn't my doctor, or my therapist, so I don't think he's subject to the same confidentiality standards," Randi defended James, not really caring that he'd outed her for seeing a therapist. "What else did he say?"

"That's when James called Charles out for not letting you be an adult and have the time and space you need to make your own decisions about your life, or to discuss private matters with your partner, and traumatizing you again by yelling at you in front of God and everybody," Diana paraphrased. "He told your dad that if he wanted to yell and scream at the person responsible for upsetting you, he should do it in a mirror."

"Actually, it was a *'fucking'* mirror," Amy corrected, using air quotes when she said "fucking" to make sure they all realized that it was a direct quote from James.

Randi couldn't help but laugh, thinking, *I guess if I can't ever cuss around my dad, James will do it for me.*

"That wasn't even the best part," Amy proclaimed, waving her hands, as if that would get Randi to quit laughing, so she could hear the rest of the story. "Stop laughing so I can tell you. I repeated it over and over in my head, so I could remember it because his parting line was so perfect."

"Sorry." Randi forced herself to stop laughing and pay attention.

"He said, and I quote, 'And get out of my way, because I don't care if she's pregnant or not pregnant, or if she wants to marry me or live in sin for the rest of our lives, I'm gonna go mend my Angel's broken wings, so I can be the man to watch her fly to her greatest heights and achieve all her dreams,' end quote. It was like watching a movie and seeing the hero up close and personal as he was going to rescue his lady love."

"Well, it was certainly better than his chocolate cream pie promo," Kay chortled, as they all giggled like schoolgirls at James's sappy sweet line.

"Now I really feel guilty for not answering his calls while I was walking back to the ranch," Randi admitted as they started to unbuckle their seat belts, since they'd just parked at the mall.

"I'm sure you can make it up to him by going home with him after the rehearsal dinner tonight." Kay wiggled her eyebrows suggestively as she grabbed her purse to exit the vehicle.

Yeah, if he can forgive me for ignoring him again, Randi sighed as she got out of the vehicle and joined the others on the walk into the mall. *And if the confusion about who's test that was is cleared up by then.*

The subject changed yet again as they all started shopping. They were all brainstorming ideas for what to buy their loved ones for Christmas and having fun trying to find the best deals.

Randi was much more restrained in her shopping than the women she was shopping with, wanting to pick out something meaningful for her loved ones, but not wanting to deplete her savings to do so. That meant that while she'd seen a few things she might consider buying for her family for Christmas, she didn't purchase them yet, wanting to take the time to think about the appropriateness of each item, and whether or not her finances could currently cover the expense.

While she was optimistic that she'd be able to start her new job on Monday and replenish whatever she spent relatively quickly, she wasn't as certain of the job as she'd been before the embarrassing incident the day before. If her new boss changed his mind about hiring her after the scene she'd been in the middle of, then she'd need to save as much of what she had in the bank as she could until she could find another job.

As the worry about possibly not getting to work for the GWA after all started to fill her mind, Randi decided she needed to get her sister alone for another talk. *After working with the GWA for the last couple of months, surely Kay will know if yesterday's craziness will affect my job offer.*

Unfortunately, it took a while before Randi was able to get Kay away from the rest of the women they were shopping with to ask her about it. While the others had moved toward the women's wear section of the third store they'd entered, Randi asked Kay to head over to men's wear, so she could help her pick out something for James for Christmas.

"So, what are you thinking about getting him?" Kay fondled a few items as they strolled past a display of men's suits.

"I have no idea," Randi admitted sheepishly. She wasn't quite sure how to word her inquiry, so she stalled for time by picking up a tie from the next table they passed. "I really just wanted to get you alone for a minute to ask you something."

"Okay," Kay drew out the word, studying her sister intently.

"Do you think I still have a job with the GWA?" Randi glanced up from the purple tie in her hand to see Kay's confused facial expression. "After yesterday?"

Kay's eyes widened as realization dawned on her that the pregnancy mix-up could have some unexpected consequences for both of their jobs. It took her a moment to reply, and it looked to Randi like she was carefully thinking about her words before she opened her mouth to speak.

"Yes, I think you'll still be able to start work on Monday," Kay declared in a measured tone that was a little stiff to Randi's ears. "Even if yesterday caused Rick to have some second thoughts about hiring you, once everything is cleared up, it will be my job that's affected, not yours."

Randi felt slightly relieved by her sister's words, but then she wondered exactly how Kay's job would be impacted by her pregnancy. She expressed her concern for her sister and asked what Kay thought would change about her job.

"Well, if this time is anything like the first two," Kay sighed, rubbing a hand over her still flat belly. "Then I won't be able to fly in the last trimester. I'll have to find out what maternity leave covers. I think it's only for after having the baby, but I'll need three months off before having the baby plus the two months of recovery that it normally covers after a C-section. If it's not all covered under maternity leave, I'm not sure what we'll do."

"Do you know if the GWA has paternity leave, too?" Randi was worried about what her sister would do with Anthony away while she had to stay on the ground for five months. "Will Anthony be able to take that time off with you?"

"No clue," Kay shrugged. "Yet another thing we'll have to talk about soon."

Randi felt a little guilty for being relieved that it was Kay and Anthony having to have that talk, instead of her and James.

"Speaking of things ya'll need to talk about soon…" Randi trailed off, putting down the tie she hadn't really looked at and starting to walk through the racks, so they'd be out of the flow of traffic around them. "Have you figured out how and when you're gonna tell him about…" Randi's voice trailed off again as she waved her hand in the general vicinity of Kay's midsection, indicating the baby nestled in her womb.

"No," Kay confessed, shaking her head. "It's hard when we can't seem to get any time alone because of everything going on this week. By the time we fall into bed at night, talking is the last thing either of us wanna do."

"Yeah, well, that sounds like the perfect time to tell him," Randi quipped, stopping by a dress shirt display. "When he's nice and relaxed after a little bow-chicka-wow-wow." Randi lifted her eyebrows suggestively as she smiled at her sister.

"Too bad I'm not capable of conscious thought or able to form a coherent sentence then," Kay laughed.

Randi reflected on the out-of-body experiences she'd had with James earlier that week, and understood why Kay hadn't been able to talk to Anthony yet, if that was the only time they'd been alone since she took the test.

"Maybe I can send the girls to the church with Mom and Dad or Hazel and Bob while we go get our marriage license this afternoon," Kay pondered aloud. "Then we'd have a few minutes alone in the truck to talk."

"That sounds like a great idea," Randi agreed with her sister, even though Kay didn't sound too confident in that plan. Noticing one of Anthony's sisters coming their way, she decided it was time to change the subject. "What do you think of a dress shirt for James? I know he has to wear them all the time for work."

"Yeah, but he just bought a few last month when we went to get him and Dean measured for their tuxes." Kay fingered one of the shirts in front of her. "Actually, I think a few of those shirts required cufflinks, so he had them shipped to his house since he couldn't wear them until he got a pair. Maybe you can get him cufflinks for Christmas?"

"Oh, I like that idea," Randi decided, looking around to see if she could see a display of cufflinks in the area of the store where they were standing. "Do you think they'd be here by the dress shirts? Or maybe over by jewelry?"

"What are we looking for in jewelry?" Becky inquired as she got close enough to overhear Randi's last few words.

"Cufflinks," Randi replied, smiling at Anthony's sister, and hoping none of the earlier conversation with Kay was showing on her face. "James bought some dress shirts last month and had them sent home instead of taking them with him because he needs cufflinks to wear them, so I think that's what I'll get him for Christmas."

"Oh, that's a great idea," Becky beamed, grinning at Randi. "And I think you're right about them being in the jewelry department."

By the time the three of them made their way to the jewelry department, the rest of the women had caught up with them. Once they were all informed of what Randi was looking for, they inundated her with questions, trying to narrow down which pair to pick.

"Do you know his favorite football team?" Jen pointed to a section of the cufflink display. "They have the entire NFL lineup."

"Are you thinking silver or gold?" Charlotte inquired.

"They have several with a single initial. Do you want a J or an H?" Diana piped up.

"Or you can get them engraved with all three of his initials," Deanna suggested.

"Do you know his middle name to be able to do that?" Becky looked at Randi, a hurt expression crossing her features as Randi nodded that she knew James's middle name.

Randi thought back to the conversation they'd had when he'd told her that he never shared his middle name with anyone. He thought it was weird that his parents had used the last name of James Dean's character in **Rebel Without a Cause**, Stark, as his middle name, and gave his brother the actor's actual middle name. While everyone figured out that the Hunter twins were named after their parents' favorite actor based on their first names alone, they didn't share their middle names with anyone unless they had to, so they didn't expose the true depths of their parent's fanaticism over an actor who died before they were even born.

It made Randi feel special that James had shared his full name with her from practically the beginning of their relationship. Because it was such a private thing for James, she wasn't sure she wanted to expose his secret middle name to the women around her by having his initials engraved on a set of cufflinks. Seeing the almost two-hundred-dollar price tag on the sterling silver engravable set she liked best convinced her to wait to get those for him after she was sure of her new job and increased income. And with nobody else around when she had the engraving done. And only after she'd talked to him to determine whether or not he would like his initials engraved on something for everyone to see.

"While I like that idea, I don't think he likes his middle name enough to wanna see that initial on his cufflinks," Randi stated decidedly, moving over to a case of unusually shaped cufflinks.

Instead of the square, rectangle, round, or oval standard shapes that could be engraved, the case she looked at next contained several unusual items. There were some decorative knots, coffee cups, elephants, several logos she didn't recognize, and a few superhero symbols she thought he might like. But when her eyes landed on the sterling silver, infinity symbol set, she knew which ones she wanted to get him.

She hadn't managed to say those three little words to him yet, but she knew he'd understand her feelings for him were infinite when he saw them. "That's the pair for James," she announced as she pointed them out to the clerk, not even caring what the price tag read.

"Oh, Randi," Kay gasped, covering her mouth when she saw the pair her sister was picking out.

"You know what that symbol means, right?" Julie prodded with a single raised eyebrow.

"Of course she does," Amy snapped, coming to her defense, though Randi wasn't sure it was necessary. "They're perfect for the two of you, Randi. And all the infinite possibilities of your future together."

"Yeah, they are," Kay agreed.

Randi blocked them all out as they were discussing the meaning behind her present for James, focusing instead on the salesclerk who was ringing up her purchase. Seeing the initial two-hundred-and-twenty-dollar cost almost caused her to waver in her decision, but the one-hundred-and-fifty-dollar Black Friday discount sealed the deal. It seemed to Randi as fate stepping in to make sure she got the perfect gift for James.

Now I just have to figure out where I'm gonna hide them until Christmas. If I can actually wait until Christmas to give them to him.

~~~

Friday, November 23, 2018, 5:00 p.m.

James was a little anxious about how the Lees would greet him as he walked into the church for the wedding rehearsal. As much as he longed to see Randi and show her that he'd be by her side and support her no matter what the situation entailed, he really hoped they could avoid another confrontation with her father and brother.

As soon as he entered the sanctuary, he saw Randi standing on one side of the room surrounded by the Burleson girls, her friend Amy from Tulsa, the other bridesmaid Deanna, and her sister-in-law Diana. All the women around her paled in comparison to her ethereal beauty. She wore a pink dress that came down to an asymmetrical hem at mid-calf with a little slit on her right side that barely exposed her knee as she walked. That little slit was the sexiest part of the dress. Otherwise, it was a very conservative dress with a neckline that barely dipped below where her collarbones met her sternum, and it had elbow length sleeves.

The modest dress didn't stop James from looking over every inch of her from across the room, though. His eyes explored her from the loose waves of her platinum hair hanging over her shoulders, over those luscious curves he longed to lavish with affection, and all the way down to the sexy black fuck-me pumps she had on her feet. He was glad he'd opted to wear the jacket with his navy-blue suit to hide his body's reaction to seeing her, as his gaze returned up her body and finally landed on her angelic face.

They smiled at each other when they locked eyes. James felt the weight of the world lifted off his shoulders when he realized she was happy to see him, and not upset with him for the events of the day before.

He started to walk in her direction, only to stop in his tracks when Pastor Harrison directed the wedding party to meet in front of the pulpit and everyone else to take a seat. Since James was closer to the
~~~

center aisle than the aisle on the right side of the church where Randi was standing, he followed the pastor's directions to go straight to the pulpit, while Randi went up the aisle to the right of the pews. Deanna followed Randi and Dean came up from the left side of the church, where he'd been talking with some of the other guests.

"While we're waiting for Anthony and Kay to get back from the courthouse, we'll go ahead and have our deacons, Doc Hayes and Joe Harper, help the families and guests find their seats," Pastor Harrison announced to everyone before turning to the two bridesmaids and two groomsmen, who were gathered in front of the pulpit, where he was standing. "Ladies, if you'll please line up to my right. Gentlemen, to my left."

As the four of them moved into the positions where they would stand during the ceremony, James realized that Tia and Maria should be up there with them as well. He looked around to find them and noticed them fussing with their grandparents sitting in the front row on the bride's side of the church. Not wanting to exacerbate the issues between himself and Charles Lee by calling the girls over from where they were seated by their grandfather, James turned to Pastor Harrison and spoke quietly to the man he'd known since childhood. "Should Tia and Maria be up here too, since they're walking their mother down the aisle?"

Pastor Harrison looked first at James, then over to the girls and their grandparents, before speaking in a much louder voice than James had used. "Tia and Maria, please come line up where you'll stand for the wedding tomorrow."

"See, Grandpa, I told you we're supposed to be up there and not sitting with you," Tia scolded her grandfather before she ran up to stand beside James.

James did his best to hide his smile at the precocious girl correcting her grandfather, but he couldn't contain it when he saw Randi giggle at her niece's statement. He knew Charles couldn't see Randi's reaction because she had her back to him, and Deanna was standing between them. But with the space between them being left open for where Anthony and Kay would stand during the ceremony and the fact that James wasn't completely turned away from the congregation, James knew Charles probably saw at least part of his smile. So, he wasn't surprised by the way the older man glowered at him when he saw him from the corner of his eye.

"Once the bride and groom arrive, we'll show you to the rooms where you'll get ready and practice the processional," Pastor Harrison explained. "But we can go ahead and talk our way through the whole ceremony now, and hopefully, clear up any questions you all have about where you're supposed to be or what you're supposed to do while we're waiting for them. We'll start the music Anthony has prepared to let everyone know to take their seats. He said the first track on the playlist is a ten-minute instrumental piece that should give everyone time to be seated. When the song changes, Anthony will walk in from the side, followed by James and Dean."

"Are you not doing a traditional processional where everyone enters from the back of the chapel and begins with the mother of the bride?" Charles Lee's voice boomed throughout the church.

James noticed how Randi stiffened at the sound of her father's voice and wished he was close enough to comfort her. He looked at her, trying to offer his silent support, and was gratified by seeing her shoulders relax as their eyes met. He didn't hear Pastor Harrison's explanation to Charles about what they were doing for the processional as he was solely focused on Randi until she dropped her eyes to look down at Maria beside her. James looked down to see what had drawn Randi's attention away from him and noticed that Maria had taken Randi's hand, apparently also realizing her aunt needed comfort at that moment. With the potential crisis averted, James turned back to the pastor, who was continuing his talk through of the wedding.

"Once the three of you reach the end of the aisle," Pastor Harrison explained, specifically speaking to Tia and Maria about what would happen when they walked their mother down the aisle the next day. "I'll ask, 'who gives this woman to be joined in holy matrimony to this man?' and the two of you will say 'we do,' before moving to stand where you are now."

"No, that's not right," Maria argued, shaking her head.

"We're not giving our mom away," Tia protested, putting her hands on her hips defiantly. "We're claiming Anthony as our dad."

"You might wanna change that line in the ceremony, Pastor," Dean chuckled.

James tried to stifle his own laughter, but when both bridesmaids giggled and he heard a few more people behind him laughing, he couldn't hold it back.

"Why don't we ask the bride and groom how they want it to go since I think that's them coming in the church now?" Pastor Harrison stepped down from the pulpit to go to the back of the room to greet Anthony and Kay. Tia and Maria took off down the aisle in front of him to welcome their parents to the rehearsal.

James stood there feeling awkward while waiting for the pastor to talk to Anthony and Kay. As he turned and started walking back up the aisle with Anthony, his wife came from the side of the room to get Randi and Deanna to follow her to the back of the church.

"You don't look nervous at all." Dean chuckled as Anthony stepped to the front of the pulpit where he and James were standing.

"I'm not nervous," Anthony replied.

Pastor Harrison directed Anthony, James, and Dean to follow him out a side door that led to the small changing room beside the baptismal where the men would get ready for the wedding.

Anthony handed Pastor Harrison the flash drive with the music for the wedding, which he passed along to someone else, who would get it started, so they could make sure they had the correct song for each part of the ceremony as they went through the rehearsal.

The pastor reviewed the timing of how they would walk out, which they then practiced once the long instrumental piece was stopped abruptly to switch to the processional song that Anthony had picked.

Once he was in place between Anthony and his brother, James turned to look down the aisle as first Deanna, and then Randi walked down. Their eyes met briefly, and James imagined it was their wedding day, with Randi walking down the aisle in a white satin dress to become his wife.

I hope she doesn't make me wait too long to make that dream come true, James prayed as the music changed to the bridal march.

Tia and Maria walked down the aisle with Kay in between them. "Beautiful," Anthony reverently whispered beside him, and James knew it was a special moment between his best friend and his bride-to-be.

"This is when I'll start announcing we're here for the marriage of Kay Lynn Lee to Anthony Ray Burleson. Did I get the middle names right?" Pastor Harrison looked back and forth between Kay and Anthony.

"Yes," "yes," both Anthony and Kay replied at the same time.

"And we'll be skipping any reference to giving away people like possessions," Pastor Harrison joked, and several people chuckled.

The pastor continued on explaining each of the things they would do, starting with a declaration of intent when the couple were to answer with "I will," before going into the vows, where they would each say the personal ones they wrote before saying "I do," to the ones the pastor would recite. They planned to play the song Anthony wrote for Kay while all four of them lit a family unity candle. That would be followed by the blessing and exchanging of rings, the pronouncement of husband and wife, their first kiss as a married couple, and the presentation of the new mister and misses. They pantomimed the physical acts and skipped saying the vows that they were writing themselves, so they would be a surprise during the actual wedding.

"At this point, I'll ask, do you Anthony Ray Burleson, take Kay Lynn Lee to be your lawfully wedded wife, but with a little more prose," Pastor Harrison quipped with a small grin.

"I do," Anthony answered, his smile so big James could hear it in his words.

"Do you Kay Lynn Lee, take Anthony Ray Burleson to be your lawfully wedded husband?" Pastor Harrison played along with continuing as if they were in the actual service.

"I'm pregnant," Kay blurted. She slapped her hand over her mouth as soon as the words left her lips, as if she was in shock that she said it. Her eyes were wide, and she looked mortified.

The entire room erupted in laughter, except for Kay and Anthony, who stood there looking at each other as if frozen in shock, and James and Randi, who momentarily locked eyes as realization dawned that the pregnancy test they all saw the day before might not have been Randi's.

"So, this is a shotgun wedding?" Bob Burleson teased as his laugh died down to just a light chuckle.

"No, I left my shotgun in Oklahoma," Charles Lee disagreed, still laughing boisterously, like he thought Kay being pregnant was great news. "Maybe I can borrow one from you, Bob?"

Leah Mae Wright

James wasn't sure how to take the extreme dichotomy of how Charles reacted the day before, when it was Randi with a pregnancy test, and that moment, when Kay announced that she's expecting. *I guess it's okay because they're getting married tomorrow?* James fumed, fighting back his irritation at the man to get through the rest of the wedding rehearsal.

"Um, maybe say 'I do' in the actual ceremony," Pastor Harrison advised, trying to get them back on track for the rehearsal.

"I do," Kay choked out, dropping her hands to reveal her pink cheeks. "I'm sorry, I didn't mean to tell you this way."

"You're really pregnant?" Anthony gasped out the question. "How?"

"Dude, if you don't know how that happens," Dean started saying before James punched him in the arm to shut him up.

"I'm guessing your doctor was wrong." Kay shrugged her shoulders and looked at Anthony as if she was unsure of his reaction to the news.

Holy shit! Was that really Kay's pregnancy test? James wondered, looking past his friends at Randi. She gave him a wide smile and nodded, like she'd read his mind and was answering his unspoken question.

A huge smile spread across Anthony's face as he pulled Kay into his arms. He picked her up and pressed his lips to Kay's in a kiss too passionate for their surroundings. Her legs went around his waist, like she couldn't stop herself from latching onto him. Anthony cradled her to him with one hand on her low back and one hand on the back of her neck.

"You're supposed to wait until I tell you to kiss the bride," Pastor Harrison admonished with a chuckle. "And maybe keep it a little more chaste in the church."

Anthony appeared reluctant to stop kissing her as he pulled his lips from Kay's, but took a moment to spin her around in a circle before setting her back down on her feet. They both straightened their stance as they turned back to look at the pastor. He reached out and took her hand in his, while the pastor reviewed the rest of the ceremony.

James was happy for his friend, who was going to be a father of three soon, but he was a little melancholy as he realized that he and Randi weren't expecting their own bundle of joy.

When they went to walk back down the aisle, Anthony scooped Kay up with one arm under her knees and the other behind her back to carry her down the aisle. Her arms went up around his neck.

"I think I'm supposed to walk beside you," Kay giggled.

"Nope." Anthony chastely kissed her nose. "You aren't doing anything strenuous until the doctor checks you out and tells me it's safe. I'll carry you everywhere until then."

As Anthony carried Kay down the aisle, Pastor Harrison directed Tia and Maria to follow them. Then Randi gripped James's arm as they walked behind the girls down the aisle.

When they got to the back of the church, James noticed that Anthony had walked straight to Doc Hayes, who was there in his role as a church deacon to help with the wedding rehearsal.

"Doc," Anthony greeted. "Do you think you could open the clinic for a few minutes to do a quick exam? I wanna make sure Kay and our baby are safe."

"Sure, we can do that," Doc Hayes replied. "Do I need to check you out, too?"

"Why would you need to check me out too?" Anthony arched an eyebrow at the doctor.

"Well, I was always a little confused by the records the Navy sent me when you got out," Doc Hayes admitted, looking around as if he wasn't sure he should discuss Anthony's medical records with so many people around.

"Yeah, why?" Anthony didn't seem to care that half the town was listening to their conversation.

"They listed sterility as one of your injuries, but they didn't include the results of a sperm count test," Doc Hayes stated. "It seemed odd. You were dealing with so much more at the time that I didn't think about it to request another semen sample to test myself."

"That's because they didn't do a sperm count test." Anthony's expression looked to James like he was thinking back to his time in Germany at the hospital after the accident. "I was pretty out of it on pain meds from the broken arm and they were more worried about the collapsed lung. I was told about the sterility, but I don't really know why they said that. I thought it was because the explosion affected the nuclear power plant and everyone on the ship was exposed to radiation."

Leah Mae Wright

"Did you give them a semen sample?" Doc Hayes inquired.

"No," Anthony replied. "Unless they took one while I was knocked out?"

"Naw," Doc laughed. "That's a DIY sample extraction." The doctor turned to look at Kay, who was still cradled in Anthony's arms. "Are you feeling lightheaded?"

"No," Kay replied. "Anthony is just being an overprotective Daddy and insists you tell him I'm perfectly capable of walking while pregnant."

"I just wanna make sure both she and the baby are in perfect health," Anthony explained sheepishly.

"How about we schedule something in the clinic in the morning? Unless she's having symptoms of concern, she's perfectly capable of walking and doing all her normal activities, including going to the rehearsal dinner."

"We're actually scheduled to see you on Wednesday morning." Kay shrugged when everyone looked at her. "I figured we'd both need some tests run when the home test came back positive, so I called on Tuesday to schedule the first available appointment. We'll be cutting it close to fly out for work, but it was all that was available, since we'll be on our honeymoon on Monday and Tuesday."

"Speaking of that home test…" Randi prompted, still standing beside James, but directing her words at her sister. "Please finish clearing up the rest of that confusion."

"Sorry, Sis," Kay apologized to Randi before turning back to face Anthony and asking him to please put her down. Once she was back on her feet, she took Randi's free hand in hers and turned them back to face the rest of the people still in the church. "My sister has been an awesome friend this week. She not only helped me realize that I could be pregnant, but she also helped maintain my privacy by going outside of Heart's Destiny to buy the test for me, sneaking it to me so I could take it without being questioned by all our family, friends, and coworkers, and then hiding it for me when I needed some time and space before telling Anthony because I'm already so stressed out with everything else going on this week."

Kay turned to look directly at Randi before continuing. "Thank you, Randi, for everything you've done for me this week."

"That's what sisters are for." Randi released James's arm to hug her sister. They embraced for a long moment before they stepped apart and Randi reached for James's hand.

He laced their fingers together as Kay turned back to the crowd and directed her comments to her father. Putting both hands on her hips, she demanded, "Daddy, you need to apologize to Randi and James for acting like a total butt nugget yesterday. Neither one of them deserved the way I heard you treated them while I was taking care of Maria's skinned knees, even if that had been their positive pregnancy test."

"Kay," Charles started, her name coming out sounding like a warning that made James want to punch the man for how he talked down to his daughters.

"Don't you *Kay* me," Kay seethed, putting special emphasis on her name similar to how Charles had said it previously. "I used to think Randi was the outgoing one and I was the introvert, but it was recently pointed out to me that she's only outgoing when you're not around. I don't know what happened to make her afraid to be herself around you, but until she's ready to tell you to shut up when you start ranting, I'll step in as her big sister and do it for her."

"Whoa!" Randi exclaimed, squeezing James's hand, and looking shocked at her sister's words.

Kay didn't even seem to notice Randi's reaction, she just kept speaking to their father. "I know you love Randi, just like you love me, but you have got to stop acting like we're still children. It's time that you accept the fact that your little girls have grown up, and we don't have to have your permission or approval to do what we want, whenever we want, and with whoever we want. We get to live our lives how we see fit, and we don't have to do it your way."

James quit listening to Kay's speech as he pulled a trembling Randi into his arms. "Are you okay, Angel?" James whispered in her ear. She shook her head against his chest as her arms went around his waist, and James just held her tighter, wishing he could make everything better for her. "What can I do? How can I help you?"

"Make them stop yelling," Randi sobbed, burrowing her face into the space between his chest and shoulder like she wished she could crawl inside him and hide from everything around them.

James moved to cover her ears with the palms of his hands before shouting, "Stop!"

Kay and Charles both stopped their bickering and turned to look at him, similar looks of shock on both their faces.

James lowered his voice as he asserted, "This isn't the time or the place for this discussion," so that the majority of the people in attendance couldn't hear him. He removed his hands from Randi's ears to make sure she heard his next words. "Kay, I appreciate you wanting to stand up for your sister, but another shouting match isn't what Randi needs."

"Like you know what my daughter needs," Charles scoffed, disgust in his voice, but at least he wasn't yelling anymore.

James looked down into Randi's glossy emerald orbs and smiled. "I know exactly what she needs," he professed, speaking to her more than replying to her father. "She needs to be loved and accepted for the wonderful woman she is, unconditionally. She needs the freedom to explore the world and all the options she has open in front of her, so she can fulfill all her dreams. And while most of the time she's a badass, independent woman, who is more than capable of doing it all on her own, once in a while, she needs a partner she can lean on to take care of her while she recharges her badass batteries. If I'm really lucky, maybe she'll let me be that partner."

"We might be able to negotiate that," Randi quipped, a small smile tilting up the corners of her mouth. "But I'd rather that be a private conversation between just you and me, not with an audience of half the town."

"I think we've done all we need to do here this evening," Hazel declared before James could reply to Randi, looking at Pastor Harrison like she wanted to confirm they didn't need to do another rehearsal of the wedding.

"Yes, I think we're all set for tomorrow," Pastor Harrison agreed with Hazel before turning toward Charles and continuing. "But my door is always open to any of you who might be in need of family counseling."

"Then let's all go on over to the ballroom before our dinner gets cold," Hazel commanded, starting to usher people out the door.

"Wanna ride?" James smiled at Randi, leaning his head to point in the general direction of the bed and breakfast.

"Yeah, I'd like that." Randi smiled back at him, her vibrant green eyes clearing up to reflect her smile. "Just let me grab my purse from the pew where I left it while we were practicing for tomorrow."

James bent to give Randi a chaste kiss before releasing her from his arms, so she could go pick up her bag. He watched her walk over to the area where she'd been standing when he first arrived to get her things, never taking his eyes off of her as she put on a sweater that he hadn't even realized she had with her, picked up her purse, and walked back to his side. He laced their fingers together, so they could walk out to his truck hand in hand.

"Sorry, I should've driven one of the cars," James apologized as he opened the passenger door and helped her up into the tall vehicle.

"No, I like the height of your truck." Randi grabbed his tie and pulled him in for a kiss.

Fuck yes! She's not mad at me if she's kissing me like this, James shouted in his head, loving how Randi nibbled his lower lip to get him to deepen the kiss. She may have initiated it by pulling him in by his tie, but James took over once their tongues tangled, both hands delving into the soft waves of her hair. She tasted amazing, like chocolate and mint, making him wonder what she'd eaten right before the rehearsal.

For a moment, James forgot where they were. He was so lost in the passion of their kiss, enjoying the feeling of Randi's arms around his neck and shoulders, pulling him down so her pillow soft breasts were pressed into his chest, that he almost didn't recognize the sound of the horns blaring around them as his friends and neighbors were trying to get his attention as they pulled out of the parking lot.

"Why are they all honking?" Randi pointed at the passing vehicles with her head as he pulled back.

"Dean probably started it." James stepped back and shut her door. He walked around and got in the driver's side before continuing his explanation. "The GWA guys are all pretty bad about ribbing each other, but Dean has made it his mission in life to embarrass me any chance he gets since we were kids. Little does he know that I'm not the least bit embarrassed by him pointing out to everyone that I'm kissing you."

"Yeah, I recognized that they all liked to embarrass you with the way they were acting at the Camelot." Randi smiled at him as they both remembered the day they met.

"Yeah, well, I've made it clear that they need to behave better around you, but if they forget and do something that bothers you, let me know and I'll talk to them again." James took her hand in his after starting the truck.

"I'm not worried about them." Randi shook her head, squeezing his hand in hers. Well, squeezing as much as she could with her hand being so much smaller than his. "I'm more worried about us. Can we sit here for a minute and talk before we go face everyone again?"

"Of course, Angel." James turned the truck back off and turned in his seat to face her. "We don't even have to go to the dinner if you wanna skip it."

"No, I wanna go and be there for Kay and Anthony." Randi grasped his hand again. "I just wanna make sure we're okay first. I know you had to be freaked out by how I ran away yesterday."

James took a moment to breathe while he figured out how to explain his feelings about the events of the day before. "I was actually more worried about your safety than freaked out. I knew you were doing just like your therapist has recommended and walking away from your dad, so you didn't have to listen to him yelling."

"Yeah, but I shouldn't have walked away from you, too." Randi had a sad expression crossing her features. "I honestly didn't really hear everything that was being said, and I probably misheard whatever you said about us getting married. After thinking about it for a while now, I think I lashed out and ran from you too, because I thought you were agreeing with him that we had to get married because of a baby we're not actually expecting."

"No, I was definitely not agreeing with him," James grumbled a little louder than he intended. He lowered his voice before continuing, not wanting to trigger Randi by raising his voice like her father. "I was trying to point out that us being together isn't disrespectful or disgraceful because I'm not the player he accused me of being. I said I hope we'll be getting married eventually, but not until you're ready for us to take that step in our relationship. And after you left, I might have said something about us happily living in sin for the rest of our lives if you don't ever wanna marry me."

"Oh, I bet he loved hearing that," Randi giggled.

James shrugged, not caring what her father thought of him or anything he had to say, at least not for his own sake. He wouldn't actively try to piss the man off because he didn't want to make things worse for Randi, but he also wouldn't hold his tongue when he felt the need to defend Randi from her father's verbal assholery either.

"Your opinion is the only one that matters to me, Angel." James reached over to gently stroke her cheek with the hand not holding hers. "And I meant every word I said when I told him I wanna be your man, supporting you and standing proudly behind you while you achieve your dreams, regardless of whether we get married or not, or if we have babies or not."

"Oh, James," Randi sighed as a single tear slipped from her eye down her cheek.

"I love you, Angel." James swiped his thumb under her eye to wipe away the wetness. "I fell head over heels for you the first moment our eyes locked across the restaurant as you walked up to our table, and I just keep falling deeper and deeper in love with you every day since."

"Oh, James, I love you, too." Randi bounded over the center console to throw herself into his arms.

Their lips met in a passionate kiss that was cut way too short for James. But he understood that having the center console digging into her abdomen wasn't comfortable for Randi, not to mention the fact that they were still parked in the church parking lot, which was a completely inappropriate place for everything James wanted to do with Randi at that moment.

"Sorry, this wasn't exactly the romantic way I wanted to say those three little words the first time," James confessed as Randi sat back into the passenger seat. She gave him a quizzical look, so he elaborated. "I wanted to take you somewhere for a romantic candlelight dinner to tell you I love you the first time."

"Yeah, well, you'll just have to save that for the proposal," Randi suggested offhandedly, buckling her seatbelt like she was ready to get on with the night. "Sometime next year, not anytime soon, and only because we love each other. That's the only reason I'll ever get married. Kay and her ex are more than enough proof that getting married because you're expecting a baby is a bad idea."

"Agreed, Angel." James buckled his own seatbelt and started his truck. The reminder of his incorrect assumption about her being pregnant triggered a thought that he should have asked her more about the other day. "Speaking of babies, after seeing the test in your bag

Monday night, I thought the only thing we needed to worry about on Tuesday was that we're both clean…" His voice trailed off. He didn't know how to ask what their chances of conceiving that day were without either sounding like an asshole who didn't want a baby now, or a jackass who hoped he'd knocked her up.

"Because you thought I was pregnant already?" Randi finished his thought for him. James nodded, the lump in his throat preventing him from forming words of any kind. "And now you're wondering if it's possible since we didn't use a condom on Tuesday?"

James nodded again, glad that he hadn't shifted into gear, or actually pulled out of the parking space yet, since he couldn't take his eyes off Randi to be able to pay attention to the road to drive them to the rehearsal dinner.

"Well, no form of birth control is one-hundred percent effective, so I suppose it's possible." Randi slightly lifted one shoulder in a sort-of half-shrug. "But since I'm only a month in on my birth control shot that's supposed to last three months, it's probably less than a one percent chance. If that's too much of a risk for you, we can go back to using condoms if you want."

"No," James protested, probably too vehemently. "I mean, unless you want me to," he quickly corrected. "I just didn't know if you were on any kind of birth control. And I know you said you don't wanna have kids for another five years, so I wanted to make sure I wasn't derailing your plans. But I'm sure your shot is more effective than condoms, so I'm good with just one level of protection, if you are."

Shut the fuck up! James told himself, feeling like a perv for wanting to keep going bareback because of how much better it felt with no barriers between them, when that might not be what Randi wanted.

"I'm good with just the shot," Randi giggled, just as an alarm blared from her purse. Randi pulled her phone out and turned off the alarm. "Now we should probably go to dinner, so I can get something to drink to take my medication."

"Oh, um, yeah," James sputtered, shifting the truck into gear, and focusing on driving them to the plantation house.

As soon as they arrived, he made a beeline to the kitchen to get her something to drink to take her medicine. Once that was done, they walked hand in hand into the ballroom where the rehearsal dinner was already underway. Kay waved them over to the main table, where she was sitting with Anthony, her daughters, and the other two members of the wedding party.

James noticed that their parents were all seated at a separate table from the wedding party, and was glad that he wouldn't have to sit at the table with Charles Lee and act like all was good.

Kay jumped up and grabbed each of their free hands as they approached the table to take their seats. "I'm so sorry," Kay apologized, looking like she might start crying any second. "I didn't mean to make things worse earlier. I don't know what came over me. It was like one minute I was defending you," she pointed to Randi with a tip of her head. "And the next I was saying all the things I should've told Dad thirteen years ago." Her voice broke on the last word, giving Randi an opening to reply.

"Don't worry about it, Sis." Randi pulled Kay in for a one-armed hug while still holding James's hand with the other. "I just hope it won't take me thirteen years to finally be as brave as you and say my own piece."

"Yeah, I don't recommend bottling it up for that long, but with a little help from Pastor Harrison and Anthony's parents, we've called a truce until after the wedding, so maybe don't blow up like I did until Sunday." Kay returned Randi's hug.

James found himself pulled into a group hug with the sisters as Randi agreed. After a minute or two, they all pulled back and moved to take their seats. Dinner was served and toasts were given, and overall, it was a relatively good night.

James really wanted to bring Randi home with him for the night, but she insisted he take her back to Charlotte's house when the party was over, so she'd be close to her sister for all the beauty rituals they planned for the next morning in preparation for the wedding.

Maybe I can convince her to move her stuff to my place tomorrow night after the wedding? James pondered as he drove home after a way too short goodnight kiss.

Chapter Seventeen

Randi was surprised to be woken up by the sounds of a few of Charlotte's friends arriving first thing Saturday morning. She thought the plan was for all the women to meet up at Kay's by ten that morning to start getting ready for the wedding, but apparently Charlotte had recruited a glam squad for the lot of them and with so many women needing to rotate through the hair, nail, and makeup chairs, they needed to get started much earlier.

After some confusion as to whether Cassidy, Kayla, and Lexi would be going from house to house on the ranch, or if they would set up in one place and have all the ladies come to them, they decided to kick Anthony out of his house, so the glam squad could set up there to be at the bride's beck and call. The rest of the women who wanted to partake of the professional services would have to go to Kay's house to be worked into the rotation.

Randi wasn't sure why Charlotte insisted she go with them to Kay's before seven in the morning, still half asleep from being up late the night before, but she complied. She'd barely walked in carrying her makeup bag and preferred hair products when her alarm went off for her to take her morning medication.

She'd changed her medication times from six in the morning and six in the evening to seven in the morning and seven in the evening after talking to James about the GWA travel schedule. Their conversation had made her realize that she wouldn't have to get up as early with her new job as she had when she'd needed to be at the Camelot for the first morning shift.

After a quick pitstop in Kay's kitchen for a bottle of water to wash it down, Randi was the first one in the chair for Lexi to give her a manicure and pedicure. As she applied a pretty mauve polish to Randi's nails, Lexi told her all about the nail salon, Nailed It, that she'd opened in town the year before. Lexi was a bubbly brunette a couple of years older than Randi. If she spent much more time in the cute little town, Randi could imagine they'd be fast friends.

Lexi was only about half finished with Randi's nails when Randi realized why they needed to get started so early. They'd set up the three beauty stations in Kay's bedroom, and even though it was a large master bedroom, it was quickly filling up with women waiting in line for their turn for each part of the day's beauty regimen. It wasn't just the wedding party and immediate families wanting to get ready with Kay. Randi counted almost twenty people who had converged in Kay's bedroom for the professional beauty services.

Guess it's a good thing we have eight hours until the wedding to be able to get everyone all dolled up, Randi thought as she got up so her niece, Tia could take her place in the mani-pedi chair. When she walked over to chat with her best friend, Amy, where she was sitting on the bed waiting for one of the other chairs, she realized that all three of the beauticians were doing nails.

"So, how is all this gonna work for our hair and makeup?" Randi was trying to figure out if she needed to go find a free bathroom, so she could do her own hair and makeup. *Maybe the downstairs bathroom?* She thought, knowing that Kay was in her master bathroom showering and Maria was occupying the girls' bathroom, which was the only other bathroom on the second floor.

"Sorry, we didn't explain things better for those of you who haven't known us forever," the woman she remembered being introduced to as Kayla apologized without looking up from where she was painting Deanna's nails. "Cassidy, Lexi, and I all went to cosmetology school together, so we're all licensed to do all the services we're offering today. Since there are so many people who need to get ready, it would be impossible for us to get everyone ready at the same time if we stuck to just doing the specific services we normally offer in our own businesses. So, we're doing everything today in a specific sequence, so we can get everyone ready at about the same time. It's nails first, then hair, and finally makeup. We should have everyone done just in time to head to the church and change, or change and then head to the church, depending on their part in the wedding."

"Oh, yeah, that makes sense." Amy bobbed her head, and Randi nodded her head in agreement. "You must do this a lot to have a system worked out so smoothly."

"We started back in middle school when we were getting ready for dances," Kayla explained as she capped the nail polish and indicated to Deanna to put her hands under the UV light to dry her nails. "Once we graduated it just kind of morphed into a part of our individual business plans, but it's mostly still been for Proms and such. This is the biggest wedding group we've done so far."

"Lexi said she's usually at the nail salon," Randi mentioned, catching up her friends who weren't close enough to hear her conversation with the nail tech. "Where can we find you for future appointments, Kayla?"

Randi wasn't sure if Amy or Deanna would ever use the services of the Heart's Destiny beauty businesses, but she assumed that she would be spending at least a little time in the small town with both her sister and her boyfriend living there. So, she wanted to know where to go for future girls' days with her sister and nieces.

"I rent space in the Cut & Curl," Kayla answered as she moved to start working on Amy's pedicure. "We're all three on Arabian between Longhorn and Brangus. The Cut & Curl is in between Nailed It and Beautiful Destiny."

"Nailed It," Deanna chortled, smiling. "That's an awesome name for a nail salon."

"That's what I thought when Lexi told me about it," Randi agreed with her sister's best friend.

"And Beautiful Destiny is where your other friend works?" Amy inquired.

"Yeah, Cassidy does makeup consultations, mostly for people coming in to shop in the beauty supply section of the store, and she does full face makeup, like we're gonna do today, by appointment for special occasions."

"Miss Cassidy helped us pick out the makeup and stuff we got for Mommy for her birthday," Maria announced, coming over to stand by Randi. "She's a lot nicer than the lady at the grocery store who wants to date Uncle Bobby."

"You met a lady at the grocery store who wants to date Uncle Bobby?" Hazel suddenly appeared in their circle of people. Randi wasn't sure how she heard Maria from across the room and got to her side so quickly, but it was impressive. "Do you remember her name?"

"Daddy said her name was Tammi." Maria wrinkled her nose in disgust. "But Uncle Bobby doesn't like her either, so he won't go on a date with her. That's why Daddy said she was so rude to us at the store."

Hazel's excited expression vanished in the blink of an eye.

"Sorry, Hazel, you'll have to figure out someone else to fix Bobby up with," one of Anthony's aunts, whose name Randi couldn't remember, chuckled with a shake of her head and a mischievous smile.

The talk around them turned into a matchmaking mess that Randi was ready to escape. She kind of felt sorry for Amy and Deanna as they were being asked their opinions on the various Burleson boys and the likelihood of them moving to town and dating them. Randi took advantage of Maria asking her to help detangle her hair and snuck out of the awkward conversation to Maria's room. She was grateful for the excuse of needing to use her detangling spray to escape the fix-up discussions.

Once she was done getting Maria's hair combed out, Randi ran into her mother on the way back into the bedroom, where everyone was being beautified.

Crap on a cracker, Randi thought, not wanting to risk an argument with her mother in the middle of everyone.

"Randi, darling!" Mary reached out to stop Randi from walking past her. "Can we talk privately for a moment?"

Just breathe, Randi mentally told herself. *Inhale, two, three, four, five. Exhale, two, three, four, five.* After a couple of rounds of the calming breathing exercise her therapist had taught her, Randi finally quavered, "Sure, Mom."

They took a few steps down the hall, so they weren't directly in the line of sight of anyone in Kay's bedroom, before Mary finally started talking again.

"I wanted to apologize to you for the way your father has behaved the last couple of days." Mary's expression was remorseful.

"Thanks, Mom, but it's not your job to apologize for him." Randi was surprised to realize that she wasn't mad at her mother for staying silent during her father's recent outbursts.

"No, I know that," Mary wavered, reaching out to take her daughter's hand. "But I feel partly responsible for his behavior, since my giving him daughters is what he feels changed his opinion on sex before marriage."

"I guess you did kinda start the anti-sex lecture back when I was in high school," Randi admitted, not really sure that her mother's part in that was the root cause of her issues. "But you didn't make him yell and scream and make a scene. I can handle us not having the same morals or values or whatever differences of opinion. It's the yelling and not listening to reason that I can't deal with anymore."

"I've talked to him a couple of times already, about how hypocritical he's being," Mary admitted, shaking her head, and squeezing Randi's hand.

"Hypocritical?" Randi snorted, not thinking that was the right word to describe her dad's actions of the last couple of days.

"Yes, hypocritical," Mary asserted forcefully. "We didn't wait to get married thirty some years ago, so getting mad because our daughters also didn't wait for marriage is hypocritical."

"Ewww, Mom, T. M. I. I don't wanna think about you and Daddy, before or after marriage." Randi shuddered at the gross factor of thinking about her parents having sex. It didn't matter that she wouldn't be there if they hadn't, she didn't want to think about it.

"Yes, well, that ick factor goes both ways, daughter," Mary lightly laughed. "I just wanted you to know that he's already planning to apologize to you tonight after the wedding. I'll make sure he knows that he needs to make it an apology for his aggressiveness and won't mention how much of a hypocrite he was being."

Randi couldn't help but laugh at the ornery smile on her mother's face, knowing her pious father would never admit to premarital sex in an apology, regardless of what her mother claimed.

"Thanks, Mom." Randi hugged her mother before they both went back in for the next round of beauty treatments.

Randi enjoyed the rest of the day, laughing and chatting with the roomful of new family and friends. She especially enjoyed the fact that she and James weren't the center of the gossipy gabfest. The Burlesons, specifically Hazel and Susan, were adamantly trying to recruit both Deanna and Amy to come work for them in the local office of Burleson Incorporated, so they could fix them up with their sons. And when they weren't working on convincing Deanna and Amy to move there, they were asking Kay and Randi to make sure all the wrestlers, specifically the single ones they could match up with their kids, knew they were welcome to come to the ranch for every holiday break they had.

Once everyone had their nails done, the beauty consultants cleared their folding tables of polish and UV lights and set up curling irons of every size. It was a whirlwind of a day getting them all fixed up with everything from elaborate updos to cascading waves of curls.

It was another seamless transition from hair to makeup, with the ladies who had to go home and change before the wedding finishing up first and the wedding party being the last to leave the makeup chairs. They loaded up their garment bags to change in the bridal suite at the church, with the glam squad following them over there in case they needed any last-minute touch ups.

They got to the church thirty minutes before the wedding was supposed to start and wasted no time in getting changed into their wedding finery. Randi loved the dress that Kay had chosen for the bridesmaids. Some of her friends had picked out hideous bridesmaids' dresses that Randi had hated wasting money on because she would never wear them again. But the dress that Kay had picked was something Randi could imagine wearing multiple times, being more of a semi-formal style that matched Randi's normal aesthetic taste.

"Oh, Kay," Randi gasped as her sister stepped out of the changing room in her wedding gown. "You are the most beautiful bride I've ever seen."

"Mommy is a princess bride," Maria announced, bouncing around in her dress that matched the one Randi was wearing.

"No, Mom's dress is prettier than the dress from *The Princess Bride* movie," Tia retorted.

"Yes, Kay, you are the most beautiful bride," Deanna agreed, fanning herself like she was trying to prevent herself from shedding a tear. "I'm so glad I get to see you living out your happily ever after."

Their parents popped in for a brief moment with Kay. After their congratulations and a round of pictures, her father pulled her aside to say, "I'm sorry, baby girl," before they left to take their seats. Without the time to really talk, Randi just nodded at her father as they gave each other a quick one-armed hug on his way out the door.

Leah Mae Wright

"Are we all completely ready?" Deanna waved an arm around at the women in the room.

"I think so." Kay looked around at the four ladies in blue surrounding her.

"Do you have all your old, new, borrowed, and blue stuff?" Tia probed her mother.

"Yes, my engagement ring is old, and my clothes are all new," Kay replied, smiling at her daughter. "I borrowed this necklace from Hazel, and my garter is blue."

"What about the penny in your shoe?" Randi chimed in, remembering the silly way her grandmother had finished the ritual at the wedding of one of their aunts back when she was young enough to participate as the flower girl.

"What?" Kay looked at her like she'd lost her mind.

"Don't you remember when Aunt Lolo got married and Grandma Lee said the whole poem was 'something old, something new, something borrowed, something blue, and a sixpence in her shoe', and said that since we're American and not British our family changed it to a penny instead of a sixpence?" Randi reminded her sister.

"No, I completely forgot about that!" Kay exclaimed, shaking her head.

Randi went over to her purse to dig through her wallet for a penny, handing it to her sister to slip in the side of her shoe.

"Oh, wow, I didn't realize there was more to that saying." Deanna looked down at her phone, where she'd apparently looked it up. "I didn't realize the meaning of each of the items, either."

"What are their meanings?" Tia, being her ever studious self, had to know the reasoning behind the traditions.

"The something old is supposed to provide protection for the baby to come after the marriage," Deanna read from her phone. "The something new symbolizes optimism for the future. An item borrowed from another happily married couple provides good luck. The color blue is a sign of purity and fidelity. And the sixpence is a silver coin that symbolizes prosperity and is supposed to ward off evil done by frustrated former suitors. Too bad you don't have a silver half dollar to use instead of a penny, since it's closer to the value of a sixpence in today's currency."

"No, I think I'll stick to our family tradition," Kay declared with a self-deprecating smile. "A half-dollar coin wouldn't fit in my shoe."

"That's because your feet are tiny," Deanna laughed, pointing to Kay's size five shoe, where she was tucking Randi's lucky penny. "Okay, now that all that's done, it's time to toast you and your groom."

"Yes," Randi agreed, moving to the side table to pour their drinks.

The ladies used sparkling grape juice, in lieu of champagne, to toast to the continued happiness of the family that was forming on that special day. Apparently, Kay's baby news the day before led to a scramble for finding the substitute that would be served alongside the champagne at the reception later.

It seemed that they'd barely had time for the toast before they were being instructed to grab their bouquets and line up for the processional. They reached the vestibule just as their parents stepped into the sanctuary, the last to take their seats.

They heard the music change and waited off to the side of the doors for Mrs. Harrison to signal them that it was time to start walking down the aisle. Mrs. Harrison waited until Anthony, James, and Dean were all in place at the altar before indicating to Deanna that it was her turn to walk in. When Deanna was most of the way down the aisle, she signaled Randi to follow.

As soon as Randi stepped through the door to the sanctuary, her eyes locked with James's, the rest of the room blurring from her field of vision. He'd trimmed his beard and his long hair appeared to have been straightened from his normally wavy style. Randi didn't like the royal blue tuxedo as much as she had the black one he'd worn for a Halloween costume, but she still thought he looked hot in a tux no matter the color.

Slowly walking down the aisle, Randi imagined herself walking to James as her groom. She wasn't sure she wanted a wedding as elaborate as Kay was having with Anthony. *Maybe when we're finally ready to take that step, we can do it when the GWA has a show in Vegas?*

Randi realized that she must have smiled at that thought, since James's smile widened at the same time. *If he only knew what I was thinking,* she thought as she took her place beside Deanna, leaving room between her and Anthony for Kay and Maria, similar to how James had left room between him and Anthony for Tia.

She turned like everyone else in the room to look at the door to the sanctuary as the bridal march began. The double doors opened to reveal Kay standing between her daughters, their elbows linked, so they could each hold their individual bouquets. The three of them made quite an entrance as they walked down the aisle, beaming smiles on all their faces.

When they reached the end of the aisle, the preacher began his opening remarks. When he got to the part where he announced, "We're gathered here today to join Anthony Ray Burleson and Kay Lynn Lee in holy matrimony," Maria interrupted.

"And we're here today to claim Anthony Ray Burleson as our Daddy," the precocious eight-year-old declared loudly, inciting a wave of laughter throughout the church.

Tia reached out with her free hand and grasped Anthony's hand, physically showing her claim on her new dad, but she didn't say anything more to add to the laughter of the crowd.

"How about we change that line?" Pastor Harrison winked at Maria. "We're gathered here today to join Anthony, Kay, Tia, and Maria as a family."

Maria nodded at him in agreement as he went on to deliver a short speech about the sanctity of marriage and the love of a family. After a few moments, he asked Anthony and Kay to join hands, so Randi took Kay's large bouquet to free her hands for this part of the ceremony.

"In honor of the Baptist faith of the bride, we will begin with the declaration of intent of the couple." Pastor Harrison looked past Anthony and Kay at the wedding guests. "For those of you who have attended weddings here in the past, this may sound like a second set of vows, but these statements are meant to be the verbal representation of signing the marriage license. It is the couple's public declaration that they are knowingly and willingly entering the contract of marriage. Their oral consent to participate in the wedding, if you will."

He turned his focus back to Anthony and Kay before continuing with the declaration of intent portion of the ceremony.

"Anthony, will you have Kay to be your wife? Will you love her, comfort and keep her, and forsaking all others remain true to her, as long as you both shall live?" Pastor Harrison requested Anthony's declaration of intent.

"I will," Anthony responded, smiling down at Kay.

"Kay, will you have Anthony to be your husband? Will you love him, comfort and keep him, and forsaking all others remain true to him, as long as you both shall live?" Pastor Harrison repeated the declaration of intent questions for Kay.

"I will." Kay's smile matched Anthony's.

"Anthony and Kay have chosen to write a portion of their own vows to one another." Pastor Harrison motioned to Anthony to begin his part of the ceremony.

"My beautiful Kay," Anthony began. "I've loved you longer than I've actually known your name."

Randi heard a few snickers throughout the room, and wondered how many people actually knew about the dreams Anthony had about his soulmate for over a year before he and Kay met.

"Every day, my love for you grows stronger than the day before," Anthony continued. "And not just for you. For the daughters you've already given me and for the sons we'll have in the future, as well. You are literally my dreams come true, my much better half."

"Third," Tia interjected, shaking her head at her dad. "You are twice her size, so she would be a third of the two of you combined."

"I stand corrected by our brilliant daughter," Anthony chuckled along with about half of the guests. "You're the best third of our union. I will spend the rest of my life, and the eternity of my time in heaven after this life, loving you, cherishing you, and thanking God for making you mine."

When Anthony stopped speaking, Pastor Harrison continued his vow portion of the ceremony. "Anthony Ray Burleson, do you take Kay Lynn Lee to be your lawfully wedded wife, to live together in marriage? Do you promise to love her, comfort her, honor and keep her, for better or worse, for richer or poorer, in sickness and health, and forsaking all others, be faithful only to her, for as long as you both shall live?"

"I do," Anthony declared with a huge smile down at Kay.

The preacher turned to Kay and nodded at her to say her portion of the vows she'd written for Anthony.

Leah Mae Wright

"Anthony," Kay started, sounding a bit choked up. "You came into my life when I wasn't sure I was ready for you. But no matter how much my brain argued that our timing was off, my heart knew from day one that we were inevitable. I may have told my sister on the day after we met that you were a Jedi, who used the Force on me to get me to go out with you."

She was interrupted by a few chuckles from the audience. Seeing James's curious expression directed at her, Randi smiled and nodded at him, confirming Kay's statement for everyone in attendance.

"But the truth is that I knew, even then, that you aren't a Jedi. You're just the perfect man for me. Make sure you recognize that clarification of 'for me' on that statement, because we've already established that nobody's perfect."

Randi loved the way both Anthony and Kay had embraced a bit of humor in their declarations of love. She envisioned doing the same with James when they finally tied the knot.

"You're my versions of a knight in shining armor and Prince Charming all rolled into one. I think that's why you're so tall, because all of your wonderful qualities couldn't fit in a shorter man. You may claim that I'm the best, um, third of our union, but you're one-hundred percent of the heart of our family. I love you so much and look forward to spending the rest of eternity by your side."

Anthony bent to punctuate Kay's words with a quick peck of their lips together.

"We're not to that part of the ceremony yet," Pastor Harrison playfully chided as the room filled with giggles from those assembled there to witness the wedding.

When Anthony straightened, Pastor Harrison turned to Kay to finish her portion of the vows. "Kay Lynn Lee, do you take Anthony Ray Burleson to be your lawfully wedded husband, to live together in marriage? Do you promise to love him, comfort him, honor and keep him, for better or worse, for richer or poorer, in sickness and health, and forsaking all others, be faithful only to him, for as long as you both shall live?"

"I do," Kay spoke the words reverently.

"In addition to joining Anthony and Kay in marriage, this wedding is also joining a family of four," Pastor Harrison announced.

"And soon to be more," Randi heard a deep voice a few rows back say, causing a few more chuckles through the crowd.

"At this time, Anthony and Kay would like Tia and Maria to join them in lighting a family unity candle, with the musical accompaniment of a song that Anthony wrote and recorded for Kay," Pastor Harrison continued without regard to the heckler in the audience.

Maria handed her small bouquet to Randi before stepping off to the side with her parents to where there was a table set up with four blue taper candles surrounding a white pillar candle. Randi adjusted the two bouquets she was already holding, so all three handles were close enough together that she could hold all three of them as one.

Tia watched her aunt struggling to hold the bouquets for a second before turning to James and handing over her bouquet to have him hold it, so she could light her candle without the flowers being in the way. Randi couldn't help but giggle at the sight of the big burly wrestler holding the little girl's flowers while they watched the unity candle portion of the ceremony.

Any laughter from the crowd was soon drowned out by the sound of a guitar playing a beautiful melody. After a short intro, Anthony's voice joined the strumming of the acoustic guitar as he sang the lyrics to the song he'd written for Kay, telling her that he loved her more than she'd ever know.

Randi watched as Anthony joined the recorded version of himself, singing to Kay and the girls as they each lit their individual taper candles, and then their flames joined as one to light the family unity candle. It was a truly touching moment that brought a tear to Randi's eye.

She was genuinely happy for her sister and nieces to have found Anthony to complete their family. But she also hoped for a similar future for herself and James. She wanted it all, the wedding, the loving marriage, the kids, and, most especially, to grow old with him, knowing that her heart was safe with him forever.

Randi's eyes locked with James's just as that tear slipped down her cheek. Seeing the concern on his face at her show of emotion, and knowing that everyone in the audience was focused on the family unity candle, Randi mouthed, "I love you," thinking it would ease his worry about her.

Leah Mae Wright

James smiled and mouthed, "I love you, too," just as the music ended and the new family made their way back to their places at the altar. Randi returned Maria's bouquet to her just as James returned Tia's.

Randi thought she heard Tia whisper, "Thanks, Uncle James," as she took the bouquet, but she spoke so softly that Randi wasn't sure if she correctly heard her niece using the relationship moniker.

Pastor Harrison asked for the wedding rings, so they could begin the ring exchange portion of the ceremony. Anthony unbuttoned the collar of his dress white uniform from when he was in the Navy, and pulled a necklace out from under it.

"You should've put them in your pocket, so you didn't have to get undressed at the altar," a deep voice from the groom's side of the church boomed out, causing another wave of laughter to spread throughout the sanctuary.

"I figured Pappaw Jerry knew the safest place for them, so I followed his lead." Anthony gave a slight shrug as he removed a necklace with the rings on it from around his neck. He handed the preacher the rings before putting the necklace back on and rebuttoning his uniform.

Once Anthony was back to rights, the preacher spoke about the significance of the rings. "They are made of a precious metal to remind us that love is not cheap or common; but indeed, love is very costly and dear to us. The rings are also made in a circle, and their design tells us that we must keep love continuous throughout our whole lives, even as the circle of the ring is continuous. As you wear these rings, whether you are together, or apart for even just a moment, may these rings be a constant reminder of the promises you are making to one another this day. Let us pray. Father, bless these rings which Anthony and Kay have chosen to be visible signs of the inward and spiritual bond which unites their hearts. As they give and receive these rings, may they testify to the world of the covenant made between them here."

A collective "amen" was echoed throughout the church along with the pastor.

Pastor Harrison held out his hand for Anthony to take Kay's ring as he spoke to him. "Anthony, will you please take this ring and place it upon the third finger of Kay's left hand, and holding her hand in yours, please repeat this promise to her, saying after me: With this ring, I thee wed. I seal my promise, to be your faithful and loving husband, as God is my witness."

"With this ring, I thee wed. I seal my promise, to be your faithful and loving husband, as God is my witness." Anthony slipped the ring on Kay's finger.

Pastor Harrison extended his hand with Anthony's ring to Kay and directed, "Kay, will you please take this ring and place it upon the third finger of Anthony's left hand, and holding his hand in yours, please repeat this promise to him, saying after me: With this ring, I thee wed. I seal my promise, to be your faithful and loving wife, as God is my witness."

"With this ring, I thee wed. I seal my promise, to be your faithful and loving wife, as God is my witness." Kay placed Anthony's ring on his finger.

"Kay and Anthony, you have come here today before us, and before God, and have expressed your desire to become husband and wife," Pastor Harrison continued the ceremony, as Randi handed back Kay's bouquet. "You have shown your love and affection by joining hands, and have made promises of faith and devotion, each to the other, and have sealed these promises by the giving and the receiving of the rings. Therefore, by the power vested in me by the State of Texas, I now pronounce that you are husband and wife. Anthony, you may kiss your wife."

With a hand on either side of her waist, Anthony lifted Kay off the ground to bring their lips together. Kay flung her arms around Anthony's neck, looking like she almost hit James with her bouquet from Randi's vantage point. With the way Kay's arms went around Anthony as they passionately kissed, Randi almost expected her sister to wrap her legs around him, even in her wedding dress in front of the church. But Anthony actually behaved and kept the kiss mostly chaste, and put her back down before Kay could wrap around him like a monkey climbing a tree.

"Ladies and gentlemen, it is my privilege to introduce to you for the first time, Mr. and Mrs. Anthony Burleson," Pastor Harrison announced as the music for the recessional started.

Anthony took Kay's hand and brought it to his lips for another kiss before they walked hand in hand down the aisle. Tia and Maria joined hands to follow their parents.

James offered his right elbow to Randi, which she gladly grasped before they followed the happy new family to the back of the church. Now that the pomp and circumstance was all over, Randi was looking forward to being at his side the rest of the night.

As the guests all exited the church, the wedding party stayed back at the church to take pictures, giving everyone time to find their place at the reception before the bride and groom arrived. Since Randi and Deanna had ridden to the church with Kay and the girls, and Anthony had ridden over with his dad, there were some musical chairs to be played to get the whole wedding party back to the ballroom for the reception. Anthony ended up driving Kay's Jeep with their daughters in the backseat, while Deanna rode with Dean and Randi rode with James.

Since it was the first time she'd had to be alone with James all day, Randi was tempted to ask him to go pick her stuff up from Charlotte's house, so they could go straight to his place after the reception. But since they needed to enter the reception before Anthony and Kay, they didn't have time right then.

Oh, well, I can always tell him after the reception that I'm ready to spend all my nights with him from now on.

<div align="center">~~~</div>

James loved being able to be close to Randi for all the wedding party pictures, both at the church and once they got to the plantation house before the reception. He would have to make sure he got copies of several of them with her in that sexy bridesmaid's dress. Once they took all the pictures Kay wanted on the porch of the plantation house, the wedding party was instructed to go take their places at the doorway of the ballroom, so they could make a grand entrance.

Kay had thought it would be fun if everyone danced their way into the room and up to the table where they would be sitting. Just like at the rehearsal dinner the night before, the wedding party was seated together at the head table, with the rest of their families and friends being relegated to the other tables. But unlike the rehearsal dinner, the head table was located on one end of the ballroom beside the cake table, with a space between them and the rest of the tables set up as a dance floor. The band was set up in the corner on the opposite side of the cake table, but since they weren't playing during dinner, the wedding party was basically alone at the end of the room for the first part of the reception.

The head table was set up with all eight of them sitting on one side of the long table facing out towards the dance floor and guests. James and Dean had planned the way they would direct the seating at the table when they stopped by to check the set up before going to the wedding. Once they were through dancing their way across the room, James would stop at one end of the table and pull out the two seats closest to the center seats Anthony and Kay would occupy for Tia and Randi. Once they were seated, James would take the end seat beside Randi. Dean would do the same with Deanna and Maria on the other end of the table, so they'd leave the two seats in the middle for Anthony and Kay, with Tia and Maria flanking them.

What they weren't expecting was that their boss would take over emcee duties, and instead of just announcing each of their names as they entered the ballroom and started their dance to their seats, he'd channel his inner wrestling ring announcer and rib them all a little.

As the pre-recorded music started, Dean opened the door to escort Deanna inside. They'd barely stepped through the door when Rick's obviously microphone enhanced voice boomed out, "Ladies and gentlemen, entering the ballroom first, standing an inch shorter and weighing in twenty pounds lighter than his wrestling persona, we have Dean Hunter! Beside him is the beautiful best friend of the bride since they met in the sixth grade, Deanna Wolfe!"

"Oh my!" Kay exclaimed with a bark of laughter. "What on earth is Rick doing?"

"He's giving us each our own ring entrance," Tia explained, smiling at her mother.

"I wish we were already in there to see it," Kay pouted, trying to peek through the sliver of space between the doors.

"We can watch the video later," Anthony informed her, signaling to James that it was his and Randi's turn to enter the ballroom.

James grabbed her hand, planning to swing her around the dance floor for their entrance. He didn't know what any of the steps were called, but he'd liked the way she'd taught him a few dance moves at the bachelor and bachelorette party. They were moves she remembered from her cheerleading days that to him resembled some of those ballroom dance competition shows he'd seen on television, and he thought that would be the best entrance for them. He didn't have a chance to start dancing before Rick started announcing again.

"Next into the ballroom, we have the silent but deadly half of the Dangerous Twins, James Hunter!" Rick began, making James laugh as he started his version of a swinging two-step dance across the room with Randi. "Swinging him across the dance floor, we have the sister of the bride, Radiant Randi Lee!"

"I think Rick just gave you your ring name for when you're ready to make your wrestling debut," James told Randi as he pulled her in close to pick her up for a lift and spin.

Randi just laughed as they continued their playful spin around the dance floor. Just before they got across the room to the table to take their seats, the door opened again for Tia and Maria to make their entrance.

"Next up, we have the future women's wrestling champion of the galaxy, Tia 'the Terminator' Burleson!" Rick announced as the girls started their version of a gymnastics floor routine combined with what looked to James like ballet without the painful looking shoes.

"Oh, I hope they know better than to try to do the flips in dress shoes on hardwood floors," Randi grimaced, catching a glimpse of her nieces just before she and James reached the table.

"Accompanying her is her sister, future award-winning artist, Princess Maria Burleson!" Rick announced.

After the girls were through pirouetting, tumbling, and jump-splitting their way across the room, the music changed to a new song for Anthony and Kay. They came in doing their version of a dance that James thought he recognized from a movie, but he wasn't sure.

"Ladies and gentlemen, our guests of honor this evening," Rick announced. "TOPGUN pilot Anthony Ray Burleson and his perky flight attendant wife, Kay Lynn Burleson!"

"Are those your real jobs or just what ya'll will be role playing on your wedding night?" one of the Walker's shouted from the back of the room. James couldn't tell which one from where he was sitting at the head table on the other side of the room.

Several people laughed as "Aiden" was called out by a feminine voice as needing a switch for vulgar talk in a room full of children. Aiden's apology was drowned out by the "oohs" and "awes" of the crowd when Anthony and Kay's dance ended with him lifting her overhead to imitate the airplane he flew for the GWA.

"Wow, I thought for sure Mom would chicken out of doing the lift," Tia commented as she watched her parents finish their dance right in front of the table where the wedding party were sitting.

"Nope." Kay smiled and turned toward Tia once her feet were back on the ground. "No reason to be a chicken when I know Anthony would never drop me."

"A round of applause for the newly married, Mr. and Mrs. Burleson," Rick announced.

The couple took a bow as a cacophony of clapping and whistling erupted throughout the ballroom. They took their seats as Rick brought the wireless microphone to their table for all the toasts and speeches.

Champagne or sparkling grape juice were distributed to everyone assembled, and since neither set of parents were seated at the head table to start the speeches, Randi grabbed the microphone first.

"Good evening, everyone," Randi began, standing from her seat with the microphone in one hand and her champagne glass in the other. "I know it's normally the parents who kick off the toasts and speeches to the bride and groom, but since the bride and groom are the only parents at this table, I figure it's my job as Kay's bratty little sister to get us started tonight."

She paused to allow for the laughter of the crowd. "I've always looked up to my older sister, Kay, even though I now have to sit down to do it since I'm half a foot taller than her. Though I suppose we could just have Anthony carry her around over his head all the time like he did for that dance, so we can all look up to her constantly."

James chuckled with the rest of the audience at Randi's silly suggestion.

"Seriously, though, if there ever was a woman who deserved to be put up on a pedestal and treated like a queen, that woman is Kay. For the last couple of months, every time I've talked to her, Kay has told me how Anthony has done just that, each and every day. It's wonderful to see how happy and in love you are, not just as a couple, but as a family. Here's to your endless happiness and everlasting love. Cheers!"

A chorus of "cheers" went around the room as everyone took a sip of champagne, or sparkling grape juice for those who were underage or chose not to imbibe alcohol for whatever reason.

Randi sat back down, leaned over, and kissed James on the cheek as she handed him the microphone.

Shit, I thought Anthony said I was supposed to give my speech last, James cursed in his head as he looked down at the microphone in his hand. Not knowing who was actually supposed to make the next speech, he stood to go ahead and get his out of the way.

"I know I'm probably doing this out of order, but I figured I'd go ahead while the microphone is at this end of the table, and then pass it down to Dean and Deanna, so they can say a few words." James hoped the microphone didn't slip out of his sweaty palm, and hated that he still got nervous speaking in public, even after years of performing in front of much larger audiences in the wrestling ring. "I've literally known Anthony longer than I can remember. For those of you who aren't from around here to know, Dean and I are five months older than Anthony and five months younger than Becky, so the four of us often ended up in the same playpen or crib whenever our moms would get together when we were all babies."

"Don't forget the same bathtub when you were toddlers who tried to sneak off to play in the mud," Hazel shouted from across the room.

"Mom!" Becky squealed at her mother.

"Not you, just the boys," Hazel corrected loudly while waving her hand at the table where James, Dean, and Anthony were all sitting. "Though you did share a tub with Jen and Julie a couple of times as a toddler."

James stifled his chuckle at his friend Becky's embarrassment and tried to get back on track with his speech. "Anyway, my point is that I've literally known Anthony all his life and all but five months of mine, so I've seen him through all the ups and downs of life. The good, the bad, and the ugly, if you will. And in the twenty-five-plus years that I've known him, I've never seen him as happy as he's been since meeting Kay. Even when outside forces tried to cause trouble for them, the love Anthony and Kay feel for each other was evident in their secret smiles and longing looks at each other."

James turned to look directly at his best friend and his new bride, directing the end of his speech specifically at them. "The love you share is inspiring, and it has been since the moment you met. I wish you infinite happiness in your long lives together." James raised his glass as he turned back to look at the audience. "To Anthony and Kay!"

"To Anthony and Kay," the wedding guests repeated in unison before taking another sip of their drinks.

"Heads up, Bro," James warned into the microphone before tossing it like a football to Dean at the other end of the table.

Luckily, Dean caught it easily without bumping into the woman who was walking behind him to deliver their dinner plates. *Oops!* James thought as he took his seat. *That could've been a mess if Dean didn't have such good reflexes.*

Randi reached over to clasp his hand in hers once he was seated. *Wonder if she realizes I've been trying to always sit on her right side, so we can hold hands while we eat?* James thought as he wrapped his large hand around her small one and focused his attention on her delicate heart-shaped face.

Deanna began her speech, but James didn't hear a word of it. He was too lost looking into Randi's emerald, green eyes. It felt like they were the only two people in the room, communicating their feelings for each other only through their gaze.

Neither of them seemed to notice when their plates were placed in front of them, or when the speakers changed. They'd completely disconnected from the world around them, until Tia elbowed Randi to let her know it was time to drink the next toast.

James tried to reengage with the reception, but he found it hard to focus on anything but Randi. He hoped that he at least looked like he was present in the moment as he went through the motions of eating the meal that he didn't even taste. He was too busy trying to memorize every detail about the beautiful woman at his side, and daydreaming about their own storybook wedding.

Eventually the speeches concluded with the father of the bride instead of starting with him. Kay shrugged it off as a family quirk of doing everything backwards. When their plates were cleared, the band began playing for all the special dances. James loved getting another chance to hold Randi in his arms on the dance floor when the wedding party was invited to join the bride and groom.

Anthony and Kay were way too polite in delicately feeding each other their first piece of wedding cake, at least according to Randi. *I'm gonna have a beard full of icing when we get married,* James thought as he smiled down at her, loving how she was relaxing and showing her mischievous side.

The cake was served while the band played and the dance floor was opened up to everyone. James quickly ate his slice of the five-tiered blue and white confection, so he could get Randi back out on the dance floor. They danced to everything the band played, from the few rock songs they knew to the two step and country line dance songs that James hadn't attempted since high school. But James's favorites were definitely the ballads when he could hold Randi close and have whispered conversations about their plans for later that night.

All too soon, the band took a break from playing, so Kay could toss her bouquet and Anthony could toss Kay's garter. When Randi caught the bouquet, James made sure all his friends knew that they weren't getting a chance to catch the garter and pose for a photo with his woman on their lap. Even though several of them acted like they were ready to fight over the garter, Anthony showed them all the strength of the lifelong friendship he and James had by sling shotting it straight at James.

James had thought he was doing good at only being half hard all night, even with Randi in his arms on the dance floor. But his ability to control his cock was lost the instant Randi sat on his lap for the bouquet and garter photo. She was sitting sideways on his lap with his left arm supporting her back and her right arm around his neck. But instead of sitting on one thigh with her legs draped over the other, she sat with her ass cradled between his thighs, directly on top of his rapidly growing erection. She wiggled her tight little ass on his lap, and his cock stood at full attention, pressing against his zipper, and demanding to be let out to plunder under her dress.

"Angel," James growled in a low warning tone, his lips close to her ear so only she could hear him. "You're being a very naughty girl, getting me hard in front of such a large crowd."

Randi turned her face, so she could whisper in his ear. "Then you'll have to think of a fun way to punish me when we get to your house tonight, Jimmy."

James imagined all the ways he could tie her to his bed and tease her for hours before finally making her come harder than she ever had before. While he enjoyed the fantasy, it didn't help him control the situation in his pants, which would be very embarrassing in a few minutes when the photographer was done getting them to pose just the way he wanted.

The photographer finally positioned the bouquet in Randi's left hand the way he wanted it in her lap, with James's right hand holding the garter over her thigh beside the bouquet, so he could step back and take the pictures. The first one he took with Randi and James still looking into each other's eyes. Then he had them look up at the camera for a second.

Thankfully, looking up at his and Randi's families standing behind the photographer was enough to redirect enough blood flow back to his brain, so he was back to only a half-chub when she jumped off his lap. He was able to stand and hide the evidence of his arousal under the long suit coat of his tuxedo before they were surrounded by family and friends filling up the dance floor again.

They spent the rest of the evening alternating between dancing and interacting with the rest of the guests at the wedding. The Lees waited until after Anthony and Kay left for their three-day honeymoon on Padre Island to approach James and Randi.

Randi stiffened in her seat beside him as her parents approached the table, where they were sitting and talking to his parents. James had been indulging his need to constantly touch her by holding her hand most of the night, and he was glad for that connection to her, when he was able to reassure her that he was there for her with a gentle squeeze that only the two of them noticed.

"Randi," Charles addressed them as he and Mary stopped a couple of feet away from the table. "James, can I have a moment to speak to the two of you privately?"

James looked to Randi for the answer, knowing that he could handle whatever the man had to say either privately or publicly, but wanting Randi to be comfortable with their discussion, if and when it should happen. Her wide, green eyes looked up at him with concern, making him instantly want to say "no," and whisk her away from the ongoing party.

"It's entirely up to you, Angel." James spoke directly to Randi, so she'd know he would support her in whatever decision she made. James watched her expressive face as all her emotions flowed over her features, stoically keeping his eyes on her as she contemplated what she wanted to do. When her expression turned resigned, like she'd decided how she wanted to answer her father, James lifted their joined hands to his lips, kissed the back of her hand, and then nodded at her to show he was there for her no matter what.

Randi turned to look at her parents before speaking. "No, Dad. Anything you have to say to us, you can say here and now."

"Very well." Charles motioned to the two empty chairs to Randi's left, like he was asking permission to sit. When Randi nodded, he pulled out a chair for Mary first before taking his own seat. Once they were both seated, he turned back toward James and Randi. "I owe you both an apology. I'm sorry for the way I've behaved the past few days. I'm having a hard time accepting that my daughters are grown up, and don't need me to take care of them anymore."

Randi opened her mouth as if she was going to say something, but Charles held a hand up to stop her from speaking.

"I know that's no excuse for my behavior," Charles continued in a remorseful tone. "I just want you to know that I understand why I acted out, and I'm working on dealing with all the recent changes in our family dynamics, so that I don't take my irrational feelings out on anyone else again. I am truly sorry for yelling, for trying to control your life, and for not respecting your ability to make your own decisions. I hope you'll be able to forgive me for the last couple of days, when I completely lost my mind."

"Of course, I forgive you." Randi pulled her hand out of James's grasp to lean over and hug her father. "I love you, Daddy."

"I love you, too, baby girl." Charles embraced his daughter.

James wasn't sure what to say, if anything. He wasn't mad at the man for the shit he'd spewed at him because he understood overprotective fathers a lot better after his talk with Rick a couple of days before. He'd been offended on Randi's behalf because the ferocity of the altercation had upset her, and since she forgave her father, James didn't think there was anything more he needed to add before the scene was put behind them.

When Charles and Randi pulled apart, Charles looked James in the eye before saying, "James, I'm sorry for all the things I accused you of the other day. I don't even remember half of what I said, but I know I didn't mean any of it."

"Yeah, I don't remember exactly what was said either," James admitted with a self-deprecating chuckle.

"So, we're good?" Charles implored.

"Like I told you the first time we spoke," James referenced the time when Anthony had called Charles and James put himself in the doghouse with Randi by speaking to him, grinning at Randi before turning back to Charles. "My intention is to make sure Randi is happy. So, if she's good, I'm good."

James shook Charles's hand before making sure his parents and Randi's parents had been formally introduced to each other. They spent another half hour visiting with their parents and filling everyone in on Randi's new job.

Charles made a face when Randi mentioned needing to go back to Charlotte's house to pick up her things to take them to James's cabin where she would be staying until flying out on Monday morning with the GWA, but he quickly covered it, so Randi didn't see her father's uncertainty about her being intimate with James. James knew it would take the man time to get used to having an adult daughter, who most definitely didn't fit in the virginal mold he wanted her in. So, he let Charles's momentary show of disapproval go, not wanting to rock the already shaky boat they'd boarded that night.

He had much better things to do right then, specifically getting Randi back to his house, so he could tie her up and taste every inch of her.

Chapter Eighteen

Randi floated on cloud nine after spending most of the rest of the weekend in bed with James. When she'd playfully suggested he punish her for arousing him at the wedding, she'd envisioned a light spanking before a hard fucking. But she had to admit that his idea of punishment was much better than hers.

He'd pulled several old ties from the back of his closet and used them to tie her up and blindfold her for hour after hour of erotic torture. She still wasn't sure what all he'd used to tease her in ways she'd never even imagined. He'd touched and kissed her everywhere, but in addition to his hands and mouth, he'd also used things that tickled and things that felt sharp, a little pokey but not painful. He found erogenous zones on her body that she didn't even know she possessed.

He worked her up to the edge of orgasm over and over, backing off, or switching implements, just in time to keep her from coming. At first it was frustrating, but as he altered the sensations, and found new ways to play her body like an instrument that only he could master playing, Randi had embraced that constantly-on-the-verge feeling. It was euphoric, even before he made her beg for what she wanted, and gave her the most explosive orgasm she'd ever experienced with the first plunge of his hard shaft inside her wet, quivering core.

She wasn't sure if it was one hour-long intense orgasm, or a hundred climaxes building on top of each other with each stroke of his cock into her pussy, but it was an other-worldly experience. She'd floated outside of her body for quite a while, not even remembering him untying her or carrying her into the shower to clean her up from all the liquids he'd covered her with and extracted from her body.

She'd revived for round two in the shower, then took extra time with her nightly routine while he changed the sheets, so they could sleep without being covered in the sticky mess they'd made on the first set.

They'd only left the bed on Sunday long enough to replenish their fluids, fuel up for the next round, and for her to see her family and friends off as they returned to Tulsa and Wichita. They wouldn't have taken as long of a break to go to the ranch before everyone left, if it wasn't for the fact that she and Amy needed to talk about their housing situation with them each starting new jobs.

Amy had accepted a job at Burleson Incorporated, and was only going back to Tulsa to turn in and work out her two-week notice at her old company. Then she was planning to pack up all her stuff and rent a truck to move to Heart's Destiny. Since Randi felt like it was a waste of money for her to pay rent and utilities on a house she wouldn't even see for at least three-hundred-and-twenty days a year, she planned to spend part of her Christmas vacation packing up her own things to put in storage, until she decided where she wanted to live when she wasn't traveling for work. Amy was going to give their landlord their thirty-day notice on the first of December when she paid their last month's rent.

James had suggested that she split the cost of the rental truck with Amy and move in with him, but Randi didn't want to risk the tentative peace they'd reached with her father within the first twenty-four hours by announcing that she and James were basically living together while not married. While she had every intention of sharing a hotel room with him nightly, her parents were still under the assumption that she'd have her own room. And until her father had completely come to terms with the fact that she was a grown woman and capable of living her life however she pleased, she didn't want to disabuse him of that notion.

She wasn't sure the not quite four weeks she'd be working before going back to Tulsa on her Christmas break would be enough time for her father to be ready to help her load her stuff into a truck to move in with James either. But she had a feeling it would be more than enough time for James to change her mind about putting her stuff in storage. Especially since he and Dean had spent their entire ride into San Antonio to the airport talking about how they could get James's truck to the Tulsa airport for them to have to drive during the Christmas break because James was planning to spend the break with her in Tulsa.

Randi had no idea where he'd sleep the five days she was scheduled to be at her parents' cabin in River's End. *Too bad we're basically staying on the east coast between now and then,* Randi thought, looking at the schedule she'd been given when she boarded the plane. *If we had a day in Vegas before our Christmas break, James and I could get married, so Mom and Dad wouldn't have a problem with him sharing my room.*

"I'm really impressed with how well your medication is working." James grinned at her from his aisle seat beside her. "Not only are you not freaking out, but you're actually smiling while flying."

I probably shouldn't tell him it's not the flight that has me smiling, Randi mentally giggled. *After telling him to wait a year or so to propose, telling him that I'm thinking about getting married within the next month would probably confuse him and make him think it's okay to rush the proposal. And I really do think I need at least a few months to make sure we're a hundred percent compatible before I'll really be ready to get married.*

"Yeah, I was shocked at how well it worked, even with the layover in Dallas last week," Randi finally replied, so the silence didn't stretch too long. "And it's even better today knowing that I only have to take the one flight. But I still think I'd get sick if I tried to ride backwards like Dean."

"One thing at a time, Angel," James chuckled. "Give it a little while working on your anxiety before we test it on any potential motion sickness from flying in a rear-facing seat."

"There are plenty of us who like facing the back of the plane," Dean chimed in from his seat across from James. "So, you won't ever have to risk getting sick if you don't want to."

"And even if the guys revert to their normal jackass personas, I'll always make sure you never have to sit in a seat that would make you uncomfortable," James reassured her, raising their joined hands to his lips, so he could kiss the back of her hand.

Even with her meds working for her flight anxiety, Randi was glad to have him by her side to hold his hand, especially during take-off and landing. She'd noticed that anytime they were seated somewhere, James sat to her right side and held her hand throughout whatever they were doing. She wasn't sure if he'd consciously done that, realizing that she was left-handed and he was right-handed, so they could still use their dominant hands while holding hands or not, but she liked how it had quickly become their thing.

She was brought out of her musings by the group of people across the aisle getting louder in their discussion about the identity of one of the wedding guests.

"I'm telling you, Jana, that's the missing heiress." One of the women pointed to her phone as she showed it to the woman sitting across from her.

"They do look a little bit alike, but the woman who checked into the B and B right before the wedding had black hair and brown eyes," Jana replied, pointing to an image on her own phone for her friend. "Brooklyn Barns has blonde hair and blue eyes, so I don't think she's hiding out in a small Texas town and using an alias."

"Wait, are ya'll talking about the woman Mom coaxed into coming to the reception, instead of trying to walk into town for dinner since her car broke down?" Dean inquired of the women on the other side of the plane.

"Yes." Jana turned her phone toward them, so Randi, James, and Dean could see a picture of the missing heiress from Georgia. "Emily claims that she's actually this missing woman, but I think they just have some similar features, but are two completely different people."

Emily turned her phone toward them next, putting it side by side with Jana's, so they could see pictures of both women.

"Oh my Dog! They do look alike," Randi exclaimed, pointing back and forth between the photos. "You think she dyed her hair and put in colored contacts to change her appearance?"

"Yes," Emily shouted, pumping a fist in the air in excitement at their sleuthing skills. "Not only that, but she introduced herself to us as Brie Brooks, a children's book author. And the missing woman's name is Brooklyn Brielle Barns. Brooklyn. Brooks. Brielle. Brie. Seems like a play on her own name for a pen name that she's now using as an alias to me."

"Definitely," Randi agreed, nodding her head. "Wow, I wish I would've gotten a chance to talk to her at the reception. I'm dying to know what's really going on with her soap opera like story."

"Me, too!" Emily contradicted her statement by shaking her head. "But I chickened out of flat out asking her who she really is."

"You think we should message Bobby, so he can look into her situation?" James arched an eyebrow, looking at Dean.

"I don't know," Dean shrugged his shoulders. "I mean, she didn't really look like she'd been kidnapped since she was there alone. Obviously, we'd call him if she looked like she was being held against her will, but with changing her appearance and trying to hide in a small town, I don't know. It's not really against the law to run away from home, ya know."

"You're talking about Anthony's brother, the police officer?" Jeff asked, from his seat beside his wife, Jana.

"The police chief, actually," James corrected. "And obviously, he wouldn't arrest her for running away from her fucked up family situation, but maybe he could help her shut down the media circus, and guide her through the legal channels needed to keep from being forced to marry that old dude."

"You're probably right." Dean pulled out his phone like he was going to call Bobby right then.

"Don't you have to wait until we land to call him?" Randi pointed to Dean's phone, thinking it was kinda hard to make a phone call while on a plane with no cell service.

"Yeah, there's no cell service in the air, but the plane has Wi-Fi, so I can pull a few links on the story and email him," Dean told Randi before turning to Jana and Emily and asking them to email him the photos they had of Brie from the wedding reception.

Randi made a mental note to ask Kay for an update from her new brother-in-law when she joined them on tour, as she leaned back in her seat to enjoy the rest of the flight into Tampa to start her new job. *Not just a new job,* Randi mused. *A whole new life!*

~~~

James loved being able to show Randi the ropes of life with the GWA, guiding her through the airports, car rental, and hotel check-in procedures before driving her to the arena in downtown Tampa for her first day of work. Instead of staying near the airport, or the arena, like
~~~

they did in most cities, the GWA crew was booked into a hotel near the local amusement park, so the families who wanted to take advantage of the midday time off would have easy access. James was glad for the location of the hotel because that put him closer to the adult toy store he'd looked up online the night before, so it was easy to make a pit stop there on the way to the arena after lunch and weight training at the hotel.

"Why are you pulling in here?" Randi looked around from the passenger seat in the SUV he'd rented at the airport as he pulled into The Todd and parked. "Aren't we supposed to go to the arena early for some training time before work?"

"We're still gonna have plenty of time to train in the ring before you have to start working," James assured her, kissing the back of her hand that he'd been holding on their drive before getting out of the vehicle and walking around to open her door for her. "But I thought we might pick up a couple of things to celebrate your first day on the job."

He grinned suggestively as he took her hand again and walked her into the store.

"Oh!" Randi's mouth formed an O and her eyes widened as they walked in the door.

"Don't look so nervous, Angel." James smiled down at the adorable woman by his side. "We don't have to try anything you're not interested in. I just thought it would be fun to walk through the store and get ideas of what you might like. Maybe buy a couple of the ones you like most. But we don't have to buy anything if you don't want. No pressure, we're just looking around."

"Oh, no." Randi shook her head as they walked down the first aisle of lubricants and sensual oils. "I've just never been in a place like this, so it's a bit overwhelming to see so many, um, things, all at once. But I know you'd never pressure me into doing something I don't wanna do."

"Good." James brought her hand up to his lips for another kiss.

"We should probably look at some of this," Randi suggested, waving her free hand at the shelf of lube, and blushing slightly. "So, we can do more of what we did in the back of your truck the other day."

Leah Mae Wright

"Mmm-hmm, I like the way you think, Angel," James agreed, trying desperately not to let his cock go past half-mast as he remembered playing with her tight little asshole in the bed of his truck.

Fuck, why fight it? I'm probably not the only guy sporting wood in this room. I just have to make sure it goes down before the guys show up in the ring for rehearsals.

They looked at a few different bottles and debated whether or not they needed a flavored lube before deciding on a couple to try. They moved around to the next aisle and Randi's eyes became saucer sized when she saw the variety of butt plugs.

"No," Randi vehemently objected, shaking her head, and pointing to an extra-large one that James didn't think could ever realistically be used by a human being. "Just. No."

"Yeah, I think we can skip this aisle for now," James laughed, lightly pulling her around to the next aisle. "I'd rather just use my fingers to get you ready for my cock."

After an aisle of rubber phalluses that Randi referred to as "clown cocks" because of the multitude of colors available, they finally made it to the area of the store that James had most wanted to explore with Randi. On one side of the aisle was a variety of small vibrators and clitoral stimulators that were designed to be used while going out on a date, or otherwise in public, and came with remote controls. The other side of the aisle showcased the various tools for sensation play while a partner was bound and blindfolded.

Considering how much Randi had enjoyed their sensation play Saturday night, when he'd had to make do with his old ties and various household objects to tease her, James felt Randi would be most interested in the various items there. While nothing on the shelves there would replace the soda he'd sipped from her navel, or the warm chocolate and caramel sauces he'd licked from her nipples, he imagined the Wartenberg wheel would certainly be more erotically enticing than the pen cap he'd scraped across her skin to give her just a hint of sharpness in the spectrum of pleasure and pain.

"Which of these things did you use on me the other night?" Randi motioned towards the sensation play toys.

"None," James admitted as he moved to stand behind her, where she was looking closely at the display of items ranging from blindfolds and feathers to floggers, paddles, and various electrical stimulation devices. He wrapped his arms around her middle and rested his chin on her shoulder, so he could whisper in her ear, wanting only her to hear his confession about his ingenuity on Saturday night. "I had to improvise with a microfiber duster I hadn't ever used to clean the house, instead of a feather. And I used the cap off a ballpoint pen and the edge of my debit card to give you the sensation of knife play. I don't ever wanna actually use knives, but I thought you might like one of these wheels."

His voice trailed off as he pointed to the Wartenberg wheels off to the right of where they were standing with one finger. "Or maybe some of these other things look more appealing to you?"

"Yeah, we can definitely try one of those wheels," Randi confirmed his suspicion of what she'd enjoyed previously, speaking in that sexy, breathy tone he loved, which never failed to arouse him as she relaxed back into his embrace. "And maybe one of those floggers instead of a feather? I've read a few books that mention them and how they can be used in different ways to be either soft and tickly or harder and right on the verge of painful."

"I'll have to watch some how-to videos and practice to make sure I give you the sensations you want without actually hurting you with one of those." James looked at the colorful variety of floggers to the left side of the display. "But I'm more than willing to try anything you want, Angel."

Randi reached up and ran a hand through the strips of leather and rubber on the end of a couple of the floggers. James released his hold on her as she stepped down the aisle to feel several others. He watched her face as she tactilely made her selection for what she wanted them to try. He could tell when she found the one she liked best based solely on her expression.

Once she'd placed it in the basket with the lube they'd already picked out, she moved over to pick out a wheel, a small box of candles, and a blindfold. *Fuck, tonight's gonna be fun,* James mentally exclaimed as they turned to look at the other side of the aisle.

"So, um, are these for you to use on me while I'm tied up, too?" Randi perused the collection of butterfly vibrators and clitoral stimulators that mimicked a sucking mouth.

"They can be," James offered, stepping back up behind her, unable to fight off his need to touch her a moment longer. "Or for you to put in your panties when we get to the arena, so I can tease you anytime we're close enough for the remote to activate the toy of your choice while we're working."

Randi shivered in his arms and James didn't think it was because she was cold. "Like that idea, Angel?" James's warm breath caressed her neck as he spoke.

"Yes, but maybe not on my first day on the job," Randi confessed, breathlessly.

They picked out one of each of the small devices to see which Randi preferred in the future before moving on through the store. They browsed through the lingerie section of the store, picking out a few bra-and-thong sets for Randi to tempt him with by wearing them under her prim and proper wardrobe.

When they reached the back of the store, James turned to walk up to the checkout, knowing he didn't need a penis pump or blow-up doll, which was all he'd seen on the back wall. Randi stopped him from taking more than one step toward the front of the store by grabbing his hand and dragging him down the last aisle.

"If you get to tease me at work with the remote-control toys we've already picked out, then I need to be able to tease you at work with one of these." Randi pointed to the display of vibrating cock rings in the back corner of the store.

"Angel, I'm not sure how I'm gonna hide my hard-on from being in the same room with you in my wrestling tights as it is," James protested. "There's no way I could keep the guys from noticing if you teased me with one of these, too."

Randi looked up at him, grinning and giggling. *Fuck, how can I object to anything she wants to do when the idea makes her that happy?* He looked over the various options in front of them and grabbed the largest one with a remote control, resigned to the fact that he'd suffer any embarrassment for the woman at his side.

"How about we just use this one on the plane?" Randi suggested as they made their way up to pay for their purchases. "That way it's not as obvious as it would be in your wrestling tights."

"I'll use it anytime you want, Angel," James agreed, pecking her lips with his as they got in line to check out. "But the one I picked looks like it will also stimulate you if I wear it while I'm buried inside you, so maybe not *only* on the plane." He emphasized the word "only," so she would know he intended to use it when he fucked her that night.

"Oh, I can't wait to see how that works," Randi practically purred, wrapping her arms around his neck and pulling him down for another kiss, which was probably a little more impassioned than appropriate for a public setting.

"Next," the store clerk called out, sounding a little irritated that they were making out in his store.

"Sorry," James apologized as he stepped up to the counter and started placing their purchases on it to be rung up.

"No worries, man," the cashier chuckled as he looked down at Randi blushing by James's side. "If I had a woman that pretty, I'd have a hard time controlling the PDA, too."

Randi's blush deepened at the cashier's words and James felt a slight twinge of jealousy at someone else eliciting that response from her. It quickly dissipated as she laced their fingers together and looked up at him with a smile.

He kept his eyes locked on hers while the clerk scanned their items, trying to convey without words the reassurance she needed that their public display wasn't shameful like she'd been taught in her teenage years. If hearing that she was desirable from more than just him was necessary to rid her of her unwarranted guilt, he'd hold his jealousy at bay, so she could receive those roundabout compliments from random strangers once in a while.

James finally looked away from Randi and made eye contact with the clerk when the other man gave them their total. He pulled his wallet from his back pocket to get out his card to pay for their purchases, just as the clerk and Randi blurted "holy shit," "holy shit," in unison.

He looked at Randi to see that her eyes were bugged out from looking at the total on the cash register at the same time the clerk gushed out, "You're James Dangerous! Holy shit, I can't believe you're here in my store. I have tickets to see you wrestle tonight."

Any objections Randi wanted to vocalize about him spending several hundred dollars on sex toys were drowned out by requests for autographs from not only the clerk, but also a few customers and other employees of the store. James swiped his card and signed the credit card reader with his real name first before taking a marker from the clerk to sign a few slips of paper, a couple of shirts, and even a cellphone case with his James Dangerous moniker before they left the store.

"Does that happen often?" Randi questioned the experience once they were back in the SUV with their bag of toys in the back seat.

"What?" James hoped she wasn't imagining him buying sex toys with another woman before he met her. While he'd played around with a few things in the past, they'd always been things the woman brought with her on their one-night stand, and never anything that James had purchased.

He'd been honest with Randi when he'd told her about the random hookups in his past, and knew that she'd questioned his fidelity to her at first because of it. He hoped his comfort level in the adult store didn't trigger her to question his honesty about his sexual history, or how special their relationship was to him.

"Being recognized and mobbed for autographs," Randi finally explained, relieving him of his fear that she was having doubts about them.

"Oh, um, yeah," James admitted with a shrug. "I guess, maybe a couple times a week. Usually in the restaurant or club we go to after a show. Sometimes in the hotel. But I don't normally get recognized while shopping, unless I go to a mall somewhere near a college where I'll be surrounded by our major demographic of eighteen- to twenty-five-year-olds."

"So, that's the first time you've been recognized while shopping for sex toys?" Randi blushed, the corners of her mouth turning up in a shy smile.

"Well, since that's the first time I've ever been shopping for sex toys," James gladly admitted, reaching over to hold her hand while he drove toward the arena. "Yeah, that was definitely the first time I've been recognized and asked for an autograph in an adult store."

"I thought that one woman was gonna lift her shirt and ask you to sign her bra," Randi giggled.

"Yeah, that's only happened a couple of times," James chuckled, remembering more than one indecent autograph request he and Dean had received when they first got started wrestling. "And only in bars so far."

"Oh, I bet you've been asked to sign more than bras while hanging out in bars after work." Randi was still smiling, even though her laughter had died down at the reminder of how much he'd partied before meeting her.

"You would definitely win that bet," James confirmed, shaking his head at the memories. "But one of the first lessons we learned when we started working with the GWA was to never sign body parts."

"Really?" Randi looked confused by the rule James still followed. "Why?"

"Prevents any potential legal issues," James shrugged before filling her in on all the reasons someone could sue him for signing his autograph on their body. "It's ridiculous to think about how litigious our society has become, but I don't wanna be sued for someone being allergic to the ink, or risk jail time or the sex offender registry, if the girl who asked me to sign her boob is underage. That's why even when I'm asked to sign someone's shirt, I only sign them when they aren't being worn."

"You know I thought it was weird when you said that in the store, but figured it was because you wanted to put them on the counter, so you had a hard surface to write on." Randi's expression turned quizzical. "What was up with those people carrying an extra shirt around in their bags?"

"No clue," James chortled, shaking his head, not wanting to think about the lives of the fans that required them to carry extra clothes throughout the day. "Maybe they have jobs like we do and need to change clothes a couple times a day? I hadn't ever thought about it, since I normally only sign shirts when people have just bought them at our merchandise table in the arena."

They spent the rest of the trip discussing their plans for the rest of the day. They would go change into workout clothes as soon as they got to the arena, so they could spend some time in the ring with James training Randi on how to run the ropes and reviewing the basic bumps he'd gone over with her and Tia the previous weekend. If they had time before the guys arrived for rehearsals and Randi had to go report for her first day on the job, he'd start teaching her basic maneuvers and how to choreograph a match.

They planned to break from work at the same time to eat dinner in catering together, but James was mostly looking forward to after the show was over, when they went back to the hotel for the night. He'd stashed the extra ties he'd used to tie her to his bed in his suitcase and couldn't wait to use them and the new toys they'd purchased to give them a night they'd never forget.

Fuck! I have to quit thinking about all the kinky things I wanna do with her tonight in our hotel room, or I'll never make it through wrestling tonight without embarrassing myself with an obvious boner in my tights. It's gonna take every ounce of self-control I possess to compartmentalize my desire for her and keep it locked down while we're at work. But I'm not gonna risk both our jobs by behaving in an unprofessional manner while we're in the arena.

Breathe. Focus on your job. Think of Randi as a coworker and treat her accordingly. Keep your fucking hands to yourself. You are now James Dangerous, not James Hunter. Only James Hunter can touch Randi, so you can't treat her like your girlfriend while you're James Dangerous.

Fuck! I hope I can maintain a professional distance from her until we get back to the hotel and I can be myself again with the woman I love.

<div align="center">~~~</div>

Randi had a great first day at work with the GWA. She'd known she would enjoy her new job before she'd even interviewed for it, but the reality of working with the GWA was way better than she'd envisioned. Everyone was super friendly and welcoming on the plane that morning, even the people she'd just met that day because they hadn't been in Heart's Destiny for the wedding.

After the smooth flight into Tampa, she'd spent the midday with James. They had lunch at the hotel, spent some time in the hotel weight room, and grabbed a snack before leaving the hotel to go to the arena.

The extra stop he'd made on the way to the arena at the sex toy shop had been a surprise, but one she'd most definitely enjoyed. She couldn't wait to play with their new toys, even though she wasn't sure how she'd made it through everyone who'd asked for James's autograph seeing what they bought without dying of embarrassment.

Once they got to the arena, they'd both quickly changed clothes (again) to head to the ring for her first actual in-ring training to become a professional wrestler. It took a few tries for her to get the timing right to run the ropes the way James instructed her to, but she eventually got the hang of it. She'd remembered everything he'd already taught her about taking bumps and was able to demonstrate them for him with perfect form.

She knew she'd be a lot more sore after taking those bumps in the ring than she'd been from learning them on the thick mats James had put down in his home gym to originally teach them to her and Tia. Not only was the ring a lot harder than she expected, but the ropes were also stiff and painful to run into. When she showered and changed clothes after their training session to get ready for work, she noticed rope shaped bruises lightly forming on her side from slamming her body into them so many times while learning how to run across the ring.

The adrenaline rush she got from being in the ring and learning the first few moves was more than enough to offset any residual discomfort she had from the physicality of the training. It was better than any runners high she'd ever gotten from training for other activities in the past. She didn't think anything would be able to wipe the smile off her face at how happy she was learning her new craft.

Her new boss had even commented on her perpetual smile when they were sitting in catering on their dinner break. "If she's constantly smiling like that in the ring, we'll never be able to book her as a heel to team up with you," Rick had told James.

"Sure we can, Boss," James had replied, grinning at her. "She can either be the over-the-top super bubbly cheerleader that annoys the shit out of everyone, or we can book her as a psycho who grins when normal people would grimace, and laughs in her opponent's face while they're beating on each other."

They'd all laughed before going back to work, but the conversation had caused Randi to start thinking about what kind of character she wanted to portray as her wrestling persona. The perky cheerleader that James had suggested would be an easy role for her, since that's what she'd been all through high school and college. But she kinda wanted to go against the ingrained role and show her acting range by playing the badass biker babe supporting her man and fighting dirty.

Her first day of work had actually been pretty easy. Rick had handed her a tablet with a schedule for the show that night and introduced her to the other production assistant, Joel Baker. Joel had then shown her how to go through the schedule to determine what needed to be set up for each match. If the wrestlers needed some gimmicked props for specific spots in their matches, they were noted on the schedule beside their match.

While the wrestlers were rehearsing for their matches, Randi's job was to go through the list of props and make sure they were all in place prior to the doors opening for fans coming into the arena to watch the show that night. That meant that she got to watch as the performers rehearsed, and as soon as they were done practicing what they needed with their props, she'd make sure the props were put back where they needed to be for the actual show that night, usually under the ring or somewhere at ringside.

They took their dinner break once everything was in place. She'd enjoyed eating dinner with James, even though he hadn't held her hand all through it like he had when they'd sat together at the rehearsal dinner and wedding. She chalked up the lack of affectionate touching to maintaining a sense of professionalism while they were working, and tried not to feel hurt by the loss of contact.

After dinner, Randi followed Joel as they did a final walk through of the area around the ring, double checking that everything was either under the ring or in its place at ringside. The rest of the night was spent backstage, keeping track of who was performing in each match, that they were sticking to their allotted performance time, and alerting the next performers when it was time for them to go to the gorilla position to make their ring entrances for their turn in the ring.

Since it wasn't a televised show, the wrestlers hadn't worn the extra parts of their costumes, like the Dangerous Twins' leather jackets, that the production assistants would be responsible for taking backstage during a televised show. Joel had still shown her how to get to the area under the stage to be able to go down to ringside beside the ramp, instead of walking on it like the wrestlers did. So, she knew where to go and how to sneak in and out of the ringside area the next night, when she'd be the one clearing the costumes from the ringside area without detracting from the performance going on in the ring.

While it wouldn't be the same as actually performing on the show, Randi was looking forward to all the running back and forth between the ring and the backstage area. She'd even texted Amy to tell her to watch to see if her friend could spot her on TV the next day.

She was still feeling wired from the excitement of the show when she and James got back to their hotel room that night. Thankfully, they'd chosen to share a room, so Randi knew how she'd be working off her excess energy to be able to wind down to be able to go to sleep later.

Knowing what was coming didn't help her feel any less awkward as she waited for him to initiate their intimate evening. It wasn't that the silence between them was unpleasant. Randi actually liked the fact that they didn't have to constantly chatter on about nothing just to fill the space with noise. It was nice to feel comfortable being quiet with someone.

The reason she felt awkward was because it was her first night of hotel life, and it was throwing her off of her normal routine. Randi felt a little silly asking James what her new nightly schedule should consist of, so she watched him for clues as to what she should be doing. It was uncomfortable for her because she really just wanted to rip their clothes off and climb him like a tree, begging him to fuck her against every flat surface in the room, but she wasn't mentally prepared to be that sexually aggressive, even with James.

As soon as they got back to the room, James was focused on rearranging the things in his various bags to make sure he had all his dirty clothes in a bag to be laundered at the next hotel and clean items in the bags he'd take to the arena the next day. It felt like he was still maintaining that professional distance between them, even after they'd left the arena and were alone in their room.

She'd expected him to be more insistent about taking her to bed first thing when they got back to the room, so when he didn't, Randi sat quietly on the bed, just watching him, unsure what she should be doing. After a couple of minutes of feeling lost, she decided she should probably follow his lead, and put her dirty gym clothes in with his for the laundry, and put clean gym clothes in the small bag he'd insisted she carry to the arena for the next day.

She hung the hotel towel, which she'd taken to the arena to use when she rinsed her workout sweat off before work, on the towel rack in the bathroom. Since she didn't wash her hair twice a day and knew she'd never have time to redo it after a shower in the arena, she only had to make sure she had one of the small bottles that she'd bought and divided her bodywash into in the bag with her clean workout clothes for the next day. She'd wait to get a clean towel at the hotel in Orlando to put in the bag for after her workout the next day.

She was done long before James, who was still sorting out his wrestling gear and gimmick wear when she was finished prepping for the next day. She wasn't sure if she should go ahead and go through her nightly rituals to get ready for bed, or if she should wait until after he was done with everything else, so they could have sex first.

Never having spent the night with anyone other than James, Randi hadn't ever had to figure out how to mesh her routine with that of her significant other before. And the few nights she'd spent with James in the last week, he'd taken the lead to guide her through combining their daily domestic tasks.

I guess his first night back, he's just instinctively going about his normal routine, Randi thought as she leaned against the bathroom doorway watching him. *He's not used to sharing his space with anyone else, so he doesn't realize I need him to help me make "his routine" into "our routine," or at least act like he knows I'm here, and give me some indication that we still have plans for playing with our new toys tonight.*

Great, now I'm even sounding clingy and needy in my own head. I'm not a narcissist that needs his undivided attention twenty-four-seven. At least I don't wanna be that kind of woman, Randi decided as she started to turn to go into the bathroom to start on her normal bedtime routine.

I know he's had just as long of a day as I have, so I'm sure he needs some time and space to wind down, too. I'll just go do my thing and let him do his. And when he's ready to have sex again, I'm sure he'll let me know.

"I can hear you thinking from way over here." James finally broke the silence, just before Randi took that first step into the bathroom.

Randi stopped in her tracks, but didn't turn back to face him. She didn't know how to reply to his statement since he hadn't actually asked her what she was thinking. *Not that I wanna tell him how bratty my thoughts were anyway.*

"You okay, Angel?" James wrapped his arms around her from behind, surprising her in how quietly he'd walked across the room.

"Yeah," Randi squeaked, hating that her uncertainty was evident in her unsteady voice.

"Then what's got you so deep in thought tonight?" James's warm breath blew across her ear and sent tingles throughout her body.

Randi shrugged, feeling silly for her childlike thoughts and need for guidance, when she should be able to figure it all out for herself at twenty-five years old. She knew age play wasn't her kink, but she didn't know another analogy to use to explain her need for a guide in the new world she found herself in.

I'll sound like an utterly helpless idiot if I tell him I need him to give me instructions for what I'm supposed to do each night when we get back to the hotel.

"Talk to me, Angel," James implored, pulling her back into his hard body. "I can't fix whatever's bothering you if you don't tell me what it is."

"I feel stupid," Randi admitted, closing her eyes, unable to handle seeing his response to what she was about to say.

"You're not stupid." James kissed the top of her head.

"I was so hyped up all day," Randi choked out, still keeping her eyes tightly shut. "Then when we got here, I expected that excess energy to be channeled into intense bedroom activities."

"And when I didn't immediately toss you on the bed and have my way with you, you had an adrenaline crash," James finished her thought in a way she hadn't expected.

"Yeah, I guess," Randi admitted. "I just feel lost. Confused. Not sure what I'm supposed to do."

"You don't have to do anything, Angel." James rested his cheek on the top of her head.

"Yeah, I do," Randi protested, turning in his embrace to look up into his steel-gray eyes. "I can't just sit still and do nothing. Even when I'm sitting and watching TV, I have to be doing something else to feel productive. And watching you, I was able to figure out that I needed to get my stuff ready for tomorrow. But once that was done, I was right back to being lost because I don't know the schedule for the rest of the night."

"There's not a schedule for the rest of the night, Angel," James chuckled. "We're free to do whatever we want until nine a.m. tomorrow, when we're supposed to head to the airport."

"Yeah, I know that, James." Randi's words came out in a huff because she was exasperated at not knowing how to explain her frustration to James. "But I thought we still had a plan for what we were gonna do when we got back to the hotel. But you seem to be following what I assume is your normal routine when you get to your hotel room each night, instead of what I thought we were planning when we went shopping this afternoon, and I have no idea where I fit into that routine. I mean, am I supposed to strip, dig into our goody bag to start playing by myself, and wait for you to notice? Or should I go ahead and wash my face, brush my teeth, and get ready for bed while you go about your nightly routine, and wait for toy time when we haven't had such a long day? I'm good either way. I just need to know the plan, so I can get into a normal routine and not feel lost."

"Oh, Angel," James crooned, squeezing her to him in a tight hug. "I'm sorry. I didn't mean to make you feel lost. I was just trying to get everything ready for tomorrow, so I could spend the rest of the night and as long as possible tomorrow morning balls-deep inside you, without risking being late for our flight or unprepared for work."

Randi started to open her mouth to tell him that she understood that, but she didn't get a chance to say anything as he continued explaining his behavior since they arrived at the arena earlier that day.

"I realized on the way to work that I had to separate my feelings for you from our time in the arena, or I'd never be able to get through the day. It was extremely hard to control my natural response to being in the same room with you." James pressed his erection into her belly to emphasize the meaning behind his words. "I mean, *extremely hard*," placing extra emphasis on the last two words, so Randi understood his double entendre.

"I basically had to pretend I'm two people and get into character as James Dangerous, to whom you are completely off limits, so I could act professionally, and not like a teenager with an uncontrollable hard-on. I guess I didn't leave the character at the arena like I should have. I should've been back to being your man, James Hunter, holding your hand on the drive and kissing you the instant we were alone. I'm sorry I didn't think about it being your first night on the road and a new routine for you. I should've explained what I was doing and filled you in on the plan, so you wouldn't have felt lost. I can't promise I won't screw up like that again, but I will try to keep you better informed, so you don't ever feel off kilter like that again."

Before Randi could respond to his statement, James covered her mouth with his, kissing her like he needed her more than he needed air to breathe. He picked her up and carried her over to the bed, where he'd dropped their bag of goodies earlier. By the time he broke the kiss to put her down and start stripping off their clothes, Randi had forgotten what she was going to say.

Any minor feelings of being ignored, or neglected, were quickly banished from Randi's mind by the intense desire she saw in James's gaze as he devoured her with his eyes.

"Fuck, Angel," James groaned, trailing open mouthed kisses down the column of her neck as he picked her up to carry her onto the bed. She wrapped her arms around his neck and her legs around his waist as he walked on his knees to the center of the king-sized bed. He laid her down, covering her body with his own and kissing his way back up to her ear. "I know we were planning to play with all our new toys tonight, but they're gonna have to wait for round two. I need to be inside you too bad to take my time with them right now."

"Oh, yes, Jimmy," Randi replied just before he fused their mouths and bodies together.

It was a tight fit as he burrowed his cock into her channel, but even without foreplay she was wet enough that it wasn't painful in any way. He took his time working her open for his deep penetration, but Randi didn't mind the first few minutes being slow, sensual lovemaking. She knew James could only maintain that gentle rhythm for a short time. Needing the same passion and intensity that she craved, he would soon be driving into her with a wild abandon that would take them both over the edge to oblivion.

"Fuck, Angel, you're so, fucking, tight. So, fucking, wet. So, fucking, perfect."

James continued talking dirty the whole time, even when Randi was too breathless from multiple orgasms to form coherent thoughts, much less words. They maintained eye contact in a way that felt like their souls were connecting as much as their bodies. Randi couldn't tell where she ended and James began, truly feeling like they were one being as they exploded in a simultaneous climax.

They clung together for several long moments as they floated back down to earth and caught their breath.

"Wow," Randi breathlessly breathed out the word, unable to describe how wonderful being with James felt in any other way.

"Wow, indeed, Angel," James chuckled as he picked her up and carried her to the bathroom.

He proceeded to clean her up from head to toe, just as he had the previous two nights when Randi had stayed with him at his cabin. Once their shower was over, he dried her off and detangled her hair before having her brush her teeth, wash her face, and do anything else she needed to do for her nightly routine. Then he scooped her up into his arms to carry her back to their bed to look over their new toys, and pick a couple to play with during round two.

They didn't manage to get out the ties for him to tie her down while he administered another night of erotic torture, but after sanitizing everything they'd bought, they did find a couple of things they both quite enjoyed.

"We're gonna have to try the rest another night, Angel," James declared after a couple of hours.

"No," Randi protested, even though she was struggling to keep her eyes open after their long day traveling, working, and playing.

"We don't have to do it all in one night," James chuckled as he put everything back in the bag and set it on the floor beside the bed. "We have the rest of our lives to try something new every night, Angel."

"Mmm, I like the sound of that," Randi agreed as she succumbed to slumber. "The rest of our lives together sounds pretty nice."

"Yes, it does." James laid back down and pulled his sleeping beauty into his arms.

Chapter Nineteen

Friday, December 14, 2018

After almost three weeks of traveling with the GWA, Randi was comfortable with her schedule and enjoying her job. She'd had to reschedule her therapy sessions for earlier in the day, instead of her previous four o'clock times, so she could do them in the hotel room and start working at four each afternoon. But Kelly hadn't had a problem with doing that, especially when she saw such a dramatic improvement in Randi's anxiety issues and confidence level from how happy she was in her new career.

She took that hour once a week when James was in the weight room to talk to her therapist about everything that had happened with her parents, how her relationship with James was going, and how she was opening up and no longer repressing her sexuality as her parents had raised her to do. Randi had even worked out a plan with her therapist about how she was going to handle seeing her parents again at Christmas.

Instead of going to their cabin in River's End as soon as she got to Tulsa on the twenty-second, Randi and James were planning to stay at her house in Tulsa. They would spend three days packing up all her stuff to be ready to move right after Christmas. Early on Christmas Day, they would go to the cabin for the holiday with her family and return to Tulsa that night, so there wouldn't be any conflict with her parents about Randi and James sharing a bedroom.

Then, they planned to rent a truck to load everything up on the twenty-sixth and twenty-seventh. Once the house was cleaned and Randi turned in the keys to the landlord, they were driving from Tulsa to Heart's Destiny.

Leah Mae Wright

Somehow in the last three weeks, James had convinced her that there was no point in paying to store her stuff in Tulsa, when he had plenty of room for her things in his house. When she tried to argue with him about it being too soon for them to move in together, he pointed out that they were basically already living together on the road, so why not make it official at home? Unable to refute his argument, Randi caved and planned for them to move her things on their long Christmas and New Year's holiday break.

Randi had learned that with the end of year holidays they would actually be flying into New York on the twenty-first and would be off work until they flew out of New York on the second of January, giving them eleven days off instead of the normal nine they got for holidays. Since they technically had to fly in and out of New York on the first and last day of their vacation, Randi still only considered it nine days off, not counting the travel days as days off like her sister did.

Randi had enjoyed having her sister and nieces at the arena with her ten (really twelve if you count the travel days when they arrived to start their flight rotation) of the nineteen days she'd worked with the GWA. She'd not only had time to have some sister time with Kay, but she'd also spent some time in the ring training with Tia. Even though Tia had missed a week when she would've been there to train, so she could take the acceleration tests to be able to skip high school and start college courses in the new year, she was still pushing Randi to be able to keep up with their training.

When Tia wasn't there to practice with Randi, a couple of the female performers had stepped in to help train her. At first, she was jealous, thinking that they were just trying to make time with James, but once she got to know them a little better, she realized that they saw her as someone they would eventually be working with in the ring, and were trying to welcome her into their circle of friends. Randi could see herself becoming really close friends with a couple of the women wrestlers, especially Allissa Walters, who wrestled under the ring name of Victoria Vicious.

Since her family was off work for the pay-per-view weekend, Randi made plans to spend some of her downtime when they got to Providence, Rhode Island with the women she hoped to be able to work with in the ring one day soon. This weekend was Randi's first experience with the way their schedules all changed on pay-per-view weekends. She was as excited for the fan expo on Saturday as she was for the two nights off with James between now and the big show on Sunday.

As she was boarding the plane with James in Boston for the flight to Providence, Rick called out, "Randi, James, sit close, so we can talk about the show this weekend."

"We'll be right behind you, Boss." James directed Randi to take the first front-facing seat behind the grouping of four seats where their boss was sitting. He stored their bags in the overhead bin and one of the rear-facing seats behind them, leaving the two rear-facing seats in their grouping of four empty.

Randi wasn't sure why he was putting the oversized suitcase they were sharing behind where they were actually sitting instead of where they could see it, but she didn't want to appear ignorant in front of the power players in the company by asking him. Dean stored his luggage in much the same way as James had stored his and Randi's before taking one of the seats across from Randi and James. By the time everyone was on board the plane and seated for the flight, one of the writers had taken the fourth seat in their section, right behind the owner of the company, Rick Robertson.

Randi recognized Ethan Abrams, the writer that had taken the seat next to Dean, because he'd been the main person she had to deal with on live-television days, when he made last-minute changes to the lineup of the show and the scripts for the promos the wrestlers had to give backstage, and she had to scramble to get the correct people in place to keep the show from going off schedule. He was the youngest of the writers that Randi had met, probably no older than thirty, with brown hair and brown eyes. At only six-foot-one, he was shorter than most of the other men who worked for the GWA, and his thin frame made it obvious that he worked behind the scenes and not in the ring.

Just like the rest of the people who worked with the GWA, Ethan had been nothing but kind and welcoming in the interactions Randi had previously had with the man. She wasn't sure why she was uneasy about whatever Rick and Ethan planned to discuss with her while on the flight, but she felt a few extra butterflies in her belly that she couldn't explain as anything other than nerves about issues they may have with her job performance.

Leah Mae Wright

I know Rick said he wanted to talk to James about the show this weekend, but that doesn't explain why he wants me to take part in the meeting, Randi mused as she squeezed James's hand on take-off. *Unless they need to go over different duties that I have during pay-per-views that aren't applicable to the normal nightly shows?*

She didn't have to wait long for her questions to be answered. As soon as they leveled off and the fasten seatbelts lights turned off, Rick stood from his seat and turned to their seating area. "Randi."

"Yes," Randi squeaked, hating her apprehensive response to being addressed by her boss.

James squeezed her hand reassuringly as Rick started speaking. "I've been watching you the past few weeks, both while you're working as a PA and while you're in the ring training."

Sugar! He thinks I'm wasting my time trying to learn to wrestle to be able to work as a performer on his shows.

"And while you've done an outstanding job as a PA, I don't think that position is the best way we can utilize your talents." Rick looked down at her from his position standing in the aisle. He continued speaking, but all Randi could hear was the pounding of her heart, and the blood rushing by her eardrums, as she had a mini panic attack at the thought of losing her job.

Randi opened her mouth to object, wanting to tell her boss how much she enjoyed her job and didn't want to lose it less than three weeks in the position, but she didn't get a chance to make a sound before James was excitedly hugging her to his side. "This is gonna be great!" James exclaimed, bringing Randi back to the moment and restoring her ability to hear the conversation going on around her. "The fans are gonna love her."

"Wait, what?" Randi looked around at the jubilated faces around her and felt confused. Needing clarification, she finally settled her gaze on her boss. "Can you repeat that, please?"

"I said that we're doing you a disservice by pulling you away from training every afternoon to work as a PA," Rick stated. "And while you're not ready to wrestle in front of a crowd yet, you'll get there a lot sooner if we go ahead and transition you to a talent position, so you have the extra time in the afternoons to train, when the rest of the roster is sparring and going through rehearsals."

"But if I'm not ready to wrestle yet and I'm not working as a PA anymore, what job am I gonna be doing?" Randi was still dumbfounded by Rick's statements.

"James told me about an idea you'd given him a couple of months ago about acting as his manager," Rick explained, smiling at her before nodding his head to Ethan and continuing. "I talked to Ethan about it last night, and from what I've seen of your performance ability, I think that will be a good way to get you started. You still need a few months to fully train for in-ring work, but we can hone your promo skills, and get you comfortable in front of our audience in a managerial role, until you're ready to wrestle."

"Oh, wow, um, okay," Randi sputtered, in shock at what was essentially a promotion with on-the-job training in less than a month with the company. "How does all this work? Like the whole changing jobs thing with my schedule and salary and stuff?"

Geez! Shut up, Randi! She mentally chastised herself. *Don't lose the new job by sounding so unprofessional and unworthy of the shot you're being given.*

"The only change to your schedule is that you'll stay in the ring to train when everyone else gets to the arena, and you'll start walking to the ring with James and Dean, being with them for promos, that kind of thing," Rick elaborated, lightly chuckling. "Ethan is going to work with you on the flight to develop your wrestling persona and plan your performance on the show Sunday. We'll have to schedule a time this afternoon to shop for your wardrobe, since I don't think you have any gimmick wear."

"Are we gonna be able to get her a ring jacket to match ours by Sunday?" James looked up from his seat at their boss.

"No, just pick her up some black leather biker gear for now." Rick shook his head. "We need to schedule a time to have her measured for any custom pieces we need to get ready for her. Is it possible for you to take her to our corporate office when we get to New York next Friday for all that? Or do you have an immediate flight out for the holidays?"

"Yeah, we can do that," James replied, pulling his phone out of his pocket, and making a note in his calendar app. "Our flight to Tulsa isn't until Saturday morning."

"Perfect." Rick nodded at James before turning his attention back to Randi. "I'll send you an email with your updated salary, since it will be bumped up to our talent minimum. The rest of the benefits all stay the same. Any other questions before I turn you over to Ethan to prep for your first performance?"

My salary will be bumped up? Holy cow! I'm happy with my current salary, but I'm not gonna balk at a raise.

"No," Randi squeaked around the lump in her throat. After quickly clearing it, she continued. "No, sir, no questions. Thank you for this opportunity to move up in the company."

"You are more than welcome," Rick gave her a beaming smile before turning to go back to his seat.

As Rick focused on talks with the other talent and writers that were seated around him in the first two rows on the plane, Randi, James, Dean, and Ethan discussed the plan for introducing Randi to the GWA audience. She and James would go shopping as soon as they landed in Providence, and they would hopefully be able to find her some gimmick wear fit for a biker babe to wear to the fan expo and during the pay-per-view show that weekend.

She would have a soft introduction to the fans at the expo, sitting at the table with James and Dean when they signed autographs, and starting to interact with fans in attendance before she actually appeared on the program Sunday. She wasn't sure if she'd have anyone who wanted her autograph at the expo or not, but she had to come up with a ring name ASAP, or she wouldn't know what to sign if she was asked for an autograph.

"I say we should go with the one Rick gave her at the wedding reception," Dean suggested, smirking as they discussed her ring name.

"I'm not signing Radiant Randi for autographs," Randi protested, thinking that made her sound narcissistic.

"What about Randi Dangerous?" James leaned over and nudged her. "I mean you are coming in as our manager, so shouldn't you have the same name as us?"

"No," Ethan objected before Randi could. "That'll make it seem like you're related, like your sister, or wife, or something that doesn't work for the gimmick. She needs a badass biker bitch name for the persona we're crafting for her."

Randi giggled at being referred to as a "badass biker bitch," causing Ethan to blush and say, "Sorry, I didn't mean to insinuate that you're, uh…" He coughed to cover the end of his sentence making Randi laugh even harder. "I'm sorry, I'll try to watch my language better in the future."

"No worries, Ethan," Randi chuckled, smiling at the obviously embarrassed writer sitting across from her. "You're right, that is the type of name I need, so I can get into character."

"I've found that most people do better starting out with a variation on their own name, so they answer to it on camera." Ethan was making notes on his tablet and not making eye contact with Randi to hide his residual embarrassment. "But a lot of bikers just go by a nickname, so that could work for your gimmick name, too."

"James calls her Angel all the time." Dean pointed to the two of them. "That's a good biker chick name."

"No," Randi immediately objected, wanting to keep that special between her and James.

"I don't like the idea of anyone else calling her Angel." James shut down any further talk about his pet name for her being used as her ring name before Randi could continue her objection.

"Okay, then what's your full name?" Ethan looked up from his tablet to address the question to Randi. "Maybe we can use part or all of it to make it easier for you."

"Randi Mae Lee," Randi replied, even though she didn't think her name sounded like a good biker name.

"Damn, how'd you end up with a more country name than anyone in our hick town when you grew up in a city like Tulsa?" Dean laughed and shook his head.

"I don't know, Byron," Randi retorted, pulling out Dean's little known middle name to tease him back. "You'll have to ask my Momma about our family tradition of naming kids after our ancestors instead of actors."

"Hey, don't be spreading that name around," Dean growled in a low tone, making it obvious that he hated his middle name as much as James hated his.

"Maybe we should look at teaming you up with the Bama Boys," Ethan suggested, smiling at Randi, and getting them back on track with the ring name discussion. "Randi Mae is the perfect country girl name to work with their gimmick."

"Grr." James growled beside her, and Randi giggled at his obvious displeasure at the thought of her walking to the ring with anyone but him.

"Sorry, I left my short shorts and crop tops at home," Randi joked with a smile. "Besides, I'm looking forward to showing off my acting range and shocking my family with my new badass biker bitch image."

James shifted in his seat and leaned over to whisper in Randi's ear. "We can grab some of those Daisy Duke outfits when we're in Tulsa, but you're only allowed to wear them when we're role playing behind closed doors."

Randi felt her cheeks heat as she blushed from the mental image of cowboy and cowgirl fantasy role play with James, even though she knew he hadn't spoken loud enough for anyone else to hear what he said. She just smiled at him, hoping he could read her acquiescence in her eyes without her having to verbally respond to his role play suggestion, since she wasn't sure she could say the words without being overheard.

"How about we just go with Randi Lee for your ring name? But maybe spell it differently, so overzealous fans can't look you up online too easily?" Ethan suggested.

"You mean like L-E-A or L-E-I-G-H, instead of L-E-E?" Randi thought that sounded like the best option they'd come up with so far.

"Yeah, unless you want to use a single name that's not associated with you in any other way, like Harley," Ethan offered.

"As much as that's a spot-on biker name, I don't think I wanna risk comparisons between me and Harley Quinn." Randi passed on the suggestion, remembering James's comments on her first day with the GWA about booking her as a psycho, and how that combined with her blonde hair could be seen as a trademark infringement.

Apparently, the guys all noticed Randi's slight resemblance to the comic book character when Randi mentioned the iconic name and laughed, even as they agreed with her to avoid that potential ring name. After a few more minutes of discussion, they opted to just go with the single name of Leigh, since the pronunciation was the same as her last name, so she'd answer to it automatically, but it wasn't close enough to her name to make it easy for potential stalkers to figure out her real name easily.

Once they had her ring name figured out, they went into detail on how they would book the match on Sunday, changing the original plan for the Dangerous Twins to lose their titles to Dark Chocolate and Red at the pay-per-view. Randi was shocked that they'd change the pre-planned outcome of the match because of adding her to the event, but when Ethan explained the reasoning, she understood.

"First, we haven't been promoting the possibility of losing the titles if the Dangerous Twins are disqualified," Ethan stated matter-of-factly. "Second, if we bring you in and have you cost them the titles the first night, it'll undermine you as an asset to the team. So, Rick wants us to book it with your interference not being seen by the ref, but making it obvious to the fans that your cheating ways gained the twins the victory."

"So, I'm an evil asset," Randi cackled like a cheesy B-movie villain.

"Yes, but don't laugh like that at ringside." Ethan laughed along with Randi, James, and Dean.

By the time they landed in Providence, Rhode Island, they had a solid plan in place and had already pulled Liam and Dion into their discussion with plans to rehearse the cheap shot Randi would give Liam to end the match the next day after the fan expo. Randi was looking forward to hearing about all the interesting prop ideas the writing team came up with for them to use the next day. But not as much as she was looking forward to her afternoon shopping with James for her new badass biker bitch wardrobe for any appearances she would be making on the next week of wrestling shows.

~~~

Saturday, December 15, 2018

James was feeling pretty proud of himself for the surprise he'd set up the night before for Randi. While she was in one of the many dressing rooms trying on clothes for her new ring persona, James had texted with Anthony to get him to fly her family into Providence to see her
~~~

debut from ringside seats. Anthony had questioned his sanity when he requested the Lees attend the event, but James knew that seeing up close and personal how happy Randi was with her new career was exactly what Charles Lee needed to be able to reconnect with his daughter. And as much as he hated to admit it, Randi needed to reconnect with her dad and the rest of her family as her true self before she'd be ready to move forward with him in their relationship.

James was more than ready to propose and start planning their wedding, so he was more than willing to do whatever he needed to do to help Randi and her father heal their unwanted rift. That included being sneaky and texting back and forth with Charles any chance he could when Randi was otherwise preoccupied while they were shopping to make sure they were all on the same page for how the weekend would go.

They'd had a little bit of a disagreement about hotel sleeping arrangements and James's intention to ask for Randi's hand in marriage. But that was settled quickly when James bluntly texted Charles back, saying that Randi was her own woman and didn't need anyone's permission to live her life, however and with whoever she wanted. When he'd specifically texted saying,

"James: I don't care how you feel about me. I'm sure we'll have a lot of things we'll have to agree to disagree on in the future. My goal with inviting you to Randi's debut performance with the GWA isn't about whether you accept me as Randi's mate. It's about you getting to know who your daughter really is & accepting her unconditionally like she needs you to do as her father. If you can't do that yet, then maybe it's not time for you to see her now. But I'm hoping you're more like the man Randi described to me when we first met & talked about our families than the one we saw on Thanksgiving. If so, then come tell your daughter how proud you are of her accomplishment in earning her spot on the roster with less than a month of wrestling training. Your daughter is the most naturally talented performer I've ever seen. I hope you can see

that in her & start to heal some of the painful parts of your relationship, so she can blossom into the wonderful woman you raised without feeling ashamed of not being exactly what you want in a daughter."

Charles had called and humbly apologized to James. The older man had sobbed, sounding pained at the thought of making Randi feel ashamed of who she was as a person. James knew the weekend visit was just the beginning of the healing process, but he was hopeful that it would lead to a much happier future for all of them.

Not that he was unhappy with the way things had been going for him and Randi in the last three weeks. Since they'd first said "I love you" to each other, they'd repeated those three little words multiple times a day and physically shown their feelings for one another every night. He was living out his dreams daily with Randi by his side.

Even though he and Randi had talked about ways they could sneak in semi-public sex at the various arenas they worked at when they'd talked during the long-distance part of their relationship, neither one of them had pushed to actually try it since she'd started working with the GWA. While they both enjoyed those fantasies, they didn't want to take any risks with their jobs.

They'd talked more about it after that first day when James had realized he needed to maintain a professional appearance to their relationship while in the arena. Randi had understood his distance that day and agreed wholeheartedly that they should keep the public displays of affection to a minimum while they were working.

Now that she was transitioning from working as a production assistant to working as talent on the shows, though, James wondered if they could do away with some of that professional distance. That distance had been easy to maintain when she was running all over backstage and working more with the writers, camera crew, and prop people than with the talent. But now that she was going to be acting as his manager and would literally be by his side twenty-four-seven, James wasn't so sure he could keep his hands to himself as easily. Especially since she was being introduced to the fans as his girlfriend at the fan expo.

I'm supposed to hold my girl's hand and sneak in kisses as part of the performance, right? Fuck, maybe I should talk to the wardrobe department about making some kind of adjustments to my costumes, so my fucking hard-on isn't constantly on display when she's at ringside while I'm wrestling. Is there a way to make spandex pleather that isn't so form fitting?

"What's wrong?" Randi came out of the bathroom in their hotel room, where she'd been getting ready to go to the expo.

"Nothing's wrong, Angel." James stood up from where he'd been seated on the bed to put on his biker boots. Since the high was only in the forties in Providence, James was glad for his heavy leather coat as part of his gimmick wear that he was wearing to the arena for the fan expo. But seeing Randi in her leather pants and low-cut t-shirt made him wish she didn't have to cover up with a leather jacket of her own. "Fuck, you're gorgeous."

"Don't distract me with compliments," Randi teased as he took her in his arms. She wrapped her arms around his neck to return the embrace, but she pulled her head back, preventing him from kissing her like he desperately wanted to at the moment. "You had a weird look on your face when I came out of the bathroom. No kisses until you tell me what's wrong."

James had to stop and think for a minute to remember what he'd been thinking about since the sight of Randi in her new gimmick wear had captured all of his attention. He chuckled lightly before explaining. "I was trying to figure out if there's a way to modify my wrestling tights, so the whole world doesn't see how hard I get every time I see you when you're at ringside during my match tomorrow night."

Randi giggled before pushing up on her tiptoes and giving him a quick kiss. "Maybe you need a chastity belt instead of a jock strap? Or maybe one of those cages we saw at that store in Tampa?"

"No, definitely not," James laughed at her ornery grin when she made her suggestion. "You ready to go meet your legions of fans?"

"As ready as I'll ever be," Randi sighed as she leaned her head against his chest and moved her arms down to around his waist. "I'm nervous, but it's more of an excited nervous than a worried nervous."

"Should we have called your doctor yesterday to see about adjusting your medicine again before this weekend?" James rubbed his hands up and down her back, hoping to reassure her that she didn't have to be anxious about performing.

"No, it's not the same kind of feeling." Randi squeezed him tight for a moment. "This is a good feeling; not like I'm gonna have a panic attack or freeze up type of anxiety."

"Okay, good." James kissed the top of her head and hoped he didn't mess up the way she had her hair styled. "Just know that if at any point it feels like too much, I'm right there beside you. Say the word and we'll leave if you need to."

"I might hold your hand for reassurance, but I don't think I'll need to leave for any reason." Randi pulled back, so she could grab her coat and they could leave their hotel room to head to the arena.

"I'm definitely gonna like being able to hold your hand more at work now that you're my manager," James admitted, grabbing his own coat, and taking her hand as they left the room.

They continued holding hands as they made their way to the rental car. James tensed as they stepped out of the hotel, and he realized it was snowing. Being born and raised in South Texas, he had very little experience driving in snowy weather. He'd done it a couple of times when he'd first joined the GWA roster, but he hated it so much that he usually rode with one of the other guys, who were more adept at bad weather driving.

Since Randi had started working with the GWA, he'd been renting a car for the two of them, instead of riding with his brother or the other guys, wanting to have that time alone with her. At that moment, he wished he'd thought about needing a more skillful winter weather driver to keep Randi safe on the way to the arena.

"James?" Randi used his name as a question, probably about why he'd stopped in his tracks, instead of continuing toward the parking lot and their vehicle for the day. "Did you forget something?"

"No, Angel." James looked around to see if there was a taxi service or something that he could use instead of risking driving in the inclement weather. "I was just thinking maybe we should call a car service since it's snowing."

"Why would we do that when we have an SUV?" Randi started to pull him toward the parking lot.

"Because I don't wanna risk an accident by driving in weather I'm not comfortable driving in," James answered her, even as he followed her toward their vehicle.

"Well, it's a good thing I'm here then," Randi grinned as they reached the back of the SUV they'd rented the day before. "Half my time in driver's ed in high school was spent driving in snow and ice, so I'm well prepared to get us safely to the arena in this." She waved her hand around at the falling snowflakes before extending her hand for him to give her the keys.

Even as uncomfortable as he'd felt at the thought of being behind the wheel in a snowstorm, James relaxed contentedly in the passenger seat as Randi deftly navigated the slick roads and safely delivered them to their destination.

Fuck, she's an amazing and impressive woman, he thought as he watched her calmly performing a task that slightly frightened him. *I don't know how I got so lucky to be able to call her mine, but I'm damn glad to have her in my life.*

Their conversation was effortless and easy as usual, leaving them both relaxed as they walked into the arena for the fan expo.

James spent the rest of his morning watching Randi's flawless performance as *Leigh*, interacting with the fans at the expo, signing autographs, and even holding her own in the video game competition booth. He'd have thought she was a pro gamer, if he'd only met her that morning and didn't know it was her first time playing the GWA video game. Several of the fans had commented on how she must have been playing daily since it'd come out, to be as good as she was and whipping all of them in the electronic wrestling ring.

It was when they were in the booth playing their final game before going to the interview booth that her family finally arrived to surprise her. James slightly tensed when he saw them walking up in his peripheral vision as he looked over at Randi instead of watching the screen. He hoped she wouldn't freak out when they walked up behind her, suddenly questioning his planned surprise.

"No way my baby sister is that good at a video game," David scoffed, pointing to the action on the screen, where Randi's avatar was pinning the avatar of the teenager she was playing against.

James wasn't sure if Randi didn't hear her brother, or if she didn't respond to his comment because she was so focused on finishing the game, but she didn't turn her attention away from the kid she was high-fiving for their tag-team victory over James and the little girl's teenage brother.

"Don't feel bad, I can't beat her at this game either," James consoled his dejected, teenaged teammate as they too high-fived. He and Randi exchanged pleasantries with the kids and their parents before the kids went with their parents to the next booth and Randi finally turned her attention to the voices behind them.

"Wha-what are ya'll doing here?" Randi stuttered as her nieces and nephew all hugged her and congratulated her on winning the video game.

"We couldn't miss your wrestling debut," Kay announced, motioning with her arm toward the rest of the family, like she was presenting them as the prize on a game show. "So, we hopped on the plane to make sure everyone made it here in time for the show tomorrow."

"Oh, wow!" Randi sounded a bit choked up as she was embraced by each member of her family. Once they'd all taken a turn hugging her and offering words of praise and encouragement, Randi looked them all over, still appearing confused by their appearance. "How'd you know? I mean I just found out yesterday after you left for home." Randi motioned toward Kay, Anthony, and their daughters as she finished her statement.

"A little birdie told us," Mary confided, smiling at her daughter.

"More like a big bird," Anthony chuckled as he slapped a hand on James's shoulder.

"You told them?" Randi turned to James. "That's what all that texting was yesterday? And the phone call you had to step outside the store to take?"

"Yeah, Angel," James confessed, smiling down at her. "I remember how special it was to have my family at my first show, and I wanted you to have that same kind of love and support for your first show."

Randi launched herself at him, causing him to have to take a step back to catch her, even though she was half his size. Their lips met in a passionate kiss that was probably a little too risqué for their environment, especially since she had her arms around his neck and her legs wrapped around his waist. He tried to keep it PG by keeping his hands on her back, instead of holding her up with one on her ass like he usually would, but when she ground her leather covered pussy over his cock, he was helpless to prevent his massive arousal from being evident beneath his leathers.

"Thank you," Randi gushed breathlessly as she pulled back from their kiss. "You know me better than I even know myself." She released her legs from around his waist to hop back down to stand on the floor. James loosened his hold on her, letting her pull back to a more appropriate distance for the surroundings, but he still tried to keep her close enough to hide the hard-on he was sporting from her show of gratitude. "I didn't realize how much I wanted them all here, until the moment they showed up. I don't know how you know what I need better than I do, but I hope you'll share your secret, so I can give you epic surprises like this, too."

"I just pay attention, Angel," James shrugged, bending to give her a kiss on her temple. "To absolutely everything about you," he whispered in her ear before moving to give her a peck on the lips.

When he stood back up straight and saw her father over her shoulder, his cock instantly deflated. *Maybe I can just picture my future father-in-law every time I get a boner at an inappropriate time? If seeing him kills it when she's still in my arms, imagining him should keep me from busting out of my wrestling tights, right?*

Not wanting to dwell on that thought too long, James released Randi from his loose embrace, turning her to face her family before saying, "Now, why don't we go show your family around, since I don't think any of them have been to a fan expo before."

"Aren't we supposed to go to the interview area next?" Randi took his hand.

"Yep." James laced their fingers together and started to lead them all in the direction of the next booth they were supposed to make an appearance at that day. "That seems like a great place to start our tour."

They spent the next couple of hours going from booth to booth with her whole family following along. Randi excitedly explained everything to her family, really coming out of her shell in a way he hadn't seen around her parents before.

James felt a swell of pride in his chest at being able to bring that out in Randi. Oh, he knew he couldn't really take the credit for her finally being able to be her confident, outgoing self, without any sign of anxiety that her parents would lecture her for her choices in life. She was the one who was doing all the work in therapy, and being proactive in discussing her anxiety issues with her doctor to make sure her medication was at the proper dosage to be most beneficial. But James liked to think that knowing he was there to love and support her unconditionally played, at least, a little part in helping her feel safe to be herself, when she hadn't felt comfortable before meeting him.

He looked forward to spending the rest of his life watching her continue to grow as a person and share her light with the world. Now he just had to figure out the best way to present her with the ring that had been burning a hole in his pocket since he picked it up the day after Thanksgiving.

She probably wouldn't like it if I asked her to marry me center ring after our match tomorrow night, he thought, knowing she wasn't quite ready for the proposal. *I know she said to wait to ask until "next year," but she didn't say it had to be at least a year before I propose. Maybe at the* **Saint Valentine's Day Massacre** *pay-per-view?*

~~~

Sunday, December 16, 2018

Randi pinched herself to confirm she wasn't dreaming her fabulous life as she was getting dressed in the locker room at the arena in Providence, Rhode Island, that was named after a popular donut brand. She just couldn't believe that she was really going to be making a six-figure salary as a performer for the Galactic Wrestling Association, barely a month after being fired from her previous waitressing job. Or that she was making her debut with the support of her family, who were sitting ringside for the show thanks to her boyfriend extending an olive branch to lessen the conflict with her father.

As if the first pinch wasn't enough to convince her that she was wide awake and really working in her dream job, Randi pinched herself again to verify that her relationship with James wasn't a delusion either. *Nope, it's all real. He's real. Our coupledom is real. The job is real. Even my parents being happy for me and supporting my choices in life is real. I'm actually living my own real-life fairy tale!*
~~~

If anyone had told her six months prior how the year would turn out for her, she would've told them they were crazy, completely unable to believe she would figure out what she wanted to do for a career, much less that she'd meet the man of her dreams and stand up to her overbearing parents to have both him and her dream job.

But somehow, against all odds, she'd crawled out of the rut she'd been living in for most of her adult life in the eleven weeks since she'd met James. Now, she not only had the man and the job, but she also had the confidence in herself to live a fulfilling life that she hadn't even realized she'd been missing.

Even a week before, she'd only felt like she was working toward the life of her dreams, believing it would take her at least another year to achieve it all.

Who am I kidding? Three days ago, I still thought it would be six months, or a year, before I could move to the talent roster, and a whole lot longer than that before I'd feel like Mom and Dad really support me in following my dreams.

Having her father hug her and tell her how proud he was of her for following her heart, when he first showed up at the fan expo the day before, had gone a long way to mending any hurt feelings she had from his disapproving lectures in the past, and relieved any residual anxiety she had about being her true self in the presence of her parents. She probably still wouldn't curse in front of them, but that was more as a way of showing her respect for them than because she was afraid that they'd reprimand her for it, like it had been in the past.

She'd shown that she no longer had a problem standing up for herself with them, when she told them about her change of plans for Christmas at dinner after the expo. They'd stayed after the fans all left to watch her practice hitting Liam with a folding chair, so she'd be ready for her debut as the villainess manager of the Dangerous Twins at the **Christmas Chaos** pay-per-view. Once everyone with the GWA was convinced that she had the timing down for the spot that would decide the winners of the match, Randi and James had gone back to the hotel for dinner with the family.

Much like the family dinner the night before Thanksgiving, it felt natural to be partnered up with James, while her parents and siblings were all partnered up with their spouses. Only this time, Randi wasn't trying to act like the little girl her parents wanted her to be. Through medication, therapy, and knowing James was there to love and support her no matter what, Randi had learned to be comfortable in her own skin in the past few weeks, and was finally able to show her parents who she really was deep down inside.

She'd calmly explained that she needed the days leading up to Christmas to pack up and clean the rest of the house she'd shared with Amy for the last few years, so they could turn in the keys. When her mother had said something about being able to pack up everything in the remainder of her time off between Christmas and New Year's Day, in an attempt to get her to stick to the original plan of being at their cabin from the twenty-second to the twenty-sixth, Randi had stood her ground instead of caving to her parents' wishes. She explained that she needed those days to drive her things to James's house in Texas and unpack everything.

Randi didn't give her parents the chance to object to her moving in with James. She stated plainly that it was her life, and nobody else had the right to decide where she should live it. In the end, her parents had actually offered to stay in Tulsa for Christmas to help her pack. She'd declined their offer, making sure they knew that while she still had only a limited time available, she wanted to celebrate the holiday at the cabin with them.

Kay had spoken up then as well, helping her get her parents on board with them going about their already scheduled holiday plans, while Randi followed her new schedule. Kay wanted to show Anthony the cabin and that part of Oklahoma while they had the chance. Kay's words had made Randi realize that she wanted to show James some of the same things, so he could have the chance to see some of her favorite places from her childhood, as she'd seen his when they were in Heart's Destiny.

Maybe we'll even make a return trip to Chandler Park when we're in Tulsa, Randi mused as she closed her locker. She grinned at the thought as she made her way out of the women's locker room to find James sitting with his brother and their opponents for the night.

"Feck, lass," Liam lilted as she walked up to the four of them at a table in the catering section of the backstage area. "You sure you don't want to swerve and hit James with the chair tonight and run off with me instead?"

Before Randi could respond to the over-the-top flirting of the Irishman, James growled at him while reaching out and clasping her hand to pull her down into his lap. He covered her mouth with his, staking his claim on her in front of the whole company with his kiss. Randi instantly melted into him, returning his fervent kiss with equal passion.

The sounds around them vanished as Randi felt her world shrink down to just her and James. Normally, she felt calmed by his touch. When he held her hand or hugged her, he grounded her in stressful situations. But anytime he kissed her, he wiped everyone and everything else from her mind, whisking her away to their own little world where only they and their love existed.

When they finally broke the kiss to breathe, Randi vaguely registered that the conversation around them had continued, but she was still too focused on looking into James's stormy gray eyes to comprehend what was being discussed by her coworkers. As she realized just how public their display had been, she smiled at him. "I guess we're doing away with that no PDA at work rule?"

"Yeah, I can't maintain a professional distance when these clowns are hitting on my woman," James declared with a smirk. "And since Rick said you can't wear that *Property of James Dangerous* t-shirt as your primary costume, I'll have to just keep staking my claim by thoroughly kissing you multiple times a day, regardless of who's around to watch."

"Speaking of that shirt," Randi whispered, her voice husky with desire. "I was thinking of ways I could cut it and a few of the others to make them sexier to fit the gimmick, but I didn't wanna ruin the ones you sent me. Think we could sneak off to one of the merchandising tables to get some extras, and maybe find an office with some scissors, so I could show you my ideas?"

"Are you trying to tempt me to go off to a secluded office, Angel?" James gave her a sexy grin. "Maybe a semi-private area where we can both get off?"

"Well, we do have a couple of hours to kill while we're waiting to *perform*," Randi replied, putting special emphasis on the last word to hint that she wanted them to have a private performance before their scheduled match on the pay-per-view.

"Oh, we'll definitely be *performing* before and after your television debut." James's eyes filled with lust as he stood, picking her up and carrying her out of the catering area.

There were several catcalls and whistles coming from the wrestlers that had been surrounding them in catering, but James and Randi ignored them. It didn't take him long to find an exit from the backstage area out to the mezzanine around the arena, where the merchandise tables were set up waiting for the doors to open for fans to shop before taking their seats.

James sat her down on her feet, unable to search through the display for what they were looking for while holding her in his arms. They quickly grabbed a few t-shirts and made their way back to the closed off section of the building where the business offices were located. With it being Sunday, the arena employees who worked in the offices were not in the building, off enjoying their weekend instead of working. James found the first unlocked office and urgently ushered her inside.

The door had barely shut behind them when James pushed Randi up against it. The shirts were dropped to the floor as their lips collided and their tongues tangled. They didn't even bother trying to find a light switch, both so desperate for one another that they didn't care if they were going at it like rabid animals in the dark. The only light in the room was a sliver of moonlight coming in from a window on the other side of the room, but it was enough for them to see what they needed to start removing their clothing.

Randi tugged at James's t-shirt while he frantically unfastened her leather pants. They only broke their kiss long enough to get both of their shirts up and over their heads, needing to make sure that anything they were going to be wearing to the ring later was out of their way, not wanting any of their clothing to be spotted with bodily fluids while they were on worldwide television later.

"Fuck, we need to switch you to leather miniskirts, Angel," James groaned against her lips when he struggled to get the leather pants down her legs. "I need easier access to you than these fucking pants."

Randi giggled when he got them down to her knees and realized her biker style boots were also an issue. "We probably should've done this before getting ready for the show." She bent down to unbuckle her boots. "How about I take off my boots and you take off yours?"

"Fucking wrestling boots," James grumbled as he pulled up the ends of his wrestling tights to get to the laces of his boots.

As soon as he got his boots off, James stripped off his tights and briefs, laying them over the same chair behind him where he'd already put his and Randi's shirts. Randi finished removing her clothing and handed it to him, so her pants, panties, and bra could join the rest of their clothing, out of the way of any mess they would soon be making.

As soon as they were naked, other than their socks, James lifted Randi back into his arms and pressed her back against the office door. She wrapped her arms and legs around him as he speared his tongue into her mouth. The hand he had on her ass slipped down between her thighs. One long finger slid into her opening, testing her wetness to make sure she was ready for more.

"No time for foreplay, Angel," James moaned between kisses. "This is gonna be hard and fast. You okay with that?"

"Oh yes, James," Randi panted out, eager for him to give her exactly what he was describing. "Fuck me. Now. Please."

With one quick thrust, he impaled her on his cock. Even though she was dripping wet, Randi felt the slightest discomfort from being stretched open so suddenly.

"Fuck," James groaned as he held still deep inside her. "How are you still so fucking tight when I spend hours every night opening you up with my cock?"

Randi hoped that was a rhetorical question because she had no idea how to answer. Instead of trying to reply, she dug her fingers into his hair, pulling his mouth back to hers, and shutting them both up with another searing kiss.

James trusted her legs around his waist and the door behind her to hold her up, using both hands to fondle her breasts as he started to move in and out of her. He may have tried to be gentle by allowing her a moment to adjust to his size before moving, but once he started thrusting, all semblance of gentleness left the building.

The door started banging in the doorframe in time with his pounding rhythm. The combination of his drugging kisses, the tantalizing feel of his hands on her breasts, his pubic bone hitting her clitoris with every deep thrust, and his cock repeatedly hitting that spot deep inside her, which only he'd been able to find, soon sent her soaring through an intense climax.

"James, yes, James," Randi chanted as the waves of her release flowed over her.

"Fuck, yes, Randi," James growled between open mouthed kisses down her neck. "I love feeling you come on my cock. Don't stop. Keep coming. Be my good girl and keep squeezing my cock."

"Yes, James, fuck, yes, James," Randi panted breathlessly, riding wave after wave of what seemed like a never-ending orgasm.

"You want my cum, Angel?" James shoved in deep as Randi felt his cock seem to swell inside her. "You wanna work your first match full of my cum?"

"Yes, James, yes." Randi was barely able to get the words out, having held her breath during the most intense portion of her own orgasm.

"Randi, fuck, Angel," James repeated several times as he filled her with his release.

James wrapped his arms around her, cradling her to his chest as she collapsed forward. Randi rested her head on his shoulder, unable to hold herself up on him a moment longer. She felt completely boneless in her satiated state, and had no idea how James was still standing, if he felt half as good as she did after their primal joining.

James somehow walked backwards to the desk in the center of the room, resting his bare ass on the edge while still holding Randi until they both recovered.

"Wow!" Randi exclaimed when she finally caught her breath, slowly disentangling from James, so they could start getting dressed. "How do you keep making it feel better and better every time? Surely, we have to hit a plateau at how good it can be at some point. Or have an off day when it's not earth-shatteringly amazing."

"Not us, Angel," James disagreed, grabbing some tissues from the box on the desk to wipe them up a little. He tossed them in a nearby trashcan before grabbing their clothes to redress for the show. "We're too good together to ever plateau, or have an off day between us."

James held out her panties for her to step into them. Once he'd caressed her legs to put them in place, he picked up her pants and repeated the process to redress her. Since his underwear and tights were next in the stack of discarded clothing, she grabbed them to do the same for him, liking how much easier his tights went on than her leather pants.

Leah Mae Wright

James found out that putting a bra on wasn't as easy as removing it, so he let Randi finish dressing herself, since she complained about being uncomfortable in the cups when he tried to do it for her. He slipped his t-shirt on and sat in the now empty chair to put on his wrestling boots while Randi adjusted her bra and put on her own shirt.

When James got up from the chair to pick up the shirts Randi wanted to cut up to make into gimmick wear for her at ringside, Randi took the chair to put on her own boots. They didn't bother looking around the office for a pair of scissors to make the design changes to the shirts in James's hand, opting to find a pair later when they weren't rushing back to the locker rooms to fix their hair and Randi's makeup for the show.

Once they were back to looking ready to work, they met up outside the locker rooms to go join the rest of the company in watching the **Christmas Chaos** pay-per-view on the backstage monitors. When Joel came over to where they were seated to let them know it was almost time for them to make their entrance, they donned their leather jackets and made their way to the curtain for their ring entrance.

"Come on, Angel." James laced their fingers together as their intro music started playing. "It's time for me to introduce the wrestling world to my sexy-as-fuck girlfriend."

Stepping through the curtain was surreal. The stage lights made it impossible for Randi to make out the faces in the crowd, but she would always remember the roar they made as she walked down the ramp to the ring for the first time.

The ringside seats were close enough that she could clearly see her family as they cheered for her. She wanted to laugh and remind them that they were supposed to be booing her heel persona and the bad boy tag team she managed. But she somehow maintained her character as a badass biker bitch, even as she fawned over James and demanded a chair to place his and Dean's leather jackets in beside her at ringside.

When the match started, she stood on the side of the ring facing the hard camera, knowing that she needed to be on that side of the ring, so none of the fans could miss her using that chair to knock out Red when the time came. She yelled and screamed, slamming her hands down on the ring apron several times, cheering on her team and distracting the referee when they needed her to, so they could get in a few dirty moves without being caught.

She'd been a little worried about being able to play the part of the "bad girl" alongside her "bad boy" boyfriend and his brother. It was definitely a role way outside the norm for her. But after only a few minutes in character, she understood why James said he preferred to work as a heel. It was surprisingly freeing to purposely act in a manner completely opposite of the way she was raised, to be evil instead of good.

She was having so much fun getting into a verbal altercation with a fan behind her that she almost missed her mark for the most important part of the match. Luckily, James screamed, "Keep him out of the ring!" loud enough for her to hear him, so she could turn around in time to see the referee pushing Dion back into his corner on the other side of the ring to know it was time.

She quickly dumped the guys' jackets to the floor, so she could pick up the folding chair and get into position. James did some kind of tripping maneuver to cause Liam to fall into the ropes with his upper body hanging out between the top two ropes around the ring.

Just as Randi hit Liam with the chair while he was draped over the ropes, she heard her father shout, "That's it! Clobber him, Leigh!"

She was so shocked at her dad's outburst that she couldn't maintain her character. She burst out laughing and prayed Rick would remember James's suggestion to portray her as a little bit psycho to cover her slip-up at the announcer's table.

As Randi was schooling her features to try to hide her reaction to her straightlaced, uber religious father going against his normal morals and cheering for her to cheat to win, James rolled Liam up for the pin and grabbed the referee's pantleg to get him to turn around and give him the three count. Randi jumped up on the ring apron as soon as the ref declared the Dangerous Twins the victors.

James grabbed her for a kiss that hadn't been planned as part of the show, while Dean held up both of their title belts for the crowd. When they broke the kiss, Dean handed James his title belt, which he promptly draped over his left shoulder. They got out of the ring and Randi handed them each their leather jackets before they started toward the ramp to the backstage area.

James took his jacket in his left hand and bent down using his right to put Randi up on his right shoulder.

Leah Mae Wright

Good thing I'm not afraid of heights, Randi inwardly giggled as James walked up the ramp with her on one shoulder and his title on the other. She held on to his hand on her thigh with her right hand and around his neck with her left. Even though she knew James would never drop her, she still felt safer holding on to him, too.

"Dean, James," the ring announcer shouted, stopping them on the stage at the top of the ramp, just before the curtain to the backstage area. He obviously wanted to do an interview to close the show, but Randi wasn't sure how that would go, since she hadn't been given any kind of script for it, the way she had for the one they'd recorded the day before to play during the show to introduce her to the crowd before their match.

"No time to talk, Chad," James smirked at the camera positioned just over Chad's shoulder and focused on them. "Gotta get my ol' lady back to the hotel to celebrate."

James turned and continued carrying Randi toward the curtain heading backstage just as Chad turned his attention to Dean. "Do you have anything to say to the fans about the way the Dangerous Twins won tonight?"

"Yeah," Dean laughed into the microphone being held out to him. "With the luscious Leigh in our corner, our undefeated streak is gonna stretch out for many, many years to come."

Randi ducked through the opening in the curtain, so she didn't hit her head on the metal framework holding it up under the jumbo screen, where the fans had watched their recorded promo earlier. Dean was only a few steps behind them as they stepped into the backstage area.

"Dude, did you just call my lady luscious?" James chopped his brother's chest as he put Randi down backstage. "That sounded like you've got a thing for my girl."

"Sorry, Bro," Dean chuckled. "It just came out. I didn't mean to make it sound like we're tag-teaming her."

"Good, 'cause you know that's never gonna happen," James growled, shaking his head at his brother.

"Great job, everyone!" Rick yelled, just as Dion and Liam walked through the curtain to the backstage area. "Randi, that burst of laughter as you hit Liam was the perfect way to play your character as a little crazy. The fans ate it up."

"Really?" Randi gaped at her boss. "That was actually me breaking character because I was shocked by what my dad said."

"Yeah, I was glad I had my back to the camera, so hopefully, nobody noticed me breaking character then, too," James chuckled beside her.

Liam and Dean agreed that they'd almost laughed then too, explaining to Rick what Charles had shouted at ringside to throw them all off.

"Well, I guess that means you don't have to worry about him objecting to your relationship anymore," Rick shrugged. "Hit the showers and have a good night. I'll see you all in the morning on the plane to Worcester and we'll start drafting the changes to Tuesday's show in the aftermath of tonight."

"I guess there's no rest for the wicked, huh?" Randi giggled as they walked toward the locker rooms.

"Oh, my wicked Angel," James crooned, pulling her into his arms just as they reached the door to the women's locker room. "I can guarantee you won't get much rest tonight."

He kissed her soundly before letting her go, so they could each get cleaned up and changed in their separate locker rooms.

"Looking forward to it, Jimmy," Randi grinned, giddy with excitement for what was to come for them as they lived out their fantasy life together.

Epilogue

James paced nervously in the men's locker room at the San Antonio arena as he got ready for his match on the ***Saint Valentine's Day Massacre*** pay-per-view. He had absolutely no worries about his performance in the ring. After years of working as a professional wrestler, he'd long since worked out any issues with stage fright he'd had early on in his career. Absolutely every ounce of apprehension he felt was because of the way he planned to close out the card with an in-ring proposal that Randi wasn't expecting.

Oh, she knew that she was supposed to get in the ring at the end of the match to comfort him after the title loss, but she had no idea he planned to go down on one knee, once they were the last two people left in the ring. Since he didn't have a safe place to carry it in his wrestling tights, the engagement ring that he'd carried in his pocket since Black Friday was already safe and sound in Meemaw's pocket at ringside.

He'd worked out the plan with his brother and the friends they were working the match with for how he'd get the ring when it came time for the proposal. Dion and Red would throw Dean out of the ring in front of where Meemaw and PopPop were sitting, so they could double team James at the end of the match. Dean would retrieve the ring from Meemaw and pass it to James when he got back in the ring to save James from their excessive beatdown after the pin. Once Dion and Red had left the ring with the titles, Randi was supposed to come into the ring to check on him and that's when he planned to drop to one knee and ask her to marry him. He would do it without a microphone, so he could use her real name and not her ring name when he asked the question. But holding up the ring would give the fans in attendance a glimpse of their real lives.

Fuck, I hope she realizes that it's a real proposal and not scripted for the show, he worried as he made probably his fiftieth lap around the locker room.

"Dude, you need to chill out or she's gonna know something's up before we even make it to the ring." Dean stopped James from continuing to pace around the room.

"She's gonna know this is a real proposal, right?" James beseeched his twin for reassurance. "She won't think it's something we changed in the script last minute and didn't tell her about, will she?"

"Naw," Dean replied, shaking his head. "She's worked with us long enough to know that even last-minute script changes are reviewed with everyone multiple times before they're implemented. She'll know it's real. Hell, she may even be expecting it since you have her whole family sitting ringside, when she doesn't even know they're in town."

"Yeah, well, I'm hoping that having them sitting on the other side of the ring instead of right behind her will keep her from noticing them," James confided, knowing that was probably not going to be the way it played out.

Fuck, I hope seeing her folks at ringside won't keep her from saying yes, James pondered a new worry about his proposal plan. *But she's been really good about standing up to them and making her own decisions about our lives the past couple of months. And I've filled Charles in on the plan, so he won't freak out and object when I ask her. So maybe it'll all be okay?*

"Yeah, well, maybe the lights in her eyes for the cameras will keep her from recognizing them while she's on the floor on the opposite side of the ring during the match, but I'm sure she'll notice them once she's in the ring." Dean shook his head, looking like he thought James's plan was flawed. "But it's too late to worry about that now. You need to pull it together, so we can go meet her in catering. Get into character as James Dangerous, like you did when she first started working as a PA, if you have to in order to keep her from getting suspicious of your nervous behavior."

"Are you kidding?" James glared at his brother, incredulous at Dean's lack of understanding of the dynamics of being in a relationship. "If I go back to avoiding our normal PDA, she'll really know something's up. I just have to quit thinking about the proposal for the next couple of hours and stick to our routine of sneaking off for a quickie before the show."

"Dude, I do not need to know what ya'll do when you sneak away from the rest of us," Dean groaned, holding up a hand to silence James. "I love ya, Bro, but I think of Randi like a sister, and don't want those images in my head."

James laughed at his brother's overacting, knowing darn good and well that Dean had seriously been attracted to Randi when they'd first met her back in September. Of course, he also knew that Dean quit thinking of any other woman as attractive as soon as he met Allissa in October, but that didn't necessarily mean all Dean's female friends were categorized as family like a sister, instead of just going into the friend zone. "Not sure when you suddenly developed brotherly feelings for Randi, but you don't have to worry about me sharing any dirty details about our sex life."

They were still laughing when they got to catering and found Randi sitting with her sister, brother-in-law, and nieces. James had actually set it up for them to have ringside seats too, but since it was their flight rotation with the GWA, they opted not to use them, so it wouldn't be obvious when they weren't backstage as usual. One of the production assistants was going to walk them out to ringside through the not so prominent entrance beside the ramp the performers used during the main event match, so they wouldn't miss the proposal.

Seeing the newlyweds and expectant parents sitting with Randi helped James get his mind off his upcoming proposal. He was able to focus on his friends and everything going on in their lives and put his own plans for the night to the back of his mind, while he filled his plate and took his seat beside Anthony.

At four months along, Kay was just starting to show the slightest little baby bump. While James could see what everyone talked about with pregnant women glowing when he looked at the woman he already considered his sister-in-law, he was more interested in seeing how his best friend acted as an expectant father. Anthony had doted on Kay from the first moment they met, but since finding out she was carrying his baby, he'd gone a little overboard with taking care of her every want and need, so she didn't risk overexerting herself.

Knowing he would one day be the same way with Randi, he observed his friends as often as possible, so he could learn how to straddle that line of being overprotective, without making her feel like he was stifling her independence. Since the sisters were so much alike in their need to be self-sufficient, James figured Anthony was a good example of what to do and what not to do for him to remember in the future.

He wasn't sure how it would work with their wrestling careers, but James couldn't imagine his life without raising at least a couple of kids with Randi. Unlike his family, who seemed to want him to have boys to carry on the family name, James wanted girls who looked just like their mother.

But maybe we should have a boy or two first to help me run off all the boys who wanna flirt with my girls, James thought when he noticed Cooper's son, Connor, watching Tia from across the room. *Shit, she just turned thirteen. That's way too young to have to worry about boys and their bad intentions.*

"Hey, um, Anthony," James whispered quietly, so he only alerted his friend to the situation at hand. "You see what I see goin' on over there?" He nodded his head in Connor's direction, trying not to be too obvious that he was pointing out the kid making eyes at Tia.

Anthony turned his head to look where James had directed him and chuckled lightly. "Oh, yeah," Anthony whispered, so only James could hear. "We've already had a couple of discussions about those puppy dog eyes. Supposedly, they only talk about science when they chat in the classroom, but I think he's interested in doing a lot more than talking about other things outside the classroom. Thankfully, Tia's too analytical to express an interest in boys yet."

"What are you two whispering about?" Randi moved between James and Anthony like she wanted in on the secret.

"Just offering to help Anthony if he wants backup to scare the boys away from Tia." James pulled her into his lap and pointed with his chin toward Connor.

"Oh, don't you dare," Randi whisper-shouted a little louder than he and Anthony had been speaking. "They're so cute together. The way he follows her around like a little lost puppy, and she tries to be patient teaching him about complex scientific principles that confuse the crap out of all the parents and tutors is absolutely adorable. They're making great memories of young love."

"My daughter is too young for love, even puppy love," Anthony protested a little too loudly, drawing the attention of several people around them.

"And how old were you and Nancy when you first started dating?" Kay arched an eyebrow at Anthony, leaning into his other side, so she could include James and Randi in the conversation.

"I was fifteen," Anthony stated adamantly. "So, we've got a couple more years before Tia's old enough for her first taste of puppy love."

"Yeah, but wasn't Nancy fourteen?" James teasingly poked the beast inhabiting his best friend. "And Connor's fourteen now…" James intentionally let his statement trail off, knowing his friend would get the implication without him having to say it out loud.

Anthony growled, causing the rest of them to laugh. "Just wait." Anthony pointed at James, his lips turning up in the slightest smirk. "Your day will come when you have teenage daughters, and I'll remind you of this conversation."

"Yeah," James conceded with a grin, hugging Randi close. "In fifteen or twenty years when your girls are already married, I'll let you get out your overprotective daddy tendencies by helping me scare the horny teenage boys away from our daughters."

"Daughters?" Randi looked at James questioningly. "Just how many kids do you think we're having?"

"As many as you're willing to give me, Angel." James pecked her lips with his and hoped it would get him out of the doghouse for thinking about having more children with her than Randi was ready to discuss.

"One boy and one girl," Randi conceded as soon as he lifted his lips from hers. "And if they can come as fraternal twins, so I only have to take time off work to be pregnant once, even better."

"Remind me when we turn thirty, so I can send your request to my swimmers when we're ready to start trying." James's statement caused another round of chuckles.

"Yeah, don't tell them now when we're just practicing," Randi sputtered through her giggles. "They might think we're ready now and override my birth control."

"How does that work with you not being able to go to Tulsa every three months for your shot?" Kay leaned around Anthony to look at Randi. "Actually, how do you get any prescriptions when you don't have time off to go home to get them?"

"We use a specialty pharmacy that mails our meds," Randi explained. "At first, it was confusing with having to plan the deliveries for where we're gonna be. But once we explained our travel schedule, the pharmacy switched everything to overnight delivery, so it would be a definite delivery date and not a window of dates the package could be delivered. Now we can give them the hotel address for whatever city we're going to on the delivery day and it's easy-peasy. Well, as long as this one doesn't freak out over having to stick me with a needle."

In Randi's typical way of talking with her hands, she motioned toward James with her thumb when she said, "this one," so Kay would know it was James that administered the shot back in January. He hated the thought of hurting her more than anything, but she still picked on him about his fear of needles, like that was the issue he had with giving her the injection.

After he'd pointed out that he couldn't have a fear of needles and been capable of getting all his tattoos, she'd finally relented and accepted his valid feeling of being afraid of doing it incorrectly. She'd gotten her doctor on a telehealth appointment to walk him through the first one via video, so he felt more comfortable with his ability to continue administering them in the future.

"I'm good with it now that your doctor walked me through the first one," James reminded her, tickling her lightly to get her back for making him sound like a wuss the first time. "I can handle poking you with a needle once in a while, even though it's not nearly as enjoyable as what I prefer poking you with."

"Stop, stop, stop," Randi squealed through her laughter at being tickled.

James immediately complied, so she wouldn't scream out "octothorpe" and cause him to have to explain safe words to her nearby nieces. Just the thought of her using her safe word caused his cock to engorge, overriding the fact that there were kids present, which he'd been using to keep his arousal under control.

Leah Mae Wright

"Speaking of poking," Randi whispered in his ear as she wiggled her ass on his lap, making it even harder for him to hide his body's response to her. "Shouldn't we be sneaking off while everyone's eating dinner and otherwise occupied?"

"Absolutely, Angel," James growled softly in her ear.

They cleared their plates from the table and feigned excuses for what they needed to do to prepare for the show to make their escape from the crowd of coworkers in the catering area. It didn't take long for them to find a secluded supply closet down a long hallway toward the opposite end of the arena from the portion set up as the backstage area for the show. The light in the small room came on as soon as they opened the door, apparently motion activated.

As soon as they were locked safely inside, out of the view of any potential prying eyes, James pushed up Randi's miniskirt with one hand while using the other to clasp the back of her neck to pull her in for a soul-scorching kiss. He wanted to spend at least a few minutes on foreplay, touching and tasting her sweet pussy until she came a couple of times before taking his own pleasure, but Randi had other ideas.

She shoved his tights and underwear down to his thighs before jumping up to wrap her legs around his waist. With one hand on his shoulder, she used the other hand to push her sexy thong panties to the side and line him up with her entrance. He couldn't even voice his protest to slow things down with their tongues still dueling for control of the kiss, as she slid down his length encasing him in the velvet glove of her body.

He lightly swatted her ass with the hand that had been on her little leather skirt, breaking the kiss to say, "Such a naughty little slut, taking what you want and not letting me play first. I'm gonna hafta punish you for this when we get back to the hotel tonight, Angel."

When she'd first asked him to call her a slut and punish her during sex, James had been adamantly against it, not wanting to make her feel guilty or ashamed of what they were doing. But when she'd explained it was her way of taking away the negative connotations to the words and replacing them with their own loving meanings, he understood her reasoning. When she went on to tell him that it was partially her therapist's idea, and partly her being inspired by his super-hot dirty talk and how it made her feel, he couldn't argue against it and finally embraced the idea. He only called her a slut when she was brave enough to take the lead sexually, and their playful punishments were really more rewards for both of them. Even spankings were pleasurable when they were more light little love taps.

"Oh, yes, Jimmy!" Randi chanted between nibbles on his neck.

He loved the feel of her teeth and nails biting into his flesh, knowing that whatever marks she left would be visible to the world when he wrestled. "Fuck, yes, Angel, mark me for all the world to see," he moaned as he gripped her hips with both hands, so he could control the way she bounced up and down on his dick.

Randi still had a tendency to rush things whenever she took the lead in their lovemaking. James knew it would take more than the few months they'd been together for her to completely get over her feelings of guilt for enjoying sex, so he tried not to make a big deal out of it when she acted frantic like that. He just quietly took control, setting a slower, gentler pace for however long it took for her to completely open up for him. He'd maintain control over his inner caveman and give her a few mini O's to make sure she was good and ready before he released his inner beast for the primal, animalistic pounding they both craved.

"Fuck, Randi, ride my cock, Angel," James growled just before sucking on the sensitive skin just below her ear, leaving his own mark on her for all the world to see. "I love how fucking tight you get when you come on me. Even as slippery wet as you are, when your cunt clamps down on my dick, it's next to impossible to move. Like you're gonna hold me deep inside you and never let me go."

"I'm never gonna let you go, Jimmy," Randi purred in that sexy, breathy tone he loved so much, as the vise-grip of her inner walls started to relax around his cock. "You're just as much mine as I'm yours."

"Damn straight, Angel," James agreed as he resumed moving in and out of her slick channel. "I'm yours and you're mine. Forever, Randi. For. Fucking. Ever." He punctuated each of his last three words with a powerful thrust of his rock-hard cock into her velvet pussy. "And the whole fucking world is gonna know it when you're standing ringside with my cum dripping down your legs."

"Oh, fuck, James!" Randi screamed as she was overtaken by another, more intense climax than the last few. James covered her mouth with his, swallowing her cries of ecstasy, so their coworkers and her family wouldn't hear her from the other side of the arena. He plunged his tongue into her mouth, mimicking the way his whang was ravaging her between her lower lips.

The feel of her coming undone around him, squirting her release against his groin, was pure heaven for James. He couldn't hold back any longer. He shoved his way as deep inside her as possible. When he felt the head of his cock pushing against her cervix, he gave in to the tingle that started in his spine and quickly moved to his balls. He held himself still, as far inside her as he could possibly be, and released his seed directly into her womb.

James knew with the shot he'd administered less than a month before that Randi wouldn't actually get pregnant from his deep deposit. But knowing that his cum wouldn't immediately flow out of her body from their carnal coupling filled him with a sort of primal pride, as if a part of his DNA would be permanently embedded in the woman he loved.

James held Randi in his arms for several long moments, as they each recovered from their intense orgasms. Once their breathing returned to normal, he slowly slipped out of the warmth of her body before setting her down on her feet. He kept his arms around her until he knew her wobbly legs would hold her up. Then he grabbed a roll of paper towels from one of the shelves in the room to clean them up as best he could.

"Yeah, I'm gonna have to go back to the locker room and change my panties now," Randi giggled as she started righting her clothing. "These are so wet and stretched out, they're completely useless."

"I'll buy you some new ones tomorrow, Angel," James chuckled as he pulled up his wrestling tights and underwear, noticing the hem of his t-shirt was wet from where Randi had gushed her cream. Since the milky white substance was obvious on his black shirt, James knew he'd have to go change as soon as they left the supply room, but he couldn't resist teasing Randi about it first. "You think this will dry before our match?" James pointed down at the creamy stain over his abs. "It'll be too obvious if I change my shirt now, since I don't have another one like this clean."

"No," Randi gasped, her mouth opening in a perfect O at the end of the word before she covered it with her hand. "You're definitely changing your shirt ASAP. If anyone asks about the different shirt you can tell them you spilled something on it at dinner. And this," she motioned between them to refer to the wild romp they'd just had, "won't be nearly as obvious as it would be if they see what actually soiled your shirt."

James couldn't maintain a straight face at seeing her reaction. "Yes, Angel, whatever you want, Angel."

They were both laughing as he opened the door, and they stepped out of their secluded space to go change for the show. Any anxiety James had previously had about proposing later that night had been completely vanquished by their time alone together.

This is gonna be the best night of our lives so far, James decided while watching Randi enter the women's locker room. *I'm sure it'll be topped by the night she becomes my wife, and every time she gives birth to one of our children, but I'm gonna enjoy every moment of the night I'm finally able to slip that engagement ring on her finger.*

<div align="center">~~~</div>

Randi was having the time of her life working side by side with James for the past couple of months. Even though her wrestling training was progressing to the point that she'd be able to start working as a wrestler before the Memorial Day break, she hoped the writers would keep her in her current role as the manager of the Dangerous Twins, while allowing her to also wrestle with the guys in her corner the way she stood in their corner currently.

Or at least with James escorting me to the ring and standing in my corner, Randi thought as she slammed her hand down on the ring apron and yelled at the referee for a made-up offense. *I want him to know how much fun this part of the show is, too, not just the wrestling part.*

The crowd noise was deafening as half of them called her out on trying to cheat by distracting the ref and the other half tried to defend her honor to the rest of the arena. For a second, she thought she heard her father's deep baritone voice as part of the latter half of the fans, but she quickly shook off that thought when she couldn't see his face in the seats closest to her. With the way the lighting was set up for the

Saint Valentine's Day Massacre pay-per-view, she couldn't see the people on the opposite side of the ring well enough to know if he was over there, but she knew if her parents had actually come to the show, Rick would've made sure they were sitting on her side of the ring. So, she blew off her auditory hallucination as nothing more than her briefly thinking back to the last pay-per-view, when she'd made her debut as Leigh, the manager for the Dangerous Twins.

"Pay attention Ref!" Randi shouted her disapproval of the referee focusing on Dean, who'd been thrown out of the ring on the opposite side from where Randi was standing, instead of the action in the ring. "These lowlifes are double teaming James! Unless you're helping Dean up to even the odds, you need to turn around and disqualify Dark Chocolate and Red!"

The referee finally turned around, hitting the mark that Randi alerted him to with her shouting, just in time to count the pin against James.

"No, no, no!" Randi shouted, jumping up and down with each instance of the word, feigning her anger at the outcome of the match. She knew the Twins were scheduled to lose their titles, but she had to sell it to the fans that it was a disappointing loss.

Dean jumped back into the ring to defend James from a post-bell beat down by the supposed babyface team. Randi wasn't sure how the writers could claim that Liam and Dion were the good guys in their feud when they cheated just as much as she and the Dangerous Twins on any given night, but she didn't argue with her boss or his writing staff about the psychology of the show. She just tried to stay in character and enjoy her job, even when it was hard not to laugh or shake her head at the inconsistent antics of her fellow performers.

The referee finally raised the victors' hands and gave them the title belts, so they could leave the ring. As soon as the other team had vacated the ring, Randi jumped up onto the apron and stepped through the bottom two ropes to go console her man as they'd scripted. Just as she moved in to hug him as planned, James stepped back and dropped to one knee.

"What are you doing?" Randi whisper-shouted, not sure what to do when James wasn't following the script.

"Something I've wanted to do for months, Angel." James reached out to take her left hand in his right, which was backwards for how they normally held hands and confused Randi even more. "I started falling for you the moment I first saw you walking across the restaurant toward me back in September. I was completely head over heels for you by the time I dropped you off at your house the next morning. Being on the road away from you was excruciating, and made me question my career and priorities in life, but luckily, we were able to overcome that obstacle to our relationship. Well, you were, anyway. You're the strongest woman I know, brilliant in ways that blow my mind, and you make me wanna be a better man to keep earning your love. I love you more than I even knew was possible to love someone, and that love just grows stronger each day. I don't ever wanna spend a day without you in my life. I claimed you as mine the night we met, but what I didn't tell you that night was that I also gave you my heart with that declaration. Now I wanna make it official. Let the whole world know that you're mine and I'm yours. Randi Mae Lee, will you marry me?"

James held up his left hand, presenting her with a gorgeous three stone ring on a platinum band. Randi was speechless for a moment, covering her mouth with her right hand as tears of joy streamed down her cheeks. *Yes, yes, James, I'll marry you,* she thought, unable to figure out how to form the words that were running through her head. She tried nodding, but wasn't sure she was successful in her affirmative head movement.

"Say the words, Angel," James commanded, smiling up at her. "Please, I need to hear you say yes."

"Yes!" Randi finally shouted, fanning herself with her right hand like that would help her be able to talk. "Yes, James, I'll marry you!"

Even without a microphone in the ring, she screamed the words loud enough that even the fans in the cheap seats could hear her. The arena exploded in cheers for them, as James slipped the ring on her finger, stood up, scooped her up into his arms, and sealed their engagement with an earth-shattering kiss.

Randi was so lost in the throes of the passionate embrace with James that she didn't realize the ring was filling with people. It wasn't until he pulled back from the kiss and let her slide down his body that she noticed they weren't alone in the ring. As soon as her feet hit the mat, she was pulled out of James's arms and embraced by several members of their families as they offered their congratulations.

Leah Mae Wright

The house lights came up and the fans started leaving the arena before she and James were able to come back together in the center of the ring after all the hugs and handshakes of their combined families. Randi couldn't help but laugh when she realized she'd actually heard her father during the match after all.

"I can't believe you're all here." Randi looked around to the family members surrounding her and James in the middle of the ring.

"I couldn't propose without everyone we love here to witness it." James encircled her waist with his arms while standing behind her.

Randi leaned her head back onto his sweaty chest, tilting her chin up enough that she could look up into his eyes as he gazed down at her. "Thank you for knowing me so well that you knew I'd want them here, again."

"Always, Angel." James smiled at her before pressing their lips together in an awkward upside-down kiss. One of many they would share over the course of their lives together. "Always."

Want more of James and Randi?

Download your free copy of <u>***Wrestling with Randi Bonus Scenes***</u> to get three bonus epilogues, including their wedding night, their surprise honeymoon location, and a glimpse of their plans for the future. SPOILER WARNING: <u>***Wrestling with Randi Bonus Scenes***</u> contains spoilers for events that happen in **Adoring Amy**, **Charlotte's Wedding**, and **Dean's Darlin'**, so you may want to read those books before you read these bonus epilogues. It also contains graphic sex scenes and profanity, which is intended for adult audiences (18+) only.

Next in the Heart's Destiny Series

<u>*Bobby's Bride*</u>

Bobby Burleson enjoyed the bachelor life and all the perks that came with being a member of one of the founding families of his small hometown. He had his own home on the Burleson Ranch, plenty of money in the bank from his dividends and salary as a board member of Burleson Incorporated, and his pick of the buckle bunnies that hung out at Tully's Roadhouse after the rodeo almost every weekend. Though his family money made him wealthy enough to never have to work a day in his life, he'd worked his way up from a small-town cop to the police chief position with the Heart's Destiny Police Department.   Between his duty to the town and the extra work he did for his family business, Bobby didn't have time for his meddling mother and her friends' matchmaking mischief, much less the relationship they wanted him to find.

Brooklyn Brielle Barns was a mostly naïve heiress who lived a sheltered life, unaware of her inheritance from her mother. After her mother died when she was four, she was raised by the household staff, who provided her with a home-school education. Her father neglected her, except when he expected her to play the part of the dutiful daughter at social events. After earning her online degree in English with a special focus on creative writing, she was excited to start her career as an author of children's books. Before she could tell her father her plan for the future, he announced that he'd set up an arranged marriage for her. She was to wed one of his colleagues, a man more than twice her age, whether she liked it or not.

480

Brooklyn spent six months playing the part of the blushing, virgin bride, attending all the society events her father insisted she should with her unwanted fiancé, while secretly starting her writing career under the alias of Brie Brooks. She stashed her income in secret online accounts, only dipping into it so the household staff, who acted more like her foster parents, could help her buy a car to make her escape from the forced marriage. The unknown heiress became a runaway bride a little over a week before the wedding, hoping to stay hidden away from her oppressive father's evil plans.

When Bobby saw the kidnapped heiress headlines and heard the opinions of his family and friends on the young woman's fate, he felt compelled to investigate. Not because of his duty as a police officer, since a kidnapping in Georgia was way outside his jurisdiction, but because of the strange feeling in his chest when he saw Brooklyn Barns' photos. His inner alpha wanted to rescue the damsel in distress.

When Brooklyn's car broke down in a small Texas town, she felt a sense of safety and home that she'd never felt before. She accepted a job as a live-in cook and housekeeper on a ranch to supplement her author income. It was virgin instalove the moment she met her new boss, but she wasn't sure she could tell him who she really was without risking him sending her back to her unwanted old life.

When Bobby met the woman his mother hired to be his cook and housekeeper, he felt as drawn to her as he did to the images of the Georgia heiress that he no longer believed was kidnapped. As he got to know Brie, he started to see the similarities between her and Brooklyn.

Would he figure out that the two women he was drawn to were one and the same? Would the small-town hero be able to protect his lady in hiding? Could this unlikely couple find their happily ever after?

DISCLAIMER: This small-town cop, damsel in distress, unlikely couple romance book contains references to childhood neglect, profanity, and graphic sex scenes. It is intended for adult readers (18+) who are not easily offended.

Next in the GWA

Fighting for Fiona

Book One in the Galactic Wrestling Association Series

Rick Robertson lived his dream life as the second-generation owner and promoter of the world's most successful sports entertainment company—the Galactic Wrestling Association. As a single dad and billionaire boss, his life was spent traveling the world with his twelve-year-old daughter and the crew he considered a second family. But seeing his staff and talent falling in love made him realize there was still one thing missing in his life—his soulmate.

Fiona Harrison was tired of living the sheltered life of a preacher's daughter in a small Texas town. She craved adventure and excitement, like she read about both with her middle school English students and alone at home. She wanted to get out of Heart's Destiny and see the world. And maybe meet a man who could make her feel more than the friendly affection she felt with the guys she grew up with.

Fiona jumped at the chance to travel with the GWA when her coworker and friend told her about the traveling English teacher position. She interviewed for the job when the GWA was in Heart's Destiny for a wedding over Thanksgiving break. She was scheduled to start her new job at the beginning of the new year, and hoped the instant attraction she felt when she interviewed with the owner of the company wouldn't make the working conditions too uncomfortable.

Rick didn't think his attraction to the new English teacher, who was ten years his junior, would be a problem. She was too young to be interested in a single father with too much responsibility on his shoulders to ever have time to take her out and treat her the way a beautiful young woman like her deserved. He considered himself to be more than man enough to appreciate her beauty from afar and keep all their interactions professional.

Then he went home to New York over Christmas break and hired a male history teacher closer to Fiona's age. When the two new teachers both started work in the new year and seemed to be spending an awful lot of time together, Rick struggled to fight his natural alpha tendency to claim Fiona as his own.

Which battle would Rick win? The battle with himself not to pursue Fiona? Or the fight for Fiona's heart?

DISCLAIMER: This single dad billionaire boss, teacher, age gap, sports romance book contains references to fertility issues, profanity, and graphic sex scenes. It is intended for adult readers (18+) who are not easily offended.

Books by Leah Mae Wright

Heart's Destiny Series

A Brief History of the Founding Families of the Fictional Small Town of Heart's Destiny, Texas – Free eBook
Courting Kay – Anthony Burleson and Kay Lee
Courting Kay Bonus Scenes – Free eBook
Wrestling with Randi – James Hunter and Randi Lee
Wrestling with Randi Bonus Scenes – Free eBook
Bobby's Bride – Bobby Burleson and Brooklyn Barns
Adoring Amy – Justin Burleson and Amy Lawton
Charlotte's Wedding – Ian Campbell and Charlotte Burleson
Joshin' Around – Josh Burleson and Cait Campbell
Dion's Dream Girl – Dion Davis and Julie Burleson
Destined for Deanna – JJ Burleson and Deanna Wolfe (Coming Soon)
Lights, Camera, Ashlyn – Darius Davis, Ashlyn Lawton, and Cade Starling (MFNB Trio Romance, Coming Soon)

Galactic Wrestling Association Series

About The Author

Leah Mae Wright lives in Florida with her husband and fur babies. Her head has been filled with romantic stories for as long as she can remember, beginning with fairy tales as a small child growing up in Oklahoma and carrying through to countless ideas of her own throughout the years, as she's moved around to live in several different states. Now that her children are grown and life has slowed down, she's letting them out of her head, so they can join the libraries of her fellow fans of romance. Leah's literary world is a wonderful place that has no Covid, no real politicians, and a few unreal towns. Her favorite part about her characters living in her literary world is knowing that they are guaranteed a happily ever after.

You can keep up to date with Leah's future book plans at: www.leahmaewright.com – Be sure to sign up for the Newsletter to receive emails about new releases, sales, and freebies.
www.facebook.com/LeahWrightAuthor
www.amazon.com/author/leah_wright
https://www.instagram.com/leahmaewrightauthor/
https://www.pinterest.com/LeahMaeWrightAuthor/

Provide your feedback to the author at:
Leah's Literary World Facebook Group
LeahWrightAuthor@gmail.com
Leah@LeahMaeWright.com

You can also review Leah's books on Amazon, Apple Books, Barnes and Noble, Bookbub, Fictiondb, Goodreads, Google Play Books, and Kobo.